One N...
Hc...

KELLY HUNTER
SUSAN STEPHENS
KATE HARDY

First Published in Great Britain 2016
By Mills & Boon, an imprint of HarperCollins*Publishers*
1 London Bridge Street, London, SE1 9GF

ONE NIGHT WITH HER EX © 2016 Harlequin Books S. A.

The One That Got Away, *The Man From Her Wayward Past* and *The Ex Who Hired Her* were first published in Great Britain by Harlequin (UK) Limited.

The One That Got Away © 2013 Harlequin Books S. A.
The Man From Her Wayward Past © 2012 Harlequin Books S. A.
The Ex Who Hired Her © 2012 Harlequin Books S. A.

ISBN: 978-0-263-92047-5

05-0116

Our policy is to use papers that are natural, renewable and recyclable products and made from wood grown in sustainable forests.The logging and manufacturing processes conform to the legal environmental regulations of the country of origin.

Printed and bound in Spain
by CPI, Barcelona

THE ONE THAT GOT AWAY

BY
KELLY HUNTER

Accidentally educated in the sciences, **Kelly Hunter** has always had a weakness for fairytales, fantasy worlds and losing herself in a good book. Husband. . .yes. Children. . . two boys. Cooking and cleaning. . .sigh. Sports. . .no, not really—in spite of the best efforts of her family. Gardening. . .yes. Roses, of course. Kelly was born in Australia and has travelled extensively. Although she enjoys living and working in different parts of the world, she still calls Australia home.

Kelly's novels *Sleeping Partner* and *Revealed: A Prince and a Pregnancy* were both finalists for the Romance Writers of America RITA® Award, in the Best Contemporary Series Romance category!

Visit Kelly online at www.kellyhunter.net.

PROLOGUE

THERE were limits—but Logan couldn't remember what they were.

He lay on the bed, stripped-out and trembling, his body screaming out for oxygen and his brain not working at all. The woman splayed beneath him looked in no better condition. Boneless in the aftermath, just the occasional twitch to remind them that there was substance there, the shallow rise and fall of her chest that accompanied her breathing.

He looked to her skin; it had been flawless when he undressed her but it was flawless no more. There were marks on it now from his fingers and from the sandpapery skin of his jaw. Marks on her wrists and her waist and the silky-soft underside of *her* jaw.

He'd met her in a bar; that much he could remember. Some student hangout near the hotel he was staying at. This hotel. This was his room; he'd brought her back here. She'd given him her number but that hadn't been enough for him. The hotel nearby. He'd walked her back to it. Invited her back to his room.

And those golden eyes had seen straight through to his soul and she'd tilted her lips towards his and told him to take what he wanted, all he wanted, and more. And he'd done so and discovered himself utterly in thrall.

'Hey,' he said gruffly, and reached out to drag his thumb across her stretched and swollen lips. Their last close encounter had been the wrong side of rough, and he felt the shame of it now, the black edge of guilt encroaching on the insane pleasure that had gone before. 'You okay?'

She opened her eyes for him, and, yeah, she was okay. He smoothed her inky-black hair away from her face, tucked it behind her ear, combed it back from her temple. He couldn't stop touching her. Such a beautiful face.

He stroked her hair back, smoothed his hand over the curve of her shoulder. 'Can I get you anything?' he offered. 'Glass of water? Room service? Shower's yours if that's what you want.' Whatever she wanted, all she had to do was ask.

And she looked at him and her lips kicked up at the corners and she said, 'Whatever you just did to me... whatever that was—I want more.'

CHAPTER ONE

'You could marry me,' said Max Carmichael as he stared at the civic centre drawings on Evie's drawing table. The drawings were his, and very fine they were indeed. The calculations and costings were Evie's doing, and those costings were higher—far higher—than anything she'd ever worked on before.

Evie stopped chewing over the financials long enough to spare her business partner of six years a glance. Max was an architect, and a visionary one at that. Evie was the engineer—wet blanket to Max's more fanciful notions. Put them together and good things happened.

Though not always. 'Are you talking to me?'

'Yes, I'm talking to you,' said Max with what he clearly thought was the patience of a saint. 'I need access to my trust fund. To *get* access to my trust fund I either have to turn thirty or get married. I don't turn thirty for another two years.'

'I have two questions for you, Max. Why me and why now?'

'The "why you" question is easy: (a), I don't love you and you don't love me—'

Evie studied him through narrowed eyes.

'—which will make divorcing you in two years' time a lot easier. And (b), It's in MEP's best interest that you marry me.' MEP stood for Max and Evangeline Partnership, the construction company they'd formed six years ago. 'We're going to need deep pockets for this one, Evie.' Max tapped the plans spread out before them.

She'd been telling him this for the past week. The civic centre build was a gem of a project and Max's latest obsession. High-profile, progressive design brief, reputation-enhancing. But the project was situated on the waterfront, which meant pier drilling and extensive foundation work, and MEP would have to foot the bills until the first payment at the end of stage one. 'This job's too big for us, Max.'

'You're thinking too small.'

'I'm thinking within our means.' They were a small and nimble company with a permanent staff of six, a reliable pool of good subcontractors, and the business was on solid financial footing. If they landed the civic centre job they'd need to expand the business in every respect. If they got caught with a cash-flow problem, they'd be bankrupt within months. 'We need ten million dollars cash in reserve in order to take on this project, Max. I keep telling you that.'

'Marry me and we'll have it.'

Evie blinked.

'Shut your mouth, Evie,' murmured Max, and Evie brought her teeth together with a snap.

And opened them again just as quickly. 'You have a ten-million-dollar trust fund?'

'Fifty.'

'Fif— And you never thought to *mention* it?'

'Yeah, well, it seemed a long way off.'

He didn't *look* like a fifty-million-dollar man. Tall, rangy frame, brown eyes and hair, casual dresser, hard worker. Excellent architect. 'Why do you even need to *work*?'

'I *like* to work. I want this project, Evie,' he said with understated intensity. 'I don't want to wait ten years for us to build the resources to take on a project this size. This is the one.'

'Maybe,' she said cautiously. 'But we started this business as equal partners. What happens when you drop ten million dollars into kitty and I put in none?'

'We treat it as a loan. The money goes in at the beginning of the job, buffers us against the unexpected and comes out again at the end. And we'd need a pre-nup.'

'Oh, the romance of it all,' she murmured dryly.

'So you'll think about it?'

'The money or the marriage?'

'I've found that it helps a great deal to think about them together,' said Max. 'What are you doing Friday?'

'I am not marrying you on Friday,' said Evie.

'Of course not,' said Max. 'We have to wait for the paperwork. I was thinking I could take my fiancée home to Melbourne to meet my mother on Friday. We stay a couple of nights, put on a happy show, return Sunday and get married some time next week. It's a good solution, Evie. I've thought about it a lot.'

'Yeah, well, I haven't thought about it at all.'

'Take all day,' said Max. 'Take two.'

Evie just looked at him.

'Okay, three.'

It took them a week to work through all the ramifications, but eventually Evie said yes. There were provisos,

of course. They only went through with the wedding if
MEP's tender for the civic centre was looking good. The
marriage would end when Max turned thirty. They'd
have to share a house but there would be no sharing of
beds. And no sex with anyone else either.

Max had balked at that last stipulation.

Discretion regarding others had been his counter
offer. Two years was a long time, he'd argued. She didn't
want him all tense and surly for the next two years,
did she?

Evie did not, but the role of betrayed wife held little appeal.

Eventually they had settled on *extreme* discretion
regarding others, with a two-hundred-thousand-dollar
penalty clause for the innocent party every time an ex-
tramarital affair became public.

'If I were a cunning woman, I'd employ a handful of
women to throw themselves at you to the point where
you couldn't resist,' said Evie as they headed down to
Circular Quay for lunch.

'If you were that cunning I wouldn't be marrying
you,' said Max as they stepped from the shadow of a
Sydney skyscraper into a sunny summer's day. 'What
do you want for lunch? Seafood?'

'Yep. You don't look like a man who's about to in-
herit fifty million dollars, by the way.'

'How about now?' Max stopped, lifted his chin, narrowed his eyes and stared at the nearest skyscraper as
if he were considering taking ownership of it.

'It'd help if your work boots weren't a hundred years
old,' she said gravely.

'They're comfortable.'

'And your watch didn't come from the two-dollar shop.'

'It still tells the time. You know, you and my mother are going to get on just fine,' said Max. 'That's a useful quality in a wife.'

'If you say so.'

'Dear,' said Max. 'If you say so, *dear*.'

'Oh, you poor, deluded man.'

Max grinned and stopped mid pavement. He drew Evie to his side, held his phone out at arm's length and took a picture.

'Tell me about your family, again,' she said.

'Mother. Older brother. Assorted relatives. You'll be meeting them soon enough.'

She'd be meeting his mother this weekend; it was all arranged. Max showed her the photo he'd just taken. 'What do you reckon? Tell her now?'

'Yes.' They'd had this discussion before. 'Now would be good.'

Max returned his attention to the phone, texting some kind of message to go with the photo. 'Done,' he muttered. 'Now I feel woozy.'

'Probably hunger,' said Evie.

'Don't you feel woozy?'

'Not yet. For that to happen there would need to be champagne.'

So when they got to the restaurant and ordered the seafood platter for lunch, Max also ordered champagne, and they toasted the business, the civic centre project and finally themselves.

'How come it doesn't bother you?' asked Max, when the food was gone and the first bottle of champagne

had been replaced by another. 'Marrying for merce-
nary reasons?'

'With my family history?' she said. 'It's perfectly
normal.' Her father was on his fifth wife in as many de-
cades; her mother was on her third husband. She could
count the love matches on one finger.

'Haven't you ever been in love?' he asked.

'Have you?' Evie countered.

'Not yet,' said Max as he signed for the meal, and
his answer fitted him well enough. Max went through
girlfriends aplenty. Most of them were lovely. None of
them lasted longer than a couple of months.

'I was in love once,' said Evie as she stood and came
to the rapid realisation that she wasn't wholly sober any
more. 'Best week of my life.'

'What was he like?'

'Tall, dark and perfect. He ruined me for all other
men.'

'Bastard.'

'That too,' said Evie with a wistful sigh. 'I was very
young. He was very experienced. Worst week of my
life.'

'You said best.'

'It was both,' she said with solemn gravity, and then
went and spoiled it with a sloppy sucker's grin. 'Let's
just call it memorable. Did I mention that he ruined me
for all other men?'

'Yes.' Max put his hand to her elbow to steady her
and steered her towards the stairs and guided her down
them, one by one, until they stood on the pavement outside. 'You're tipsy.'

'You're right.'

'How about we find a taxi and get you home? I promise to see you inside, pour you a glass of water, find your aspirin and then find my way home. Don't say I'm not a good fiancé.'

'Vitamin B,' said Evie. 'Find that too.'

Max's phone beeped and he looked at it and grinned. 'Logan wants to know if you're pregnant.'

'Who's Logan?' Even the name was enough to cut through her foggy senses and give her pause. The devil's name had been Logan too. Logan Black.

'Logan's my brother. He's got a very weird sense of humour.'

'I hate him already.'

'I'll tell him no,' said Max cheerfully.

Minutes later, Max's phone beeped again. 'He says congratulations.'

It couldn't be her. Logan looked at the image on his phone again, at the photo Max had just sent through. Max looked happy, his wide grin and the smile in his eyes telegraphing a pleasurable moment in time. But it was the face of the bride-to-be that held and kept Logan's attention. The glossy fall of raven-black hair and the almond-shaped eyes—the tilt of them and the burnt-butter colour. She reminded him of another woman…a woman he'd worked hellishly hard to forget.

It wasn't the same woman, of course. Max's fiancée was far more angular of face and her eyes weren't quite the right shade of brown. Her mouth was more sculpted, less vulnerable…but they were of a type. A little bit fey. A whole lot of beautiful.

Entirely capable of stealing a man's mind.

Logan hadn't even known that Max was *in* a serious relationship, though, with the way Max's trust was set up and Max's recent desire to get his hands on it, he should have suspected that matrimony would be his younger half-brother's next move.

Evie, Max had called her. Pretty name.

The woman he'd known had been called Angie.

Evie. Angie. Evangeline? What were the odds?

Logan studied the photo again, wishing the background weren't so bright and their faces weren't quite so shadowed. The woman he'd known as Angie had spent the best part of a week with him. In bed, on their way to bed, in the shower after getting out of bed... She'd been young. Curious. Frighteningly uninhibited. There'd been role play. Bondage play. Too much play, and he'd instigated most of it. Crazy days and sweat-slicked nights and the stripping back of his self-control until there'd been barely enough left to walk away.

At a dead run.

He'd been twenty-five at the time, he was thirty-six now and he doubted he'd fare any better with Angie now than he had all those years ago.

He squinted. Looked at the photo again. *Could* it be Angie? They were very long odds. He'd never kept in contact with her; had no idea where she was in the world or what she was doing now.

No, he decided for the second time in as many minutes. It wasn't her. It couldn't be her.

'She pregnant?' he texted his brother.

'Hell, no,' came Max's all-caps reply, and Logan grinned and sent through his all-caps congratulations. And then deleted the picture so that he wouldn't keep staring at it and wondering what Angie—his Angie— would look like now.

* * *

Evangeline Jones felt decidedly nervous as Max helped her out of the taxi and followed her up the garden path to his mother's front door. It was one thing to agree to a marriage of convenience. It was another thing altogether to play the love-smitten fiancée in front of Max's family.

'Whose idea was this?' she muttered to Max as she stared at the elegant two-storey Victorian in front of them. 'And why did I ever imagine it was a good one?'

'Relax,' said Max. 'Even if my mother *doesn't* believe we're marrying for love, she won't mention it.'

'Maybe not to *you*,' said Evie, and then the door opened, and an elegantly dressed woman opened her arms and Max stepped into them.

Max's mother was everything a wealthy Toorak widow should be. Coiffed to perfection, her grey-blonde hair was swept up in an elegant roll and her make-up made her look ten years younger than she was. Her perfume was subtle, her jewellery exquisite. Her hands were warm and dry and her kisses were airy as she greeted Evie and then retreated a step to study her like a specimen under glass.

'Welcome to the family, Evangeline,' said Caroline, and there was no censure in that controlled and cultured voice. 'Max has spoken of you often over the years, though I don't believe we've ever met.'

'Different cities,' said Evie awkwardly. 'Please, call me Evie. Max has mentioned you too.'

'All good, I hope.'

'Always,' said Evie and Max together.

Points for harmony.

In truth, in the six years she'd known him, Max had barely mentioned his mother other than to say she'd never been the maternal type and that she set exceptionally high standards for everything; be it a manicure or the behaviour of her husbands or her sons.

'No engagement ring?' queried Caroline with the lift of an elegant eyebrow.

'Ah, no,' said Evie. 'Not yet. There was so much choice I, ah…couldn't decide.'

'Indeed,' said Caroline, before turning to Max. 'I can, of course, make an appointment for you with *my* jeweller this afternoon. I'm sure he'll have something more than suitable. That way Evie will have a ring on her finger when she attends the cocktail party I'm hosting for the pair of you tonight.'

'You didn't have to fuss,' said Max as he set their overnight cases just inside the door beside a wide staircase.

'Introducing my soon-to-be daughter-in-law to family and friends is not fuss,' said Max's mother reprovingly. 'It's expected, and so is a ring. Your brother's here, by the way.'

'You summoned him home as well?'

'He came of his own accord,' she said dryly. 'No one makes your brother do anything.'

'He's my role model,' whispered Max as they followed the doyenne of the house down the hall.

'I need a cocktail dress,' Evie whispered back.

'Get it when I go ring hunting. What kind of stone do you want?'

'Diamond.'

'Colour?'

'White.'

'An excellent choice,' said Caroline from up ahead and Max grinned ruefully.

'Ears like a bat,' he said in his normal deep baritone.

'Whisper like a foghorn,' his mother cut back, and surprised Evie by following up with a deliciously warm chuckle.

The house was a beauty. Twenty-foot ceilings and a modern renovation that complemented the building's Victorian bones. The wood glowed with beeswax shine and the air carried the scent of old-English roses. 'Did you do the renovation?' asked Evie and her dutiful fiancé nodded.

'My first project after graduating.'

'Nice work,' she said as Caroline ushered them into a large sitting room that fed seamlessly through to a wide, paved garden patio. The table there was set for four. Perfumed roses filled several large vases, their colours haphazard enough to make Evie smile.

'I had a very demanding client who knew exactly what she wanted,' said Max. 'My ego took such a beating. These days I only wish all our clients could be that specific.'

'Max tells me you're a civil engineer,' said Caroline. 'Do you enjoy your work?'

'I love it,' said Evie.

'And this new project you're quoting on? You're as enthusiastic about it as Max?'

'You mean the civic centre? Yes. It's the perfect stepping stone for us.' *Us* being the business. 'The right opportunity at exactly the right time.'

'So I hear,' said Caroline, with an enigmatic glance for her son. 'I hope it's worth it. Let me just go and tell Amelia we're ready for lunch,' she said smoothly, and swanned out of the room before anyone could reply.

'She's not buying it,' said Evie. 'The whirlwind engagement.'

'Not so,' said Max. 'She's undecided. Different beast altogether.'

'You don't take after her in looks.'

'No,' said Max. 'I take after my father.'

'You mean tall, dark, handsome and rich?' Evie teased.

'He's not rich,' said a deep voice from behind them. 'Yet.'

That voice. Such a deep, raspy baritone. Max had a deep voice too, but it wasn't like this one.

'Logan,' said Max turning around, and Evie forced herself to relax. Max had a brother called Logan; Evie knew this already. It was just a name—nothing to worry about. Plenty of Logans in this world.

And then Evie turned towards the sound of that voice too and the world as she lived in it ceased to exist, because she knew this man, this Logan who was Max's brother.

And he knew her.

'Evie, this is my brother,' said Max as he headed towards the older man. 'Logan, meet Evie.'

Manners made Evie walk puppet-like to Max's side and wait while the two men embraced. Masochism made her lift her chin and hold out her hand for Logan to shake once they were finished with the brotherly affection. He looked older. Harder. The lines on his face were more deeply etched and his bleak, black gaze was as hard as agate. But it was him.

Logan ignored her outstretched hand and shoved his hands deep into his trouser pockets instead. The movement made her memory kick. Same movement. Another time and place.

'Pretty name,' he rumbled as Evie let her arm fall to her side.

He'd known her as Angie—a name she'd once gone by. A name she'd worked hard to forget, because Angie had been needy and greedy and far too malleable beneath Logan Black's all-consuming touch.

'It's short for Evangeline,' she murmured, and met his gaze and wished she hadn't, for a fine fury had set up shop beneath his barely pleasant façade. So he'd been duped by a name. Well, so had she. She'd been expecting Logan Carmichael, brother to Max Carmichael.

Not Logan Black.

Logan's gaze flicked down over her pretty little designer dress, all the way to her pink-painted toenails peeking out from strappy summer sandals. 'Welcome to the family, *Evangeline*.'

Max wasn't stupid. He could sense the discord and he slid his arm around Evie's waist and encouraged her to tuck into his side, which she did, every bit the small, sinking ship, finding harbour.

'Thank you,' she said quietly, restricting her gaze to the buttons of Logan's casual white shirt. It wasn't the first time she'd taken shelter in Max's arms and it wasn't uncomfortable. It was just…wrong.

'How long are you staying?' Max asked his brother.

'Not long.'

Logan ran a hand through his short cropped hair and the seams of his shirt-sleeve strained over bulging triceps. Evie shifted restlessly within Max's embrace, every nerve sensitised and for all the wrong reasons.

'Did you have to travel far to get here?' she asked Logan. Not a throwaway question. She needed him to be based far, far away.

'Perth. I have a company office there. Head office is based in London. Have you ever been to London, Evangeline?'

'Yes.' She'd met him in London. Lost herself in him in London. 'A long time ago.'

'And did it meet expectations?' he asked silkily.

'Yes and no. Some of the people I met there left me cold.'

Logan's eyes narrowed warningly.

'So what is it that you do, Logan? What's your history?' Rude now, and she knew it, but curiosity would have her know what he did for a living. She'd never asked. It hadn't been that kind of relationship.

'I buy things, break them down, and repackage them for profit.'

'How gratifying,' said Evie. 'I build things.'

No mistaking the silent challenge that passed between them, or Max's silent bafflement as he stared from one to the other.

'Max, do you think your mother would mind if I took my bag up to the room?' she asked. 'I wouldn't mind freshening up.'

'Your luggage is already in your suite,' said Caroline from the doorway. 'And of course you'd like to freshen up. Come, I'll show you the way.'

Five minutes ago, Evie wouldn't have wanted to be alone with Caroline Carmichael.

Right now, it seemed like the perfect escape.

Logan watched her go, he couldn't stop himself. He remembered that walk, those legs, remembered her broken entreaties as she lay on his bed, naked and waiting. He remembered how he was with her; his breathing harsh and his brain burning. No matter how many times he'd taken her it had never been enough. Whatever she wanted, whenever she wanted it, and he hadn't recognised the danger in giving her whatever she asked for until the table had given way beneath them and Angie had cut her head on the broken table leg on the way down. 'I'm okay,' she'd said, over and over again. 'Logan, it's okay.'

Eleven years later and he could still remember the warm, sticky blood running down Angie's face, running over his hands and hers as he'd tried to determine the damage done. That particular memory was engraved on his soul.

'An accident,' she'd told the doctor at the hospital as he'd stitched her up and handed her over to the nurses to clean up her face. 'I fell.'

And then one of the nurses had eased Angie's shirt collar to one side so that she could mop up more of the blood, and there'd been bruises on Angie's skin, old ones and new, and the nurse's compassionate eyes had turned icy as she'd turned to him and said, 'I'm sorry. Could you please wait outside?'

He'd lost his lunch in the gutter on the way to get the car; still reeling from the blood on his hands and the sure knowledge that accident or not, this was *his* fault, all of it.

Like father, like son.

No goddamn control.

Angie hadn't known he was Max's brother, just now.

Logan didn't think anyone could conjure up *that* level of horrified dismay on cue. Or the hostility that had followed.

'So what was that all about?' asked Max, his easy-going nature taking a back seat to thinly veiled accusation. 'You and Evie.'

'Do you really intend to marry her?'

Do you love her, was what he *meant*.

Do you bed her? Does she scream for you the way she did for me?

'Yes,' said Max, and Logan headed for the sideboard and the decanter of Scotch that always stood ready there. He poured himself a glass and didn't stint when it came to quantity. Didn't hesitate to down the lot.

'I'm guessing that wasn't a toast,' said Max, and his voice was dry but his eyes were sharply assessing. 'What is *wrong* with you?'

'Did you protect your money? Has she signed a pre-nup?'

'Yes. And, yes. We also restructured our business partnership to reflect proportional investment. Evie's no gold-digger, Logan, if that's what you're thinking.'

'You're in *business* with her too?'

'For the past six years. She's the other half of MEP. You know this already. At least, you would if you'd been paying attention.'

'I did pay attention. I knew you had a business partner.' He'd known it was a woman. 'I just…' Didn't know it was Angie. 'So this marriage…is it just a way to get your hands on your trust money?'

A simple no was all it would take. A simple no from Max, and Logan would dredge up congratulations from somewhere and be on his way. All Max had to do was say no.

But Max hesitated.

And Logan set up a litany of swear words in his brain and reached for the decanter again.

Leave it *alone*, an inner voice urged him. It's past. It's *done*. Plenty of other women in the world. Available women. Willing women.

Angie had been willing.

'Does she *know* you're marrying her to gain access to your trust money?' he asked next.

'She knows.'

'She in love with you?'

'No. I'd never have suggested it if she was. It's only for two years. And we'll be working flat out for most of it.'

'Right. So it's just a marriage of convenience. No broken hearts to worry about at all.'

'Exactly,' said Max.

Leave it alone, Logan. Keep your big mouth shut.

But he couldn't.

No way he could have Evangeline Jones for a sister-in-law and stay sane. It was as simple as that.

'And if I said I already know your soon-to-be wife? That I met her a long time ago, long before she ever knew you? That for a week or so we were lovers?' Logan's voice sounded rough; the firewater was not, so he drank some more of it before turning to face his brother. 'What then?'

Max stared at him for what seemed like an eternity. And then turned and strode from the room without another word.

Caroline Carmichael lingered once they reached the suite; a glorious eastern-facing bedroom with en suite, bay windows overlooking the garden and a sweet little alcove stuffed with a day-bed, and alongside that a bookcase full of surprisingly well-worn books.

'It's very feminine, isn't it?' murmured Caroline. 'I've never put Max in this room before. Then again, he's never brought a fiancée home either.'

'I'm sure we'll be fine.' One big bed, one day-bed. Evie couldn't have asked for a more suitable room.

Logan Black was Max's brother. Everything was just fine.

'Because I can put you in the adjoining room if you'd rather not be together before the wedding.'

'Whatever you're comfortable with, Mrs Carmichael.' Evie made no false claim to virginity. She doubted she could have pulled it off. Besides, she could only manage one lie at a time, maybe two.

'Please, call me Caroline,' said Max's mother easily. 'It's just that it occurs to me—as Max must have known it would—that your upcoming union might be a marriage in name only. A way for Max to access the money his father left him.'

'Yes, Max warned me you might think that.'

'Oh, there's affection between you, anyone can see that,' continued Caroline as she tugged at the curtains to make them absolutely even. 'But I'm not seeing love.'

Evie eyed the other woman steadily. 'What does love look like?'

'Depends on the type,' said Caroline Carmichael. 'My first great love was Logan's father and by the time we'd left the battlefield, love looked like a wasteland. But there was passion between us, passion to burn by. My second husband knew how to coax forth a steady flame, one that warmed me through and I thanked him for it every day of his life. But you and Max… Forgive me for being so blunt, but do you really intend to share this bed?'

'None of your business, Mother,' said Max from the doorway, determination in his voice and something else. Tightness. Anger. Max so rarely got angry. 'I need to speak to Evangeline alone.'

Caroline left with a concerned glance for her son and Max shut the door behind her. Evie stayed by the bookshelf, arms crossed in front of her and her chin held high.

Surely Logan would have kept his sinner's mouth shut.

Wouldn't he?

'Logan tells me he's met you before,' said Max.

Guess not. 'Yes.'

'When?'

'Ten years ago, maybe more. I haven't kept count. We met in passing. I was on a study exchange programme at the University of Greenwich. Your brother was doing something or other in London. I never did ask what.'

'He's the one, isn't he?' said Max. 'The one who ruined you for all other men.'

'I'm thinking *ruined* is too strong a word,' said Evie. 'I was definitely exaggerating and possibly maudlin when I mentioned that to you. I'm not ruined. I don't feel ruined. Do I look ruined?'

Max took his time looking her over.

'You look flustered,' he said grimly. 'You never get flustered.'

'Not true. C'mon, Max. I had a fling with a man called Logan Black more than ten years ago. Five minutes ago you introduced him to me as your brother. I'm calling that one fluster-worthy.' Heat flooded Evie's cheeks and distress fuelled her temper. 'I'm sorry, okay? I'm sorry my past has come back into play. It was a

pretty tepid past.' With one notable exception. 'It doesn't
have to impact the present.'

'It just did.'

Hard to argue with that.

'Do you still want him?' asked Max.

'No.' And as if saying it louder would somehow
make it true, 'NO.'

'Because he sure as hell still wants you.'

'If your brother had wanted me, Max, he'd have
found me. That much I do remember about him.'

But Max just shook his head and ran his hands
through his hair. He didn't look much like Logan except for his dark hair and olive skin. Their features were
quite different. Their mannerisms not similar at all. No
way she could have known...

'I can't believe he even told you,' she muttered. 'Why
would he *do* that? What could he possibly hope to gain?
Does he not like you? Is that it?'

'We get on well enough,' said Max.

'Then *why*?'

'Maybe he thought you were going to say something.'

'Yeah, well, he got that wrong.'

Max cut her a level glance. 'Honesty not really your
strong suit these days, is it?'

'Or yours,' she snapped back. 'You said you had a
brother—I *thought* I'd be meeting Logan Carmichael.
You never told me you had a half-brother named Logan
Black,' she said as her legs threatened to fold and she
sat herself down on the day-bed. *Think, Evie. Think.*
But her mind had left the building the moment she'd set
eyes on Logan, and it hadn't yet returned. 'Your mother's hosting a cocktail party in our honour in just over
seven hours,' she said, and put her head to her hands

and the heels of her hands to her eyes and pressed down hard. 'What's the plan here? What do you want to do? Because I can go find her and apologise and tell her the engagement's off, if that's what you want.'

'Evie—'

'Or we could put in an order for a time machine. I could go back in time, find your *half*-brother and spurn his advances. Failing that, I could at least wring his neck afterwards. That'd work too.'

'Evie—'

'Because after that I'm fresh out of ideas, Max. I don't know how to fix this without making even more of a mess.' Evie's throat felt tight, her eyes started stinging. 'I didn't know. I *didn't* know he was your brother. I would *never*... If I'd known. The business.... *God*.'

The horror in Logan's eyes that last time they'd been together when she'd cut her head on the too-sharp table leg. The trembling in his hands, the fear and self-loathing in his eyes. He'd taken her to the hospital and by the time they'd arrived Logan had pulled himself together, standing silent and sombre by her side until the nurses had asked him to wait outside.

'There's no problem here,' she'd told concerned nurses firmly. 'None.'

But they'd given her a business card and on it had been a number to call and she'd shoved it in her handbag rather than argue with them any more.

Logan had taken her home and she'd known something was wrong but she hadn't been able to reach him. 'Logan, it was an accident,' she'd told him as he'd walked her to her door. 'You *know* that, right?' And she'd thought he was going to reach for her then and make everything all right, only he'd shoved his hands in his pockets instead and nodded and looked away.

Last words she'd ever said to him, because the following day Logan Black was gone from her life as if he'd never existed.

'God,' she whispered.

And then Max's hands were circling her wrists and he was crouching before her and pulling her hands away from her face. 'Hey,' he said gently. 'Drama queen. Don't go to pieces on me now. We can fix this.'

'How?'

'We just have to know what everybody's intentions are, that's all. Yours. Mine. Logan's. Because I'll stand aside if I have to, Evie, but only if there's a damn good reason for doing so.'

'That I slept with your brother isn't good enough?'

'Well, it's not ideal...' Droll, this fake fiancé of hers, when he wanted to be. 'But I've got fifty million good reasons to get over it. Question is, can you and Logan? You need to talk to him, Evie.'

'We just did. You were there. It didn't go well.'

'You need to talk to him *again*. In private. Minus the element of surprise.'

'I really don't.'

'How else are you going to know if you're over him?'

'I'm over him.'

'Yeah. And he's over you. That's why he's downstairs mainlining Scotch and you're up here falling apart.'

'He's mainlining what?'

'Says the voice of disinterest. Corner him after lunch. Let him corner you.'

'He thinks we're getting *married*, Max. He's not going to come anywhere near me.'

'I think you might be underestimating the effect you have on him, Evie. Besides, he knows this is a marriage of convenience.'

'He *what*?' Evie was having trouble keeping up with who knew what. 'How?'

'I may have mentioned it. Before he mentioned knowing you. He was concerned for me. Or possibly for you. Not sure which. He asked me straight whether our marriage was to be one of convenience.'

'You *told* him? What happened to the game plan? The "I want to pretend it's real in front of my family" plan?'

Max had the grace to look discomfited. 'Couldn't do it,' he said finally.

'You are the worst. Liar. Ever.'

'Yes, well, now we know that.' Max was getting surly, a sure sign that he'd been caught wrong-footed. 'Look, I'll go and beard my mother, tell her what's going on. But you have to talk to Logan and find out what he wants. What *you* want. See if you can imagine him as your brother-in-law.'

She really couldn't.

'Just talk to the man, Evie.'

'Okay,' she said. '*Okay*. But if I need saving, you'd better come save me.'

'I will.'

'And I'm still your business partner.'

'I know.' Max eyed her steadily. 'That's not up for renegotiation, regardless of what happens with the engagement.'

'You hold that thought,' Evie said doggedly. 'No matter what Logan tells you, you hold that thought.'

CHAPTER TWO

EVIE came back downstairs five minutes later, hoping to find everyone already gathered for lunch, but there was only Logan, with his back towards her as he stared out at the garden beyond. Evie paused in the doorway, not ready for this confrontation, dead scared of this particular ghost, but he turned and there was nothing for it but to take a breath, straighten her shoulders and move forward. 'Where are the others?'

'Down in the cellar, choosing a bottle of wine,' said Logan. 'They were discussing the merits of marriages of convenience along the way. They could be a while.'

'Oh.' Happy conversations all round. And where to begin with Logan? 'I knew Max had a brother called Logan,' she said awkwardly. 'I didn't know it was you.'

'Fair enough. Now you do.'

His voice. How could she have forgotten that voice?

'What do you want from me, Logan?'

'You,' he said, and Evie's breath hitched. 'Gone.'

'We leave on Sunday.'

'From my life.'

'As far as I can be.'

'It won't be far enough, Angie. Not if you marry my brother. Not if you stay in business with him.'

'I'm not Angie,' she said with quiet firmness as thick black lashes came down to shield Logan's eyes. 'I grew up after you left me. I finished my studies and went to work on site in the construction business. I learned how to stand my ground. People call me Evie now. Evangeline when they're cross.'

'And is my brother cross with you, Evangeline?' Logan's black gaze swept up and over her, searing her. Lingering just a little too long on her hairline and the fringe that hid the faintest trace of an old, old scar.

'It's hard to say. What do you want from me, Logan? You didn't have to tell Max you'd bedded me. It's been ten years. More. Why didn't you leave that memory in the past where it belongs?'

He didn't answer her, just moved towards the drinks sideboard and poured clear liquid from a jug into two highball glasses. 'It's just water,' he said. 'Want one?'

'Thank you.'

So he picked them up and came over to her, and wasn't *that* a bad idea? Because now she could smell him and it was a scent that had haunted her, and now she could see the faint stubble on his jaw and the fine lines etched into his face. Older now, and wiser. Less inclined towards a smile.

He had a heartbreaker's smile when he chose to use it.

He held the glass out towards her and she stared at it and the strong, long fingers that held it. Go find out what he wants, had been Max's directive. Find out what you want.

So she reached for the water and deliberately brushed her fingers against Logan's in search of the fire that had once poured over her at his touch.

And came away scalded.

One sip of cool water and then another as she held Logan's gaze and fought that feeling of helplessness.

'The trouble with memories like ours,' he said roughly, 'is that you think you've buried them, dealt with them, right up until they reach up and rip out your throat.'

Some memories were like that. But not all. Sometimes memories could be finessed into something slightly more palatable.

'Maybe we could try replacing the bad with something a little less intense,' she suggested tentatively. 'You could try treating me as your future sister-in-law. We could do polite, and civil. We could come to like it that way.'

'Watching you hang off my brother's arm doesn't make me feel civilised, Evangeline. It makes me want to break things.'

Ah.

'Call off the engagement.' He wasn't looking at her. And it wasn't a request. 'Turn this mess around.'

'We need Max's trust-fund money.'

'I'll cover Max for the money. I'll buy you out.'

'What?' Anger slid through her, hot and biting. She could feel her composure slipping away but there was nothing else for it. Not in the face of the hot mess that was Logan. 'No,' she said as steadily as she could. 'No one's buying me out of anything, least of all MEP. That company is *mine*, just as much as it is Max's. I've put six years into it, eighty-hour weeks' worth of blood, sweat, tears and fears into making it the success it is. Prepping it for bigger opportunities and one of those opportunities is just around the corner. Why on earth would I let you buy me out?'

He meant to use his big body to intimidate her. Closer, and closer still, until the jacket of his suit brushed the silk of her dress but he didn't touch her, just let the heat build. His lips had that hard sensual curve about them that had haunted her dreams for years. She couldn't stop staring at them.

She needed to stop staring at them.

'You can't be in my life, Evangeline. Not even on the periphery. I discovered that the hard way ten years ago. So either you leave willingly...or I make you leave.'

'Couldn't we just—'

'No.' And then he leaned forward and brushed his lower lip against the curve of hers, and she closed her eyes and tried to pretend that her response didn't belong to her. That the thrill of pleasure that screamed through her belonged to someone else and that the hint of whisky on his lips wasn't intoxicating.

'You can't marry my brother, Angie. Don't even *think* it,' he murmured against her lips, and brought his hands up to cradle her face, and they were gentle but the tongue that stroked the seam of her mouth open was not, and the kiss that followed was not. The kiss spoke of ownership and anger and a helplessness that Evie knew all too well.

Logan's fingers tangled in her hair as he tilted her head back for better access to her mouth and the kiss continued. Not tentative. What Logan wanted, he took—that was just his nature, but the way he took it... oh...the sensual way he feasted... She'd never forgotten how deeply his enjoyment of sex had run. A pleasure seeker without equal. Giving it. Taking it. Owning it.

And then he drew back, breathing hard, and wiped the shine from her lips with his thumb, and his breath hitched and Evie plain forgot to breathe at all.

But she could still move, and she needed to move before Max and his mother returned, and there was something else she needed to know as well, so she wrapped her hand around his wrist and dug her nails into the vein, and watched for that tiny flare of pain and what he would do with it. Whether he'd resist it or chase it, and the increased pressure of his thumb crushing her lips into her teeth said chase and chase hard, but the curse that fell from his lips told of a resistance that ran equally deep.

Still fighting his own nature, then. Still that mad mix of sybarite and saint.

'You have to go,' he said.

He wasn't begging. Logan Black did not beg. But it was close.

'You hate it, don't you?' she murmured. 'What I make you want. What I make you feel. You've always hated it.'

'Yes.'

'Was that why the only place you made for me was on my knees in front of you?'

'Not *only* on your knees,' he offered roughly. 'I might be on mine.'

Which didn't help.

'Break the engagement, Angie. Find a way out of my brother's business and go far, far away. *Stay* away,' he said and abruptly let her go, moving back a step or two for good measure.

'And then what?'

'And then nothing.'

'Being left with nothing doesn't suit me these days, Logan.' Evie kept her voice steady and her back straight. No way he could know how her legs trembled and her heart thudded against her ribcage in the aftermath of his touch. 'I'm not the person you once knew. I'm stronger now. I'm a fighter now and I know what I want. The answer's no.'

'So,' said Caroline Carmichael as she swept into the room, with Max behind her brandishing a bottle of champagne in one hand and a bottle of white in the other. Evie stood on one side of the room, Logan on the other, and Caroline noted the distance between them, and probably the flush on Evie's face, with measuring eyes. 'Max mentioned we have a slight problem on our hands. I trust everything's been sorted?'

Logan said nothing. Instead, he let the silence stretch so thin you could see through it to the turmoil below.

'Well, one could hope,' said Caroline dryly. 'Do sit down to lunch, everyone. I, for one, can't problem-solve on an empty stomach. And make no mistake, this problem does need solving.' She eyed her eldest son sternly. 'Or would you prefer a fractured family?'

Logan's havoc-wreaking mouth was a thin, grim line, but he pulled out his mother's chair and saw her seated.

'Max, you'll pour?' said the widow Carmichael and Evie caught a glimpse of the iron will behind the amiable mask.

Max cracked the white and filled his mother's glass and then Evie's. 'You want me to get the Scotch?' he asked his brother.

'I'm done with the Scotch,' said Logan. 'Scotch is

for shock.' So Max filled Logan's wine glass with the pale, straw-coloured chardonnay too, and then his own.

So civilised.

They filled their plates in silence. Evie had never felt less like eating. And then Caroline looked across the table at Evie and said mildly, 'I hear you and Logan have met before.'

'Yes.' As Evie fought a blush and lost. 'It was a long time ago.'

'I heard that too,' said Caroline, and lapsed into silence while Evie sliced a spear of asparagus into half a dozen little pieces.

'It seems to me,' continued Caroline, 'that if you want this farce of a marriage to Max to continue, the best course of action would be to forget you and Logan ever met.'

'Yes,' murmured Evie. 'I thought that too.' Twelve tiny chunks of asparagus on her plate now, all lined up to make the whole. Very orderly.

'Logan?' said Max, and Evie looked up. No mistaking the question in Max's eyes or the resistance in Logan's.

'Or you can call off your engagement, I buy Evie out of your business and finance you until your trust fund comes in,' Logan told Max curtly.

'And where would that leave Evie?' asked Max.

'Gone.'

Why was there always a part of her that agreed with Logan? Why?

'I'm right here,' she said tightly. 'No need to talk around me. And you can have my share of MEP when I'm dead, Logan. I thought I made that clear. MEP is mine just as much as it is Max's and I will not give it up. Not to you. Not to anyone.'

'No one's saying you have to give it up,' said Max soothingly. 'No one but Logan's saying you have to give it up.'

Evie reached for her wine glass, only to change her mind before her fingers reached the glass. Her hands were too shaky; now was not a good time for alcohol.

'I think it's a *very* good time for alcohol,' murmured Logan, as if reading her mind.

'I'm not you,' she bit back.

'They can't even be in the same room with each other,' said Max to his mother.

'So I see,' murmured Caroline. 'Logan, I do think you're being a touch unreasonable,' she offered, before turning back to Evie. 'It's his father's fault. My first husband was utterly vulnerable to his emotions once they were roused. It used to scare him witless too.'

Only a mother could have that take on this situation. 'Logan doesn't strike me as particularly vulnerable, Mrs Carmichael.'

'Please, call me Caroline. I insist.' Caroline turned to Max. 'Do you *have* to have access your trust-fund money now?'

'We need ten million dollars to kick off the civic centre build, and they want to see our financials,' said Max. 'We've already explored several other avenues of financial backing. They weren't attractive.' Max speared Logan with a level gaze. 'Make us an offer that's attractive and Evie and I won't need to get married.'

'I just made it,' said Logan.

'Then the answer's no,' said Max with a tight shrug. 'When it comes to my marital status, I'm prepared to humour you. When it comes to MEP, Evie's an integral part of it. She stays.'

Impasse.

'Why so much float money?' asked Caroline finally. 'I don't know much about the construction industry, but it seems excessive.'

'Because we don't receive first payment until we're out of the ground on this one,' said Evie. 'It's a common enough clause in building contracts. But most of the foundation work for this particular build will have to be done underwater. Makes it expensive.'

'Sounds like you're out of your league,' said Logan.

'No, just our price range,' said Evie.

'Then get your client to advance you the funding for stage one.'

'They won't.'

'Then find another client.'

'You're right.' Evie eyed Logan steadily. 'Would you like us to build *you* an innovative, high-profile civic centre?'

'I wouldn't employ you to build me a bookshelf.'

'What do you think she *did* to him all those years ago?' Max asked his mother, dividing his gaze between her and Logan warily. 'He's not usually this intractable.'

'You should have seen him as an infant,' said Caroline. 'He could be extremely recalcitrant if he didn't get his way. I like to think I nudged it out of him. Perhaps not.'

'I'm right here,' said Logan, between gritted teeth. 'No need to talk around me.'

His mother studied Logan with sympathetic eyes. Max just studied him, and then, as if judging a walnut that would not be cracked, Max turned to Evie.

'So what'd you do to him?' asked Max. 'Did you reject him?'

'No,' said Evie quietly. 'I did everything your brother asked of me.'

'Never a good move,' said Caroline gently, and Evie shrugged and returned the older woman's gaze and thought she saw a glimmer of understanding.

'I'm still not seeing the reason for the extreme hostility,' said Max. 'You haven't seen each other in years. You were together for one week and then you parted ways. How bad can it be?'

He'd never been in thrall, thought Evie gently. He'd never known obsession. Ignorance was bliss.

'Would you like to tell him or shall I?' said Evie when the silence threatened to smother her.

'By all means, let's hear your take on it,' said Logan with exquisite politeness.

'Our time together was all-consuming,' she offered, and wore Logan's burning black gaze and didn't flinch. 'I was very…malleable, and Logan liked it that way. The combination worked a little too well for us. And then one day someone held a mirror up to our actions and Logan didn't like what he could see, and so he left and spared us both.' Evie arched a slender eyebrow and Logan met it with a bitter twist of his beautifully sculpted lips. 'Am I close?'

Logan inclined his head.

And for once, neither Max nor his mother had anything to say.

CHAPTER THREE

THE problem with the truth was that people so often hated hearing it. Logan was no exception. He didn't want to admit the darker aspects of his nature. The possessiveness. The passion that coursed through him, unbridled and deep. He'd only ever lost himself in a woman once and that was with Angie. Never again.

Not once since then.

His mother knew how dark he ran on occasion. Mothers knew. Half-brothers who were eight years the younger did not always know such things, and the furtive glances Max kept giving him set Logan to seething.

'Don't judge until you've been there,' he snapped.

'No judgment here,' said Max quickly. 'None. Just trying to figure the best way forward.'

'Get rid of her.'

'He means the best way forward for *everyone*,' his mother said pointedly.

His mother was not the weakest link at this table. Neither was Max.

Logan turned once more to Evangeline. 'You really want to cross me?'

'What I *want* is for MEP to land the civic project and for you to stop being such a dog in the manger,' she said evenly. 'You don't want me, and that's fine. I get it. I got it ten years ago when you walked away. So stay away. Stay out of my business and I'll stay out of yours.'

'You're in my *home*.'

'Actually,' his mother said gently, and reached for her wine, 'this is *my* home.'

'Logan, you'll be gone in a couple of days,' said Max carefully. 'Evie and I will be back in Sydney. Out of sight, out of mind.'

'No,' said Logan curtly. 'She won't be out of mind, she'll be within reach, and if you think your sham of a marriage will keep me in check, think again.'

'You still want her,' said Max slowly.

Logan didn't want to answer that question. For over ten years he'd avoided that particular question, contenting himself with less, always less. Touching no one too deeply and making damn sure no one tapped the darkness in him.

'Yes,' he admitted through clenched teeth, and pushed back from the table, intent on leaving before he made a bad situation worse. 'It appears I do. Which is why if you have any care for her whatsoever you'll get her the hell out of my way.'

Evie gave up all pretence of eating once Logan had stalked from the room. 'I'm sorry,' she said. 'I'm sorry.'

'Stop it, Evangeline,' said Caroline Carmichael sharply. 'When you've done wrong you can apologise. But I see no reason for you to apologise for the behaviour of my son.'

'We can call off the wedding,' said Evie. 'I'm happy to call the wedding off. This isn't going to work.'

'No kidding,' murmured Max.

'There'll be other civic centres,' she said, and almost believed it. 'Better ones.'

'Evie, you *know* how often projects like this one come up,' said Max tightly. '*Don't* lose sight of the bigger picture here for you and me and MEP. I'll talk to Logan again. He'll come round, I know he will. Because that wasn't my brother, just then. That's not who he is. He's just…jet-lagged or something.'

Evie said nothing. Caroline said nothing.

And Max drank deeply of his wine.

'*Are* you strong enough to withstand my eldest son's desire for you?' Caroline asked her bluntly.

'No.'

'Are you still submissive?'

'No.' Evie smiled faintly. 'I was very young. I found my strength.'

'You might want to consider ramming that particular development down Logan's throat,' said Caroline.

'I thought I just did.'

This time it was Caroline's turn to offer up a faint smile. 'Harder.'

Evie stood.

'Where are you going?' asked Max.

'To abuse your brother's throat.'

She found him in one of the bedrooms, slinging clothes into a suitcase with little care as to how they landed.

'Get out,' he said when he saw her in the doorway.

'No.' Evie made herself continue forward, shutting the door behind her, and moving forward again until she was well into the room, but not so close as to be within reach. 'You're being childish, Logan. You're letting your fear of behaviours long gone colour your vision of the

present. You need to learn how to deal with the person
I am now. I need to learn how to deal with you.'

'*Childish?*' he said incredulously.

Was that *really* as far as he'd got with her words?
'Don't forget fearful.'

He pinned her with a fierce gaze.

'Why else would you be running away?' she pointed
out as gently as she could.

And received silence in reply.

'Do you feel guilty about some of the things we did
together? Is that it? Because you shouldn't. You had
my consent.'

'I know that, Angie.'

'Is it because you exposed your deepest desires to
me, and I just fed them to your family?'

'Those desires started—and finished—with you.
They don't belong to me any more. And, yeah. You
could have kept them to yourself.'

'Maybe I thought your family needed a better explanation than the one they'd been served. I didn't realise
you were only interested in being truthful up to a point.'

'You should have.'

She wanted to rattle him, Evie realised. Pick away
at his anger and his armour and see what was underneath. 'You can't dominate me any more, Logan. You
need to realise that.'

'I don't *want* to dominate you,' he muttered. 'I never
wanted that.' He shoved his hands in his trouser pockets and looked away. 'But it happened.'

'I thought I was in love with you. Week one of an
intensely sexual, sensual relationship,' she argued. 'So
much to feel and to learn and, yes, my focus was on
pleasing you. I like to think I'd have regained my equi-

librium at some stage. That the relationship dynamic would have evened out in time. But I guess we'll never know.'

'I don't want to dwell on the past, Angie. I just want you gone from my life *now*.'

'Which is in itself an exercise in enforcing your will over mine.' Evie moved forward until she was crowding his space; nothing weak about that move. 'That seem right to you?'

'You can't marry him, Angie.'

'You really think Max would still have me after the fuss you just made?'

'He's got fifty million reasons to ignore the fuss I just made,' said Logan gruffly. 'You don't. You need to end this now.'

Logan's hand went to the back of his neck. From there, it was only too easy for Evie to let her gaze run over the hard angle of his jaw, the stubble just starting to show, and from there to his lips. A woman could fixate on those lips.

'Don't,' he warned huskily.

'Don't what?' Wonder if she could coax them open? Wonder what it would take to make them say the name Evie instead of Angie? 'Don't tempt you? Don't wonder what we might have had if you'd stuck around long enough to find out? Because I do wonder what we might have had together, Logan. I can't help it. And I'm sure as hell wondering it now.'

'Nothing good.'

'You don't know that. You barely know *me*. What if I *am* a match for you now? Ever thought of that?'

'No.'

'Maybe you should,' she cautioned gently, and

touched her fingers to his lips and he went still as a statue but he let her do it. 'What if we *could* bring this passion between us under control?'

'We'd get lost,' he muttered as her fingertips strayed to his jaw. '*I'd* get lost and I can't afford to, Angie. I can't.'

'What if I know the way?'

'Do you?' he asked, and then his hands were on her waist, dragging her towards him, and his lips crushed down on hers, desperate and tortured, no half-measures with this man and there never had been. It was all or nothing, and his kisses inflamed her as desperation turned into desire hot and sweet. And then he took his tongue to her mouth and lit an inferno.

A step backwards towards the bed for him as Evie set her palms to his chest and drank deeply of his passion and his pain. A step forward for her, and then they were falling, and he was beneath her, and his eyes were closed and his ravenous mouth never left her skin.

Her dress proved a poor barrier against Logan's clever hands, the thin shoulder straps sliding down, and then he swept the bodice down to reveal the swell of small breasts and the tips of her nipples. He set his tongue to one, and then lips, and suckled hard and Evie gasped as he took her to the edge of pain, and he knew exactly where that edge began, damn him, and when to retreat and bring pleasure coursing in its wake.

Palms to his shoulders, with only the warm cotton of his shirt in the way and she wanted his clothes gone, and hers, but when she tried to undo his shirt buttons he wouldn't let her, pushing her hands away with ruthless efficiency. 'No,' he muttered.

And then he slung his arms beneath her thighs and

slid her up and over his chest and onto his mouth and licked his way past her panties and into her, and if she thought he'd been a skilled lover ten years ago it was nothing to the expertise he wielded now.

With tongue and with hands he opened her up and drew her out, until her gasps became pleas and her pleas turned into a breathless stream of nonsense as she rode him, no room for his pleasure now, it was all about Evie, and what this man had always been able to do to her in the bedroom, and that was make sensation the only thing that mattered and self-control nothing more than a wispy memory.

This wasn't submission, she thought hazily, sliding her hands down to tangle in his hair, holding him exactly where she wanted him and it didn't take long, not long at all, before Evie shot to orgasm, wave after wave of pleasure so fierce and fine that her body arched like a hunter's bow.

He let her rest, momentarily. He let her catch one breath, maybe two, and then, just when recovery seemed possible, Logan clamped his mouth over her again and came at her sideways with his tongue and slung her skywards once more.

No control over her response whatsoever as she cried out her release and prayed she hadn't been too loud, but it wasn't submission. Evie clung to the faintest of hope that surrendering to pleasure wasn't submission. It was just…

Sensitive now as she toppled forward, her forearms landing on the bed above him and her head resting on her arms. A tremor shook her, a juddering reminder of where she'd just been and what Logan had just done to get her there.

'That wasn't submission,' she said breathlessly as she tried to think of a smooth move that would get her body back down level with *his* body.

There was none.

'I was on top,' she said as she crawled back down his body the clumsy way. 'I *am* on top.'

Which sounded lame, even to her ears.

'I could have done anything with you, Evie. *Anything,* and you'd have let me.' He worked his mouth across her nipple again and had a little party there and all she could do was whimper and strain against him and hope to hell he got it into his head to party harder. 'What *is* that if not submission?' he muttered.

'Participation,' she said. 'Participation resulting from stimulation. You need to work on your definitions.'

And she needed to work on him. Cautiously, Evie inched her way further down Logan's big body until her face was level with his and her hair fell around their faces like a curtain.

He didn't look rested or anywhere close to content. Evie closed her eyes and rested her forehead gently against his, breathing in the scent of him and the scent of her still on him. He tasted of her too, as she licked at his mouth, coaxing and cajoling until he did what she wanted, which was open for her with a groan, but when she went to undo his belt, he clamped her wrist and dragged her hand back up to his chest.

'Don't,' he said against her lips and she pulled away, just a fraction.

'Why not?'

'No condoms.'

Which sounded a lot like an excuse. 'Another way, then. Same way you did me.'

'I want—'

Yes, he did want. She could feel him rigid beneath her, digging into her. 'Hard,' she murmured.

'Yes. I want hard.' As if the admission of specific needs and desires was something to be ashamed of. 'And rough.' He licked at her lips as if soothing away fresh wounds. 'Too rough for your mouth. Don't want to hurt you.'

'Hands,' she offered. 'Yours *and* mine. Rough.'

He shuddered beneath her, but he still wouldn't let her hand go any lower than his chest. 'No.' With their lips barely touching and a shield of black lashes concealing his eyes. 'You need to leave, Angie. Now. I can't do this.'

'Why not?' She could think of plenty of reasons. They were in his mother's house. She was—supposedly—still engaged to his brother. Not that it had stopped him. And then there was this fear he had of dominating her, of hurting her, and *that* was the resistance he couldn't get past. Same reason they'd parted all those years ago.

'I don't understand you.' Evie backed off a little, pulled the straps of her dress back up her shoulders. 'Condoms can be purchased. Needs can be satisfied without anyone getting hurt. And my doing as you ask and leaving your room is *not* submission. It's listening and responding and it's action born of concern. For you. For whatever's going on in that hard head of yours.' He wouldn't meet her eyes, so she put a gentle forefinger to his chin, and leaned down and gently forced eye contact. Turmoil there, and plenty of it. Black eyes blown with darkness and desire. 'You savour me with one breath and turn me away with the next. Want to tell me what that's all about?'

'I really don't. Angie, please—'

'I know,' she said. 'Just go.'

Time to smooth down her dress with fumbling fingers and hope to hell no one saw her on the way to the guestroom. She didn't understand this man who lay so unmoving on his bed, one arm behind his head, one hand hooked over his belt as he watched her through slitted eyes, his erection still straining against his trousers. Her gaze fastened on his lips next; he had such sexy, snarly lips.

'Your mother said something about your father being a man of strong passions.' Uncontrollable passions, maybe. Caroline had implied that Logan had similar issues. Mothers knew these things. 'Are you close to him?'

'My father's dead,' answered Logan flatly.

'Oh,' she said with a grimace. 'I'm sorry. I didn't know.' So many things about this man that she didn't know.

'No great loss. He died when I was ten.' Logan closed his eyes and shut her out, put his forearm over his eyes for good measure. 'My father was an abusive, controlling bastard. When my mother finally worked up the guts to leave him—and me—he blew his brains out.'

Evie stared at him in horrified silence. What did a person say to that? Where did a person even start? 'Logan—'

'Go,' he muttered gruffly. 'Please, Evangeline, just go.'

And this time Evie complied.

CHAPTER FOUR

LOGAN remembered to breathe again once Angie had gone and the door snicked shut behind her. He shouldn't have told her. It wasn't something he talked about. Not with his mother, not with the psychologists his mother had taken him to once she'd had him back in her care.

It was okay to be angry, several of them had told him gently. Maybe he could examine his anger; start with the little things, they'd coaxed, while his ten-year-old self had sat there and studied his ragged, chewed-off fingernails and told them he wasn't angry, not him. Not with his father for topping himself, not with his mother for leaving them. She'd come back, hadn't she? Once the old man was gone? She'd come back for her son who was volatile, and controlling and needy, just like his father, and she'd never once called him those things, just started praising all the *other* traits he possessed and sent him to shrinks to keep the crazy in check.

Why had he *told* Angie that? Why couldn't he have left it at his father was dead?

She'd run now, if she had any sense. Away from this family. Away from *him*.

Evangeline Jones didn't understand the stakes in this game, but Logan did. He knew how it went; the breaking of a woman's will. Drip by tiny drip until it was all gone and she jumped at the sound of a footfall and flinched whenever someone moved too fast. He *knew* those games, knew every move.

Second hand.

Time to take himself in hand, thought Logan grimly as he sat up and ran his palms over his face. Do something about the want first. Take the edge off; the needy, greedy edge. Stay focused on the end game, which was staying strong and staying sane.

Hurting no one.

Hurting everyone.

Evie made it back to her room without encountering anyone. She made it to the en suite and stood there staring at the carnage Logan had wrought. Lips swollen from kisses that had gone too deep, complexion still rosy from the afterglow of good sex and her eyes dark with a mixture of shock and desire.

If a man tries to warn you over and over again that he's damaged goods he probably is.

If he tells you that he has his reasons for not wanting too hard then he probably does.

If he tells you outright that he doesn't want to hurt you, it's because he knows that some day he will. Maybe not today, or tomorrow, but he will, and he's given you fair warning.

Evie turned her back on the face in the mirror and closed her eyes and tried not to remember the crazy things Logan made her feel. Time to forget the feelings and *listen* to what the man had to say and get out of his life as best she could. Tell Max she'd see him at work on Monday, make her apologies to Caroline Carmichael and *leave*.

She stripped off her dress and her underwear and tossed them over the edge of the bath. She headed for the shower and turned it on hot and hard and stood and let the water wash away the stench of cowardice that clung to her skin.

'Walk away, Evie,' she whispered, and set her palms to the wall in front of her and her face to the spray to wash away the sting of tears. 'Run.'

And then the shower door behind her opened and Logan stepped in, fully dressed, and reached for her and she went to him without hesitation, wanting to comfort and be comforted, wanting his touch more than she wanted anything in this world. Riding that slippery slope of obsession and longing as the water poured down on them both and he pressed a condom packet into her hands and pushed her back against the wall and started kissing her.

Rough was the wrong word for what he wanted. *Intense* was a better word. All-consuming, as she helped him shed his clothes and laid hands to him, learning him all over again. Condom on and then Evie on as she put shoulders to the tiles and locked her legs around Logan's waist and he was slow and forceful as he entered her, and the skin on his jaw tasted salty and a little bit rough, but his movements weren't rough, not rough at all. His movements spoke of worship and wonder and a slamming, heartbreaking need as he claimed her body and offered up his own for her pleasure.

His touch was deft and agonisingly sensual as he cupped her and tilted her just so against him. Such tenuous control once passion came to play, and Evie was no help whatsoever, because wherever Logan led she went willingly.

He wanted her mindless to everything but his touch; and he succeeded.

He wanted her convulsing against him, with her mouth on his shoulder her only tether to this earth; and he succeeded.

She wanted him with her and this time he came when she did, eyes blazing, and his body straining, matching her gasp for gasp, with his mouth on hers, but only just, and his hand on the back of her neck as if he would never let her go.

'Sorry,' he muttered when his breath had slowed enough for speech. 'Angie, I'm sorry.'

'Don't be.'

'For the mess I made of my time with you. For the mess I'm still making.'

'Don't be.'

She unlocked her legs from around him and set toes to the floor and he held the condom on and slipped out of her and turned away. No words of affection for her, no smile of reassurance, just a need he couldn't voice and old fears made new again.

She stepped on his clothes on her way out of the shower. Looked at them and looked back at him. 'Impulsive,' she said with the tiniest of smiles.

'Always.' As he cut the water and she handed him a towel. 'Around you.'

'I try to control it,' he said gruffly, a moment later. 'I *need* to control it.'

'Yes, I guess you do.' An indirect reference to his past. The history that had shaped him. This *had* been controlled for Logan. He could get way more lost in desire than that. 'Lots of baggage, Logan.'

'More than you can handle?'

'Are you asking me to have a relationship with you?' Evie wiped her face down with the towel and started in on her dripping hair.

Logan said nothing, just slung the towel around his hips and stepped from the shower, avoiding the question, avoiding her eyes so Evie figured that for a no, and wasn't surprised. He'd retreat now, he always did, and she should have felt used and confused, but she didn't. Instead she felt sad as she let her gaze wash over his naked form. Sad for him. Sad for herself. But not abused.

She didn't even know how he came to have a body like that. What sports he played, what he did to blow off steam. The list of things she didn't know about this man seemed endless. And the list of things she did know about him was short and anything but sweet.

'Do you play sports?' she asked, and when he lifted his eyebrow at the inanity of the question she shrugged and tried not to be too distracted by the thin line of hair that ran south from his belly-button and disappeared beneath that low-slung towel.

'I climb,' he said. 'Snow and water ski whenever I get the chance. Sail catamarans competitively.'

That'd do it.

'Does this have anything to do with the amount of baggage I can carry round?' he asked with the ghost of a smile.

'No,' she replied with a rueful smile. 'I just wanted to know a little more about you, that's all. Something little. Something…'

'Normal?' he offered.

It was as good a word as any. 'I don't know what to do. From the moment I first saw you again, I haven't known what to do.' Truth, and if it signified weakness on her part then so be it.

'You need to call off this wedding, Evangeline.'

'I know that, Logan.' Evie glanced towards the shower. 'Is that what the sex was all about? A demonstration of my weakness when it comes to your touch? Because if it was, it wasn't necessary. I already knew.'

'It wasn't that.' Logan turned away to pick up his soggy clothes and wrung them out. 'It was need.'

And there was the appeal of this man and the danger in him. That stinging, searing, all-consuming need—and his fear of it.

'What if we start again?' she offered quietly. 'I call off this wedding, MEP finds some other way to finance the civic centre bid and you and I, we start again. Clean slate. You might, for example, come to Sydney one weekend and ask me out on a date. We might see a movie or go for coffee in the park. You could bring me a bunch of black-eyed daisies or a paper parasol. I might feed you chocolate-cherry mud-cake with my fingers by way of thank you.'

Logan's eyes had darkened again.

'Easy as,' she said lightly. 'And your call.' She wasn't the one carrying a dead father and a battered mother around. 'What kind of cocktail party does your mother throw? Fairly formal?'

'Yes.'

'Are you planning to attend?' she asked next.

'Are you?'

Evie nodded. 'Got to try and explain my engagement to Max away somehow.'

'Just tell them my mother made a mistake. Tell them you're celebrating a business milestone rather than a personal one.'

'Yes. Something like that.' She eyed him steadily. 'We could use your help to sell it. You could aim for civilised.'

'Yes,' he said with a smile she didn't trust at all. 'I could.' And handed her back the towel and stalked from the bathroom and then from her room without another word.

'So what happened between you and Logan?' asked Max for the umpteenth time as Evie plucked a midnight-blue gown from a clothing rack and flattened it against her body.

'We talked,' she said calmly. 'Too formal?'

'No,' said Max. 'Does he still want you to go live in Antarctica?'

'Probably,' said Evie, and withdrew a sleek little black dress from the rack. 'But he knows he can't make me, so he's just going to have to learn to live with disappointment. Too severe?'

'Yes.'

Evie draped it across her arm of potential dresses anyway. Little black dresses could be deceptive. A deceptively demure black-and-caramel-coloured dress caught her eye next. Demure could be deceptive too. 'What about this one?'

'Evie, just pick one,' said Max.

'Or I could take an early flight home and forget about your mother's cocktail party altogether,' said Evie. 'As long as we're talking contingency plans, I'm liking that one a lot.'

'No,' said Max steadily. 'We ride this one out together. Kill the speculation stone dead now.'

'Maybe you can tell them I'm gay,' murmured Evie.

'They wouldn't believe me. Not if Logan's anywhere in the room.'

'Okay, then. You can be gay.' Evie eyed a plum-coloured gown with a plunging neckline and a thigh-high side split speculatively. 'What about this one?'

'Evie, just *pick* one.' And then Max looked at the dress. 'But not that one.'

Evie slid it back on the rack. 'I vote we tell your mother's friends that we're celebrating the success of our business partnership and hopefully the beginning of bigger and better things for MEP. We smile and shake our heads and say we're sorry people got the wrong idea but we're not engaged and not about to be. We keep it simple. Deny everything.'

'You really think that's going to fly?'

'Put it this way,' she said. 'You got a better idea?'

The cocktail party was every bit as awkward as Evie thought it would be. Elegant, wealthy people, all set to welcome Evie into their lives at Caroline's behest, and politely puzzled when it became clear that they didn't have to.

Civilised. It was all so very civilised, but no midnight-blue cocktail gown in the world could shield her from Logan's powerful presence as she stood by Max's side and talked business goals and achievements with strangers.

Logan didn't approach her. He stuck to his side of

the room and Evie stuck to hers. She didn't watch him out of the corner of her eye. Instead she stuck to finding him in reflections in mirrors, of which there were plenty. In the shine of tall silver vases. How could one man assault her senses the way he did, just by being in a room? One man, dressed in black tie, just like every other man in the room.

'Evie, stop fidgeting,' said Max.

'I'm not fidgeting.'

She *was* fidgeting, so with a smothered curse she stopped.

'And swearing,' murmured Max, highly amused. 'You could stop that too.'

'I'm not—damn!' Evie swore rather than add chronic lying to her list of sins too. 'How much longer do we have to stay here?'

'Until the bitter end,' said Max cheerfully. 'I'm guessing around midnight.'

She'd been sticking to mineral water until now. Maybe it was time she swapped over to something with a little more kick. Then again, the argument against alcohol was a strong one. She'd already been quite uninhibited enough today.

'You could marry someone else,' she told Max during a moment they had to themselves—just business partners sharing a quiet moment out on the patio, drinks in hand and smiles at the ready. 'A childhood friend. Someone who knows this life and how to live it. Someone who'd be happy to accommodate you for two years and then move on.'

'Absolutely not,' said Max with a shudder. 'I'm over marriage for the time being. I might try being in love with the person next time. Just a thought.'

'How are we going to get the money for the civic centre bid?'

'Overdraft for some of it,' said Max. 'I'll put my place on the market.'

'I'll put mine on,' Evie said with a sigh. 'We're still going to come up short.'

'Business loan,' said Max bleakly. 'Here, before I forget.' He fished in his pocket and pulled out something small and round and silver-coloured, those bits of it that weren't a dazzling, glittering blue. It was a sapphire ring the size of Texas. Evie didn't understand. 'My mother wants you to have this as a memento of our engagement. Something about payment for your trouble.' He held it out towards her.

'No.' Evie took a hasty step back. 'Whatever your mother's opinions are, just…no. I'm all for forgetting we were ever engaged.'

'I told her you'd say that.' Max reached for her right hand and slipped it swiftly on her middle finger. Not her ring finger, not even the proper hand. 'She seems to think I owe you a ring. That we were engaged, however briefly, and that you deserve some kind of compensation. Wear it. Flog it. I don't care. Just take it. I'm a man in search of family harmony and my mother wants you to have it.'

'I don't want it,' muttered Evie, tugging the ring off just as swiftly as it had gone on. It was too bulky anyway. Too much the reminder of bad decisions too hastily made. 'Please, Max. Just give it back to her. Tell her I don't want it.'

But Max's attention had drifted to a point just over her shoulder, his eyes narrowing fast, and Evie knew, even before she looked over her shoulder, that Logan was heading their way. 'Take it,' she said, trying to push the ring into Max's hand, only he wasn't having it, and then Logan was upon them and Max automatically moved to make room for him.

'Change of heart?' murmured Logan, looking at the ring, and shock flared deep in his eyes; right before those same eyes turned bitter and then carefully blank.

'This isn't what it looks like.' Max's words came low and fast. 'It's not an engagement ring. We're not engaged. The wedding's off and it's staying off. You know that.'

'Where'd you get the ring?' asked Logan, and didn't wait for Max's answer. 'She give it to you? Our mother? She tell you to give it to Evangeline?'

'Yes.' Max looked uneasy. Evie *was* uneasy.

'Take it,' said Evie urgently. 'I don't want it. Would someone please just take it back?'

But Logan wanted no part of it. He knew that stone, the ocean-reef-blue of it. He'd seen it before. He looked towards the small crowd of people in the adjoining room. Those who hadn't drifted out onto the patio or into the gardens and his mother was one of them. What was she doing? What the hell was she thinking giving Evie this particular ring? She had that look about her; the one that said I'm worried about you and I'm scared of what you'll do and he wished to hell she'd just *stop looking at him like that!* Look to her own flaws, for once, and not only to his.

'Logan?' said Evie, and put her hand to his forearm to draw his attention, and something twisted deep in his gut. 'Logan, what's wrong?'

'Nothing.'

'Bull,' she snapped, calling his bluff. 'You're hurt.'

'No. It's her ring. What do I care what she does with it?'

'Logan, *who* gave your mother this ring?' Evie asked tightly.

But Logan refused to answer her.

'It's the one your father gave her, isn't it?' said Evie.

'No,' said Max.

'Doesn't matter.' He wouldn't let it matter.

'Logan, this *can't* be that ring,' continued Max doggedly. 'She wouldn't do that.'

But she had.

Max wouldn't recognise it; she'd never worn it in front of him. Different lifetime. Different family. Caroline Carmichael had got it right the second time round. A gentle, supportive husband and a loving, well-balanced child.

Max thought their mother was wonderful.

And then the bitter blackness spewed forth, and, for the second time that day, Logan let it engulf him.

'She likes to remind me of him whenever she thinks I've gone too far.' He sought Evangeline's gaze. Evangeline in the midnight-blue gown that accentuated her flawless skin and slender curves. The same skin he'd put mouth to not so long ago. The same curves he wanted to caress again with an intensity that bordered on obsession. 'Have I gone too far, Evangeline?'

'No,' she said slowly as her fist clenched around the ring. 'It's not you who's gone too far.'

And before Logan had any notion of what she was about to do, Evie twirled and flung his mother's ring into the shadowy garden, into the shrubbery far, far away.

The pregnant silence that followed threatened to engulf them all.

'Good arm,' said Max finally.

'It was given to me,' she said raggedly. 'And I've done what I wanted with it. No one needs that kind of reminder in their life. *No one.*'

He couldn't cope. Logan stared at her, his every defence shattered, and something passed between them, something dark and sticky and breathtakingly savage. He didn't cope well with emotion; his mother was right. Sometimes his feelings just got too big for him to hold.

'Excuse me,' he muttered, before he did something unforgivable like drag her from the room, lock her in his arms and never let her go. 'Excuse me, I have to go.'

Evie watched him leave, her heart so full of lead she was surprised she was still standing up. 'I did the wrong thing,' she whispered to Max. 'Said the wrong thing.'

'No,' said Max and his arms came around her comfortingly, urging her to turn and focus her stricken gaze on something other than the door Logan had just exited through. 'You did exactly the right thing. He's feeling too vulnerable, that's all. He never stays when he gets that way.'

Evie didn't want to stay either. Not that she wanted to run after Logan, because she didn't. Assuming she even caught up with him, what would she say? How was she supposed to heal hurts inflicted so long ago? If they hadn't healed by now, chances were they never would.

'Max, may we leave early too?' she asked shakily. 'I've had enough. I really have.' Of the assault on her senses and on her mind. Of the impossible situations that just kept coming, and of the helplessness she felt in the face of this family's hidden pain. 'I want to go upstairs and pack, then call a taxi.'

'Where do you want to go?' Max's usually laughing brown eyes were dark with concern.

'Back to Sydney,' she said. 'Away from here. I want to go home.'

CHAPTER FIVE

WALKING away from Logan that Saturday night at the cocktail party wasn't the hardest thing Evie had ever done. Staying sane the following week was the hardest thing she'd ever done. Sane when Max looked at her sideways and kept his mouth firmly shut. Sane as she worked on project proposals and tried not to wonder what Logan was doing and what he was thinking, and whether she'd ever see him again.

How she could have handled things better.

What she might have done to make Logan stay.

'What?' she demanded in exasperation as Max walked into her office unannounced for about the tenth time that morning.

'Touchy,' he said.

'Bite me.'

'Not my buzz,' said Max, and placed a sheet of paper on top of the drawings in front of her. 'You'd be wanting my brother for that.'

He wasn't wrong. 'I'm working,' she said and picked up the sheet and held it out for Max to take back. 'Whatever it is, you deal with it.'

'Read it,' he insisted, so Evie turned it back around with a sigh.

A bank deposit notice, but not a bank she regularly dealt with. Max's personal account, by the looks of it. With deposit into it yesterday of ten million dollars.

'Trust fund?' she asked.

'Logan.'

Evie's heart skipped a beat. 'Terms?'

'Three per cent below market interest rate.'

'Handy.'

'You don't mind?' asked Max.

'Do you?'

'He stole my fake fiancée and messed with my business plan,' said Max dryly. 'I'll take his money.'

'Yay for brotherly love,' said Evie. 'As long as the loan is between you and Logan and the money comes into the business through you alone, I have no objections.'

'That's how it'll work.'

'Lucky MEP.'

'Any other questions?' asked Max.

Evie shook her head.

'You don't want to know where Logan is? What he's been doing lately?'

She *did* want to know where Logan was and what he'd been doing lately. But she sure as hell wasn't going to ask.

'PNG,' said Max, as if reading her mind. 'Sorting out the mess some mining company has made of their operation there. Sometimes Logan troubleshoots for others. For a hefty fee.'

'The devil will have his due.'

'He's a good man, Evie.'

'I know that, Max.'

'You should call him. Might improve your mood.'

'There is *nothing* wrong with my mood.'

'Carlo would beg to disagree.'

'Carlo ordered twenty-eight thousand dollars' worth of reo we don't need,' she said curtly. 'He's lucky I let him keep his *job*.'

'And Logan thinks you meek,' muttered Max beneath his breath. 'God knows why.'

Evie knew exactly why. 'Was there anything else?'

'Could be Logan will need a place to stay for a few days when he returns at the end of the week and before he heads back to London. Could be I'm thinking of offering up my apartment for him to use while he's here.'

'Why? You think he's short of cash?' asked Evie dryly.

'What I *think*,' said Max with admirable restraint, 'is that if you want to see him again, you shouldn't wait for him to call you. Call him. Arrange something. Don't assume that he knows what he's doing when it comes to relationships, especially important ones, because he doesn't.' Max plucked the bank note from her fingers and waved it in front of her face. 'This, for example, might as well have "*Evie, I want to see you again*" written all over it.'

'But it doesn't,' she countered sweetly, and Max sighed and dug his mobile out of his pocket and started in on the touch screen before handing it to her with a flourish.

'Tell him you've been mooning over him all week and want to see him again.'

'I will *not*.'

'All right. Then tell him I want my chief engineer's head back in the game and that I'm blaming *him* for the fact that it's not.'

Evie glared at Max's hastily retreating back, silently wondering just how many problems she'd solve if she brained Max with his phone. Probably not that many.

'Tell him I said thank you,' added Max.

'Tell him yourself,' she yelled after him, and then put the phone to her ear just in time to hear the man who currently inhabited most of her dreams—sleeping and waking—say his brother's name.

Which necessitated some sort of reply.

'Um…hi. It's not Max,' she said awkwardly. 'It's Evie. Evie on Max's phone. How much did you hear?'

'Everything from "thank you" onwards.'

'Oh,' she said, more than a little relieved. 'Good. Because that about covers it. Your bank transfer came in and Max's just showed it to me and we wanted to say thank you. Which I'm sure Max will do in person when he sees you next. Thank you, that is.' And if Max said anything else to his brother about Evie's recently distracted state she'd strangle him. 'And I'd like to thank you too. The money's going to help the civic centre bid's chances a lot, and Max's set on winning it and can take it from here, and I can get on with the rest of the work and let the prima donna do his thing…so thank you.'

'You often make business phone calls like this?' asked Logan.

'Never.'

'Good to know,' he murmured.

'Bite me.'

Silence after that, heavy and waiting. Evie took a deep breath. 'Max tells me you're flying into Sydney later this week, and I was thinking…'

Evie had no idea what she was thinking.

'…I was thinking that Max probably wants to invite

you into the workplace so you can look around. Which would be fine by me. If you wanted to, that is.' Evie closed her eyes, leaned back in her chair and thumped her head repeatedly against the headrest, scrabbling for confidence in the face of Logan's silence and coming up empty. 'I was thinking you might need to be picked up from the airport. I could do that. Take you wherever you wanted to go.' Excellent. Now she was officially babbling. 'How's PNG?'

'Hot, sticky and politically messy,' he said. 'Largely bereft of plain speaking.'

Evie was largely bereft of plain speaking too.

'Would you like to have dinner with me while you're here?' she asked with her eyes closed tightly shut, and figured it for as plain spoken as she was going to get. 'I know some good casual eating places. Nothing fancy. But the food's good.'

Asking a man out on a date was hard. Harder still, when the man in question said a whole lot of nothing in reply.

'This is the part where you say yes or no,' she prompted quietly.

'I don't get into Sydney until late Friday night,' he said finally. 'There'll be a hire car waiting for me.'

Of course there would.

'And I don't need the workplace tour.'

Of course he didn't. 'Let me just find Max for you, shall I?'

'Dinner on Saturday evening I could do.'

'Pardon?' Evie was halfway to the door. She probably hadn't heard him correctly.

'Dinner,' he said. 'Saturday night. Something low-fuss and easy. That I could do.'

'There's a place called Brennan's in Darlinghurst. It's a bar and grill. Very casual.'

'I'll meet you there at 6:00 p.m.,' he said. 'Evie, I've got to go. I'm meant to be in a meeting.'

Interrupting his work. Not exactly a high priority in his life. He couldn't have made it any clearer if he'd tried. But he'd said yes to seeing her again, although God knew why.

'Bye, then,' she said. And hung up before he could, and went to tell her meddling business partner that her head—far from being back in the game—was now officially screwed.

Served Max right.

Saturday came and Evie spent the bulk of it trying to forget that she'd ever asked Logan out in the first place. She went to Coogee Beach and swam in the surf and then in the rock pool with a uni friend she often caught up with on weekends. They walked the cliff walk round to Bondi and had an ice cream and then she caught the bus home. Which still gave her three hours to fill in until six and her dinner with Logan. She put on a movie and steamed through her ironing basket and did a fast tidy-up of her apartment. And then she hit the shower and saw a slightly sunburned domestic goddess, which wasn't all bad because now she could turn up at the grill looking as if she'd been enjoying her weekend, rather than just waiting for six o' clock and Logan to come around.

No woman in her right mind would pin too many hopes on Logan.

So it was well-worn jeans and a white cotton top that gathered at the hip with a multicoloured scarf that she wore to meet him. Add to that an inexpensive blue-bead necklace, half a dozen thin silver bangles, sunglasses perched on her head and Evie figured herself plenty casual as she walked into Brennan's at five to six. If Logan didn't show…if he'd changed his mind about seeing her again…well, there was food here aplenty and she wouldn't go thirsty.

But Logan was already there when Evie arrived, sitting by himself in a corner booth with a half empty beer in front of him and lines around his eyes that told of fatigue, but he smiled when he saw her and hell if she didn't melt at the sight of it. She'd never seen him in jeans and scuffed work boots before and he wore them just as easily as he wore a custom-made suit. His shirt was black, and seemed to suck in the light and women watched him from the corner of their eyes. Watched him because he was black-eyed and beautiful and sexuality clung to him like a second skin.

He stood as she approached. He took her hand and leaned closer and kissed her cheek and then withdrew. 'First date,' he murmured. 'Easy as. That's what I'm aiming for,' he added and sat back down after she sat, and placed an elegant square box, about the size of her hand, on the table between them. 'I couldn't find any black-eyed daisies or paper parasols.'

The lid came off and the sides of the box folded down to reveal a life-sized origami hummingbird sipping from a bell-shaped flower.

'It's beautiful.' Evie leaned closer for a better look, not game to touch it, so delicate was the detail. 'Exquisite. But you didn't get this from Papua New Guinea.' This was a museum-quality offering, not a last-minute little something from a handy airport gift shop.

'No.' He gave a small shrug. 'I got it today. I know I cut you short on the phone the other day, Evangeline. It was unavoidable. I know I should have called you back. I just didn't know what to say.'

'It's okay, Logan. I don't know what I want from you either.' And it was far easier to say that in person than on the phone. Evie boxed the gift back up with gentle fingers and set it on top of her handbag in the far corner of the bench seat, far away from where the food would be placed. 'Thank you for your gorgeous gift.'

Logan shrugged, shrugging it off. Don't make such a fuss over it, he might as well have said. Doesn't mean I *care*.

He'd seemed that way with his mother too, and Max to a lesser extent. Desperately trying *not* to care about them too much. If you didn't care, they couldn't hurt you. Oh, Evie knew that defence. She knew it well.

'How was business in PNG?'

'Unpredictable,' he murmured. 'In need of a strong hand.'

'So it suited you,' she countered, and he smiled that lazy wicked smile of his, the one that made her blood heat and her pulse quicken.

'Yes.'

Hard not to admire a man who worked to his strengths. 'Are you rich?' He had to be wealthy in order to slip Max ten million so quickly, but exactly *how* wealthy was a question Evie hadn't yet asked and Logan hadn't yet answered.

'You want a monetary estimate?' he asked, and she nodded, and he named a figure that made her sit back and blink. 'I inherited money early,' he said. 'My mother handed over every last cent of my father's wealth the minute I turned eighteen and I took it and put it to work. The money doubles on a regular basis and that's the way I like it.'

'Because you never want to go hungry again?' she asked.

'Because I'm addicted to power and the wielding of it.'

'Wow,' she murmured. 'A man who owns his flaws. That's really rare.'

'I wouldn't call them flaws,' he murmured with a crooked smile. 'Exactly. What about you, Evie? Are you rich?'

'Not at all, compared to you. I own my own apartment. I can sometimes afford an expensive treat but I don't make a habit of it. As far as family goes, my father's respectably well-off but not effortlessly wealthy; probably because he's on his fifth wife. My mother was wife number three. I have twelve half siblings, no full siblings, and my mother's now on husband number three. Max thinks I have no strong ties to family and no respect whatsoever for the institution of marriage. He's probably right.'

'So if a man wanted to marry you…'

'I'd take some convincing.'

'How long did it take Max to convince you?'

'Ah, but Max had good monetary *reason* for wanting to get married. And it benefited me too. And it wouldn't have been a proper marriage anyway. It was more of a business transaction. With a two-hundred-thousand-dollar windfall clause for the injured party every time one of us strayed.'

'Honour system?' asked Logan with a touch of incredulity about him.

'No. The clause only kicked in if the straying became public knowledge.'

'And Max *agreed* to this?'

'I *know*,' said Evie, making good use of her eyelashes. 'I figured Max would be up for at least a couple of million before we were through, and that's being conservative. Your brother's got a short attention span.'

'And no contract sense whatsoever.'

'I had his back though,' murmured Evie. 'If Max got too far in debt to me I was going to start matching him, indiscretion for public indiscretion.'

Logan's eyes narrowed. Evie smiled and sipped at her just-arrived soda. 'You're pulling my leg,' he said finally.

'Someone's got to. You take life entirely too seriously.'

'No, I take *contracts* seriously. There's a difference.'

'If you say so.'

'You're sunburnt,' he said and Evie nodded agreeably.

'That's because I've been to the beach.'

'Was it good?'

'Very good.'

'Maybe there should have been sunscreen involved.'

'There was. Though possibly not enough.'

'What else do you do in your down time?' he asked.

'I like to travel. Explore new places. Even a new-to-me suburb will do.'

'On your own?'

'It's better with friends. But sometimes on my own.'

'Any special friends I need to know about?' he asked.

'You mean lovers?' she said and he nodded, his eyes

narrowing. 'No. I may not be marriage-ready, but one lover at a time will do.'

'Am I currently the one?'

'I don't know.' Time for truth and if it burned then so be it. 'I guess that's what I asked you here to find out.'

'I'm only here for a week, Evie.' His voice held a quiet warning.

'Sounds familiar.' Hers held quiet challenge. 'I like you, Logan, in case you hadn't noticed. Baggage and all. It wouldn't be a hardship to spend another week with you. Might even be fun.'

'As opposed to…'

'Intense, confusing, and ultimately heartbreaking. I'd like to think that we have enough experience between us now to keep those elements out of play.'

'You don't like intense?'

'You're right. There's a lot to be said for intensity. That one can stay.'

'You calling the shots now, Evie?'

'Only some of them. Feel free to voice your requirements too.'

'I want exclusivity,' he said.

'The feeling's mutual.'

'And freedom.'

'I'll do my freely exclusive best.'

'Obedience.'

'And sometimes you'll get it.' Evie edged closer, elbows to the table, so much for manners. 'You don't want to dominate me completely, remember? Or am I wrong about that?'

'Just keep reminding me when I forget.' He had his shoulders to the padded black vinyl of the booth bench and one arm stretched out on the table towards her.

He looked gorgeous and confident and he leaned forward with a look that spoke of barely contained hunger. 'C'm'ere.'

Evie inched closer because she wanted to. Opened her lips beneath his, because she wanted that too. The taste of him, not knowing what type of kiss she'd get from him, and she wondered if he mixed his kisses up deliberately—needy and greedy one time and slow and savouring the next. Whether he ever had a plan...

Evie *never* had a plan once he laid siege to her, but that would have to change.

Just as soon as this gentle whisper of a kiss finished.

'You talk a good game, Evie,' he murmured, and eased away slowly. 'I'm tempted to give you that week.'

'This coming week is the one on offer,' she said with a gentle smile as she sat back and browsed the blackboard menu. 'Let me know what you decide. I think I'll have the salmon, spinach leaves and pear salad. You?'

'Rib eye.'

'They do a nice one here.' Small talk to settle her nerves. And then the waiter came for their order and a side of bread arrived shortly after that and Evie nibbled on it and her stomach settled further. The civic centre bid had been submitted, she told him. Max was doing the follow-up courting. Three bread-and-butter projects were out of the ground and well under way. Plans for a luxury harbour-side residence were on the drawing board. Business as usual. Enjoyable as always, that mix of creativity and calculation. There was an eco house up in the Blue Mountains that she wanted to see. Canton tower in Guangzhou, China. Hell, why not a world tour of giant Ferris wheels and fabulous hotels?

'That what you want to do this coming week?' he asked quietly. 'Because we could.'

'Maybe *you* could,' she said after a moment's startled silence. 'The rest of us get to save for years, finesse the dream and carry the sweet scent of achievement around with us when finally such a trip comes to pass. But if it's filling this coming week that you're interested in, I still have to work seven till three, Monday to Friday. Wednesday afternoon I might be able to clear. How do you feel about roller coasters and fairy floss?'

'That's your idea of a dream date?'

'You don't like roller coasters and fairy floss?'

Logan shrugged. 'It's been a while.'

For her too. Maybe it wasn't such a good combination. 'Does Max know you're having dinner with me?'

'Not unless you told him.'

'I didn't.' Which led to the next question that needed asking. 'This week you're currently considering sharing with me—do you care if people know about it?'

'Do you?'

'No. But then, I'm not the businessman wheeler and dealer with control issues.'

'I wouldn't call them issues, exactly.'

Maybe her multimillionaire wasn't so self aware after all. 'Would you want to stay at my apartment?'

'I'm staying in a serviced apartment at the Quay,' he replied. 'You could come there.'

'Yes, but it's not your home, is it? Last time we did this I was living in a student dorm and you were living out of a hotel penthouse. We spent most of our time in that penthouse naked. Beyond our sexual compatibility I had no real sense of you as a person. And you had none of me. I wonder if that was a mistake.'

'Do you really want me in your home?' he asked.

'Yes. My bed. My kitchen in the mornings. My life. For a week.'

'What if we're not compatible?'

'Then there's nothing to worry about.' Evie sat back and regarded him solemnly. 'The question you *should* be worrying about is what if we are?'

Logan ended up at her place for coffee. No word from him yet on what he would do this coming week. No more words from Evie either, regarding their relationship. Instead she invited him in and stood back and watched him as he entered her apartment. Nothing special by his standards, but more than adequate by hers. She wondered if Logan would recognise his brother's touch when it came to the design, but if he did he didn't say anything. Max had made his early reputation by converting row upon row of inner-city warehouses into spacious three-storey apartments and this was one of them. It was how they'd met. She'd asked Max for some structural changes and he'd heard her out grudgingly. About halfway into the collaboration Max's reluctance had turned to enthusiasm.

'There's three floors,' she said. 'Kitchen, living area and utilities are on the ground floor, office and spare room on the first floor and my bedroom and living quarters are up the top.'

'You have a three-storey fire pole,' he said.

'Did I mention I like rides?'

Logan just looked at her.

'I have stairs too.' Gorgeous, floating stairs she'd designed herself—one of the modifications she'd asked of Max. She'd started out with grand plans for a minimalist lifestyle, but that was half a dozen years ago now and homely clutter had moved in. Not a show-piece, this apartment, but a home. Comfortable sofas in mismatched colours. Mismatched cushions too. Lots of colour to balance the unpainted concrete walls and exposed girders. Logan was looking up at those roof-top girders now.

'What are you looking for?' she asked.

'Trapeze.'

'Huh.' She'd never considered a trapeze before, though she had considered bungee apparatus. 'You think I'd need a net?'

'That or a last will and testament. You know, I never *once* figured you for a thrill seeker.'

'Really? You don't think me sliding so willingly up and down the pleasure-pain endorphins might have clued you in?'

Logan shrugged. 'Not sure I was thinking at all when I was with you before, Evangeline.'

'And now?'

'Well, I can still remember my name,' he said. 'That's got to be a good sign. Have you given any thought to what might happen *after* our week is up?'

'Logan, I'm not sure we're even going to get through *today*. There's still three hours of it left, and forgive me for saying so but you don't seem to want to be here.' Evie was nervous. Logan looked nervous. Hardly an ideal combination.

'It's just…this is your home.'

'Yes.' She eyed Logan speculatively. 'Logan, have you ever *been* in a woman's home before? Apart from your mother's?'

'I have aunts as well,' he murmured.

'You know what I mean.' She meant had he ever been to the home of a woman he'd bedded, or intended to bed.

'No.'

'Nervous?' She turned to a high kitchen shelf and pulled down a bottle of half-empty Scotch. Good Scotch. Glasses came next and then she unscrewed the lid and poured generously.

'You really think that's the solution?'

'I'm willing to give it a whirl,' she murmured before lifting a glass and tilting it towards him and then downing it in one hasty swallow. 'That one was for courage, and here's what we're going to do. You're going to go over to the lounge, turn on the television and channel surf until you find something you want to watch. I'm going to put some nibbles on a plate and bring them over and sit down beside you and relax. There's a slim chance you might relax too.'

'Don't count on it.'

'I'm not,' she said dryly. 'What do you think the courage was for?'

Logan shot her a smile and picked up her glass and his and the Scotch bottle too before sauntering over to the lounge.

She joined him a short time later, dimming the lights on the way. Easier to ignore all the bits and pieces she'd filled her life with after that. Not so easy to ignore the effects of Logan's nearness, the subtle scent of sandalwood on his skin. The strong, sensual shape of his lips or the ripe red colour of them. He was so very kissable.

And clearly he felt completely out of place.

Two minutes she lasted. Two minutes before her hands were roaming his chest and Logan's hands were in her hair as he laid silent, lazy siege to her mouth.

Evie knew she was coming apart under Logan's touch but there was nothing she could do to prevent it. Did he *know* how closely attuned to each other they were in their lovemaking? How rare that was? Rare for her, at any rate. Maybe for Logan it was perfectly normal. Maybe he made every woman he bedded feel as if she were the only thing that mattered to him in this world.

Maybe that was just his way.

Vocal—that was new. The husky oaths that fell from his lips like endearments. The groans that sounded like prayer.

On her back now, because that was where he wanted her, with her legs drawn up on either side of him and his mouth not leaving hers. Sinuous, his movements as he rubbed up against her. Sensuality his weapon of choice.

And he used it with devastating effect.

Kissing was easy, thought Logan. Kissing was a hell of a lot easier than talking or trying to fit into a life that was not his.

His shirt came off, and Evie's would have too, but she slid out from beneath him and pushed him back against the sofa with a palm to his chest as she straddled his hips.

'My house,' she murmured. 'My rules.'

She pushed his arms back until they rested outstretched along the back of the sofa and set her lips to his triceps and he shuddered beneath her touch and closed his eyes and let her play. Pure pleasure, no pain, and he craved this just as much as he'd ever craved the other. Such a slow and easy slide into sensation. The wet lick of tongue against sensitive skin. The brush of soft hair over hardened nipples. The slow creep of moisture and heat and the tightening of his balls when finally she freed him from his clothes and loosened her own and he slid slowly into her.

Not always rough and fighting for control. Sometimes—when the mood was upon him—he could be exquisitely, unthinkingly…

Gentle.

Evie woke the next morning in her bed. She'd lured Logan there eventually and the slight shift of her head confirmed that he hadn't yet left. He lay sleeping instead, and in the quiet half-light of dawn Evie studied the man she'd tangled with so exquisitely last night. More beautiful asleep than awake—and always had been. Less guarded when he was asleep and far more innocent-looking. Slept on his tummy with his hands beneath the pillow and his head and one knee crooked towards her. As if he'd watched her slide into slumber before surrendering to it himself.

Fanciful notion, and she knew it. The man had been sated towards the end. He would have closed his eyes and been asleep within moments, just as she had. No time for analysis of the lovemaking that had taken place. The frightening, soul-stealing beauty of it.

That was what morning-afters were for.

Slowly, so as not to wake him, Evie slid silently from the bed, slipped a robe from its hanger and headed for the stairs, no need to put it on now. She'd shower downstairs where the noise would not wake him. No need to wake him for, once she did that, Logan might go.

She had a feeling he'd want to go.

'I'd kill for coffee,' he said as her toes touched the first step.

Evie turned and found herself in receipt of a sleepy gaze that swept her from head to toe. Not the full-wattage smile; he wasn't even trying and *still* he warmed her through.

'In house or out?' she asked lightly. 'Because if you're fussy, there's a place on the corner that does fancy coffee.'

'Not fussy,' he rumbled as his eyes closed once more. Not quite awake either. 'Just need something to wake me up. Evie?' he murmured.

'What?'

'Morning.'

Logan gave himself over to a few more minutes of shut-eye before rolling onto his back and setting the heels of his hands to his face in an attempt to make his eyes stay open. He shouldn't be jet-lagged; he'd only flown in from PNG. No, the tiredness came from not being able to leave Evie alone last night. Of reaching for her one last time, and then another. Of going slow and savouring every caress.

Last night he'd been given a gift. A chance to make amends for all that had gone before, and he'd done it, replaced old memories with new. Better memories that he could examine without shame. Memories he could hold on to without feeling the stain on his soul.

He looked around the room, looking for clues as to the type of person Evie was at home and finding it in the rough concrete finish of the walls and the exposed plumbing and air-con. No hiding of mechanics behind pretty painted walls for Evie. She seemed to want to strip life back to basics so she could keep an eye on it—everything exposed, even the clothes cupboard, or what there was of it, for her clothes hung on hangers over a long stretch of metal bar, not a cupboard wall in sight. The clothes were colour co-ordinated—sort of—and clearly some thought had gone into the mix and matchability of them. Lots of black and grey, and what colours there were had a vividness about them. No pretty pastels for Evie. Clearly that wasn't her style.

He was contemplating getting out of bed but hadn't quite got there yet when Evie returned with the coffee, robe on and hair gathered casually atop her head. The robe slid off one shoulder as she set the tray down on the bed and she raised her arm to slide the robe back into place with the absent-mindedness of someone who repeated that particular action often.

'Lot of space up here,' he said as she settled down carefully on the other side of the tray.

'I know,' said Evie. 'It bothers some people. They'd rather sleep in a cave with the ceiling and walls tucked in close.' She eyed him curiously. 'Does it bother you?'

'No.' But parts of her statement did. 'What people?'

'The one or two people who've been invited up here over the past half a dozen years,' she said evenly, lifting her coffee to her lips and taking a tiny sip. 'Are you asking me how many men I've had in this bed?'

'No.' None of his business.

She looked at him and her eyebrow rose just a fraction.

'Maybe,' he admitted gruffly.

'How many would you think?'

'Not going near that one, Evie.'

'Six,' she said sweetly. 'Though not all at once.'

Six was okay. Given Evangeline's charm and enjoyment when it came to the pleasures of the flesh, six lovers in as many years was downright picky.

'Anything else you'd like to know?' she offered.

'*Really* don't want to know,' he said quickly. Only a madman would ask her for details and he had no intention of doing so, and besides…he'd *wanted* her to explore her sexuality after he'd left her, hadn't he? Wanted her to be sure of her preferences and to know her own mind.

Still did.

He looked around the room again and thought of the woman-child he'd once known and the woman Evie was now. 'Tough profession, engineering,' he said mildly.

Evie nodded, letting him change the subject.

'Why'd you choose it?'

'I wanted in on a highly paid and flexible profession that had the potential to take me anywhere. No relying on anyone else for my financial well-being or my status in society.'

That need *hadn't* started with him. At least, Logan didn't think it had. 'Why the overwhelming need for independence?'

'My mother's been a trophy wife all her life. It's hard work. Soul-destroying, at times. I guess I simply grew up *not* wanting it.'

'Is that why your bedroom's so spartan? Because you're rebelling against the perfect-homemaker label?'

'I hope not,' she murmured. 'Because that'd be stupid, considering I made this home for me. No, I just really like the minimalist aesthetic. Which is not to say I'm totally against a lavish touch at times, because I guarantee you'll find one in the bathroom. Bubble bath, scented candles, fluffy towels…'

'Sensualist,' he murmured and Evie shot him a slow smile.

'Rich, coming from you,' she said. 'I've never known anyone who savours sensuality the way you do. Who cherishes touch the way you do. Anyone would think you'd been starved of it as a child.'

'My mother wasn't demonstrative,' he offered blandly. Evie had seen for herself what kind of relationship he had with his mother. His father's hand had usually been hard and punishing, but those memories he kept to himself. Better a fist than no touch at all—that was the way the crazy ran for him at times. The reason why he'd taken so instinctively to pain play during lovemaking. He hadn't needed a psychologist to tell him the why of that.

But not last night. Last night's lovemaking with Evie had been positively, effortlessly normal.

'Do you have any plans for today?' he asked, and Evie shook her head and the vivid red silk robe slid from her shoulder again.

Pretty.

He bit into the cinnamon roll Evie had brought up with the coffee and it tasted sweet and flaky and sticky on his tongue.

'I could show you round Sydney if you feel like playing tourist,' she offered.

'Can there be jet boats on the harbour involved?'

'Yes.'

'With me at the wheel?'

'No.' Evie rolled her eyes at him. 'For that you'd have to buy the boat. Bridge climb?'

'Too slow.'

'Skydiving?' she offered next. 'I'm in a club.'

'Why am I not surprised?'

'Because you're getting to know me,' she offered dulcetly. 'But in the interests of full disclosure, we could also head for the Botanic Gardens this morning and lie on the grass and listen to buskers play lazy Sunday-morning songs. That'd work for me too. I guess it all depends.'

'On what?'

'On whether you plan to stick around and slay a few more demons this week or whether after last night you already consider them vanquished, in which case my money's on you leaving some time in the next ten minutes.'

Not only did this woman know her own mind, Logan thought uncomfortably, she also had a fair and accurate reading of his. 'Do you want me to leave?'

'No.' She was breaking the other cinnamon roll into bits and he couldn't see her eyes for eyelashes, but the steadiness of that no was reassuring.

'You said you'd give me a week,' he said.

'And I will, if that's what you want.'

She still wouldn't look at him.

'I do want,' he said and leaned forward and snaked his hand through her hair and kissed her gently, and then a whole lot more thoroughly, on the lips. 'But with wanting comes fear—of my nature and of yours and of the path we took last time. You scared me, Evie. With your compliance and with what you were prepared to give. You have no idea how much I wanted to take it *all*. And then demand more.'

'You're right,' she said quietly and the gaze she pinned on him was dark and knowing. 'I didn't know the dangers of that particular road we were on. But I do now.'

'If I break you I'll never forgive myself.'

Truth.

'You won't break me, Logan. I know what I'm doing. I've got your back.' As the gentle touch of her tongue to the corner of his mouth threatened to undo him. 'And your front.' Her hand slid slowly down his stomach, searching for stiffness and finding it. 'Your measure.'

And he prayed to God that she did.

CHAPTER SIX

Sunday passed in a blur of tangled limbs and bed sheets and Monday morning came around way too fast. Up at six, with Logan up and ready to head back to his serviced apartment for the day. Scalding-hot coffee and marmalade on sourdough toast as Evie slipped into her work clothes and scowled at the clock. Not a morning person after a night chock-full of Logan. Not a sensible thought left in her head other than she was determined to show him what her life was like, and that her life—on the whole—involved generous quantities of work.

Evie was a good business partner to Max and she needed Logan to see that. She lived a busy life and she wanted Logan to see that too. She wouldn't be derailed by him the way she had been before.

Half six and out of the door, locking it behind her while Logan stood at her side and waited. She'd see him tonight for dinner. His choice of restaurant this time and he'd let her know exactly what that choice was some time during the day. Not to be controlling or to keep her unsure of his plans for the evening; he just didn't know yet—this wasn't his city.

A twenty-minute walk to work for Evie, with Logan

heading in the opposite direction. They parted with little fuss, no kisses to spare.

Businesslike.

Until Logan turned back and claimed her mouth with ruthless efficiency before heading off once more, this time wearing a devil's grin.

They did this for three days and three predominantly sleepless nights.

On the fourth day Max asked Evie where his brother was and whether he'd taken Evie's brain with him.

'My brain's right here in my head,' she said, and looked at the invoices that covered her desk. Ordering the materials for the various jobs they had on wasn't her pleasure, which was why she'd given the job to Carlo in the first place, but he'd made a mess of it and she'd taken the job back in the interest of straightening things out. 'What haven't I done?'

'You forgot to order the additional tie wire for the Henderson job.'

Evie groaned. 'You know what I want more than anything in this world?'

'Your brain back?' asked Max.

'A proper project manager. A really, really good one.'

'If the civic centre job comes through you can have one,' offered Max.

Evie just looked at him through her fringe. 'Who went and got the tie wire?'

'Carlo. He put it on the account. Said to tell you "Checkmate".'

'Carlo wants a proper project manager too,' said Evie. 'I'll grovel to him later.'

'That's my girl,' said Max.

'Anything else?' Evie glanced down at her desk

once more and sighed. 'Don't answer that. I'll have this sorted by the end of the day.'

'You seeing Logan again tonight?' asked Max, with not quite the right amount of disinterest.

'He's coming over, yes.' Assuming he'd left her apartment today at all. He'd discovered her home office and she'd said he could use it. He had his own computer but he was in love with her scanner and fax and her big shiny desk.

'Do you know what he's been doing with his days while he's here?'

'I think he sleeps.' How else did a man get to be so inexhaustible throughout the night?

'Did you know he blew off a face-to-face meeting with a soviet steel baron yesterday? Told him they could reschedule in two weeks' time or have a conference call, and that it was all the same to him.'

'You don't think Logan knows what he's doing when it comes to big business?' Evie leaned back in her chair and eyed Max steadily. 'Maybe he just doesn't want to work with this man.'

'Maybe he's off his game.'

'You don't like that he's spending time with me?'

'I didn't say that. I just happen to think that he's keeping his real life at bay at the moment. Which is hardly conducive to an ongoing functional relationship.'

'Your brother doesn't want an ongoing functional relationship, Max. He wants to prove to himself that he's over me. That he has no need to be scared of me. The minute he does that he'll be gone.'

Max eyed her narrowly. 'So what's in it for you?'

Evie shrugged. 'A fascinating house guest, for a while.' Max probably wouldn't want to know this next reason but it was a definite plus to Evie's way of thinking. 'Exceptionally good sex.'

Max winced. 'Is that it?'

'Isn't that enough?' countered Evie.

'Cold, Evie.'

'Maybe,' she murmured. 'But I've decided that I can't be in love with your brother, Max. Infatuated, yes. Willing to help him overcome a few demons, yes. But I can't fall in love with him. That'd be beyond stupid.'

'You know, I had this vision in my head that if I cut you free to be with Logan that your romance would progress in somewhat traditional fashion. Dating. Getting engaged. Marriage. What about marriage?'

'Marriage is overrated.'

'You're selling yourself short, Evie. And my mother's in town as of last night and she wants to have lunch with you.'

'Pardon?'

'Consider yourself forewarned. She'll be here in about...' Max glanced at his two-dollar watch. 'Now.'

'She's coming *here*?' Evie had a sudden and irresistible urge to be not here. 'I won't be here. I'm heading out on site. Now. Right now. I'm already running late.'

'Which site?'

'The Rogers site.'

'Mick's already there.'

'He needs help.'

'He's got help.'

'*My* help.' And Evie needed to be gone when Caroline Carmichael arrived. 'What does your mother want with me? I mean...if she's after her ring back, I don't have it.'

'I found the ring, Evie. I spent half a day looking for that bloody rock. I gave it back to her.'

'Oh.' Evie digested Max's words with a frown. 'What did she do with it?'

'I'm guessing she put it back where it came from. I didn't ask.'

'She hurt him.' Hurt Logan.

'Sometimes he brings it on himself.'

'You're defending her.'

'No!' said Max curtly. And with a twisted scowl, 'Yes. She's my mother, Evie. What do you want me to say?'

Good question. 'Do you know what Logan's father did to them? What he did to himself? What he did to his *son*?'

'Do you?' asked Max quietly. 'You know what Logan's told you, Evie. That's not the whole story. If you want another side of the story, best you get it from my mother. She's not a bad person. It wouldn't kill you to hear what she has to say.'

'She hurt him, Max. By having you give me that ring she used you, confused me and stuck a knife in Logan's heart. Anything she has to say should be said to Logan, not to me.'

'He doesn't listen to her, Evie. Maybe he'll listen to you. You're closer to him than anyone's ever been.'

'And yet I'm still so very, *very* far away.' Evie ran a hand through her hair. 'Max, I can't fix this. I can barely fix what went wrong with Logan and *me*. You're asking too much. Your mother is asking too much.'

'And yet here I am,' said a cultured, feminine voice and there stood Max's mother. Logan's mother too. Caroline Carmichael in her well-preserved flesh. 'Asking for an hour of your time and an open ear. I want you to listen—I *hope* you will listen to what I have to say.'

'This wasn't fair warning.' Evie eyed Max darkly. 'You're my *business* partner. We don't bring personal matters here. Not to work.'

'We've always brought personal matters here, Evie. We tangled those threads a long time ago.'

Maybe so, but she had never thought Max would ambush her like this. She glared at him some more and then at Caroline, who stood quietly by the door, wanting more from Evie than Evie had in her heart to give.

'You're here to tell me how you failed to protect your son?' she asked acidly and felt a flush of shame when Caroline Carmichael looked her dead in the eye and said yes.

'Everyone makes mistakes, Evangeline. Mistakes that shatter your world and lose you everything you love,' said Caroline with quiet dignity and Evie felt the sharp sting of tears behind her eyes. 'Please.'

'I can't help you repair your relationship with Logan.'

'I'm not expecting you to,' said Caroline. 'I just want you to help my son be the best man he can be. I want him to realise what a good man he is. I want him to be happy.'

As far as manipulation went Caroline had nailed her good—or maybe Max had. Someone had.

'One hour. Not a minute more,' said Evie, and again Logan's mother said yes.

'Why did you make Max give me that ring?' asked Evie when they were seated at a table for two on the shady terrace of a nearby restaurant. The table wobbled ever so slightly because of the convict-laid cobblestones beneath its feet, but the water was cold and the service was speedy, and, as far as Evie was concerned, speedy was good. 'You knew Logan would recognise it.'

'You have to understand,' said Caroline. 'Logan was a heartbeat away from walking out my door that weekend and never coming back. Because of you. Because of me. Because walking away is easier than staying and dealing and if there's one thing Logan knows how to do it's walk away,' said Caroline. 'Logan was about to turn his back on his family. I had nothing to lose.'

'But why the ring? Why shove those memories in his face?'

'Because I thought I could goad Logan into finally losing his temper with me. He never has, you know. He locks it all up inside. I've been thinking for years that if I could just shatter his self-control, just *once*, that he would realise that, no matter how deeply he feels betrayed, he will *never* raise his hand in anger. Never be the man his father was.' Caroline sat back and raised an elegant hand to her neck, rubbing wearily before seeming to realise what she was doing. Her hand returned to her lap and she sat up straighter, the perfect image restored.

'Do you have any idea how much courage it takes an abused woman to pick a fight, Evangeline? *That's* how much I believe in the goodness of my son's heart. That's how strongly I believe that Logan's fear of turning out like his father is misguided. He won't. He will *never* raise his hand in anger. I believe that with all that I am.'

Evie ran a hand through her hair and nodded, not trusting herself to speak.

'I'm sorry I used you, Evie. I used Max too and I've apologised to him as well. But you have to understand…

That weekend was the closest I've ever seen Logan to breaking. I thought that if I pushed him I could finally make it happen.'

Love wasn't meant to be this complicated, thought Evie raggedly. It just wasn't. 'But he didn't break.'

'Not on me, no. Instead, you threw that ring away and cracked my son's heart wide open. I'm calling that a win.'

'You're mad,' said Evie.

'Been called that before.' Caroline Carmichael's smile didn't reach her eyes. 'Mad and useless and pathetic. I used to believe it. I don't any more.'

The waiter came with glasses and water and took their lunch order. Salad for Caroline and a sandwich for Evie. Food that wouldn't take long to prepare, food that would get this luncheon finished with fast.

'If Logan's father was such a man as you describe…' Evie couldn't believe she was about to ask such an intimate question of a woman she barely knew '…why did you marry him?'

'If I said I loved him once with all my heart you'd call me a fool. But it's the only explanation I've got.'

Which was no answer at all and for some reason made Evie want to cry. Again.

'Has Logan told you anything about his father?' asked Caroline Carmichael after a long, long pause.

'Very little.' Evie shrugged and cleared her throat. 'He told me that you left him. That you left Logan too. And then his father killed himself.'

'Did he mention that he was with his father because I was in a hospital with two cracked ribs, a broken cheekbone and internal bruising?'

No. Logan hadn't mentioned that.

'Hospital,' echoed Evie.

'Yes.'

That explained…a lot.

'When I got out of hospital I went to my sister's. I stayed there a week, getting AVO's and legal advice about how to get Logan away from his father. How to *keep* him away from his father. His father was a rich man. He could have the best legal representation money could buy and I needed to cover my bases. I couldn't afford not to do everything *right*. I was *always* coming back for my son, Evangeline. Always. I just wasn't fast enough.'

Evie said nothing. There was nothing to say.

'Do you know what the ultimate bid for control ends in, Evangeline?' asked Caroline Carmichael. 'Death. And you might think that the last one standing is the victor, but not always. Sometimes the last ones standing wear the stain of that death for the rest of our lives. The helplessness and the guilt. The control issues. The fear of ever letting anyone get close.'

'But you married again.'

'I had the best shrinks money could buy and a very understanding second husband. He died too, from cancer, and it was fast and painful. Heartbreaking in its own way. But not my fault.'

There was the guilt Caroline Carmichael spoke of. The deeply held scars that coloured her life.

My mother's not a bad person, Max had said.

'Mrs Carmichael—'

'Caroline,' said the older woman. 'Please.'

'Caroline.' The name rolled off Evie's tongue easily enough. It was hard to keep hold of her anger when her overwhelming emotion was sadness. 'I appreciate you telling me about your past, and Logan's, but please… don't pin any hopes on me and Logan staying together, or on me being able to influence his relationship with you. *I'm* not pinning any hopes on me and Logan staying together. He's here for a week and we're halfway through it already, and after that he's going to go. And while I hope very much that Logan's been able to slay a few demons when it comes to him being too dominant and me being too submissive all those years ago, I'm going to let him go.'

'You don't care for him?'

'I do care for him. It'd be so *easy* to care deeply for your son, but I can't, don't you see? Logan doesn't *want* to fall in love with me. He wants a casual, easy relationship that he can walk away from, no damage done to either of us. *That's* how Logan knows he's not the dangerously obsessed and unstable man his father was. He doesn't trust his heart in that regard. Only his actions. He walks away. You *know* that's what he'll do.'

'But he isn't walking away,' offered Caroline quietly. 'Not from you.'

'He will.' Evie took a jagged breath. 'It won't be long now.'

'He'll be back.'

'Maybe. And then he'll go again. And again. And again. Mrs Carmichael, what do you want me to say?'

'I want you to say that you'll give my son a chance. That you won't be so busy protecting your own heart that you fail to see the love pouring out of his. *Don't* go into this thinking that Logan's only move will be away from you. I think he'll surprise you. Let him surprise you.'

Evie glanced away. She didn't know what to say.

'Anything else?' Because Evie *really* wanted to be done here.

'One more thing. One more piece of advice that perhaps my second husband might give to you were he alive today. He was a good man, Evie. A loving man and he loved my Logan as if he were his own. He'd have asked you to be generous with Logan when he makes mistakes.'

'I had lunch with your mother today.'

Logan stilled and Evie felt the headache that had been coming on all afternoon pick up. Most of the conversations she'd had today hadn't gone well. Evie didn't hold out a lot of hope for this one. 'She cornered me at work. Max was in on the plan as well, though I noticed he managed to weasel his way out of the actual lunch.' Bastard.

'What did she want?' Logan asked finally, his attention seemingly fixed on the far corner of her not-so-sparkling kitchen floor.

'Mostly to apologise for using me to get to you.'

'Sounds about right.' A muscle ticced in his otherwise rigid jaw. 'What else did she want?'

'To sing your praises, I think. She did a bit of that.' Evie wasn't sure she wanted to share the entire conversation with Logan, but she could reveal bits of it. 'She wanted to know my intentions towards you.'

Logan looked up, his gaze ever so slightly incredulous. 'What did you tell her?'

'I probably should have told her to mind her own business, but I didn't. I told her you were leaving at the end of the week and that I had no idea what we were doing after that. Does that sound about right?'

Logan cleared his throat and rubbed his neck with his hand. One of Caroline's traits too, when she wasn't busy aiming for full composure. 'Something like that.'

'Max asked me what was going on between us too. We're a hot topic of conversation within your family, apparently. I told him that you were an excellent house-guest and an incredibly skilled lay.'

Logan seemed to be having trouble with speech. Which was just fine by Evie, because she didn't particularly want to talk about where their relationship was going either.

Evie picked up a slice of apple pie she'd brought home with her and handed it to him along with her smuggest smile. 'You're welcome.'

CHAPTER SEVEN

LOGAN'S week at Evie's passed in a blur of easy smiles and sweat-slicked nights. Life was good but there was no denying that he had put the real life on hold in order to be here. Work was piling up back in London and his executives had taken to calling him in the middle of the night—his time—with increasingly urgent questions about the running of his business and opportunities arising. His executive assistant was ready to strangle him. On Friday she'd not so politely told him that if he didn't have his surly self back behind his desk come Monday, she wouldn't be there either. Apparently she'd had quite enough of his executive employees begging her for word on decisions that no one but Logan had the power to make. No one else sat at Logan's desk while he was away. He'd never *stayed* away for this long before, had never needed to structure his organisation so that he could.

Something to consider.

As for Evie, she was being very…understanding. She didn't push for him to stay and, apart from that time when she'd talked about lunching with his mother, she'd made no reference to where their relationship was headed at all. As if it was the most natural thing in the world for him to breeze into and out of Evie's world and make barely a ripple.

Not meek when it came to everyday living—Evie knew how to stand her ground and more. That message had come through loud and clear. He'd watched her putting the brakes on a new project Max had wanted to bid on—a bread and butter project that Max figured they could turn a quick profit on. Evie begged to differ. The client was dodgy—notoriously late with payments and not above changing specs mid build and expecting the builder to wear the cost. There were jobs worth taking, Evie had told his brother bluntly. This one wasn't worth their effort.

Max had thrown up his hands in a sulk. Evie had lifted one eyebrow, folded her arms in front of her and murmured, 'Really?'

And half an hour later Max had been back, the dodgy bread and butter bid abandoned, head down alongside Evie's as they nutted out an alteration to the civic centre plans that scattered her kitchen bench.

No wonder Max had refused to let her go.

But Max wasn't here now and Logan had to be at the airport early in the morning and, dammit, Evie could at least acknowledge that fact with more than a nod.

And then she pulled down a bottle of tequila from a shelf in the kitchen and two shot glasses and poured until tequila threatened to spill over onto the bench.

'Got any salt?' he said.

'Happens I do.' Evie had lemons too, and he felt all of sixteen as Evie told him to make a fist. He did and watched as Evie's hand circled his wrist and she brought his fist to her mouth, a tiny, knowing smile on her face as the tip of her tongue dipped into the V between his forefinger and thumb.

She had his undivided attention as she pulled away, poured salt over the wet part and set her mouth to him again, licking the salt off in one long, lazy swipe before picking up the shot glass and swallowing the contents fast.

Lemon came next and she scrunched up her eyes and shook her head as the lemon juice went down. Party.

'Hard day at the office?' he asked as she licked then at her own hand and poured salt on and offered it to him. Logan's body kicked as he took her wrist and guided it to his mouth. He took his time, his thumb stroking slowly over the pulse at her wrist, and then he rubbed his lips along the edge of her thumb and then his tongue. And then he took teeth to her skin and nipped and felt Evie's pulse kick and her eyes glow golden.

'Ordinary day at the office,' she murmured. 'But I'm hoping for an extraordinary night.'

He licked at the salt and she downed his tequila and he slammed his lips into hers and drank it straight from her mouth and chased it down with the sweet taste of her until the salt was all gone and the tequila was gone and all he could taste was Evie.

By the time she drew away to take a shaky breath, Logan was hard as concrete and a delicate flush of arousal had moved in on Evie's cheeks.

'More,' she demanded, and sucked her lower lip into her mouth and licked it clean.

'More of what?'

'Everything.'

So he poured them another tequila and this time Evie bypassed the condiments and went straight for the alcohol and then expelled her breath as if she was breathing fire. She probably was.

'Something you want to forget?'

'No. I want to remember it all.' Evie smiled and pierced his heart. 'I'm just working up the courage to let you go. Bear with me. It's going to be harder than I thought.'

Easy words, and an easy out if he wanted to take it. Keep it light, no deep, dark emotions required. Except that sorrow lurked beneath the smile in her eyes and challenge lived there too.

'I hope the week worked for you,' she said.

'It did. Did it work for you?'

Evie shrugged, and, for the moment, the challenge in her eyes won out over sorrow and goodbye. 'You know I'm a sucker for more.'

He knew what she wanted. His gaze skated over her face, lingered on a spot covered by the fall of her glossy black hair. He couldn't see the scar but he sure as hell knew it was there.

'No table tops,' she said. 'For this we use the bed.'

And still Logan hesitated.

He'd been good all week. So very restrained. Playing at normal and it had worked. He'd wanted normal. Needed to prove to them both that he could be satisfied with it. Tonight though, he craved just that little bit…more.

They still had a few hours left. They still had the night.

And there were so many ways to spend it.

He came around to her side of the counter and pushed her back against it, got up in her space, his arms either side of her. Lips to her cheek now, the scrape of his teeth against the sensitive skin of her ear lobe, just enough to make her gasp. One hand to her throat now as he took full possession of her mouth. Finding the pulse point the better to monitor it. Tilting her head back so that his mouth fitted hers exactly the way he wanted it to.

Mine. He let that thought reach the top of the stack and his hips responded with a slow and rolling grind.

'Mine,' he said and his voice came low and savage.

'Prove it.'

Oh, he was going to.

'Stroke me,' he said, and showed her exactly how he wanted it, and he was comfortable calling the shots, God help him, he was. Hard and rough and she leaned into him and set her lips to his jaw, and her teeth to the skin of his chin and nipped, at which point he slipped just that little bit out of sync with the rest of the world. The place he entered had far more jagged edges and ruins in it and the rivers ran red with pain beneath. Evie didn't need to be told to take the tip of him between fingers and thumb and squeeze hard—she already knew how much he liked riding that bright flare of pain right back into pleasure.

Knew because she liked that ride too.

'I want control tonight.' The words came from the deepest, darkest part of him. 'Over pleasure and pain and everything in between. *All* the control.'

Evie smiled as she palmed her way down blood-engorged hardness and stroked him again with a twist to her wrist that almost made him come undone. 'Then take it.'

He swore he wouldn't take too much; that this was just a game that when played well led to extreme plea-sure for both participants. He swore to do no harm and the kitchen counter wouldn't do, so he took her by the wrist and headed for the stairs.

The bottom of the stairs saw his shoulders braced against the wall and Logan's hands cradling her cheeks as he set his lips to hers again. They had to get up the stairs without him reaching for her along the way. There were a lot of stairs. Evie strained against him, hands cupping his buttocks and pulling him against her.

'Patience,' he whispered. 'Virtue.' And devoured her mouth, his tongue searching and sweeping and his teeth taunting and teasing, memorising the taste of her, testing the surrender in her.

It took them for ever to get to the bedroom.

Hours, in Evie's estimation. Or maybe it was just that time stopped so often along the way. Stopped when Logan got to sitting on the stairs with her knees either side of him, and wrapped one of her hands around the stair railing and made her put her other palm to the wall as he licked along the lacy edge of her bra, and the bra came off and he curled his tongue around a nipple before closing his lips around her and sucking hard.

Evie whimpered as passion caught a lick of pain and burned all the brighter for it.

She returned the favour when finally he let her put her mouth to him.

And then they got to the bedroom and slowly, surely, he stripped her down until the only thing that mattered was Logan's next touch and what it would bring, and she never knew what, only that it was always exactly right.

No thought of anything but the ride as he worked her, enslaved her.

No need to ever ask for more because she already had everything she'd ever wanted and his name was

Logan and when her sky turned black he was the only thing she could see.

This, she thought when she was a mindless mess of sensation and yearning and he finally sheathed himself inside her. This man and the razor-sharp edge he brought to things.

This was what she'd been waiting for.

Evie woke in the dark, twenty minutes before Logan had set the alarm on his phone to ring. He had to get to the airport by six. By the end of the day he'd be on the other side of the world. She didn't want to dwell on how empty that made her feel.

Instead, Evie stretched her arms above her head gingerly, and straightened her legs, testing for tenderness and finding echoes of it in unexpected places. Inner thigh muscles, upper arms, her mouth…overstretched and puffy, and she sucked at her lower lip, checking for splits and finding one. She turned towards the man sleeping beside her, only he wasn't asleep. Sleepy-eyed, yes, but not asleep, his gaze roved over the parts of her not covered by the sheet, and then he rolled over onto his elbow, flicked on the lamp by the bed before sliding the sheet down her body and studying the rest of her in the soft glow cast by the lamp's light.

'Roll over,' he ordered and Evie did as she was told and let him continue his examination. 'Bruise here,' he said, and ran the pad of his thumb over the curve of her hip. 'Red here.' A touch on her buttocks; the soft underside of her upper arms.

'Feels fine,' she said and slid her hands beneath the pillow and stretched again, working out the kinks, one by one.

His fingers touched the split in the middle of her lower lip and his eyes darkened. He'd used her hard and they both knew it.

'Sorry,' he rumbled gruffly.

She prodded at the split with her tongue. Decided that within half a day it'd be gone. 'Don't be.'

Logan moved his attention to her hair next, gentle fingers sliding through it, pushing it back off her face, out of her eyes. She let him find the scar he was looking for. Let him run his fingers over it.

'Angie—'

He hadn't called her that all week. She knew exactly why that name had slipped from his lips now, but it wasn't one she wanted to hear.

'Evie,' she corrected gently and drew his hand to the curve of her cheek instead. 'Angie didn't know how to pull all the scattered pieces of herself back together after a night like last night. Evie does.'

'Who taught you?' Possessiveness in his voice and in his eyes, and Evie thrilled to it, even as she rolled away from his touch and out of the crazily mussed-up bed.

'No one person. You more than anyone. Experience.' She sat on the side of the bed with her back to him and her fingers curled around the edge of the bed. She closed her eyes, tilted her head back and stretched her back out. 'You were right about me needing more experience all those years ago. Hindsight's a wonderful thing.' She turned her head to look at him, expecting turmoil in his eyes and finding it. 'I like the person I am now. I value every single experience that went into the making of her. Good and bad.'

'Evie—'

Her name bled from his lips, apology shot through

with regret. 'Logan,' she replied steadily. 'If that's regret on your lips for what we did last night I'd rather not hear it. You brought a lick of pain and a lot of intense pleasure along with your lovemaking last night and you like wielding both—don't tell me you don't—and I love it when you do. No analysis required. Can't we just leave it at that?'

So he choked on whatever he'd been about to say and asked her if she wanted coffee instead.

She said yes, and watched as he stepped into sweats that rode low on his hips and disappeared down the stairs, a picture of rumpled, extremely biddable masculinity. She didn't want coffee but Logan wanted to get away from her, or do something for her, or both, and who was Evie to argue?

She waited another moment and then rose and headed for the bathroom, somewhat tender in places, walking a little stiffly, to be sure, but nothing a shower and being up and about wouldn't fix.

A quick shower this morning, anticipating that Logan too would want to clean up and be on his way. Go back to bed after he left, she could do that, but Evie knew she wouldn't.

Strip the bed, put some washing on, get out of the apartment, maybe even go for a swim and let the waves wash away her tears. Keep moving, stay busy.

He came back with coffee just as she stepped from the shower and she towelled off fast and slipped into her dressing robe. Leave him with a picture of morning domesticity. A counterpoint to the memories they'd created last night.

Tossing the towel atop the clothes basket, Evie offered up a wry smile, took the coffee from his outstretched hand and headed back towards the bed, sitting cross-legged on it but pulling a sheet up around her legs to keep her honest before taking her first sip.

He'd made the coffee *exactly* the way she liked it.

Bastard.

She watched him pack in silence, wondering whether he still needed to collect things from the serviced apartment he'd rented for the week or whether over the course of the week he'd managed to bring everything here. He'd worked here—she knew that much. Using her home office to stay in contact with his London office and his Perth office. Getting up in the early hours of the morning when his phone rang and heading downstairs while an urgent voice on the other end of the phone demanded his attention. Rich man, but definitely still a working man with responsibilities she barely understood.

But they'd done well together this past week, nonetheless. He could be proud of that. They both could.

No need to do anything but smile once he was fully packed and his attention returned to her once more. He knelt down beside her bed and took her coffee from unprotesting hands and set it aside. He pressed butterfly kisses to the wing of her eyebrow, the curve of her cheek and finally her lips. Tender, this goodbye, and she reached up to trace his lips with her fingers, still obsessed with the shape and sensuality of them.

'Got everything?' she asked quietly.

'Yes. The rest is downstairs in your office.'

She leaned forward and kissed him lightly and then once more to savour him. 'Safe journey, Mr Black. Be happy.' Then she pulled him into a fierce hug and closed her eyes and memorised the feel of being in his arms. 'I'm happy. You need to know that I wouldn't have missed one moment of this past week. With you.'

His arms tightened around her, but he didn't speak, just buried his face in the curve of her neck, breathing in deep before slowly letting go.

And then he picked up his bag and Evie closed her eyes so that she didn't have to see the set of his shoulders or the shape of his resolve as he headed for the stairs.

She'd done all she could. It was up to him now.

Evangeline Jones knew exactly how to love hard and with no regrets.

She needed a man bold enough to do the same.

CHAPTER EIGHT

LOGAN couldn't get Evie out of his head. The long hours of travel couldn't shift her. The mountain of work that awaited him upon his return served only to make him more aware of how much he wanted her around *after* the day's work was done. One week after his return to London and he couldn't look at his bed without thinking of what Evie would look like in it. Passion-blind and soaring. Shiny-slick and smiling in the aftermath. He missed the brush of her shoulder against his as she cooked in her kitchen. Being in her space; having her invade his. He hadn't just tolerated it. He'd embraced it. A sucker for a soft touch, she'd teased him. Or a hard touch.

Any kind of touch as long as it was hers.

Only hers.

He didn't know what to do with a need so fierce and large. Didn't know how to make her a part of his life without demanding too much. Didn't know how to balance Evie's needs with his fear of one day losing control of his own desires and going too far. Of becoming possessive and controlling. Abusive. So many different ways to reach inside a person and tear them apart.

He'd texted her when he'd arrived back in London. 'Home,' he'd written.

And got a smiley face text in reply.

That was good, right? Not too needy or greedy on either side. Letting Evie get on with her life without him stomping all over it. Letting him get on with his.

No obsession here.

No overwhelming need to have her by his side.

Except that with each passing day Logan's need to hear Evie's voice and feel her touch grew stronger.

He lasted a week. One week before he rang his brother during Max's working day on the pretext of getting Max's opinion on converting an outer London warehouse into residential units. Max's speciality, not his. Was Max interested in taking on the project? Developing an international profile?

Was Evie?

'Since when have you been interested in redevelopment projects?' came his brother's guarded reply.

'Since staying with Evie in her warehouse apartment,' he countered. 'I didn't mind the experience.'

'Well, aren't you the lucky one?' said Max with unmistakeable bite. 'Did it ever occur to you that the reason you liked the warehouse apartment experience was because of the woman involved?'

'If you're not interested, all you have to do is say so,' countered Logan coolly.

Silence from Max's end. 'I'll talk it over with Evie,' he said grudgingly. 'I don't know that we're ready to take the company international. You looking to move on the warehouse fast?'

'Don't have to. Just letting you know it's there. Any news on the civic centre bid?'

'Looks promising,' said Max. 'There are three bids left on the table and one of them is ours.'

'Good,' said Logan. 'Good. What do you know about Sinclair House?'

'You mean Mum's latest charity? It's a safe house for victims of domestic abuse. She goes there once a fortnight and helps with meals or something. Why?'

'She hit me up for a donation. Apparently they need a new roof.' But Max's answer had piqued Logan's interest more than it had settled it. 'What do you mean she goes there once a fortnight?'

'Just what I said.'

'She needs to stop that. It's not safe.'

'It's a *safe* house, Logan. Heavy on the security windows and doors. Six-foot fences.'

'Yeah, and it's full of God knows who.'

'Mostly battered women and children, from what I can gather. What exactly do you think they're going to do?'

Logan shook his head. This was the difference between him and Max. Max had no goddamn idea what people were capable of. 'Desperate people do desperate things.'

'Yeah, and they also need help. What do you want me to do, Logan? Tell her to stop? That'd work on her almost as well as it works on you. *You* talk to her if you're that concerned about it. Heaven knows she treasures every last scrap of attention you throw her.'

'Hey, you're the favourite.'

'You know what? For all your legendary business acumen you're one blind son of a bitch.'

'Language, little brother.'

'Screw you. Don't start with me, Logan, or I'll serve

it straight back at you. Matter of fact I'm going to anyway. Why haven't you called Evie? Which, by the way,
she predicted.'

'What do you mean *predicted*?'

'I mean when I asked her if she'd heard from you
she said no, that wasn't part of the deal. What the *hell*
kind of deal is that?'

'Look, Max—'

'Don't you "look, Max" me. You spend a week inside a woman's skin, she opens up her home to you and
her life to you and a week later you can't be bothered
to give her five minutes of your precious time? What
is *wrong* with you?'

'Nothing! I was just…giving her some space.' A gap-
ing pit was beginning to form in Logan's stomach at
the thought that something might have happened to her.
'Is she all right?'

'Evie's *fine*, Logan. Just *peachy*, thanks for asking.
She does her work, she goes to the beach, she bought
a Ducati road bike that goes from zero to one hundred
in six point nine seconds, but don't let that alarm you.
She's taking road-safety lessons from a former AMA
Motocross champion called Duke, but don't let that
bother you either. His manners are impeccable and he
knows how to use a phone.'

'Hey, hold the PMS.'

'You deserve the PMS. You're treating a woman I
respect and admire like a whore and she's letting you.
Doesn't make it right.'

'If I'd wanted a sermon I'd have gone to church.'

'Go to hell, Logan. I vouched for you. I practically
threw Evie at you, and *this* is how you repay me? By
using her up and walking away without a backward

glance? *My* business partner. *My* friend. And your loss.
I'll give your regards to Duke.'

And then Max hung up on him.

'Who's Duke?' asked Evie as she strode into MEP's
outer office, head down and preoccupied, but not so
unconscious that she hadn't caught the way Max had
slapped his phone down on the desk, and there was
definitely no missing his scowl.

'Duke's the US motocross champion who's teaching you how to ride your new Ducati,' said Max curtly.
'Don't ask.'

'Huh,' said Evie thoughtfully. 'Am I enjoying the
process?'

'Immensely.'

'Good for me,' she said. 'Because it's a good idea. I
take it that was Logan on the phone?'

Max nodded.

Evie smiled; she couldn't help it. 'So what else have
I been doing?'

'Not moping,' said Max. 'As a true friend I'm doing
my level best to ignore your current state of mope.'

'Excellent,' said Evie. 'Good for you too.'

'Do you remember how peaceful life was back in
the days before we got engaged and I made the idiotic
mistake of introducing you to my family?' Max asked
with a great deal of wistfulness. 'I do.'

'Never mind, Max. You'll fall in love yourself one
day, lose all sense of purpose, struggle mightily to keep
your life on track and probably fail miserably, but trust
me; I will be there to point it out to you. It'll be my
pleasure.'

'Must be catching,' said Logan.

'What?'

'PMS.'

'Just for that I'm not bringing you back any lunch.'

'I'll remember that when I'm rich and *you* want lunch. No champagne. No caviar. No lobster.'

'No problem. I've lived on tuna sandwiches before. I can do it again.'

'Maybe I should reassure Logan that you're not interested in his money,' said Max. 'Might help.'

'Tell him whatever the hell you like,' said Evie, doing an about turn and heading for the door. 'Maybe I could be flying fighter jets next time he calls. Stunt biplanes.'

'Get me a tuna sandwich,' Max called after her. 'And I won't tell him how much you're missing him.'

'Thank you.'

Evie heard the catch in her voice, but she kept on going because if she turned around and saw sympathy in Max's eyes, her carefully constructed world without Logan in it would probably come tumbling down. 'For that I'll bring you two.'

Logan called her that night, at her apartment rather than at work, and for that Evie was grateful. Eight-thirty p.m. her time and eleven-thirty a.m. in London. Middle of a businessman's day and she wondered where he was calling from, whether he'd squeezed her in between meetings, and most of all she clutched the phone and closed her eyes and concentrated on the sound of his voice saying her name. Some time soon she was going to have to speak, but not yet. Not until he said her name again.

Which he did.

'Hey,' she said. Best she could do—she was fresh out of amiable greetings.

'Max tells me you bought a Ducati.' Guess Logan was all out of pleasant small talk too.

'So I heard,' offered Evie.

'Which one?'

'The red one that goes really, really fast.' And there ended Evie's knowledge of motorbikes and her taste for silly lies. 'I didn't buy a Ducati, Logan. Your brother's messing with you.'

'He's not the only one.'

'Could be you bring it on yourself,' she murmured. 'Best guess.'

'I should have called you a week ago,' he said.

'Only if you wanted me to feel valued.' She let her comment hang for a moment, because she was nobody's pushover and he needed to know that. 'If, on the other hand, you were sorting out a few issues, like, say, the difference between wanting to stay in touch with someone and being so unhealthily obsessed with someone that you couldn't live without them... If a little bit of thinking time bought you some clarity on that issue... I'd call that time well spent.'

She could almost hear his brain churning.

'Generous of you,' he said finally, his voice sounding as if he'd just eaten a mile of gravel road.

'For you I can be generous.'

'So how've you been?' More gravel. Filler conversation.

'Okay.' Wasn't as if he was going to call her a liar. 'Work's been slow and I'm thinking of painting the ceiling of my apartment dark red.'

'Evangeline, parts of your ceiling are three storeys high.'

'I own half a construction company, Logan. There's this equipment called scaffolding.'

'I'm assuming you have people called employees as well?'

'So speaks the multimillionaire.' Evie rolled her eyes. 'I like painting. It's therapeutic. Besides, if you want something done right, do it yourself.'

'Don't say that,' he said with what Evie could have sworn was an underlying note of panic.

'Why not?'

'Because I've just created two new senior operations manager positions and filled them and I'm now on the hunt for a senior finance manager.'

'So...you're expanding?'

'Restructuring. I was causing bottlenecks. I needed to let go of some of the decision making. We'll see how it goes.'

'You don't sound convinced.'

'If you want something done right, do it yourself.'

'So I hear,' she said with a grin. 'Just think of all the bold *new* projects you'll be able to put your mark on before handing over the boring bits.'

'There is that,' he said. 'I want another week with you.'

'Before you hand over the boring bits?'

'You're not boring, Evangeline. You're challenging and wise and I'm a little bit terrified of you, but I wouldn't call you boring.'

'Would you call me submissive?'

A long pause from Logan; as if he knew he'd be judged on his answer. 'Not in general,' he said finally. 'Although on occasion you're willing to relinquish control to a more dominant sexual partner.'

'Good answer,' she said softly.

'Come to London, Evie. Come visit me. Same deal as I had with you. A hotel room for when and if you need it and an invitation to join me at my house should you so choose.'

'Logan—'

'Don't say no. It won't cost you anything but your time. First-class travel, with a stopover at, say, a landmark hotel in Dubai?'

'Are you serious?'

'Do you feel valued yet?'

'Remind me to tell you the difference between being valued and being bought.'

'Does that mean you *don't* want to experience the delights of a seven-star hotel?'

'Wash your mouth out,' she said. 'It could mean I never actually reach London.'

'*Now* who's feeling undervalued?'

'Hey, you started this,' she reminded him. 'Will you *join* me at the hotel in Dubai?'

'You don't like us together in hotel rooms, remember?'

'I'd like us in this one.'

'How does next week sound?'

'I can't do next week,' she said with a grimace she was glad Logan couldn't see. 'We'll know if we landed the civic centre job by Wednesday next week and I want to be here to either celebrate or commiserate.'

'Hnh.' Logan sounded ever so slightly annoyed.

'Don't people ever say no to you?' she murmured.

'People often say no to me,' he countered. 'My job is getting them to change their minds.'

'I'm not going to change my mind.'

'I know that, Evie. Hence the hnh. I'm just thinking ahead to what's coming up on *my* schedule that I can move around, that's all.'

'Oh.' It wouldn't hurt for her to give some credit to the pressures of *his* job while she was busy getting him to consider the challenges of hers. 'You'll be working through the day while I'm there, though, right? Same deal as when you were here and I went to work only this time I fit in around you?'

'You don't want to spend the entire week in Dubai?'

'No. One night should do it. On one condition.'

'What's that?'

'Promise you'll play tennis with me on the helipad.'

'Max, you're wearing out the floorboards,' said Evie. 'And you're driving me insane.' It was four-thirty on Wednesday afternoon and the reason that Max was driving her insane was that there was still no word on the civic centre bid. 'No news is good news.'

'I hate platitudes,' said Max. 'We didn't get it. We almost got married for nothing.'

'You almost got married?' asked a startled Carlo, who was hovering there with them, waiting on that call. Jeremy was there too—a junior site engineer who'd been with them for two years. So was Kit, one of their electrical subcontractors. Nervous people with nothing to do but wait on a phone call that hadn't yet come.

'It's a long story,' said Evie. 'Max wanted to marry me for his money but wiser heads prevailed. Besides… that was before I met his big brother.'

'Impressive?' asked Kit.

'Be still my beating heart.'

'Evie, one more platitude out of you and violence will ensue,' threatened Max. 'C'mon phone. *Ring.*'

'A watched pot never boils,' said Kit.

'I thought it was "kettle",' offered Jeremy. 'A watched kettle never—'

And then the phone rang and shut them all up.

Suddenly it wasn't so much fun to tease Max any more. He'd thrown everything he had at this job and if they didn't get it he was going to be gutted. Carlo headed for his office cubicle, taking Jeremy with him. Kit eyed Max warily and then said, 'Got any biscuits in the tea room?' and took himself off.

Evie debated heading for her office but Max grabbed her by the wrist and mouthed 'Stay,' as he listened intently to whatever the person on the other end of that phone was saying.

Max let her wrist go when she nodded, and then Evie sat on the edge of the table and tucked her hands beneath her legs and waited. Max resumed his pacing. Evie most definitely wanted to land this job. But her heart wasn't in it the way Max's was.

'Yes,' said Max, and, 'yes,' again. All very restrained.

The smile that swept across his handsome features moments later was not so restrained. Max's smile thought it was Christmas and there was a pony under the tree.

He laughed and said he was looking forward to it. He set up a meeting for tomorrow morning. And then he got the hell off the phone.

'We got it,' he said. 'We got it!'

'Of course we did,' said Evie as Max swept her up into a bear hug and swung her around. 'MEP's architect is a visionary, the company's on its way up and the price was right. What time is it in London?'

'Ah, early morning? Seven-thirty? You calling Logan?'

'Texting him, to be safe. I'm telling him we're about to spend his money.'

'So…you're talking again?' asked Max. 'There's been contact?'

'There has. And I didn't have to instigate it.'

'That's good,' said Max. 'That's very good.' He squeezed her once more before releasing her. 'Kit,' he bellowed. 'Break out the beer.'

The party started at the office and moved to the local bar, where there was more food and a better beverage selection than the one they had at the office. Their concreter turned up with a few of his crew—nothing like the promise of more work and free drinks to raise a man's spirits. Evie's spirits too, and who cared if she got ribbed for drinking champagne rather than beer? Not her problem if her co-workers preferred beer. Not her job to tell them to cease with the swearing, although she had a feeling that most of them *did* try to curb their language around her, which boggled the mind given the curses that still slipped through.

'How about asking Juliet Grace to come and be our new project manager?' she said as Max reached past her to put his empty beer glass down and pick up a handful of peanuts. 'She's detail oriented, most of us know her, or know of her, and she can handle this lot.'

'A woman.' Max eyed her dubiously.

'Careful, Max. Your biases are showing.'

'I'm not biased. I'm thinking.'

Evie laughed; she couldn't help it. 'Do you think more beer will help?'

Logan stood outside the busy Sydney bar and watched as the slim woman with the raven-black hair and wicked smile signalled the barman for another round of drinks. Max stood with her and so did at least a dozen other men. Labourers half of them, they looked as if they'd come straight from a job. A tight-knit group, intent on celebration, and it was clear that Evie was one of them. Accepted by them. Protected by them, even if she didn't know it.

Though she probably did.

Evie had texted him that they'd won the contract. That particular message had been waiting for him when he'd got off the plane in Sydney.

He should have texted Evie back. Should have said, 'I'm in Sydney. Where are you?'

But uncertainty was riding him hard this evening and he'd texted Max instead.

It didn't look as if Max had told Evie that Logan was on his way. She didn't look like a woman who was waiting for her lover to walk through the door. Evangeline Jones had a very fine habit of extracting pleasure from the moment—no angst-ing required.

Logan envied her.

The amount of anguish that had gone into Logan's decision to get on a plane so that he could be with Evie and Max come civic centre decision time could have filled the Pacific. Would Evie find it presumptuous? Would Max? Would they want him there?

All he knew was that for the first time in his life he was reaching out and wanting to be a part of something, as opposed to keeping everything and everyone at arm's length.

Arm's length being the distance whereby he couldn't inadvertently hurt anyone and they couldn't hurt him.

Logan watched as some moron bumped Evie in the shoulder as he turned away from the bar with a tray full of drinks in hand. He watched as Max automatically slung his arm around Evie's shoulder and drew her to his side.

Logan didn't viciously resent Evie and Max's camaraderie. He didn't catch his breath and look down at the concrete beneath his feet in an attempt to manage that part of him that wanted to take Max apart, piece by bloody piece, for daring to touch what was his. Not him.

He looked back and tried to *not* want to beat his brother bloody.

Nope. Still no luck letting go of that particular desire.

He was so screwed.

Logan watched as Evie moved out from beneath Max's shoulder and settled herself on a barstool. Men at her back and beside her and the table beneath her elbow now. Protected on all fronts. Also hogging the peanuts.

What if she didn't *want* to make room for Logan in her life tonight?

Because it was one thing for Max to know that Logan and Evie were tangling. It was quite another to walk in there and stake his claim on her in front of people she had to work with. God knew he had no desire to undermine her authority.

Maybe if he *didn't* stake his claim—just went in there and kept his hands and his mouth off her…

Be Max's brother rather than Evie's lover. Keep everything casual and easy—no biting jealousy or had-to-see-you-again obsession here. If he could do that...

It was a pretty big if.

Moments later Logan's phone beeped.

'What the hell are you doing?' the message from his brother read, and he looked up and his brother was fiddling with his phone and Evie was deep in laughing conversation with the giant across the table from her.

Another text from Max. 'You want a gold-plated invitation?'

The short answer being yes. Either that or a machete to cut through the mess of thoughts and feelings roiling round inside him.

With a shake of his head, Logan pocketed his phone and headed for the open doorway of the bar. He'd know soon enough if he'd done the right thing by coming here.

And he'd take her dismay straight up, if that was what she served him.

The noise level was high as Logan stepped inside. The smell of hops permeated the air. Not exactly an upscale establishment, this one. Cheerful though. And then Max lifted his arm and gestured him over and bent to whisper something in Evie's ear and she whipped around and the smile that lit her face wrapped around Logan's heart and wouldn't let go.

Her smile said she didn't consider his presence an intrusion.

Her smile telegraphed a message Logan had waited a lifetime to hear.

Pleasure—not pain—because he was near.

Max snagged Evie's champagne glass from her as she pushed through the circle of men and headed straight for him and then she was in his arms and her lips were on his and she tasted of strawberries and champagne and generous, genuine welcome.

If ever there was a time to keep his wits about him this was it, but the kiss deepened anyway, capturing him so completely that there was no room for anything else. Only Evie.

Wolf whistles helped him to remember where he was.

Evie's reckless smile told him she knew exactly where she was and that she didn't mind laying claim to him in public in the slightest. She brushed her thumb over his lips and kissed him swiftly once more, and then took him by the arm and propelled him forward towards the group she'd been sitting with.

'Everyone, this is Logan Black. He bankrolls us from time to time. He's also Max's brother.'

Max picked up two drinks from the table—a whisky shot and a beer chaser. 'You're going to have to catch up,' he said, and handed them to Logan.

Max's casual welcome worked to soothe Logan some. The welcome said, 'I know damn well you've never been this invested in my successes before, but I'm open to it no matter what the reason. You're my brother. You want in, you're in.'

'Doesn't seem entirely wise,' said Logan, but he took the drinks anyway, sent the whisky straight down and set the beer on the table for later. 'Congratulations on landing the job.'

'Thanks.' Max clasped Logan's forearm to his. 'Couldn't have done it without you. You just get in?'

'Yeah.'

'You *knew* he was coming in?' asked Evie.

'Surprise,' said Max and grinned, warm and wide,

at Evie's narrow-eyed glare. 'Who says I can't keep a secret?'

'It was very last-minute,' Logan offered by way of lame excuse. 'Didn't know if I'd make it in time.'

'You came straight from the plane?'

Logan rubbed ruefully at his bristly jaw—he'd last shaved back in London, about thirty hours ago by his count. 'Why? Does it show?'

'To your extreme advantage,' said Evie dryly. 'You are so *pretty* when you get all tousled and unshaven. Have you eaten?'

'No.'

'Most of this lot will clear out in another hour or so. I was planning on grabbing a meal somewhere nearby with your brother. Which should in no way be construed as a date,' she added with a touch of anxiety.

'I'll keep that in mind.' He liked that little hint of anxiousness in her. He liked it a lot. And hated himself for it. His father had kept his mother anxious, always one breath away from outright fear. God, he remembered her fear. This wasn't the same.

Dear God, make it not be the same.

'You want to come along?' she asked next.

'Yeah.' Logan ran a hand through his hair and looked to the bar rather than at Evie.

'Yeah, that'd be good,' he muttered.

'What's good?' asked Max.

'Food.'

'When?'

'Whenever you're done here.'

He wasn't jealous of the bond Evie shared with Max. He *wasn't.*

'One more round,' said Max and Logan nodded.

'Max's happy,' he said as his brother turned away.

'Very,' replied Evie. 'There'll be no living with him after this. He's going to drive the workmen on this project bonkers. Fortunately, I have a solution. Her name's Juliet Grace.'

'She's going to distract him?'

'Not at all. Juliet's a construction manager with forty years' worth of high-end project management under her belt.' Evie smiled sagely. 'She's going to control him.'

Evie made Logan feel wanted. There was no other explanation for the warmth in his body and the smile that came so readily to his lips. Easy to make an effort to fit in when a person felt wanted. Cost him nothing to satisfy people's curiosity about what he did for a living and to grin and wear it when one of them asked him where he'd been all Evie's life. 'He's mine,' Evie told them more than once. 'All mine. I saw him first.'

'But I have a puppy,' called Kit. 'I bet Logan likes puppies.'

'I have goldfish,' said another pure soul.

'I have breasts,' said Evie smugly and Logan almost choked on his beer as Kit pouted and the men around him roared. She knew how to handle her subbies, damned if she didn't.

'Max, you got another brother?' asked Kit.

Max shook his head and met Logan's gaze with an affectionate one of his own. 'One's enough.'

'Cousin?' asked Kit, and Max glanced back at Kit with a quick grin.

'She's married.'

'Guess you'll have to do,' said Kit with a devil's slow grin.

And Max blushed.

Logan leaned in towards Evie and she made it easy for him by tucking into the circle of his arms. 'Did my brother just blush?' he whispered in her ear.

'You're very astute.'

'Are they—?' Shock robbed him of words.

'Not yet.'

'But has he *ever*—?' Still no words.

'You mean has *Max* ever? Not that I know of, but it wouldn't surprise me. Kit's not the type to persist when he knows the other guy's straight. And he *has* been persisting. Which means Max hasn't yet given him a definitive no.'

'Who is this Kit?' he wanted to know. 'What does he do?'

'Protective,' murmured Evie and wove her fingers through his. 'I like that. Kit's an electrician. Runs his own company. Subcontracts on big commercial jobs, mainly. Shopping centres. Stadiums. High rises. Jobs that are worth his while. Subcontracts for us every so often on jobs that aren't always worth his while.'

'Fancy that.'

'Yes, he does.'

Logan looked from his brother to the tanned, blue-eyed blond called Kit, who'd abandoned his pursuit of Max in favour of watching football on the big screen. Was Max *really* falling for this man? Did that mean he was reassessing his sexual preferences? Or had he always been looking in that direction and Logan had just never noticed? God! Logan was going to have to rethink every last memory of his brother that he had. 'How did I *miss* this? I need to get home more.'

'Your brother thinks the world of you, Logan,' said

Evie, and there was something approaching seriousness in her voice. 'Wouldn't hurt.'

Logan watched the game on the big screen for a moment or two before turning his attention back to the man who apparently had a puppy and wasn't afraid to use it. 'Hey, Kit. What's the score?'

'Nil all.' Kit shot them a darkly amused glance. 'I'll let you know if anyone scores.'

Evie grinned.

'Next time, *warn* me,' muttered Logan.

'Next time, *call* me when you're coming to visit,' countered Evie. 'And I will. They've been circling one another all week. Best show in town. Mind you, that's what Max says about us.'

'Evangeline, do you and Max have *any* distance between you whatsoever when it comes to your personal lives?'

'Some.' Evie held up her forefinger and thumb an inch or so apart and turned her head so that she could see his eyes. 'We're friends who work together. We're in each other's face all day and we know what's going on in each other's lives. There's no lust. It shouldn't bother you.' Apparently she could see that it did. 'You shouldn't let it bother you,' she said firmly, and brought his hand up to her lips and pressed a quick kiss to the knuckle of his thumb.

Eventually, the MEP crowd thinned. Max kept smiling but seemed somewhat preoccupied. The swaggering Kit had ambled over to the snooker tables in the far corner of the room and started playing. Money was changing hands. Kit looked as if he was working towards finding trouble. Logan eyed the rest of the sharks over by the pool tables. He wouldn't have to wait long.

'Ready to go find something to eat?' Max asked them, with a swift glance in Kit's direction.

'Your call,' said Logan, for it was Max's party. 'He coming too?'

Max shot him a sharp glance.

Logan shrugged and raised an eyebrow. Acknowledgement, if that was what his brother wanted. An innocent question if not.

'I—ah.' Max glanced Kit's way again and this time the other man turned around and caught his eye. Long glances were exchanged before Max turned away. 'No. I don't know what I'm doing there. Probably not a good idea to do it in front of you two.'

'Stay here, then,' offered Logan. 'See if your poolhustling friend wants to grab a bite to eat with just you and then stumble around all you want. Who's going to see?'

Max laughed tightly. '*He'll* see. Lord, I've got no experience with this. *None.*'

'Chances are Kit knows that,' offered Evie.

'You don't mind?' asked Max gruffly, and his question wasn't just for Evie. Max was looking at Logan with something that looked a lot like pleading.

'It's your call,' he said again, not knowing what other assurances to give his brother, and hell would freeze over before he started dishing out advice. 'I'll run with whatever you want.'

Max glanced back towards Kit again, and that was enough for Logan. 'We're going. You're staying. Not sure I ever want details.'

'Amen to that,' said Max and with a wry nod he headed towards Kit.

Evie tucked in beside Logan as they left the pub. She

put her hand in the crook of his arm and every time her shoulder brushed his Logan felt tension leave his body. It was the most relaxed Logan had felt in over a week. 'What do you want to eat?' she asked him.

'Thai?'

'Perfect.'

Even the way she said *perfect* was perfect. Evie embraced the *now* better than anyone else he knew.

'Damn, I'm glad you're here,' she said, bumping his arm this time and making Logan grin. 'What brings you here? Apart from me.'

Cocky. Entitled. And damned if he didn't love that about her too.

'I came because of Max too. I just wanted to be here when the civic centre decision came through.'

'Good for you,' she said. 'Good for me. How long can you stay?'

'I have a morning flight to Perth. I need to be back in London in three days' time.'

Evie stopped abruptly. '*One* day? Not even that?'

'Work's a little crazy right now. I'm sorting it.'

'Why didn't you say so earlier?' Evie's hands were on her hips, her eyes telegraphing irritation. 'We could have left that pub an hour ago. You could have been in my bed by now. Where's your brain?'

Nowhere close by.

There was a shadowy shopfront doorway just a few steps away and Logan took full advantage of it, pulling Evie into the darkness along with him and backing her up against the wall. He'd been holding back all evening, knowing that the eyes of people she worked with were on them. Never undermine the boss's authority. Golden rule of business, so he'd packed his need to stake his claim on her away and kept his hands and his mouth to himself for the most part.

But there were no work colleagues watching them now.

Threading his fingers through hers, Logan brought Evie's hands above her head and leaned in to capture her lips in a kiss so deeply consuming that he feared he might forget his own name.

Though there'd be no forgetting hers.

Evie moaned, deep down in her chest, and her fingers closed tightly over his.

A gasp from Evie as he moved on from her mouth and set tongue to that little V between shoulder and neck. A whimper from him as her body arched in search of his. Hands at her waist now, gathering her close.

'Logan, please. Let me take you home,' she whispered, with her hands in his hair and her mouth to his temple. 'Please, before I come apart. There's food in the fridge, I can feed you if you're hungry, just—the things I want to do to you—I don't want an audience. Just you.'

Logan groaned and loosened his hold. 'Hire-car keys are in my front pocket,' he told her and groaned anew when she found them. 'I swear the car's around here somewhere. Back the other way.'

So they went back the other way and found the car and Evie drove them home. He didn't touch her until the door of her apartment shut behind her. He didn't dare. And then he dropped his overnight case by the door and looked at her and then she was in his arms and sanctuary was his along with salvation.

He didn't want to have to take control tonight; he'd never be able to maintain it. But she didn't ask it of him, just got busy with the removal of his clothes until it was

THE ONE THAT GOT AWAY

skin on skin and hunger driving them, no room for any
other edges between them this time.

Too many stairs to make it to the bedroom and the
sofa was right there, soft and wide and the cushions
could go and he could be on his back with Evie sliding
over him, right there, for ever there.

Owning him heart and soul.

CHAPTER NINE

LOGAN left before dawn. 'Got to be in Perth this morning,' he whispered against her lips and Evie opened sleep-heavy eyes and smiled, because although he was dressed in a business suit and tie, the conventional clothes, he still had sex god stamped all over him as far as she was concerned.

'Do come again,' she murmured and fell back asleep in the time it took him to cross the floor and reach the stairs.

When she woke again, she woke alone, but the memory of last night stayed with her. Of Logan's acute pleasure and her own, and the memory made her stretch lazily and smile and roll over into his side of the bed just so that she could close her eyes and breathe in the scent of him on her sheets. She scrubbed her face against the pillow, ran her hand over the not-so-smooth-any-more sheets.

'Morning,' she murmured. Wherever he was.

And she wondered how long it would take him this time, before he returned to her again.

Easy enough to give a man his freedom if Evie's heart weren't truly in it and they were simply travelling the friends-with-benefits road, but that wasn't the road they were on, she and Logan.

And it was getting ever more difficult to let him go with a smile and pretend that she wasn't totally lost in him, more so now than she had ever been.

New day. A working day—at least she still had that. Not to mention a project that would keep her on her toes for the next eight months. There were management tiers to put in place. Checks and double checks when it came to the quality of the work. There were plenty of things to be going on with.

Where did Logan say he was going to be today?

Running her hand up under Logan's pillow, she felt the jab of something pointed and hard. She pushed the pillow aside and curled her hand around the brightly coloured paper thing and brought it in for closer inspection. Her lips curved when she finally recognised what it was: a folded-up paper parasol, the kind they put in cocktails. She'd asked for one once.

And Logan had remembered.

Evie rolled over on her back and popped the parasol and twirled it between her fingers before tucking it behind her ear.

Time to be grateful for the richness of life and the moments of sheer joy to be found in it. Like last night, when she'd first spotted Logan in the pub. There could be no hellos like that without a goodbye. As of last night she was very fond of Logan's hellos.

'Atta girl, Evie,' she whispered by way of a pep talk. 'Concentrate on those.'

There were five more hellos over the next two and a half months. Evie never got to go to Dubai or to London, for both she and Max had underestimated the management required to take on a big job and expand the business at the same time. Their bad; and the only way to fix it was to work their butts off and pray that the people they currently had in place would hold. Kit had been worth his weight in gold. If Max didn't make Kit family soon, Evie was tempted to do it for him.

Of those five hellos, four had been weekend stints where Logan had come to visit her. Once, Evie had spent the weekend with him in Perth. He owned an apartment there, and it was spacious and expensively furnished but it wasn't his home.

She hoped it wasn't his home for there'd been nothing of Logan in it. It had been a corporate executive's landing pad—a serviced apartment, one step up from a hotel suite. Logan had a real home tucked away somewhere. Some place that allowed him to refresh and renew.

Didn't he?

So there was sex, which ran the gamut from incandescently reverent to edgy to needy and greedy.

And there was work, and Logan knew so much more about hers than she did about his. Max had asked Logan's advice when it came to company expansion and Logan had given it, although not without fair warning that he was more used to stripping a company than growing one. He'd helped them keep the company structure lean, flexible, and Evie appreciated his input, she really did.

But their love life and her working life were becoming so entangled now. Logan being Max's brother. Logan and Max growing closer and closer and Evie loved watching that particular bond strengthen, she *did*.

So what if she woke up way too early some mornings thinking that if she lost Logan she would somehow lose everything else as well?

Too entwined for comfort. No reassurances as to where they were headed with this relationship and it made Evie jumpy and ultra-sensitive to criticism and, dear heaven, did she mention moody?

When Logan was around life couldn't be finer.

But when he left he did it with as little fanfare as possible and he never, *ever* said when he'd return.

Evie knew the why of it. She'd *known* it would be like this.

But the uncertainty was soul-grinding and the road they were travelling was a hard one and Evie was acutely aware that she'd promised Logan that she'd known where they were going with this. That she would be able to show him the way.

Fine words.

And not an ounce of common sense in sight.

'Lover boy still ignoring you?' asked Kit as he disassembled the last piece of scaffolding in Evie's living room and set about packing up his tools. He looked up at the blood-red ceiling and shook his head.

'Looks good, doesn't it?' said Evie.

'Gonna have to call you Mistress Dread.'

Kit had been coming around to her place on and off for a couple of weeks now—a result of Max still jerking him around and of Evie genuinely liking the man. They'd had enough in common for friendship to fall easily into place. Work ties. Mutual friends. Dysfunctional love lives…

'How long has it been since he last remembered your existence?' asked Kit again.

'Three weeks.' Three weeks since he'd last graced her with his presence.

'Train wreck.' Kit dropped his carry case by the door and followed her into the kitchen. 'How long you going to keep indulging him?'

'Says he whose boyfriend won't even acknowledge him.'

'That's different,' said Kit with impressive complacency.

'Yeah, because Maxxie's a *special* snowflake,' muttered Evie as she headed for the fridge, pulled out a beer and waved it at Kit, who nodded and took it from her before settling back against the bench, relaxed and easy in her company and looking decidedly more angelic than tragic. Sunlight streaming through the window and landing on blond hair, broad shoulders and blue eyes did that.

'Max has got a lot to come to grips with,' offered Kit. 'Social issues. Personal expectations. What's Logan's excuse? He doesn't even call you.'

'Logan's a busy man.'

'No one's that busy, Evie. It's a power play.'

'No, it's his safety check. It shows that he's still in control of his feelings for me. That he's not obsessed or demanding or—'

'In love,' said Kit.

'That too.' Evie offered up a tired smile. 'That's the last thing Logan wants to be.'

Kit said nothing.

'You think I should cut him loose?'

'It's an option.'

'Would you cut Max loose?'

'Thinking about it,' said Kit, and Evie choked on the water she'd just put to her lips.

'Seriously?'

Kit shrugged. 'If Max can't resolve his issues about being with me, then, yeah. Why stick around?'

'You don't mean that.'

But Kit just shrugged and set the beer to his lips. Maybe he did.

'How much longer are you going to give him?' she asked cautiously.

'That's the million-dollar question.'

'He relies on you,' offered Evie. 'He gets less stressed about the work when he knows you're coming in.'

Kit just looked at her.

'Maybe you could take a fall from a roof one day, land in hospital and see if Max comes running?' she said. 'That might work.'

'Maybe you could get pregnant with Logan's baby,' said Kit by way of reply. 'I hear that one works too.'

Evie grimaced. 'What else we got?'

'How about making Logan jealous? Bring on the other man.'

'For that Logan would have to actually be present,' said Evie. 'But I could definitely see the other man working for you. Maybe it's time for you to introduce Max to a former lover. One who relishes his extremely good life and the part you once played in it. One who still values you. Got any of those?'

'One or two.'

'I thought you might. That was a compliment, by the way. I can see why people wouldn't want to let you go completely. You're handy.' Evie gestured towards the scaffolding. 'Helpful. Pretty. And smart.'

'Please, my ego, it swells.'

'Nothing but the truth,' said Evie. 'Besides, ego is good for you. It smacks of self-esteem. I had self-esteem too, once. I had a handle on my world. Didn't spend half my life staring at the phone that never rings.' Evie traced a water trail across the counter to the ring that showed where the jug of water she'd taken from the fridge had once been.

'Evie, if it's that bad, let him go.'

'I know,' she said, but her voice lacked conviction. 'Thing is, parts of my relationship with Logan work just *fine*.'

'You mean the sex is hotter than the sun.'

That was exactly what she meant. 'I swear, all he has to do is—'

'Evie!' Nothing like a little panic from a houseguest. 'Too much information.'

'I was going to say "look at me and I'm his",' she finished dryly.

'Ah,' said Kit. 'Well, now I know that. Continue.'

'I was hoping for a little more control over my desire for Logan by now, but it's not happening.'

'That's because he keeps you hungry for him. Always leaves you wanting just that little bit more. You need to gorge on him. Get him out of your system.'

'You really think that'll fix it?'

'No, but you'll have fun.'

'You are *not* helpful. I take it back.'

'Seriously, Evie. If you want my advice, it's to stop letting Logan pick you up and put you down as he pleases. If you want to call him, call him. If you want to see him, tell him you're on your way and expect him

to welcome you. Take a little more control over this relationship. Don't keep making excuses for him.'

'You think I've lost control?'

Kit gave her the look he usually reserved for brain-
dead sheep. 'Evie, you only have to look at the man and
you're his. Your words, not mine. Did you ever have it?'

Later that evening—evening for her, Saturday morning for Logan—Evie picked up the phone and dialled
Logan's London number. If you want contact, make
contact. Step one in Evie's new and improved plan for
surviving a long-distance relationship with a busy, busy
man.

'I have a red ceiling,' she said when he answered
the phone, his voice all gravelly and sleep heavy. 'It's
kind of sexy.'

'Fits,' he mumbled.

'Did I wake you?'

'No.'

'Liar.'

'Maybe.' She could hear the smile in his voice. 'Late
night last night.'

'Party?'

'Work. Two buyers looking at mining rights I hold
in NSW.'

'You're into mining?'

'Sometimes I end up with mining assets as part of
a broader transaction. Occasionally I'll keep them a
while and bundle them before on selling but usually I
spin them off fast. Miners get to keep their jobs if I can
turn them over fast.'

'You're all heart.'

'Tell me about it. Did you want something, Evie?'

'Just to catch up.' Evie really should have gone into this conversation with a plan. He sounded marginally more awake. 'See what you've been doing. That sort of thing.'

'Work,' he said.

'Dull boy.'

Logan grunted his agreement. Or maybe it was disagreement.

'You haven't called me in three weeks,' she said. 'Why is that? And don't say work.'

'Getting pretty bossy there, Evie.'

'I prefer to call it frustrated. Sexually. Emotionally. Categorically. And that's another thing. No more leaving here without waking me. I hate it.'

'I figured it for a courtesy,' he offered warily.

'It's a cop-out. You lay me bare and yourself right along with me and then you sneak away like a thief because you don't want to deal with the fallout.'

'You really want to do this over the phone?' No mistaking the edge of ice in his voice.

'No. I'd much rather fight with you when you're here,' she said sweetly. 'But you're *not*.'

'So…You want to see me?'

'*Yes*, Logan. Yes.'

'So you can fight with me.'

'*Yes.*'

'And then what?'

'Wild make-up sex? Just a thought.'

'God, Evie!' Well, at least now he was fully awake. 'You don't think the sex gets wild enough?'

'I *do* think the sex gets wild enough. The sex is out of this world. You *know* that, Logan. I'd just happen to like more of it. More of everything.'

'We live on different continents. It's not an easy fix. I come when I can and I distinctly remember inviting you here months ago. How many times have you been?'

The answer to that being none.

The excuses for that being flimsy indeed.

'I'm not the only one who gets caught up in their work,' argued Logan. 'I've respected that. I haven't badgered you to come and visit me. I haven't pushed plane tickets on you. I've backed away from doing anything that could be construed as an affront to your independence. You live a full and satisfying life and you make sure I know it. I've been waiting for you to step into my life—take *one* step towards knowing more about me—but you don't. So don't you beat on me for being the only one who keeps their distance in this relationship, Evangeline. You do it too.'

Evie hated hearing the tight anger in Logan's voice. She hated even more that he was right.

'I can be in London next weekend,' she offered in a smaller voice than she would have liked. 'Get in on the Friday, leave on the Tuesday, maybe. Would that suit?'

'Yes.' He waited a beat. 'I promised you Dubai.'

'I don't want Dubai.' Evie was pretty sure this wasn't what Kit meant when he suggested she take a little more control of her relationship with Logan. 'I want you.'

'Evie.' She could hear the breath he took. The way it shook. 'I know I'm no good at relationships. Building them. Maintaining them. I don't even know the way. I try not to take too much. It's important to me that I don't try to manipulate you. Go all needy on you. It's essential to me that you have enough room to breathe.'

'Logan, you're not your father.' A bold statement on

Evie's part, because they *never* talked about his father. Not since that first time.

But her comment only got her a whole lot of silence in reply. 'Logan?'

'I can be like him though,' he said finally.

'When? When have you *ever* been like him?'

'In my head. Sometimes the things I want from you…'

'What things?' she asked quietly, and when he didn't answer immediately, 'Logan, what things?'

'Your attention.' His voice had gone rough. 'I crave it. More of it. Your eyes on me. Your hands on me. When you smile for me. All of it.'

'That's not so bad,' she whispered as desire pooled deep in her belly. 'Can't you see I've just asked the same of you? We've both been holding back. It's okay to want more. We can do more without tipping over into obsession and we'll both feel more content. You'll see.'

'Want you to myself sometimes,' he said next. 'Want everything and everyone else to get the hell out of my way.'

'That can be arranged, sometimes,' she murmured. 'It's not unusual for lovers to want privacy. Balance, Logan. We just have to find the right balance.'

'Sometimes I can't find it,' he murmured.

'We can deal with it.'

'Your body, for example. It's mine.'

'Yes.' No argument with him there. 'It is.'

CHAPTER TEN

EVIE made what they were doing sound so easy. She made it sound like the normal give and take that occurred within a relationship. Her needs and his; explored and explained away. Some needs indulged; no recriminations and no dismay. He'd put her front and centre of a corporate negotiation team any day, fully confident that she would return with the deal she wanted and a couple of souls besides.

Lord knew she had her fingers well and truly wrapped around his.

Seven-thirty on a chilly winter's night and Logan stood waiting by the arrival doors for the passengers from Sydney-Singapore to trickle through.

'I could get used to first-class travel,' Evie had texted him from Singapore, and if Logan had his way she would. Evie had paid for her own airfare; she'd insisted. And then Logan had had her bumped up to first. She needed to indulge him in this, he'd told her simply. This was normal give and take.

No denying that Logan was nervous when Evie finally reached him, trailing luggage-on-wheels behind her. Easy enough to take her in his arms and hold her close and smile as his lips brushed her hair. Smile some more when her lips met his, warm and full of promise.

'Good trip?' he asked her as they headed for his car.

'I slept,' she said with an air of deep satisfaction. 'On the plane—on this lay-back seat-bed chair thingy. First time for everything.'

'Glad to hear it.' She had a smile that could light up his world. A skip in her stride that spoke of enjoyment and anticipation. 'And glad you could make it.'

Evie sobered a little at this. 'Me too,' she said quietly.

The drive back to Logan's penthouse apartment at Imperial Wharf took time. Friday night, couldn't be helped, but they got there eventually and the porter let them in and bade them good evening and Evie nodded in some bemusement.

'You have a porter?' she whispered as the door closed behind him.

'The complex does.' Logan guided her to the lift. The eighth, ninth and tenth floors were his. The apartment was far too big for one person, but he could afford it and he liked living close to the Thames. He watched for Evie's reaction from the corner of his eye as he led her through the entrance hall and into the reception room with its three-storey-high floor-to-ceiling windows and one-hundred-and-eighty-degree views. Nothing wrong with his apartment, he'd paid good money for it, but he wanted her to like it and, by the look of her, she did.

'Wow,' she murmured. 'This is *gorgeous*. Max would be proud.'

'The architect of the family has already given it his seal of approval,' murmured Logan. 'Though he doesn't think much of the interior decoration.'

'It's very…white,' she said with a grin. 'I'll bring you some paint.'

'Keep your paint,' said Logan. 'I like white. Off white. Nearly white. Possibly white. Besides, not all of the rooms are white. Some of them are taupe. And the wallpaper in the master bedroom is stripy grey. You'll like it.'

'Oh, you poor love.' She stood in place and turned a slow circle. 'It really is gorgeous. I'm looking for a personal touch.'

'Yeah. Keep looking.' Evie would find no family treasures here. No photos. No favourite childhood things.

He'd left them all behind.

He collected old maps but they weren't displayed on walls. He had his favourite bath scrub and aftershave but the rest he left up to the housekeeper who came in three times a week and cooked for him and filled his fridge because she complained she had nothing to do for all the mark he left on the place.

And then Evie turned around and caught him watching her and he acknowledged the fact with a half-smile and a shrug.

'Not a lot of you in here, is there?' she murmured.

'No.' He pushed away from the doorway he'd been leaning against. 'But it's private, the fridge is full and it's quiet. I can relax here.'

'I'll take your word for it,' she murmured dulcetly. 'I can probably relax here too. May I have the tour?'

Eight bedrooms, two kitchens, two cloakrooms, a cinema room, an office, various bathrooms and a roof-top summerhouse later, Evie draped her crimson velvet coat over a nearby chair, slumped down on a pale-grey suede lounge and said, 'Enough. You can draw me a map later.'

'Have you eaten?' The fridge was full, no need to go out.

'Yes.'

'Get you a drink?' he asked next.

'No, thank you,' she said, eyes closed as she leaned her head back against the low, puffy pillows. 'I don't need anything at the moment.' One eye popped open as if reconsidering. She patted the cushion beside her and Logan watched as the pat turned into a caress as Evie's fingers moved over the pale suede. 'There's room for you.'

And then her phone rang and she got up and fished it out of her coat pocket and frowned. 'It's your brother,' she said, before putting the phone to her ear. 'Hey, Max. This better not be about the work I left on your desk. Because I left it on your desk for a reason.'

But Evie's smile faded fast as she listened to Max's reply, and her eyes cut to Logan. 'Yes, he's here. No, he's not driving. We just got in.' Moments later Evie held the phone out towards Logan. 'He wants to talk to you.'

Puzzled, Logan took it and put it to his ear. No need for introductions, he already knew who it was. 'What?'

'Hey.' One word and Logan knew something was wrong. The tone wasn't right. Tension ran through the phone line like a living thing. 'It's Mum. She's been taken to hospital. They're operating on her now.'

'What happened?' Logan had a love-hate relationship with his mother. It had been that way for a long time. But an icy prickle started at his scalp and swept down over his body leaving dread in its wake.

'I don't know,' offered Max tightly. 'Some kind of

incident at the shelter she volunteers at. The one for battered women and kids. A fight.'

'A *what*?'

Evie had come to stand beside him, her hand resting on the curve of his stomach, nothing sexual about it, just touch, soft and gentle. Keeping him upright. Stopping his guts from spilling out.

'They're saying she took a blow to the head. Logan—' Max's voice cracked. 'It's bad. I need you here. She needs you here. Can you come?'

'I'll come.' Halfway across the world and unable to even *get* there for at least twenty-four hours. More like thirty-six. And Evie was here. Evie, who'd just flown twenty-four hours to get here. 'I'll be there. Soon as I can.'

'I'll keep in touch,' said Max and hung up.

And Logan just stood there, his mind blank.

'Logan.'

A soft voice penetrated the fog that was his brain. Evie's voice, and she took the phone from him and pocketed it and then her hands were on him again, firmer this time, one to his chest, the other rubbing gently back and forth along his upper arm. 'What's going on?'

'My mother's in surgery.'

'And Max wants you there?'

Logan nodded. 'I'm sorry. The weekend. I can't—'

'All right,' said Evie soothingly. 'Hey, Logan. Easy.' Evie wasn't the one who was swaying, he realised belatedly. He was.

'A few clothes in a travel bag. That's all you need,' Evie was saying next. 'I'm already packed.'

'You can't want to—'

'Get on the next plane home?' she finished for him.

'Yeah, I can. C'mon, Logan, I can't remember where your bedroom is. You're going to have to help me out here.'

The man was in shock. No way could Logan drive back to the airport in his condition. Evie got him to his bedroom. She found a travel bag in his dressing room and shoved it on the rack in there and left him to it while she went in search of the porter. Evie had only the vaguest idea of what a porter manning the door of a swanky apartment complex actually did.

What she *needed* him to do was magic a taxi to the door within the next five minutes.

He didn't disappoint.

Thirty hours later Evie and Logan strode into the waiting room outside Intensive Care. They'd showered the travel grime off at Sydney airport and Evie was feeling more awake than she had been. Her body hadn't liked the extended flying hours, no matter how comfortable the seats had been. Her body didn't quite know which way was up, but her brain recognised Melbourne airport, the name of the hospital and Max, and that would have to do for now.

Max stood waiting for them, tension radiating from him in waves. Tension no longer radiated from Logan. Logan had left edgy behind a good sixteen hours ago in favour of an almost inhuman stillness and composure. Walling up his emotions, brick by brick, and the cabin crew had left him alone and so had Evie. The seats had been so far apart. There'd been no touching him.

He'd told her to get some sleep.

She'd tried.

'What's the latest?' asked Logan, for Max had been

texting them through updates every few hours, regardless of whether Logan could access them from the air.

'The swelling has stabilised,' Max offered gruffly. 'She's unconscious, but she has some partial awareness. She reacts to pain. She's come around a couple of times and called out a name but that's about it. The doctors say that's encouraging.'

'Whose name?' asked Logan.

'Yours.'

Logan turned away and Evie thought he might bolt back the way they'd come; through all the double doors and out of the hospital completely. But he stopped after a couple of steps as if held by some invisible force. His chest heaved and his hand came up to scrub at his face, forefinger and thumb, to press at his eyes and drag any moisture that might have gathered there away.

'You can go in,' said Max. 'There's chairs. You can sit.'

'Will you come in with me?' Logan's voice was so low she could barely hear him. He hadn't turned around. Evie didn't even know who he was talking to. She shared a glance with Max. He didn't know either.

Max gave the tiniest of shrugs, before replying. 'We can all go in. Whatever you want.'

Evie hugged her arms to her waist and stayed silent as Logan reluctantly turned back around, his bleak gaze seeking her out.

'Whatever you want,' she echoed quietly.

He nodded, just the slightest shift of his head. 'All of us.'

'Okay.'

There were six beds in the intensive care unit; six patients and ten times as many machines. Caroline Carmichael lay in the third bed on the left. There were tubes in her nose, tubes in her hand and wires running beneath the cover sheet. Max hadn't told them how swollen her face was or the way the colour was all kinds of wrong, black, crimson and blue—he could have warned them.

Evie hung back as Logan moved to the side of the bed and looked down at his mother.

'Speak to her,' suggested Max gruffly.

'Hey, Mum.' Logan didn't seem to have any idea what to say next. He shoved his hands in his jacket pockets, took them out a moment later and ran one hand around the back of his neck. 'Max said you wanted to see me.'

Caroline Carmichael's eyes twitched as if she was trying to open them, but Evie didn't think there was much chance of that. Not with the amount of swelling and bruising. God, the bruising. But then the older woman's mouth moved, as if she was trying to find her words.

'Logan?'

Caroline's hand twitched—the one with the tubes in it, and Logan reached for it, sliding his fingers underneath hers and curling them gently around hers.

'I'm here. I hear you got hit.' Logan's voice was nothing more than a tortured rumble. 'You should have got out of the way.'

'Couldn't,' said Caroline threadily. 'He went for her, see? Then her boy stepped up in front of her. Couldn't be that…coward.'

'You should have got out of the way,' repeated Logan doggedly.

'I stood up to him.'

'I know.' Logan's voice was barely audible this time

as he sank down into the chair beside the bed. 'You shouldn't have had to.'

'Thirty years too late,' whispered Caroline. 'About time…' Her mouth moved but her words didn't come to her immediately. 'Don't you think?'

Logan bowed his head and set his mother's hand to his cheek. His shoulders heaved and fat tears began to flow.

'Logan?' she whispered.

'I'm here.'

'I'm sorry.'

Caroline Carmichael had finally got her wish.

Evie watched in helpless silence, and so did Max, as Logan Black finally broke.

Three hours later and Evie sat in the intensive care waiting room, staring at the clock on the wall and the scratches in the floor and occasionally glancing over at Max who sat, eyes closed, with his legs stretched out before him and his hands in the pockets of his jeans. He had his head tilted back against the wall and every now and again he'd jerk as if he'd finally drifted into sleep only to remember where he was. Logan was still in the ward, sitting beside his mother; nothing else he could do as Caroline had slipped back into unconsciousness.

He'd leaned into the hand Evie had pressed between his shoulder blades when she told him she was going back out to the waiting room but he'd had no words for her. Just a nod.

Max didn't seem to have any words for her either.

'Did you know that he hit Logan too?' she asked finally, for it was playing on her mind.

Max opened his eyes to look at her. 'No.'

Lots of baggage, Logan. She'd said that to him once, long before she'd even known the half of it. She tried to think of the healing that might come of all of this. Caroline in there, desperate for absolution, and Logan giving it. Caroline finding her strength thirty years too late and paying for it in blood and bruises and believing it was worth it.

Hard to know what Logan believed, or what he felt beyond despair.

Max was still watching her, waiting to see what she would say next.

'You should go home,' she said. 'Get some rest. I can call you if there's any change.'

But Max just shook his head. 'I can sleep here.'

'You call that sleep?'

A tiny shrug and an even tinier half-smile. 'Polyphasic sleep experiment,' he murmured.

'I'm thinking eight solid hours would help more,' she replied dryly. 'Kit know where you are?'

Max nodded and closed his eyes again. Not going there. Butt out, Evie.

'What about food?' she asked next. 'When did you last have something decent to eat?'

'Define decent,' said Max without even opening his eyes.

'All right. I can't sit here. I'm going mad. I'm off on a food and coffee run. Works burger for you, if I can find one. Apple pie.'

'Hot chips with chicken salt,' murmured Max.

'Exactly. Comfort food. The really good bad-for-you stuff.'

Evie looked to those daunting double doors that led back through to the intensive care unit, wondering what

Logan might want by way of food or anything else. 'You think he's okay in there?'

'I think he's anything but okay, Evie,' offered Max gruffly. 'I just don't think there's anything anyone can do about it.'

Which was pretty much Evie's assessment of the situation too. 'Yeah, well. Maybe he's hungry.' Squaring her shoulders, Evie got up, took a deep breath and headed for Caroline Carmichael's bedside.

Logan had given up on sitting. He stood there, hands in his pockets and his gaze fixed on the monitors of the machines attached to his mother. He looked up as she came in and Evie's confidence grew at the flash of relief in his eyes and the tiniest tilt of his head.

'How is she?' she asked.

'No change.'

'I'm going on a food run. You want anything?'

'I'll come too.'

'You don't have to. That wasn't why I came in. Max's out in the waiting room trying desperately to stay awake. You're in here. I just want to stretch my legs as much as anything.' See whether it was daylight or dark outside. Her body couldn't remember.

'I'll come too,' Logan repeated, and followed her out into the waiting room and looked at his brother and frowned.

'Everything okay?' asked Max.

'You look beat.'

'Yeah, I—' Max ran his hands over his face. 'Yeah.'

'We're going to get some food. Bring it back here. Then you're going back to the house to get some sleep,' said Logan, every inch the big brother. 'Eight hours.

Don't show your face here again before then unless I call you.'

Max smiled faintly. 'Bossy.'

'Not exactly breaking news,' countered Logan.

So Evie went with Logan to a nearby café and they brought burgers and chips and coffee back to the waiting room—decaf for Max—and then Max left and Evie settled down to another long stint of sitting in the waiting room, this time with Logan, who took the seat next to hers.

He took her hand after a while. He played with her fingers and looked at the clock on the wall and the scratches on the floor and seemed content with silence, and Evie wanted to talk to him so desperately about so many things. She wanted to ask him if this was why he'd left her all those years ago. Whether it was the hospital that had freaked him out so, and the similarities between Evie's trip to Casualty and the trips he might have made to hospital waiting rooms as a child. She wanted to make this about *her*, and *their* relationship, and she wanted to ask him just how often he'd had to clean his mother up, or himself up, in the war zone that had been his home. But satisfying her curiosity seemed like such a selfish thing to do when Caroline Carmichael was in there fighting for her life and so Evie just sat there beside Logan and offered her hand in his or her thigh nudging his, her shoulder against his, because if anything could comfort Logan it was touch. Silence beamed their constant companion and when they did sometimes talk they said nothing of any consequence at all.

Two days later Caroline Carmichael regained consciousness and Max and Logan set about rearranging their lives around their mother's recovery. Evie watched them prepare to upend their lives for her, bring her home and keep her company here, take her to London or Sydney; whichever way they argued it, no way was Caroline Carmichael going to be alone.

They were staying at Caroline's house—making use of her cars and her facilities and eating her food. Logan and Max thought nothing of it. Evie thought it was a little bit presumptuous—not of Caroline's sons but of her—but Logan had flat out refused to let her stay in a hotel and Max had backed him and that was that.

She'd tried to make herself useful. She washed clothes and kept the fridge stocked, put new flowers in the vases and cleaned up around the home. Nothing big. Changing very little. Not her home.

She'd been on a supermarket run this evening—the fridge had been largely bare and she'd wanted to fill it before heading back to Sydney tomorrow. Max and Logan had been at the hospital when she'd headed out, but they were home when she returned, Max looking relieved and Logan wearing a scowl.

'Hey,' said Max with a smile that looked hard forced. 'We were just wondering where you were.'

Evie held up the grocery bags in hand. 'Most of the dinner ingredients are still in the car,' she offered by way of a hint. 'I thought we might have a nice meal to celebrate Caroline's most excellent prognosis, and, seeing as I'm leaving tomorrow, tonight's the night. Though it doesn't have to be if you've got something else on,' added Evie, because Logan was still scowling.

'I'll get the rest,' murmured Max and beat a hasty path for the door.

'Your phone wasn't on,' said Logan. 'You didn't say

where you were going. You don't know this neighbour-
hood and it's seven o clock at night. Next time you *wait*
for me and I'll come with you.'

Evie eyed him warily. 'Logan, I went grocery shopping. It happens a lot. It's *not* a two-person job. And
I thought I'd be back before you. Next time I'll leave
you a note.'

'And the phone?'

'The battery's probably run down. I'll charge it.'

But Logan still didn't look appeased.

'Look, Logan, there's concern for my well-being—
which I appreciate—and then there's trying to control
my every move—which is going to drive us both mad.
Are we going to have a problem with this?'

Logan stared at her for what seemed like an eon,
and then he let out a breath and ran a hand through
his hair and turned away as Max came back in hauling grocery bags.

'All good?' asked Max, and Evie glared at him and
Logan shot him a look that should have had a kill-
warning attached. 'Great,' said Max. 'That's great.'

'Any more to come in?' asked Logan and Max nodded.

'Couple of bags.' And this time Logan disappeared
to get them while Max started unpacking the ones he'd
brought in. 'Hey…Evie…'

Evie waited for Max to spit out whatever he clearly
didn't want to say.

'Look, I know Logan's being a little overprotective
of you at the moment, and I know it chafes, but he's
still pretty cut up about Mum. Can't you cut him some
slack? Just for a little while.'

But Evie couldn't. 'I know what he's doing, Max.

I know why he's doing it. But I can't let Logan start down that road with me. It doesn't lead anywhere good.'

Max nodded unhappily. 'Your call. Just—go easy, okay?'

Evie nodded. 'I will. I'll try. This setting of boundaries within a relationship—it's new for me too.'

And then Logan came in with the rest of the groceries and Evie started to prepare dinner and both men stayed to help. The opening of wine became Max's job, Logan top and tailed crunchy green beans. Max put the stereo on in the other room and music wafted through to them, warm and mellow. They could use a bit of mellow, Logan most of all.

Because he simmered, there was no other word for it. And Evie spent a fair amount of time wondering just how much longer he was going to be able to keep a cap on the emotions threatening to consume him. The man needed a release valve. And he didn't seem to have one.

Talk turned to work. Carlo had been holding MEP together but he was needed out on a job. Logan had been doing what work he could from his mother's house but essentially he was relying on the management people he'd put in place to do their jobs and manage his business.

The doctors were saying that Caroline could come home from hospital in a couple of days. There'd been talk of neurologists, physical therapists, recreational therapists and psychiatrists and Caroline's sons had said yes to them all. Max and Logan were both sticking around to help get their mother settled.

'Maybe I need to think about moving operations back to Australia,' Logan said as he skewered thick steaks onto the frying plate, his attention only half on his words. Max stared and Evie stared and Logan looked at them both and said, 'What?'

'Nothing,' said Max and Evie in unison, but Evie stopped by the cooker and pulled Logan towards her for a kiss that spoke of wordless approval and a whole lot more.

'I know an exceptionally talented up-and-coming architect, should you be wanting to build yourself a better penthouse than that monstrosity in London,' offered Max once Evie had let Logan go.

'I thought you liked the monstrosity in London,' said Logan.

'I do,' said Max. 'But I can design and build better.'

'If we started from scratch I'd want a lot of specialist electrical work done,' said Logan with a stirrer's glance in his brother's direction. 'I'd need someone competent to oversee that part of the build.'

'We have one of those,' murmured Evie dulcetly. 'He's very amenable. I'm sure someone could persuade him to bid for the job.'

'If either of you think this conversation is going to get you any information whatsoever regarding the status of my relationship with a certain electrical subcontractor, you're wrong,' said Max.

'Relationship,' said Evie. 'You used the R word.'

'I did not.'

Oh, but he *had*. And he was blushing because he knew it.

'Anyway,' muttered Max. 'Kit's got a big government contract lined up in PNG. He's not going to be around much.' Max looked to Evie. 'He wants to know if we want in on the build.'

'In PNG?' First Evie had heard of it. 'What sort of build?'

'It's a—'

'No.' Logan's voice cut across Max's, heavy with warning. 'You don't want to be building anything in PNG. As for Evie, she *certainly* doesn't want to be working there. It's not safe.'

'Well,' said Max, and shot Logan a troubled glance. 'That's one opinion.'

'It's not opinion. It's fact.'

'*You* work there,' countered Max mildly.

'I consult there every so often as a favour to a friend. I don't send my people there and I certainly don't plan to do business there. There are easier ways to lose the skin off my back.'

'What sort of build?' Evie asked again, and Logan turned on her.

'Did you hear me?' he asked icily.

'Yes.' Evie kept her voice smooth and even. 'Did you hear me? Because much as I appreciate your input on this, Logan, I'm interested in the details. Once I hear them, I may even agree with you. I may not. I may wonder what Kit is doing mixed up in this if it's as dangerous as you say. What I'm *not* going to do is let you speak for me.'

Logan said nothing.

'Logan,' she said softly. 'You have a point. The delivery's a little off, but I do hear you. Your opinion matters to me. I'm interested in hearing it. But then I get to make up my own mind.' Evie smiled a little, hoping to coax forth a smile in return but Logan was having none of it. 'You worry that I might be too meek for you.

I keep telling you that I will hold my own against you if need be. Well, this is me. Holding my own.'

But Logan was done talking. He picked up the car keys that she'd dropped on the bench, his jaw set and his every movement oh-so-carefully controlled. 'I'm going to get some beer. We're out.'

No, they weren't. And Evie was done with this man bottling everything up inside. 'So that's your answer to disagreement, is it?' Evie didn't want to do this. Not in front of Max. Not at all. But she'd had enough of tippy-toeing around the real issue. She'd had enough of Logan living in fear. 'When are you going to stop running away from your emotions, Logan? When are you going to realise that people argue, lovers argue, and emotions can run hot, *should* run hot, at times, and that it's not the end of the world?'

Logan stopped, turned towards her and she met him glare for glare.

'Stay,' she coaxed softly. 'Argue your point. Engage with me in debate.'

'I've said all I have to say, Evie. I've made my position very clear.'

'You argued your point for all of thirty seconds. What's the matter, Logan? Scared that if you stay you'll lose your temper?'

'No.' Logan shook his head, never mind the burning heat already in his eyes.

'I think that's exactly what you're scared of. What *does* happen when you lose your temper, Logan? What happens when you finally let go?'

'I don't.' Eyes like bruises and still he stared her down.

'Scared you're going to do what your daddy did and

use your fists to force obedience? Put me in hospital? Is that what you're scared of? Is that why you run?'

'Evie—' protested Max.

'No,' said Logan tightly. 'Evie, no.'

But he'd taken her to hospital once and Evie now knew exactly why he'd run. Tortured, this man of hers. He was still running. 'All that anger. All that pain. Wrap it up in a fist and call it an accident, but it never is—is it, Logan? It can't possibly be an accident if you're involved. It's in your blood.'

'No.'

'Yes. You know exactly how it's done. And it's your turn now. You won't be able to stop yourself.'

'I will.'

And Evie steeled her nerves and stepped up into his space, in his face, and pushed him some more. 'You sure about that?'

'I am *not* my father's son, do you hear me?' roared Logan. 'No matter what you do, no matter how much you disagree with me, I will never, *ever* raise my hand to you in anger.'

'I know.' Evie reached for him, one hand to the base of his neck and the other hand to his back, hugging him hard and waiting, waiting for what seemed like for ever before his arms came around her and tightened. 'I know,' she whispered against his neck. 'I've always known. I just wasn't sure *you* knew.'

She felt the tremors in him as his arms tightened around her. 'Well, I sure as hell know *now*.'

'That was kind of the point.'

'Hell, Evie.' Even Max sounded thoroughly shaken. 'Couldn't you have just asked?'

'Been there, done that.' Evie held Logan tighter and felt the beat of his heart against the thundering of her own. 'Didn't work.'

Logan rescued the steaks, Max put the food on the plates and they took them through to the dining room. The music still played soft and mellow, but the mellow mood was gone and Evie didn't think it was about to reappear any time soon.

She needed the reassurance of Logan's touch but there was food to be eaten and jobs to discuss, so Evie contented herself with tangling her legs around Logan's beneath the table and taking from that what comfort she could.

'So…' said Logan, with a half-smile for Evie and a level glance for his brother. 'How serious are you about this job in PNG?'

'I'm serious about Kit,' said Max with a wary glance in Logan's direction. 'Don't particularly think we need the job. It's a government offices refurb job. Sounds simple. Profitable. But I'm absolutely aware that it could be a mess and that the last thing we want to do is tie up our resources.'

'I can make some enquiries,' offered Logan. 'Put you in touch with some people who do business there. They can run through some of the challenges with you. It'll help.'

'Evie?' said Max. 'What do you say?'

'Truthfully, I don't see much in it for us. It's mainte-nance work. There's no status in it, just the headaches that come with having to fix other people's mistakes and a distant and sometimes dangerous work location. We're not that desperate for money.'

'We owe Logan ten million dollars, Evie.'

'No, Logan's ten million dollars is sitting in MEP's bank account and he'll get it back the minute the civic centre build is out of the ground. There's a difference. Besides, in two years' time when your trust fund turns over you won't be worried about money at all.' Evie eyed Max steadily, looking for a reaction and finding it in the tiny frown that framed her business partner's eyes. 'You asked for my opinion and I'm giving it. This PNG job sounds like stress we don't need. However... I do understand that it's not always about money or prestige. There's the working with Kit factor. Covering his back so that he stays safe and gets in and out with minimum fuss. That's a factor I don't know how to weigh up.'

'Some people might say that's not a factor I should be bringing to the business table,' said Max.

'Not me.'

'You sure?'

'Max, you've been working around my emotional baggage, and Logan's, for months. It's affected my work. MEP's finances. Your relationship with your family. I think I can cut you some slack.' Evie rolled her eyes. Even Logan looked amused, and wasn't that a welcome sight? 'It's entirely possible that part of the appeal of working in PNG is that you'd be getting *away* from me,' she continued

'What? And miss all this?' Max smiled, wide and warm and this time so did Logan.

'Get Kit to call me,' said Logan. 'I can help.'

Max nodded and more food got eaten. Not exactly smooth sailing here tonight and it probably never would be—not with Logan in the mix—but they were making progress. Logan had put his demons on leash and brought them to heel for her. Hard not to get a little breathless about that. 'We good?' she asked him quietly.

'Yeah.' Logan's gaze slid to her mouth and need flared fierce and bright inside her.

They'd argued and made up. Surely there was still room for crazy hot make-up sex in there somewhere. Because she wanted her hands on him, skin on skin, she needed his touch and—

'Stop it,' said Max firmly, and waved a bread and butter plate in front of Evie's face. 'Evie, stop looking at him like that. Don't encourage him. Logan doesn't *need* any encouragement in that direction.'

'Not that it hurts,' said Logan and the rough need in his voice made Evie altogether twitchy deep down inside.

'Don't look at her.' Max turned to his brother. 'Eyes on the plate. This is a family meal we're having here and I for one want to keep my appetite.'

'Food. Yes.' Right. Evie took the plate, wrenched herself out of devouring-Logan-land and schooled her features to reflect what she hoped was baffled innocence. 'Really, Max. It was only a little look. Slightly appreciative.'

'Highly inflammatory,' corrected Max. 'Let's have a toast.'

'To fires?'

'To family,' said Max. 'And it isn't just about blood.' They drank to that and Max gave them another one. 'To my mother's speedy recovery and good health.' They drank to that, too. 'And to my brother.'

'What for?' asked Logan gruffly.

'For being you,' said Max, and they drank to that,

too, sat in the small dining room at a table meant for four and Max started talking about speedboats on Sydney harbour and Logan relaxed and his smiles came warm and easy. How many people saw this side of Logan? The unguarded heart and the tumble of generosity.

Not many.

Safe, thought Evie, grasping at the edges of her understanding of this man. Logan felt safe here with his brother and with her.

They made it an early night. Half ten when they headed for bed, Evie having made herself at home in Logan's bedroom days ago, hanging clothes in his cloakroom and putting her toothbrush next to his.

He hadn't complained.

It had become almost a ritual, this act of showering and putting night clothes on just so Logan could peel them off.

He was sitting on the edge of the bed, elbows on his knees and his hands crossed loosely in front of him, when Evie emerged from the bathroom. He watched in silence as she headed his way.

'I'm sorry about today,' he offered when she was close enough to touch him and touch him she did, running her hand through the silky softness of his hair and tilting his head back, ever so gently. 'I lost my way.'

'No harm done,' she murmured and slid her hand to his face next and dragged the pad of her thumb across his full lower lip. 'A power of good done and you need to know that I won't ever do that to you again. I had a point to make and I've made it. I know what you are, Logan. I know what you're not. I can handle you, everything about you. And you can handle me.'

'Blind crazy about you, Evie,' he said raggedly.

'Right back at you.'

Logan reached for her, wrapping his arms around her waist and dragging her between his legs. Evie closed her eyes and let out a gasp as he turned his head slightly and pressed his lips into the base of her palm and then his tongue streaked out and skittered against her wrist.

The man was an expert at making her lose her way.

Evie tipped forward, knowing that if Logan hadn't wanted to go down on his back he wouldn't have. He wouldn't have let her look her fill if he hadn't liked her eyes on him. And then she wound her fingers through his and pinned his hands above his head and pressed whisper-light kisses from the corner of his eye to the edge of his lips before tasting him with her tongue.

She wanted to take her time. Render him aching and pliant and *hers*. Teasing kisses made way for longer play. Drugging kisses that left his lips shiny and swollen and then she moved on to his neck and felt a swift surge of satisfaction when he tilted his head to allow her better access.

If this man had a weakness it was touch. He shuddered beneath it, and every now and then—in mildest measure—she served it up with a nip of pain, and, oh, he liked that. He came undone on that.

'I've got you,' she whispered more than once, and watched his lips part and hot colour stain his cheeks. 'Watching out for you.' With every whispered word and knowing touch, Evie unravelled him just that little bit more.

'I love you,' she whispered against his lips as she straddled him and took him deep inside and he closed his eyes and let her lead the way.

CHAPTER ELEVEN

'STAY,' murmured LOGAN the following morning as Evie packed her travel bag in readiness for her flight to Sydney. The bag sat on the end of Logan's bed. Logan was still in the bed, sleep-softened and way too appealing for his own good. He'd surrendered so completely to her last night and Evie had taken the sweetest satisfaction in getting him completely and utterly lost to everything but sensation before bringing him home. She knew this game, knew how to wield the power he'd given her. She'd been taught by a master.

This morning, however, the balance of who led and who followed was shifting between them again.

'I can't stay,' she answered lightly. 'Max is staying and someone needs to get back to run MEP and that someone is me.'

Evie didn't want to argue about this. She wasn't about to change her mind. They'd already argued about Evie taking a taxi to the airport and Evie had won. There was no need for Logan to drive her to the airport. The man could use the sleep.

'Stay anyway.' There was no mistaking the rawness in his voice and it made Evie pause in her packing. Some of that rawness could be attributed to the intensity of last night's lovemaking, but not all. Maybe he was scared of being left alone.

But he wouldn't be alone.

'You're going to be busy too.' Evie abandoned the messy tossing of clothes into her case in favour of crawling across the bed and kneeling at Logan's side. She stroked the pale skin of his inner forearm with her fingertips and felt him relax ever so slightly. She brought his hand up, pressed her lips to his knuckles and felt him relax just that little bit more. 'Bringing your mother home. Getting her settled. She's not going to want a stranger in her home and you've got all sorts of family stuff to decide. I'm not a part of that process. That one's all yours and you'll be fine. You'll all be fine. The decisions you make will be good ones. You'll see.'

Logan clasped her hand in his and sat up, nudging her shoulder with his when he drew level with her. 'The decisions this family makes about the future are going to affect you too, Evie. You and me. Your work and Max's. You *could* stay. Be a part of the decision making.'

But Evie didn't want to be. 'I'm not very good at family stuff, Logan. I barely make contact with my own.'

'Any particular reason why?'

'No. My family's just…scattered. There's bits of it everywhere and I'm not anyone's priority. It's easier if I stay away.'

'You're *my* priority,' he said with another bump for her shoulder, drawing her gaze and keeping it. 'If I come back to Australia I want to base my work in Sydney. Live in Sydney. Because of you. You said you wanted more from me, but I don't know how to measure it. I just know that if you let me I'll take everything you have to give. I'm greedy like that. So I'm asking you now—before I put plans in motion that affect other people—whether you want me living in Sydney and demanding more of your time and everything else.'

'Yes.' Gut response, well in advance of rational thought. 'Yes, I'd like that. Didn't you get a ranty phone call from me demanding more of you?'

'Yes, but that was before you *had* me, 24/7. Maybe you've changed your mind.'

'I haven't changed my mind.'

'You sure?'

'Positive.'

Logan's expression moved from searchingly intent to boyishly pleased in an instant. He threw back the sheet, scrambled out of bed and headed stark naked for the en suite. Nothing boyish about the play of muscles in his back, though, or the tight globes of his buttocks. Evie tilted her head the better to appreciate the view. 'Why aren't you going back to sleep?' she called after him.

'Why would I be doing that?' The sound of the shower running followed soon after. 'When I'm taking you to the airport.'

Life and Logan treated Evie exceptionally well over the next few weeks. Logan's mother came home and pressed charges and began to mend. More weeks passed, weeks that turned into months as Logan relocated his business to Sydney, kept his Perth office running, and treated flying to Melbourne to see his mother as if it were no more onerous than stepping on a bus. Different mindset from Evie's. When money was no object a lot of things could happen with speed and relative ease.

A short-term lease on a fully furnished inner-city

penthouse apartment for Logan. A lease on the apartment across the hall for his mother and Caroline began to travel to Sydney for a couple of days each week instead of her boys travelling to Melbourne to be with her.

It had been years since a female figure had played any more than a token role in Evie's life, but Caroline Carmichael seemed determined to fix that, inviting Evie to lunches and brunches and shopping—oh, the *clothes* Logan's mother could afford. Elegant and flattering. Evie had discovered a brand-new obsession. Two pieces she bought for herself, with Caroline giving them the Carmichael seal of approval, and after that she had to stop, because that was her treat for the year and she couldn't afford more. She wouldn't let Caroline buy more for her either, no matter how often the older woman offered to.

'Shopping with your mother feeds my fascination for how some women can pull separate pieces of clothing together to create a look that makes mere mortals sigh with envy,' said Evie one evening when they were at Caroline's apartment and Logan had asked Evie how the late-night shopping trip had gone.

'Enrique's got sales on as of next Wednesday,' Caroline murmured dulcetly. 'He told me in strictest confidence. Half price. We should at least go and have a look for a coat for you. You're going to need one out on site.'

'She has a coat for when she's on site,' argued Max, for he was at his mother's place too.

'He's right,' said Evie. 'It's dark blue and puffy, with fluorescent yellow stripes. Goes with the hard hat.' Evie grinned as Caroline shuddered. 'I'll model it for you tomorrow when you come to visit the civic centre site. I might even be able to rustle up a hard hat for you too.'

'Why are you visiting the civic centre site?' Max asked his mother. 'We've barely started the foundation work. It's just a hole in the ground.'

'Architects,' teased Evie. 'They're all about the frills. Absolutely no regard for the achievements along the way. Trust me, Caroline. This is a beautiful hole in the ground.'

'And you're going to admire it why?' Logan asked his mother.

'I want to see what Evangeline does,' said his mother. 'Besides keep you two in check.'

'That is a full-time job in and of itself,' said Evie with a hard-put-upon sigh. 'Did you hear that Logan's now looking for a house with harbour frontage? And Max is encouraging him? And they're talking about buying a boat.'

'A really good boat,' said Max. 'To go with the excellently located house.'

'Logan, you didn't tell me this,' said his mother.

'But I would have,' he countered smoothly. 'I was just waiting for the half-price coat sale to end.'

'Excuses, excuses,' said Evie. 'Logan, you need a high-maintenance harbourside mansion all to yourself about as much as I need a five-thousand-dollar coat.'

'Well, maybe I just want one.' Logan smiled, slow and sure. 'You want me to buy you a coat while I'm at it? Half price?'

Sneaky man. 'No. No one's buying me a coat. I have a coat and it works just fine.'

'What about jewellery?' asked Caroline. 'Can someone buy you that? Brand-new? No memories attached? Because I have. Bought you something, I mean.'

'Really?' Evie eyed Caroline warily. The last time

Caroline had tried to give Evie jewellery things hadn't gone well for them.

'Now you're scaring her,' said Max.

'There's nothing to be scared of,' said Caroline. 'No ulterior motive whatsoever, beyond a thank you for looking after my house and my garden while I was unwell. It's just a little gift.'

Evie looked to Logan and he quirked his eyebrow as if to say why not?

'Come,' coaxed Caroline and handed a bunch of table napkins to Max. 'It's in my room. We'll do it now. It'll only take a moment.'

'Little tip for you, Evie,' murmured Max, thoroughly amused. 'We're twenty-two storeys up. If you don't like it and toss it out the window, it's gone.'

'I'm not *that* uncivilised.'

And then she caught Logan's darkly amused gaze once more and his look said, yes, yes, she was. And he liked her that way.

'I can behave,' she murmured on her way past Logan, and he caught her hand and pulled her close and pressed a kiss to her temple.

'Do I need to buy you jewellery too?' he asked softly.

'No. I just want your beating heart and your crooked soul.' Evie slipped away with a smile and Logan let her go. Easy to let go these days when she knew that come nightfall Logan would be sharing her bed and come morning he'd be in the kitchen begging the coffee machine for coffee, thick and black. Life these past few weeks had been rich and full and fun and Evie aimed to keep it that way.

'In here, Evie,' Caroline said from her bedroom as Evie stepped into the hallway and followed the sound

of the older woman's voice. Evie hovered in the bedroom doorway. The apartment was far more impersonal than Caroline's Toorak residence, but the bedroom
was still the other woman's personal sleeping space
and Evie didn't want to intrude, no matter how relaxed
she'd grown in the older woman's company these past
few weeks.

'Caroline, you didn't have to do this.'

'I know,' said Caroline and her eyes were bright.
'But I wanted to.'

'I did very little when it came to looking after your
house.'

'I wanted to,' Caroline repeated firmly and held out
a blue box with a white satin ribbon. 'And it's not about
the house, Evie. You know that. Please. Open it.'

Evie tugged gently on the ribbon, taking her time—
still wary, just a little bit, of Caroline's motives.

'First time I ever met you, you and Max had a conversation about a non-existent engagement ring that
made me smile. Diamond, you said when he asked you
what it was you wanted. White. I liked your quick thinking and I did like your style. Don't worry,' urged Caroline as the ribbon fell away and Evie eyed her warily.
'It's not an engagement ring. That's not for me to sort
out. This is simply about the making of new memories
between us when it comes to the giving of jewellery.
New memories to replace those I'd rather not remember.
I learned this trick a long time ago and it has always
stood me in good stead. So…' Caroline straightened
her shoulders and lifted her chin, but her eyes remained
full of entreaty. 'Let's make a new memory, Evie. You
and me.'

'All right,' said Evie. 'I'm in.'

Evie lifted the lid of the box and stared down at the bangle nestled within. Oh, boy. Platinum, Evie suspected. Platinum strands of varying thicknesses crisscrossing over and sidling up against one another all a tangle. In amongst the spaces between the strands sat a scattering of diamonds of all different sizes, some of them at least a carat, some of them only a quarter of that size. Brilliant cut, the lot of them, and there *were* a lot of them. Every last one of them a pure and blazing white. 'Oh, boy. I am *so* in.'

'Do you like it?'

'Oh, yes.' And Evie thought Caroline had excellent taste in clothes. 'I love it. But it's so delicate. And… amazing.' Expensive, was what she wanted to say. 'Where on earth will I wear it?'

'Anywhere,' coaxed Caroline. 'Wear it with what you have on now. Enjoy it. Take pleasure in it.'

Evie was wearing jeans and a vivid pink, fitted short-sleeved shirt and stifled a giggle as she fished the bangle from its box and slipped it on and sighed with delight.

'Yes,' said Caroline. 'Just like that. And I will be content.'

'So show us,' said Max when Evie and Caroline reappeared in the living room.

Evie showed them and Logan said, 'Like it?' and Max rolled his eyes.

'It's beautiful,' said Evie.

'It's a cunning plot to get you used to luxury living and harbourside mansions,' said Max, and Caroline smiled and Evie figured that there was a slim possibility Max was right. Not that she wanted to acknowledge it.

'Hey, you're the one who wants a really big boat.'

'Doesn't need to be big,' said Max. 'I didn't say big. It just has to be good.'

'Fast,' added Logan.

'Fast definitely falls within the definition of good,' said Max.

'Corruption is rife around here,' said Evie.

And so was the love.

Two months later, Logan still hadn't found himself the perfect home. He looked at whatever homes Max flagged for him and he usually dragged Evie along to look at them too. Invariably, the properties boasted waterfront access and harbour bridge views, piers and boat moorings. You know…for the yacht.

Easy to forget—when Logan was sprawled out on Evie's sofa in her little apartment—just how wealthy he truly was.

Not so easy when he went home hunting.

'Why do you even need a home this big? There's only one of you,' Evie grumbled as she stomped through yet another harbourside wonder. He had a key to her apartment and a clothes rack full of his clothes in her bedroom. If he wasn't travelling, ten-to-one Logan could be found at her place. 'Why not just move in with me and save yourself the trouble?'

'Home office,' he murmured. 'I want one. This place has two. And a library.'

'Greedy.'

'Evie, I'm working from a pile of paperwork stacked on your desk. That's when I haven't left half of it at my place. We need more room. *I* need more room.'

'Is this an ownership thing?'

'Absolutely. And a size thing. Possibly a status thing. Definitely a let's buy somewhere together thing.'

'What?' He'd snuck that one in fast. But there was no way she was going to let it pass without comment. 'But…I have a red ceiling. You like my red ceiling. And, more realistically, there is no way I could ever afford to buy a house like this with you.'

'Proportional investment,' murmured Logan, his eyes lighting up as if it were Christmas at the sight of the indoor lap pool and spa. Evie's eyes might have opened a little wider at the sight of them too. 'You live a comfortable life, Evie, and I'm not trying to dismiss it. I'm a huge fan of your fire pole. But here you could have a flying fox from the bedroom to the jetty.'

'Floating tennis court,' she suggested with a grin. 'I could make you make it happen.'

'You could. I'd never deny it,' he said, looking back over his shoulder at her with a con man's grin. 'C'mon, Evie. I like this one. Keep your apartment if it'll assuage your need for independence but please…' He knew exactly how much she liked to please him. 'Let's buy this one together.'

'You could buy it ten times over all by yourself.'

'Yes, and if I did you'd think of it as mine. I'm ready for something that's ours, Evie. Are you?'

'I don't know. I'm thinking about it,' she said, looking down through the branches of a gum tree to the extensive gardens below. 'Is there a doghouse?'

'Why? You thinking of relegating me to it already?'

'No.' Neither of them had been in the doghouse for quite some time. Oh, he could still do a mighty fine possessive wolf impersonation, and he did—most decidedly—have a superbly honed skill set when it came to getting his own way. But he did his damndest to listen to her views and accommodate them, and besides… Evie had a powerful negotiating weapon of her own.

Love.

Only three people in that small, select group for whom Logan would do anything. Give anything. Cut out his heart and lay it at their feet.

And one of them was Evie.

He'd turn his back on this place if Evie asked it of him. He'd downsize his life so that Evie would feel more comfortable in it. He wasn't asking her to be a trophy wife who catered to his every need. He wasn't asking her to cut back on her workload. Apart from a comment about MEP needing another project manager—which they did—Logan trusted her to sort out her work commitments for herself. What he *was* asking for was a commitment to sharing a future with him.

'Maybe I can get your brother to build us a doghouse if there isn't one already,' she said thoughtfully. 'Maybe he can convert the boathouse. Mates' rates. I'm pretty sure Kit would do the wiring for free. Maybe that could be my initial contribution towards buying this place. That and the paint.'

'Why would we need paint?'

'Logan, every wall in this place is white. I'm planning on living with you in glorious love-soaked Technicolor. Did you notice that there's a nursery? And an abundance of bedrooms?'

'I noticed,' he said gruffly.

'Want to help me fill them?'

Logan's smile came slow and full of promise. 'When?'

'Not straight away. But some day.'

'We do that and I'm going to want to put a ring on your finger, Evie.'

'Traditionalist.'

'It's an ownership thing.'

'Give you an inch and you'll take ten thousand miles.'

Damn but he had the sweetest smile. 'You can handle it.'

'Yes, I can.'

'You're very smug,' murmured Logan as he stalked towards her.

'It's a love thing. It happens when love is returned in full. With change. Speaking of which…did you want to put an offer in on this house today? Because I've got a dollar on me. No, wait. I've got two.' Evie patted her pockets, not protesting at all when Logan backed her up against the pool room door and claimed her wrists and pinned them above her head. She was going to like sharing pool space with Logan. She was going to like it a lot.

'Evie.'

Evie had no defences whatsoever against the way he whispered her name as if all the colours of his world were wrapped up in it. His lips began playing merry havoc with her pulse points and she had no defence against that either. 'What were we talking about again?' she asked breathlessly.

'This house.' Logan slid his lips across to nibble at her ear. 'Our children.' Another nibble. 'And you just agreed to marry me.'

'I did?'

'Devil's honour.'

They could argue about the devil's honour later. 'Let's go tell the estate agent we want the house,' she murmured. 'Two dollars ought to be enough to convince him of my sincerity, shouldn't it?'

Logan's soft laughter rippled along her skin as he freed her wrists and she wrapped her arms around his neck. 'It's going to take a little more than that.'

'That's okay,' she murmured and offered up her mouth for his kiss. 'I also have you.'

* * * * *

THE MAN FROM HER
WAYWARD PAST

BY
SUSAN STEPHENS

Susan Stephens was a professional singer before meeting her husband on the tiny Mediterranean island of Malta. In true Modern Romance style they met on Monday, became engaged on Friday and were married three months after that. Almost thirty years and three children later, they are still in love. (Susan does not advise her children to return home one day with a similar story, as she may not take the news with the same fortitude as her own mother!)

Susan had written several non-fiction books when fate took a hand. At a charity costume ball there was an after-dinner auction. One of the lots, "Spend a Day with an Author", had been donated by Mills & Boon author Penny Jordan. Susan's husband bought this lot, and Penny was to become not just a great friend but a wonderful mentor, who encouraged Susan to write romance.

Susan loves her family, her pets, her friends and her writing. She enjoys entertaining, travel and going to the theatre. She reads, cooks, and plays the piano to relax and can occasionally be found throwing herself off mountains on a pair of skis or galloping through the countryside. Visit Susan's website: www.susanstephens.net She loves to hear from her readers all around the world!

For the Angry Sparrow

PROLOGUE

THE SINGLE GIRL'S TO-DO LIST
All roads lead to Rome and there is only one goal here.
He sits proudly at number 10!
1. Get a job
2. Get a flat
3. Get a wax
4. Get a tan
5. Get a hairdo
6. Get a cool new wardrobe
7. Get a gym membership
8. Get a great dance teacher
9. Get a gag for her polo-playing brothers
10. Get a (non-polo-playing) man

As THE only girl in a family of four polo-playing brothers I've
had enough—and I mean ENOUGH!—of whips, spurs and
raging machismo morning, noon and night.

CHAPTER ONE

Get a job
Not exactly the job I imagined, but I have my reasons. What are these reasons?

Actually, I landed the dream job: management trainee in a top London hotel. It was the icing on the cake after achieving a good degree in Hotel Management back home in Argentina, where a career in hospitality seemed the obvious choice to me after years honing my craft on four demanding brothers. But I would rather eat my own feet than keep that dream job by sleeping with a slime-ball concierge who tried to blackmail me by threatening to reveal who 'Anita Costa' really was.

People who knew me before this diary entry might ask, what has happened to wild child Lucia, the glamorous, glitzy, fun girl who was always the life and soul of the party, and who now seems to have sunk lower than a whore's drawers? If you're one of them you'd better read on.

You will note that the one thing I have retained is my sense of humour. Just as well, as right now things couldn't be much bleaker.

No one knew better than Lucia that a nightclub in daylight was a dismal, skanky place.

She should do. These past few days it had felt as if she spent most of her life on her hands and knees, scrubbing the sticky floor beneath a stark long-life bulb. Glittering and glamorous at night beneath the coloured lights, the club, located on the wild and rugged splendour of Cornwall's most popular coastline, was high on society's hot list—thanks to the many opportunities to see and be seen both in the club and on the fabulous beach, where the many sporting activities drew the best pecs around. Lucia's own dangerously charismatic polo-playing brothers had flaunted themselves in this same area when they were younger, with their hot friend Luke.

Luke...

Was this a good time to be thinking about more muscles and intelligence than was good for a man, captured in one devastatingly desirable package?

A man who was out of Lucia's reach?

And who just happened to be a polo player. Which meant contravening number ten on her to-do list before she had ticked off numbers two to nine.

'Don't you have enough to do?'

Lucia shot up as the club manager hove into view. Van Rickter had been a star on the club circuit in his youth, as he had been at pains to explain to Lucia when she had first begged him for a job—any job. Now he was a middle-aged charmer with a chip on his shoulder the size of a rock, who liked nothing better than to bully his staff. Lucia quickly returned to scrubbing as Grace, another of Van Rickter's serfs, entered the club.

'I hear there's a big do on tonight,' Grace announced, dropping her bag on a nearby table. 'Wish I didn't have these sniffles. A red nose and leaking eyes doesn't do much for tips. I was hoping to meet someone fabulous tonight who would take me away from all this—'

As Grace gestured around Lucia reflected that not so long

ago just the mention of a 'big do' would have been a call to arms. She had loved nothing better than to tease and flirt and dance. With four brothers ready to flatten any man who so much as looked at her the wrong way, she had grown up with no concept of danger when she turned it on, and had felt free to be as flirtatious as she liked. Her instant reaction to the merest suggestion of a party would have been on with the five-inch heels, the dress at least a size too small, followed swiftly by slap, glitter, lashes and nails, all topped off by the studiously perfected party pout. But that was then and this was now, and things were very different now.

Turning to Grace, Lucia thought her friend looked unusually pale tonight. 'Let me take your shift if you're not feeling well,' she suggested.

'Another shift straight after this one?' Grace shook her head in firm refusal 'You haven't stopped working since you got here. You'll make yourself ill if you go on like this. Put on your heels tonight, walk in like you own the place, see who's around. Save one for me if there are any likely men.'

Inwardly Lucia shuddered, but as Grace laughed she wiped her hot face on her sleeve and joined in the merriment. Grace had no idea what had happened to Lucia in London, and Lucia wasn't about to burden her new friend with details of that experience.

'Uh-oh, here comes trouble,' Grace warned as Van Rickter returned.

While Grace hurried into the back to get changed for work, Van Rickter picked on Lucia. 'Hey, Anita from the block,' he sneered. 'Put some elbow grease into that scrubbing. I can always find someone to replace you.' With an ugly laugh, he spun on his Cuban heels.

Everyone at the club knew her as Anita. It was the name of Lucia's favourite Puerto Rican character from the musical *West Side Story*. Finding a surname had been easy. Sitting in a coffee bar, she'd thought, *Just lose the 'a'.* So Lucia Acosta had become Anita Costa.

Why the subterfuge?

It wasn't possible to have people treat you normally, let alone strike out for independence, when your four polo-playing brothers featured on every billboard in town.

Resting her hands on the small of her aching back, Lucia dreamed of Argentina and the endless freedom of the pampas. Her warm, safe home in South America had never seemed further away, especially when it turned out that she had a real talent for jumping out of the frying pan into the fire. Her life, since that rogue concierge in London had made staying on at her job there impossible, had been one long slide down. It made no difference that she came from a wealthy family, and anyway, she was determined to go it alone.

'Okay?' Grace trilled as she hurried past with a crate of drinks.

'Never more so.'

Brushing her hair back, Lucia returned to scrubbing. After London she was glad to have a job at a club where no one knew her. Before she died, her mother had used to say to Lucia, 'Keep your wits about you.' Well, she'd certainly failed at that in London, believing the concierge was her friend.

It was hard to believe her mother had been killed almost ten years ago in a tragic flood. Demelza Acosta had been Cornish, which was why the family had always holidayed in St Oswalds. And why Lucia had fled here, she supposed, seeking refuge in the one corner of England where she re-membered being truly happy.

Lucia's head dipped over her scrubbing brush as Van Rickter came into view.

'It's your lucky day, Anita,' he observed sarcastically. 'I've sent Grace home. No one wants to be served cocktails by a waitress with a runny nose, so you're on bar duty tonight.

And don't even *think* of complaining that your cleaning shift doesn't end until seven,' he warned. 'You'll have plenty of time to get ready.'

Half an hour to race over to the caravan, hose herself down in cold water and get back to the club. If she didn't stop to eat it should be possible. 'That's fine with me.' She needed the money.

Van Rickter's piggy eyes almost disappeared into folds of unnaturally pale flesh as he eyed her suspiciously. 'Make sure you clean yourself up. And put some hand cream on. Those wrinkled mitts are enough to put anyone off their champagne.'

'I will,' she said, flashing a smile she knew would rattle Van Rickter far more than an exhausted look. She got tips on the bar.

Being nice and clean was more important for work than a full stomach. No one wanted a stinky server leaning over them, and she sure as hell wouldn't get any tips, Lucia reasoned, teeth chattering as she tied her wild black hair back neatly. She had just showered in shriekingly cold water in the beat-up caravan that came with her other job, and with ice on the insides of the windows it would take some considerable time before she warmed up.

Yes, she'd landed not one but two jobs—though the one that came with the caravan thrown in was rather more complicated than her work at the club, as she didn't get paid. Not yet. She was trying to help Margaret, the old lady who owned the Sundowner Guest House and Holiday Park, where Lucia had stayed as a child, to get back on her feet.

Teeth chattering, she rubbed herself down on a rough towel whilst shooting anxious glances at Grace's uniform. The tiny cocktail waitress ensemble looked far too small. She had put on a bit of weight since coming to Cornwall, having been plied with more Cornish cream teas than was good for her by Margaret. Not that she hadn't been what you might call voluptuous to start with.

Thanks to her handsome Argentinian father and her Cornish mother Lucia had been built to withstand not just the terrifying winds of the pampas but the frigid cold of a Cornish winter—genes that had made her infamous polo-playing brothers giants amongst men, but which had left *her* with the short straw. Now she was more a dumpy style of windbreak. Not that being curvy had seemed to put men off in the past. In fact at one time she'd used to have men—for men read her brothers' approved friends—eating out of her hand. Safe to say in London that hand had been well and truly bitten off.

Her brothers had definitely snaffled all the best growing genes, Lucia reflected as she heaved and tugged on Grace's minuscule boob-tube. Lucia was five foot three, while each of her brothers was at least a foot taller. Their width was breathtaking, whilst hers was merely distance across.

And that distance had never seemed greater, Lucia concluded, as she attempted to stuff one breast inside the elasticated boob-tube only to have the other spring out. And she had yet to tackle Grace's hot pants. Malevolently gleaming silver beneath the flickering light, they taunted her in silent reproach for a diet high on cheap and comforting junk food.

Having finally managed to subdue both breasts, she approached the hot pants warily, like an enemy that had to be put in its place.

Ouch!

The hot pants were definitely in place.

In tank top and jeans, ripped, tanned and pumped after exercise, Luke Forster was reclining with his cowboy boots crossed on an ornate coffee table at his hotel suite at the Grand Hotel in St Oswalds when he took a call from Argentina.

'Do me a favour and look Lucia up while you're there in Cornwall?' Luke's closest friend, Nacho Acosta asked him after they had finished discussing their latest polo match.

'Lucia's in Cornwall?'

'That's what she told me,' Nacho confirmed.

Luke stalled. *Must I?* Was his first thought. Lucia was Nacho's sister, and more trouble than any man needed. As Nacho recited Lucia's number he processed some swift mental imagery that seemed to centre mainly on Lucia's breasts.

That was *so* wrong. Nacho was his best friend and Lucia was the nearest thing Luke had to a sister. Breasts were definitely off the menu.

Lucia's breasts were pretty spectacular.

'She's gone off radar again, Luke.'

He shook himself round to take in what Nacho was saying.

'Though this time my sister *has* been good enough to leave a voicemail with the news that she's revisiting old haunts.'

Luke groaned inwardly. He was doing the same thing, so bang went his excuse not to look for her. Raking tense fingers through his thick brown hair, he added a couple of days to an already crammed schedule. Juggling wide-ranging business interests with his family's huge charitable foundation, as well as playing polo at the international level, demanded enough of his time without going on some wild goose chase looking for Nacho's wayward sister. It wasn't as if Lucia going off radar was anything new. The only female in a family with four forceful brothers, Lucia had broken away as soon as she could, quickly gaining the reputation of being a party girl extraordinaire.

'I know she's all grown up now, but I still feel responsible for her,' Nacho was explaining. 'You will do this for me, won't you, Luke?'

How could he refuse? Nacho had assumed responsibility for his siblings when their parents were killed in a flood, which had worked out great for Lucia's brothers, who were all older than Lucia, and had been okay for Lucia to begin with. But when she'd hit her teens…

'I'll find her,' he confirmed. 'If she's revisiting old haunts, what about school?'

'Which school?' Nacho demanded.

They both laughed.

Super-bright and super-bad, Lucia had run several headmistresses ragged. 'If she's in Cornwall,' he murmured, thinking out loud, 'it shouldn't be hard to find her. The village is dead, apart from the club. Let me follow a hunch,' he said, remembering Lucia dancing at the wedding. That chick could *move*.

'I can't ask for more than that,' Nacho agreed.

They started talking polo again, but Lucia had taken up residence in Luke's head. Both their mothers were Cornish, which was how the two families had met each year, holidaying together at the same quaint guest house on the rugged Cornish coast. The Sundowner had excellent stables and immediate access to the beach, which had given it the edge over the rest of the local accommodation where Luke's parents were concerned. The Sundowner Guest House was intimate and private, plus the owner's quirky take on hospitality, treating every family as her own, meant it offered something money couldn't buy.

Luke loved Cornwall. He was glad to be back here doing business. It was the one place he felt free. Maybe he hadn't realised it as a boy, but when he'd galloped across the beach with Lucia's brothers he'd been true to himself. Now he was successful in his own right he wanted to recapture those feelings of elation and freedom.

'Let me know as soon as you hear something, Luke,' Nacho pressed him, adding, 'I envy you being back in St Oswalds. Do you remember tearing up the beach on those wild ponies?'

'How could I forget?' He liked that Nacho felt the same. 'Would you come back if I reinstated polo on the beach?'

'You bet I would,' Nacho assured him.

With one of the top polo players in the world on board, his plan was already starting to take shape, but as Nacho applied more pressure for him to bring polo back to Cornwall Luke was still thinking about Lucia.

He and Lucia were so different. Luke was an only child, brought up preppy and obedient, and when he was a boy the Acostas had seemed an exotic bunch to him, with their dark flashing eyes and outstanding horsemanship. He had made a point of riding on the beach at the same time as the brothers, wanting them to see his own skill on a horse. Nacho had taught him how to stand on a horse's back while it galloped, nearly killing him in the process, while Lucia had merely tossed her glorious black hair in his face and turned a dismissive back.

Remember those eyes when Lucia flashed a challenge? Those dark, mischievous eyes...

Damn those eyes! Lucia was more trouble than she was worth. 'I'll be in touch when I've got something to tell you, Nacho.'

'That's good enough for me, Luke.'

He exchanged the usual pleasantries and ended the call with Lucia firmly fixed in his mind.

He was still thinking about her later that day, remembering the last time he'd seen her at an Acosta family wedding. Expecting a temperamental teen, he had found a woman who was all grown up. And *hot*. The way she had sashayed up to him, only to veer away at the very last moment on the pretext of seeking out one of her brothers, had left him with an ache in his groin and sweet revenge on his mind.

Forget Lucia, Luke told himself sternly as he waged the endless razor war on stubble that refused to surrender. Tonight he was meeting an attractive blonde who ran an events company, which dovetailed nicely with his plan to start investigating the possibility of reinstating the annual Polo on the Beach event, which had been started way back by Lucia's father. His conversation with Nacho had crystallised his plans, and though it was a setback to find St Oswalds so run down, construction was one of the main planks of his business, so it made perfect sense for him to regenerate the village and bring the world back to its door.

And Lucia? What part would she play?

So much for forgetting about Lucia, Luke concluded, studying his freshly shaved face in the mirror. Shaving was a necessary habit rather than a purposeful exercise. Stubble was already shading his face, making him look more piratical than ever. His East Coast American father liked to protest that he could never understand where Luke's looks came from. 'All that thick, dark hair and the swarthy complexion...and those muscles! So vulgar.' That was his father's verdict. At which point he would cast an accusing glance at Luke's mother and tell her that it must be her side of the family to blame.

That was the link between him and Lucia. They were both outsiders. Lucia was the girl yearning for independence in a household dominated by four alpha males, while he was the musclebound son of Princeton. Quite how that would help him combine a business dinner with a blonde with a hunt for a wild child on the loose remained to be seen.

Lucia's body had just gone into meltdown. *Luke Forster was in the club.* It wasn't possible...

Unless there were two formidable warrior-type men who stood head and shoulders above every other man in the place, with the looks to make any pretty-boy film star pack up his bags and go home, it was a rock-hard certainty. No two men on earth looked as good as that.

So what was Luke Forster doing here?

Rooted to the spot, with a tray of drinks balanced precariously in her shaking hands, Lucia was hiding in the shadows by the bar, oblivious to the barman yelling, 'Get a move on, Anita. There's another order waiting. You know we're short-handed tonight, babe.'

'Move it, Anita!'

She leapt into action at the sound of Van Rickter's voice. Why couldn't the manager keep his voice down? Her name-change wouldn't fool Luke for a second. To make matters worse, Luke had a woman on his arm—a very glamorous woman. Lucia could just imagine them both laughing when Luke explained in his husky, mocking tone that Lucia was running away again, and this time with a name that reflected her interest in music and coffee.

'Thanks, darling,' the barman said as he passed another loaded tray across the bar. 'You're the best.'

She zipped away, taking the long route round to her table of customers to avoid Luke. She didn't want him to see her like this... Not just working here at the club. She would defend her right to work to the bitter end. But Luke knew her too well. He would sense how she'd changed. *Dirty... Defiled... Ashamed and afraid...*

But she was fighting back in her own time, and on her own terms.

Stamping down on the recent past, Lucia returned her thoughts to Luke. She had tried everything to eject Luke from her head, but nothing worked. The more she tried the more she wanted him, and everything had changed since the last time they had met when she had flirted so outrageously with him. She had invited trouble by living up to her wild-child image and now she had to pay the price. The woman on his arm was more Luke's type. Smart, sharp, businesslike and neatly packaged. Lucia doubted Luke's girlfriend would get herself into any awkward position outside a yoga class. Her only consolation was that the girl's improbably whitened teeth attracted the club's ultraviolet light in a way no one would want unless they suffered chronic delusions of being a torch.

'Where do you think you're going?'

Lucia froze at the sound of Van Rickter's voice. She had dumped the tray of empty glasses and had been hoping to make it to the stockroom before Luke spotted her. Rubbing her arms energetically, she said, 'Don't you think it's cold in here? I thought I'd turn the heating up.'

'Put some more clothes on while you're at it,' Van sneered. 'The new uniform was designed with slimmer girls than you in mind. There should be some of the old shapeless ones in the back.'

'That's where I'm heading,' she said brightly. Sloughing off Van's insults, she glanced anxiously over her shoulder. Thankfully Luke was still in deep conversation with the blonde. Luke wasn't just her brothers' closest friend, he was a fully paid-up member of their over-protective, pain-in-the-ass, let's-keep-Lucia-at-ten-years-old-for-ever gang. He certainly wasn't someone she wanted to see her dressed in too-tight silver hot pants and an X-rated top.

'Wait!' Van Rickter barked in a way she was certain must draw Luke's attention. 'If you're off the floor longer than five minutes, you're fired. Do I make myself clear?'

'Crystal,' Lucia said, backing towards the stockroom.

'Find the biggest uniform you can' was Van's parting shot.

'Thank you. I will.'

She disappeared behind the door with a gust of relief. She couldn't care less what Van Rickter thought about her. Ever since London she had wanted to be thought a sexless amoeba without cheekbones, breasts or a waist. Seeing Luke had only reinforced that desperate wish. Far from wanting to flirt with him, she would happily turn her back on all men with the greatest relief. And whatever sort of mess her life was in, *she* would sort it out. Not her brothers. And definitely not Luke.

Last year's uniform wasn't much better on her than this year's, but at least it had a skirt. Well, almost. Wriggling into it, she plucked the matching satin shirt from its hanger and slipped it on, tying it beneath her ample breasts. She hesitated over the grubby plastic camellia blossom she was supposed to pin behind her ear. There were limits.

She walked out of the stockroom straight into Luke. Just her luck—he was at the bar buying drinks. Now she couldn't breathe, let alone pull something out of the bag to defuse the shocked look in his eyes. 'Luke!' she said, feigning surprise as her heart threatened to explode. 'What are you doing here?'

'I might ask you the same question.' he said, taking a step back to eye her up and down.

Telling herself she was used to alpha males, having grown up with four of them, she lifted her chin. 'This is where we always go,' she said, gesturing around as if she was at the club with a huge gang of friends. This only succeeded in causing Luke's eyes to narrow with disbelief.

With shock crackling between them as Luke scoffed disbelievingly, she drank him in. Luke was the essence of male. Bigger and more powerful than the other men in the club, he was infinitely better looking. Luke had always been able to melt her with a glance—though at the moment that glance was doing its best to incinerate her, which for once rested more comfortably with Lucia than the smouldering, sexy look Luke was so good at. He was even bigger than she remembered— harder, tougher—though, as always, immaculately groomed, with shoulders wide enough to hoist an ox and hard-muscled legs that went on and on to…to a point from which she quickly averted her eyes.

While *she* had not only let herself go, but was wearing last year's shabby club uniform, with her hair scraped back and her face glowing red and shiny beneath the lights. Perfect.

'Lucia?' Luke rapped sternly, staring down at her with knife-sharp eyes. 'Are you working here?'

Of course she should have said, *What's it to you?* But a row might draw attention and she couldn't afford to lose this job. 'No, of course I'm not working here,' she protested with a laugh, glancing around to make sure no one had heard Luke calling her by her real name. 'I come here so often they let me hang my coat in the stockroom.'

'Really?' Luke drawled, with an even more contemptuous expression in his brooding amber gaze.

'Okay, from time to time,' she admitted, brushing it off as she continued to stare at a face that was mesmerising in its harsh masculine beauty. If you wanted *hard* there was no better hard to be had than Luke Forster—as her yearning and thoroughly confused body would now attest. But Van was prowling, Lucia noticed. 'Gin and orange for your friend?' she suggested as the blonde, having exited the restroom, made a beeline for them.

'I have ordered our drinks, thank you,' Luke said coolly. 'Vanessa,' he murmured, in what Lucia considered an unnecessarily indulgent tone, 'I'd like you to meet an old friend of mine.'

'Not so much of the old,' Lucia joked weakly, feeling awkward and ridiculously exposed when she compared herself to Luke's neatly styled friend. The blonde was even prettier close up, and was hanging on to Luke's arm as if her life depended on it.

'Do you work here?' Vanessa enquired, visibly relaxing once she had assessed Lucia and found her lacking in—well, practically everything.

'I help out here occasionally,' Lucia said carefully.

'How nice to have such a…sociable job.' The blonde looked

at Luke for approval of her assessment, but Luke was too busy
studying Lucia.

Van, having spotted money, was sniffing around. 'Have
you seen our new casino yet?' he crowed.

Van clearly imagined he had found a high-roller in Luke,
but Lucia knew Luke had never gambled in his life, and rarely
drank. Having summoned another of his serfs—a far more attractive cocktail waitress than Lucia—Van ushered the small
group away.

The only good thing about it, Lucia mused from the shelter
of the bar, was that Van was so drunk on the scent of money
he had chosen to walk backward in front of Luke—until he
collided with a table and then had to turn and chase after his
big-striding guest.

The crowd on the dance floor fell back at Luke's advance
like the Red Sea parting, and Luke paused at the entrance to
the casino just long enough to shoot a stare at Lucia that assured her this wasn't nearly over yet.

CHAPTER TWO

Get a flat
Admittedly, this is not quite the accommodation I had in mind. But, again, there are reasons. And holiday parks are all the rage, offering an unparalleled level of lifestyle, according to the ads I've read in magazines. Sadly, my des res is a leaking tin can on wheels, with no discernible braking system, parked in a ramshackle field on the edge of a crumbling cliff a good half-mile walk from the shelter of the guest house. Try that out for size in a sleet storm in winter.

SHE spent the rest of the shift swinging like a pendulum between kicking herself because Luke had caught her out and wondering how on earth to explain to her brothers' clearly bemused friend what she was doing there—without actually telling him what had happened, that was. Why hadn't she been frank with him and looked to Luke to keep her safe? He was the next best thing to a brother, wasn't he? Why hadn't she told him the truth?

Because it was none of Luke's damn business!

And because she had never felt more ashamed or more soiled in her life. He would never look at her the same way again if he knew… She couldn't be further from her dream of building her own life, independent of Luke and her brothers,

Lucia realised as Van switched off the soft lights in the club after another long night, turning on the harsh glare of factory-style strip-lighting.

There was a song about a girl from South America who was tall and young and lovely. Lucia had used to hum it beneath her breath when she was a pre-teen, never dreaming she would turn into the *other* girl from Ipanema—the one who was short and a bit too fat, plain and olive-skinned. And stupid. She had to be stupid to have got herself into such a mess in London. How could she go home and tell them the truth now? It was all too humiliating, too shameful.

So she would ride this storm out like any other, Lucia told herself firmly. She just hadn't fathomed out how yet.

She had been monumentally thrown at seeing Luke again, Lucia reasoned as she helped the barman clean the bar. She *was* making the climb back, though, however long it was taking, and she should cut herself some slack. Tonight the best thing she could do was to concentrate on cleaning up and earning a night's pay.

His attention on the blonde hadn't so much slipped as fallen down a ravine—a ravine with Lucia at the bottom of it. To say he was shocked at seeing her working here would be putting it mildly. It was a world away from the last time he'd seen her, dancing so hotly he hadn't been able to take his eyes off her. How had she gone from that to working for a toad like Van Rickter? How was that supposed to further Lucia's career? And where was she living? Who was she spending time with? What had happened to the girl who had blown him out of the water with her sass, her dancing, her brilliant smile, her world-class flirting, her breasts? Okay, so the breasts were still pretty amazing, but the rest…

What the hell had happened to Lucia?

The thought that Van Rickter might have something to do

with it made the hackles rise on the back of his neck. His call to Nacho could wait. There were a few enquiries he wanted to make first.

He glanced round impatiently as Vanessa waved an empty glass in his face. 'The club's closed,' he pointed out sharply, knowing he was the one to blame for hanging on to watch Lucia.

Making his excuses before the evening became even more uncomfortable than it had already been, he called a cab for the blonde and took Van Rickter into the back room to make a few things clear to him.

'How long has that girl called Lucia worked here?'

'Lucia?' Van Rickter seemed genuinely confused. 'There's no one called Lucia working here,' he protested, with a shifty, guilty look.

'The dark-haired girl with the attitude and—'

'Oh, you mean Anita,' Van Rickter said on a wave of relief. 'At least that's what she calls herself here,' he said, quickly covering himself in case Lucia had done something wrong. 'Don't tell me she's an illegal?' Van exclaimed, wiping his brow as if hiring vulnerable people for cash and far less than the minimum wage had never occurred to him.

'I mean Anita,' Luke agreed offhandedly. 'I must have misheard her name,' He might be all out of patience with Lucia, but this was private business. He wasn't going to give Van Rickter anything that he could hurt Lucia with, or make money out of.

'I could arrange a meeting, if you like,' Van Rickter said, in a way that made Luke's pupils shrink to arrowheads. 'All the girls owe me…'

I bet they do, Luke thought with distaste.

'She has a second job at the local guest house,' Van Rickter revealed, toadying up to him. 'The Sundowner? You might have heard of it. Maybe the owner there can tell you more.'

Luke hid his rush of triumph. Lucia wouldn't be using the alias Anita at the guest house, where the owner knew her, so Margaret must be in on Lucia's life plan—whatever that might be. But there was something else worrying him. If he hadn't known better he would have said Lucia had flinched from him, almost as if she had some communicable disease. That wasn't the girl he knew—the girl who would happily take any man down with her repartee. So what the hell was going on?

In spite of his distaste at being forced to discuss Lucia with a man like Van Rickter, he was amused at the thought of Lucia choosing the name of a Puerto Rican firecracker in a musical. It made him think back to her brothers, yelling at her to turn the caterwauling down when they had wanted heavy metal to rule the house. He could imagine Lucia had dreamed of being Anita, a woman free to express herself without four brothers drowning her out—though in his opinion Lucia had far more going for her than a fantasy figure.

Kill those thoughts. Lucia was trouble. Whatever mess she had got herself into this time, it wasn't up to him to sort it out. He'd tell Nacho he'd found her and then his job was done.

Lucia had a second job? Luke mused, turning to stare at the entrance to the club. No wonder she looked exhausted. Two lousy jobs in the wilds of Cornwall didn't come close to equalling one good job in the heart of London. So what had happened to the management position at the top London hotel Nacho had been telling him about? He consoled himself with the thought that whatever she was hiding he would find out. Lucia was living at the Sundowner, and Margaret, the owner, was a big part of his plan to revive the area.

'Luke...'

She was thrashing about in bed in that half-world between sleeping and waking where anything was possible—even a man making love to her. But this wasn't any man.

Shifting restlessly on what passed for her pillow, she pulled the scratchy blanket round her shoulders and slipped deeper into the world of dreams, where her body was still capable of quivering with awareness, with warmth and with arousal—where Luke's brooding amber gaze needed no explanation and the care in his big, strong hands was all the reassurance she needed.

Seeing Luke again tonight had been bound to lead to this, Lucia's drifting mind soothed. Her eyes were open and yet they were closed. She was sleeping, surely? The air was misty with a golden glow. Candles were flickering. Seductive scents tickled her nostrils. Luke was stripped to the waist and leaning over her. He was as magnificent as ever. His golden torso, so powerful and so shielding, made her feel small, made her feel safe, made her feel that anything was possible—even Luke looking at her with desire in his eyes…

Thrashing her head on the pillow, she knew this was wrong. Luke was taboo. She should not be lying here naked with him. Luke was older, established, confident, experienced. Luke was her brothers' friend—upright and principled.

Her body didn't care about any of that and responded urgently. Reaching out, she mapped the wealth of muscle from his shoulders to his iron-hard belly, glorying in his strength. And when Luke quivered beneath her touch she revelled in her power over him. But Luke refused to accept her dominance and, swinging her beneath him, brushed his fingertips across her breasts, watching without pity as she gasped for air and arced towards him, seeking more contact.

What was she doing? Luke was built on a heroic scale, and when he discovered the truth about her he would throw her off in disgust.

Luke knew how much she wanted him. Holding her gaze, he caressed her, and she groaned as pleasure spiralled through her body. Reaching up, she laid her palm against his stubble-

roughened cheek. Luke answered by teasing her lips apart
and taking her mouth in a scorching reminder of what else
he'd like to do to her.

'I have no other duty but to please you,' he said.

Quite right too, she thought, though the longing to pleasure Luke was overcoming her, and to be pleasured by him,
to forget her fear. But just as she reached for him he slowed
the pace. Turning away, he poured champagne, then reached
for some fruit in the bowl by the bed. He dipped a ripe berry
in melted chocolate before holding it to her lips. She sat forward. He took it away. He moved to kiss her. She moved away.
Luke's eyes held so much understanding, and when his lips
claimed hers he tasted of strawberries and chocolate. Gaining
in confidence, she rubbed her naked breasts against his chest
and felt her nipples tighten. Drawing deeply on his warm male
scent, she placed her hands flat against Luke's hard, hot torso
and drew him down.

'Tell me what you want, Lucia.'

'Kiss me,' she begged, reaching up.

'Is that all?'

'It's enough.'

'I don't believe you.'

As Luke cupped her with his hand, almost but not quite
granting her the contact she craved, a wave of pleasure stole
away her fear. But then he drove his thigh between her legs
and demanded harshly, 'What's wrong, Anita?'

Anita?

She shrieked in terror as the fantasy collapsed and instead
of Luke the fat, flabby, pale-skinned concierge loomed naked
and aroused above her, red-faced and lecherous. His reptilian
eyes glistened yellow in the light, while his fat red lips, wet
with saliva, just as she remembered them, were drawn back in
a snarl over rotting teeth. She fought him, fighting furiously
for her honour, for her life—

Waking with a start, Lucia sucked in a sharp breath, staring round fearfully. It took her a moment to realise where she was. The caravan slowly took on a reassuring form. There was no concierge. There was no Luke. There was no satin bed-linen. There were just bobbly grey sheets, and she had been slithering about on top of one of her magazines. Luke hadn't been feeding her chocolate sauce and fruit. And there certainly wasn't any champagne. There were just some dregs of hot chocolate left in the flask on a shelf by the bed.

She was still shaking as the nightmare faded. Climbing out of bed, she realised the dream was the closest she'd come to sex with Luke—was ever likely to come to sex with Luke—and even in her dreams she couldn't get it right.

Because the concierge had taken over.

Perhaps it would always be like that from now on. Perhaps her dream of becoming a strong, independent woman was just a pipe dream. Perhaps she would never be able to make love properly, because the concierge would always be waiting in the wings to spoil things for her.

And after a dream like that, how could she ever face Luke again?

It was eleven o' clock on a Friday night and the club was heaving. A whole seven Luke-free days had passed. And that was good.

Was it?

Yes, of course it was. She could do without any more of those dreams seeing Luke seemed to provoke. He had probably returned to the States by now, after taking the same trip down memory lane in Cornwall that she had. She could only hope for Luke's sake he had had a better result. She was currently putting in a second shift as another cocktail waitress had gone off sick, and she was so tired she was seriously considering nabbing a couple of cocktail sticks from the bar to prop her eyes open. There must be a convention on at the Grand, Lucia guessed, as more people poured in through the door.

'Anita.'

Van was approaching. There had been a distinct improvement in Van's mood since Luke's visit. He couldn't take the risk that Lucia had friends in high places, she supposed, though that had been wearing a bit thin this evening, as if Van suspected her influential friend might have deserted her finally.

The holiday had definitely ended, Lucia concluded, as Van snapped, 'There's been a spillage on the dance floor. Do something about it, will you?' Van's piggy eyes continued darting back and forth as he spoke, counting money as it walked through the door. *'Now,'* he spelled out, turning to glare at her. 'We have some important patrons stopping by tonight.'

'Yes, sir,' Lucia murmured, hurrying away to get her mop and bucket.

'And, Anita?'

'Yes?' She stopped and turned around.

'You need to lose weight.'

She nodded agreement. Van was always right. That was the mindset you had to have if you wanted a quiet life at the club. But in this instance Van *was* right. She felt humiliated in the too-tight boob tube and hot pants ensemble, over which she overflowed with all the glorious abundance of a chocolate fountain. But since Van had made her revert back to the original cocktail waitress uniform so she 'blended in', as he put it, she would just have to suck it up.

Emerging from the stockroom with her cleaning tackle, she grabbed a clean apron from a hook by the door. She would have preferred a tent, but that might have looked a bit obvious, and at least the apron partially concealed her body.

She had to put out cones to keep the area clear so no one would slip on the dance floor while she was working. She'd done plenty of clean-ups at the club, but this one was particularly revolting. Suffice it to say unmentionable substances, still with the distinct tang of brandy and cola about them, had spread widely across the black glass tiles. She was making good progress while customers gyrated around her unconcerned. She was invisible. Wasn't that great?

Not so great when she got stomped on a couple of times. But she was nearly finished.

Lucia's heart bounced once and then stopped. There was only one man who would have the balls to wear cowboy boots with a sharp Italian suit. She stiffened as a pair of very large feet halted within inches of her nose.

Important patron? Van had got that right. Conscious that her XXL silver-clad backside was poking up in the air, she quickly drew it down and remained quite still, as if she might somehow become invisible again.

But sadly no.

'Lucia?'

How could her life get any worse?

Luke Forster, Lucia's childhood crush, and more recently her erotic dream buddy, was back.

CHAPTER THREE

Where in my list does it say that one of the bad boys of polo can crack his whip over my head while I'm on my hands and knees in front of him?

Blech! That does not sound good.

Did that possibility even cross my mind when I was a fourteen-year-old dreamer with only gallant knights in shining armour ahead of me?

No. It did not.

'Up.'

People turned to stare. Luke's voice sounded like a pistol crack, blotting out the music as well as the overheated chatter in the club.

'Hello, Luke,' Lucia said mildly, determined there wouldn't be a scene. Van would sack her on the spot. And wouldn't Luke relish ammunition like that when he made his report to her brothers? 'How nice to see you again.' With clothes on, she amended silently, trying hard not to blink.

'Imagine my surprise to see you here *working*,' Luke countered with bite. He returned her upturned gaze with an expressionless stare.

Attack was the only form of defence in this situation. Why was she still down on her knees? Standing, she said coolly, 'You didn't think to say goodbye last time you were in the club. Oh, no—I forgot,' she added. 'You had better things to do.' A spear of inconvenient jealousy hit her as she looked in vain for the blonde.

'She's not here,' Luke said, reading her with ease. 'And you're leaving.'

'I beg your pardon?' Now she was upset. One of the up-sides of seeing Luke again was that it had restored some of her old fire. She hadn't broken free of her brothers only to be ordered about by Luke!

'You heard me,' Luke said stonily.

Breaking eye contact, she reached for her bucket.

'You're leaving that where it is,' he rapped.

'No!' Luke's big tanned hand seized hold of her arm, and it was bad enough seeing those sensitive fingers sinking into pale, plump flesh without remembering the magic those hands had wrought in her dream...

This was reality, Lucia reminded herself sharply.

But wasn't this what she had waited for all her life? Luke riding to her rescue. Luke holding her. Luke...

'Get off me,' she fired out furiously, shaking herself free. 'I'm not a horse you can grab hold of and lead where you like. I make my own plans, Luke. And I'm working. Do you want me to lose my job?'

Luke's arrogant head dipped so he could glare straight into her eyes. 'I would love you to lose your job,' he assured her grimly.

'I come off shift at three a.m. I can talk to you then, but not before,' she said, aware that Van the Terrible was lurking in the shadows, watching them.

Picking up her mop and bucket, she stalked off the dance floor before Luke had the chance to say a word.

There was only one small consolation in all of this. Her body might be trembling like a leaf, but she was earning a living, and however small that living might be when compared to

Luke's vast income she was living independently. *Two* small consolations, Lucia conceded with surprise. Confronting Luke hadn't frightened her. She hadn't backed down and slithered away to do his bidding. She had felt as if she'd been in a perpetual state of fear since London—finally she was beginning to feel alive again.

So she didn't need him. *Good.* He shouldn't get involved. He would call Nacho—let him take over. Lucia was wild and had set herself on a very different path from him. He was all about polo and business, and had no intention of being distracted or pulled down by anyone. Lucia was clearly on a downward trajectory. With every advantage in the world, she had chosen to work in a club.

Really? Did he believe that?

All he knew for certain at this point was that in his family no one went against expectation, and feelings were curbed as stringently as any horse in a dressage arena. Lucia was composed entirely of emotion. She was an untameable Acosta. He should put her out of his mind for good

Which was easier said than done. He was becoming increasingly worried about her, and in spite of the cold facts he owed Nacho.

Was that all?

So she was attractive. He would soon tire of all the drama.

Wasn't it entertaining to be around someone with so much character for a change?

Didn't he love to hunt?

He liked the chase best of all.

What the hell was he thinking?

Lucia was the kid sister of his closest friend. She was out of bounds. And, in the unlikely event that he found himself in the mood for a walk on the wild side, he'd choose someone as worldly as he was—not some pampered Argentinian princess.

Who wasn't too proud to get down on her hands and knees and scrub a filthy club if that was what it took.

And who was one hell of a good-looking woman, Luke conceded, even in the extraordinary outfit Lucia was forced to wear at work.

All the more reason for him to keep his distance. With his blood boiling in his veins she was safer away from him.

Three o'clock in the morning came and went. The last patron had left the club. They had swept up and tidied and Luke had gone. She'd been too busy to notice when he left. He had left with the blonde, she presumed, feeling sick inside. He definitely hadn't remembered what day it was today.

So what? Why should she care if Luke had forgotten it was her birthday? She didn't need him. Luke Forster could go to hell in a bucket for all she cared.

'Didn't your birthday start at midnight?' Grace asked, giving Lucia's arm a squeeze as they left the club together.

'How did you know?' Lucia asked as they took shelter for a moment before braving the rain.

'I know everything about you,' Grace teased fondly.

Including Lucia's real name. Grace was too good a friend for Lucia to want to deceive her. 'So you've heard the party-girl rumours too?'

Grace laughed. 'You don't know the meaning of the word. You're not a party girl any more than I am, Lucia. But some of our friends at the club seem to think we should lighten up a bit.'

'I hope you're not referring to Van Rickter?'

Grace frowned. 'I wouldn't call him a friend, exactly, but there *are* other nice people working at the club.'

'What are you hiding under your jacket?' Lucia enquired as they crossed the road.

'We had a whip-round for your birthday,' Grace explained, starting to smile.

'What is it?' Lucia asked, her curiosity well and truly roused.

'I'm not saying. I don't want to spoil the surprise. But I will tell you this much—everyone seems determined to tempt at least one of us off the straight and narrow this year.'

'It might take a bit longer than that for me,' Lucia admitted, shivering as the cold wind whipped around her.

'Don't be such a defeatist,' Grace teased. 'A lot can happen quickly if you're lucky.'

Lucia huffed as Grace squeezed her arm again, and then both girls screamed as they sploshed through an icy puddle in the middle of the road.

'I stuck a couple of mags in the bag as well,' Grace called out as they parted company at the entrance to the Sundowner Holiday Park. 'You might recognise one of the centrefolds. You were talking to him in the club.'

Lucia's heart went crazy with excitement. The centrefold was hardly going to be Van Rickter—unless the magazine in question was *Amphibian World*.

She ran all the way to the caravan and, throwing her shoulder against the buckled door, launched herself inside. Dropping her things on the floor, she snatched the magazines out of the gift bag and flung herself onto the lumpy bunk. Leafing through as fast as she could, she stalled at the centre page of the second magazine.

Luke Forster was *ROCK!*'s Torso of the Year.

Dropping the magazine, she threw herself back against the cold tin wall. 'You blue-blooded hypocrite!' Her main gripe was not how Luke looked—which was pretty spectacular by any standards—but the way he behaved when he was around her, as if he were a paragon of all the virtues. 'So you're incorruptible, are you?'

Now, this was worrying. Not only was she talking to herself, but she was involving a magazine in the conversation. With an angry huff, she plucked the gum from her mouth and stuck Luke's centrefold to the wall. 'Take that!' A thump from her fist secured it. Standing back, she had to concede Luke's centrefold *did* brighten things up a bit.

So where was he? Lucia wondered, going through her nightly routine of getting ready for bed in the freezing caravan by piling on more clothes. If Luke was still in Cornwall he was probably tucked up in a nice warm room at the Grand by now—with the blonde. *Ack!* And if he thought about Lucia at all it would only be to wonder if she was ready to go home yet.

'No, I'm not ready,' she snarled, glaring at Luke's poster. 'And I'm not giving up. I can't give up. I can't go home. Not like this….'

Their nice, warm kitchen in Argentina, where the roof never leaked and the floor was never cold, and she had never once had to pick ice off the insides of the windows…

Unscrewing the top of the flask of hot chocolate that Margaret left on the table each night, she scowled at Luke's centrefold as she gulped the warm liquid down. She tried not to think about the list of goals she had intended to achieve by now—goals Lucia had been so confident were achievable when she was fourteen.

Reaching beneath the bed, she drew out the precious tote full of memories and extracted the battered notebook in which, as a dreamy-eyed teen, she had written down her innermost hopes and dreams. She didn't often do this. She saved it for when things were really bad. The bag of dreams, as she called the old canvas tote, was her comforter. It contained her journal from when she was fourteen, and her rather more neglected journal from now. She pulled the old one out and started to read.

It is imperative *to follow this list to the letter if I'm* ever *going to break free from Conan the Barbarian and his gang of galloping gauchos—otherwise known as my brothers...*

Lucia smiled as she read the messy list, with all its scribbles and crossings-out. It was hard to believe she had ever been so naïve. Most of her ideas had been based on articles she'd read in teen magazines, which of course were essential reading for fourteen-year-olds with everything to learn. She would have to completely re-jig the list. Get a wax *after* she'd got a man? Well, that was wrong to start with. And, the way she felt right now, getting a wax could be number two-hundred and thirty-six on next year's list. Yes, Luke was gorgeous, but...

No. She couldn't.

She just couldn't, that's all.

But just out of curiosity, and because trips down memory lane seemed to be in vogue right now, she straightened out the much-thumbed pages and began to read.

1. Get a job!—preferably promoting a bar, which is a great way to meet new people, according to *ROCK!* magazine
2. Get a flat!—something gorgeous and stylish in the best part of town. N.B. V. close to the bar!
3. Get a wax!

She remembered that last entry being based more on dreading what her rapidly changing body might do next rather than any horrific hirsute happenings. And how many times had that entry been deferred? And why did she still shift position nervously when she read it?

She pulled a face as she got up to check her top lip in

the mirror. Flopping back down again, she remembered her mother's pale face when a visit to the beautician loomed. Perhaps that was the answer to her waxing phobia. She could still hear her young self asking, 'Are you all right, Mama?' And her mother's response: 'You'll understand one day what it means to be a woman, Lucia, and what we have to go through for our men…' Hefty sigh at that point.

All sorts of images had flashed into Lucia's young brain—nostril-hair-plucking, blackhead-excising, even earwax-removal with one of those long, pointy things—but never had she imagined that her mother was referring to that most delicate of regions, let alone that some stranger was going to view her private bits close up prior to coating them in molten wax like some medieval torturer. And it didn't finish there—as Lucia had discovered in that invaluable teenage self-help tome known to one and all as *ROCK! Magazine*. Then this female Torquemada was going to rip away at those nether regions without so much as a by-your-leave.

Youch!

No way, José!

Back to the list. The next entry after wax, was

4. Get a tan

Lucia remembered a columnist in *ROCK!* insisting that this must be subtle—a mere sun-kissed whisper that would fool any man into thinking it was natural.

5. Get a cool new wardrobe!

One that did not include a bobbly polyester uniform in a shade that might once have been white, presumably.

6. Get a hairdo

This prompted another visit to the mirror, where she lifted up her haystack hair. Most people complained that their hair was too thin or too straight. She was currently experiencing the opposite problem, known as The Inexplicable Explosion of Frizz. Without her styling products and gadgets, and without money to get it done in a salon, she was on her own.

7. Get a gym membership

First off, gym memberships cost money. And there was a more important consideration: without the hairdo, the tan, the wax and the cool new wardrobe, she was never going to make it through the door of a decent gym.

8. Get a good dance teacher—for the Samba, preferably. Someone like the old gaucho Ignacio, on Nero Caracas's ranch. Judging by the way Ignacio vaulted the fence when I decided to ride Nero's fire-breathing monster stallion bareback, Ignacio has still got some moves in him!
9. Get a gag for her polo-playing brothers—so they can't share any embarrassing secrets with any men I might attract once I've completed all of the above.
10. Get a (non-polo-playing) man

And there the list ended. Lucia smiled as she remembered Ignacio teaching her to dance the Samba, and quite a few other dances as well, bringing his ancient ghetto blaster, as Ignacio had called his battered radio, to the hay barn, where she'd been able to blunder about undisturbed. Okay. Looking on the bright side. She was still podgy and in need of a sun-tan with a frizz ball on her head, but this babe could dance.

'Cheers, Margaret,' Lucia murmured, wrapping her frozen hands around the warm flask of chocolate. This small, kind act of someone who had so little made Lucia more determined than ever to help her elderly friend.

'And hello, Luke,' she added, addressing Luke's smouldering poster just inches from her bed.

Hopping out again, she took a closer look. *Wow* hardly covered it. Lucia's brothers frequently featured on billboards, but always in full polo rig and usually mounted on a horse. They were certainly never caught half-naked, sluicing themselves down, in a shot Lucia couldn't imagine strait-laced Luke agreeing to in a million years.

'You're full of surprises, aren't you?' she murmured, taking full inventory of Luke's previously hidden assets.

And then there was the pose. Brandishing a whip as he glared into the camera, Luke was naked to his washboard waist, his hard tanned torso accessorised by nothing more than sharp black stubble and a steel watch that could probably tell his position in relation to the moon. A pair of obscenely revealing riding breeches and knee-high leather boots completed an image guaranteed to make any girl's day.

Posters were a safe way to appreciate the finer points of one of the world's fittest men. She liked that. As she jumped about and blew on her hands to keep warm before hypothermia set in, Lucia guessed the only way Luke would have been caught out in a shot like that was through the involvement of her school friend and ruthless sister-in-law Holly. Holly was a journalist at *ROCK!* magazine, and had tamed—sorry—was *married* to Lucia's brother Ruiz. Capturing Luke in such a provocative pose would have been an incredible scoop for her.

Three cheers for Holly the reporter! Lucia concluded, chalking one up for the girls. She took another look at Luke's centrefold.

Goodness, Luke was big...

No wonder she was having erotic dreams. Trying hard not to fixate on Luke's clinging breeches and the improbable-sized bulge within, Lucia shook her head. She could admire all she liked, but it certainly would never happen now. It couldn't. *She* couldn't. One thing was sure: after this unveiling he could stick his disapproval the next time they met.

The next time they met?

There was nothing on her to-do list that ruled against meetings with an approved family friend, she reasoned, climbing into bed.

CHAPTER FOUR

I wandered lonely as a cloud that floats o'er vales and hill...

I'm the only twenty-four-year-old I know who doesn't need to take her pill.

Anon.

~~Are all poets destined to end up on the (remainder) shelf?~~

Pull yourself together, Lucia!

RESTING her cheek against the cold wet glass the next morning, Lucia stopped scribbling in her journal and stared out of the caravan window at the windswept shore. If she had wanted distance from her brothers she had certainly got it here. She missed them, but no way was she going to ask them for the money to help Margaret. If she did she'd be right back to square one. Yes, she loved her brothers, but Nacho especially made no distinction between caring and smothering, which had left her gasping for freedom in the shadow of four powerful men and their saintly friend Luke.

Luke...

Did her body *have* to respond with such unbridled delight to the idea of so much stern, glowering disapproval locked inside one hot man?

Maybe she liked Luke's steely self-control too much, Lucia

reflected, glancing at his poster image. It was certainly enough to overrule her fear of men.

Most men. Picking up her bag, she made a mental note to get the strap repaired. It had suffered a few injuries when she had used it to beat off the concierge. Teeth, nails, handbag, heel of her shoe… A frantic struggle which seemed so feeble now she looked back. But at least she had got away. Eventually.

The concierge had made her feel dirty, calling her names as she ran from the room, clutching her ripped shirt together. He'd said she was asking for it, when nothing could be further from the truth. She did like parties, and she liked flirting with hot guys, but now she could see that her fun-filled reputation had done her no favours. She could just imagine Luke's scorn if he ever found out what had happened. Getting changed in the staffroom without remembering to put the lock on the door? It was such a stupid thing to do. But she had to try to put it behind her or she would never get on with her life.

Tilting her chin, Lucia gave Luke's image one last confident stare, but the ache still remained. Where was he now? *With the blonde?* Perhaps Luke had sensed she was tainted— that the concierge had had his hands all over her. *Everywhere.* It made her stomach heave just thinking about it. She could still remember his fingers intimately feeling…squeezing… probing, and his sour breath choking her as she struggled to escape. If Luke knew that he would just think, *Party girl. What do you expect?*

She jumped as her phone rang, and then frowned as she checked the number. She had to take a moment before she could answer. Talk of the devil—though Luke would have no truck with hell. *What? No air-con?* Luke would be more likely to hold a season ticket to cloud extreme, where he could strum his whip beneath the glow of an oat-fed halo. No way would he waste his time on an aerodynamically inefficient tail and a totally useless pitchfork unless he could use it to strike a polo ball.

'Luke,' she said finally, when she had calmed down a little. 'What a nice surprise. Did you leave something at the club?'

'In the unlikely event I *had* left something at the club I would go back to pick it up. I wouldn't call you.'

Well. That told her. Luke couldn't have sounded less enthusiastic had he tried. Crouched on the bench seat, with her legs drawn up, she hugged the phone. 'Of course not,' she said, injecting energy into her voice. 'So, what can I do for you?'

'I didn't see you when I left the club. You were working, I expect.'

'I'm sorry. I—'

'Strange,' he rapped over her. 'The first time I saw you at the club you assured me you weren't working there often. But the manager says you are. And he knows you as Anita. What's going on, Lucia? Why are you lying to me?'

'What I do or don't do is none of your business, Luke.'

'Nacho made it my business.'

'So you're my brother's deputy now?'

'I'm your brother's friend,' Luke argued quietly.

Luke couldn't have disarmed her faster. There was no point starting a feud with someone Nacho loved when the very last thing she wanted was a total break with her family. 'So why are you calling me?'

'I'm concerned about you, Lucia.'

'Well, don't be. And if my brothers are so worried, why don't they call? Or are they too busy playing polo?'

'Why are you always so suspicious, Lucia?'

'Because you're all joined at the hip,' she flashed. 'And because my brothers never like me to have too long a leash. Isn't that right, Luke?'

There was silence at the other end of the line.

Damn him! Luke had made her feel homesick, reminding

her of all the warmth and support she received in Argentina. It made everything here seem bleaker—the wind rattling round the caravan, the freezing cold water, the hideous episode with the concierge which she was doing her best to block out, and then her subsequent high-speed drive through the night, reckless...

And her lousy job at the club.

A dead-end job to end all dead-end jobs.

Her heart sank like a stone. She couldn't bear for gorgeous, glorious, successful Luke to know her life was a complete and utter mess. And she certainly couldn't bear for him to share that little nugget of information with her brothers. If they knew what had happened... How they would blame her for her frivolous, careless party-girl lifestyle. She deserved this, didn't she?

Sucking in a deep, steadying breath, she said briskly, 'Is this a courtesy call, or does it have some purpose, Luke?' She needed him to get off the line fast, before her voice broke.

'I've never heard you in this mood before,' he said suspiciously.

'Independent, do you mean?' Her fingers had turned white on the phone. It was one thing acting tough, but when she really wanted to cling to Luke's disembodied presence like a brainless limpet until all the bad things went away it was far better to end the call as soon as she could.

'Are you still there, Lucia?'

'I'm here.'

Luke checking up on her was nothing new. She had been an object of amusement for Luke and her brothers for as long as Lucia could remember. They thought she was a fancy, frilly little joke—a novelty, a pet they would like to keep locked up in a box until they decided to bring her out and coo over her on those rare occasions when they weren't trying to murder each other on the polo field.

'Just tell my brothers everything's fine.'

'*Is* everything fine?' Luke repeated suspiciously. 'Maybe I should check that statement for myself.'

'If you've nothing better to do. You'll only make a wasted journey. I'm working all hours.'

'Is that so?' he said.

'I do take a break from partying sometimes.'

And now tears were backing up behind her eyes. She knew what Luke and her brothers thought of her. Flighty Lucia, they had used to call her, flapping their arms and laughing. What a joke that was. And of course little Lucia was always getting herself into trouble, always needing to be bailed out, they used to say, while one of them leaned his forearm on the top of her head. Well, not this time. She was none of those things now.

Steadying her voice, she said, 'You're actually quite lucky to catch me—'

'The club opens at eight in the morning?'

'Don't pretend you don't know about my second job. I saw you getting cosy with Van Rickter. I'm sure he told you everything you wanted to know.'

And what was Luke doing in Cornwall, having meetings with a man like Van Rickter? Lucia wondered. Was Luke going to buy the club? Her stomach sank. She knew nothing about Luke or his life, Lucia realised.

'Lucia?'

'I'm still here,' she confirmed.

She wished she could tell Luke about Margaret and how things were, talk things through with him. Luke had always had a clear head on his shoulders. But his tone was brisk and impersonal and didn't invite confidences.

'Where are you calling from?' Curling into a small defensive ball, she pictured him relaxing back somewhere warm and luxurious, with his feet up and a coffee to hand as he made this duty call.

'In transit. Why?'

'No reason.' She could hardly ask where he was in transit from or to without seeming unduly interested. 'You didn't tell me why you're in Cornwall…'

'Didn't I?'

'Do you have business with Van Rickter?' she pried. 'Are you calling me from the Grand?'

'So many questions, Lucia.' The first hint of amusement coloured Luke's voice. 'I'm not far away, as it happens.'

The blonde was probably having her nails done and Luke had nothing better to do than harass her, Lucia guessed, flashing a glare at his centrefold. If there was one thing guaranteed to switch her thoughts from her own screw-ups it was wondering how one of the sharpest men on the planet had been caught in such a picture *and* by a Technicolor blonde. She had never known Luke to let his guard down before.

'So, what do you do when you're not working, Lucia?' he said.

'Oh, you know…'

'That bad?'

'I'm usually so exhausted after work I just sleep.' True, unfortunately, but definitely the safest option.

'So you wouldn't want to come to supper with me tonight?'

'With you?' Luke couldn't have surprised her more. There were so many reasons why she wanted to go out with him, and so many reasons why she shouldn't.

'Why not?' he said, adding casually, 'It *is* your birthday, isn't it?'

Her brothers must have put him up to this, Lucia realised as her heart thundered a tattoo. 'Yes, it is,' she confirmed. Matching Luke for nonchalance, she added, 'Don't tell me you're asking me out on a date?'

'You wish,' he countered, with a flash of the camaraderie they had shared before hormones kicked in. 'Well?' he demanded in the same offhand tone. 'What's your answer?'

She had to release her stranglehold on the phone and shake her hand to get the blood flowing through her fingers again before she could think straight. If she accepted, and Luke started questioning her, how would she explain to him what one part freedom in Cornwall to nine parts humiliation in London felt like? How would he react when she told him that there wasn't a chance she was going to turn her back on her new life? How would she hide from Luke what had happened in London?

And what about the blonde?

No. She couldn't accept. If she went out with Luke it would be—

What? Surrender? Defeat? Weakness? *What?*

Wasn't she guilty of overreacting just a little bit?

While she was trying to decide Luke started talking 'horse'—a language spoken exclusively by Luke and her brothers. Dreams were almost always better than reality, Lucia reflected, gazing at Luke's centrefold, thinking maybe she owed it to the Sisterhood to warn the women of the world about him. Luke's poster image suggested an impossibly sexual animal with a body designed for sin, when she knew the only type of physical activity that really got Luke's juices flowing involved a bit, a bridle and a pair of really sharp spurs.

'Well, if everything's okay your end, Lucia?'

'What?' She realised he was about to sign off. 'Don't go yet—I mean… It's um…fun talking to a dinosaur.' She laughed, hoping Luke hadn't detected the flash of desperation in her voice. No one said she had to go cold turkey. A familiar voice was like tonic wine. You drank it down and then you felt better. Right?

'*Now* you want to talk?' he said dryly. 'How about you start with what really brought you back to Cornwall? And for goodness' sake call your brothers, will you?'

'I have.' *So many times*. But they were *always* playing polo. And as for Cornwall… 'I'm just taking a break in Cornwall.'

No way was she telling Luke the truth. It would be the easiest thing in the world to howl down the phone that things hadn't turned out the way she'd hoped they would, and could Luke please lend her the money to fly home? But if she did that this climb-back of hers would be over before it had started, and she would have proved everyone right about her. Deep inside she would hate herself. She would be a failure and everyone would know it.

'Well, I hope everything works out for you, Lucia—'

'Tonight,' she cut in with one final burst of desperate lonely energy. 'That supper you mentioned?'

When this was met by an ominous silence she realised Luke had probably had second thoughts. Maybe it was time to eat some humble pie.

'I think I could make it tonight.'

'So you have no plans?' he said flatly. And when she remained silent he added, 'I never thought I'd see the day when Lucia Acosta stayed home on her birthday… But if it's a matter of money and you'd rather go out with some friends—'

'Stop that, Luke!' Money was the way her brothers had always controlled her.

'Don't be so touchy,' he fired back.

'Then get it through your head that I don't need your money. I've got everything I need right here.'

She had birthday gifts from her friends, and a few clothes if she wanted a night out. Well, she had the sale rail spectacular she'd snatched from her room before bolting from the hotel in London, together with some shoes she'd had repaired. She hadn't stopped to pack a case. She couldn't have spent a second longer than she had to in the hotel while her body was crawling with invisible insects where the concierge's hands had touched her.

'It seems you've got everything covered,' Luke was saying, while she shrank like Alice to the size of a pea. 'I'll get off your case, Lucia. I was only trying to look out for you.'

She hugged herself tighter, waiting for the line to be cut, for the silence to grow and gather. But Luke didn't cut the line.

'Are you really spending your birthday on your own?' he drawled, in a mock-weary tone.

'For goodness' sake, stop going on about it,' she flashed. 'I don't need a cake and candles at my age. I'm a big girl now.'

'Good. Then you can have supper with me at the Grand. Eight o' clock sharp. And, Lucia?'

'Yes?'

'Don't be late.'

The *Grand*? She had been to the elegant hotel many times with her parents, and the entire family had always dressed up for the occasion. She had nothing remotely suitable for an evening at the Grand in her sparse arsenal of clothes.

So was she going to turn down Luke's invitation? A warm room, a decent meal, the company of an old friend...

Her stomach growled in anticipation of its first proper meal in a long time that didn't include scones, cream and jam, fries or hot chocolate. 'Don't worry, Luke. I won't be la—'

Luke had cut the line.

What on earth had she agreed to? The Grand was one of those seriously exclusive hotels that attracted seriously exclusive guests. And if she was going to brave it in her sale rail spectacular, did she *really* want to prove the fact that sun-starved olive skin looked no better than sun-starved pale white skin?

Lucia's gaze strayed to the well-past-its-sell-by-date bottle of fake tan on the shelf, which had been there when she'd moved in. She had to do something to make herself feel better. She couldn't possibly look any worse than she did now, she reasoned, reaching for it.

CHAPTER FIVE

Get a Tan

You will have noticed that The Tan was actually item number four on my to-do list, appearing after item number three: The Wax. I think you'll agree that's proof positive that the list was written by my fourteen-year-old-self long before the ramifications of turning fuzzy black leg hair a strange shade of green with the overuse of chemicals had actually occurred to me.

You will also know that a fake tan takes time to develop—something else I had yet to learn. With my olive skin I was naturally sun-kissed in Argentina, thanks to the lovely weather, and even when I was at school in England there were always half-term holidays and trips home, so I was a bit of a fake-tan virgin. When one application didn't seem to work I applied another... and another...figuring that since it was past its sell-by date maybe it wasn't as strong as normal.

I couldn't have been more wrong.

I decided to wear my sale rail spectacular for the birthday supper with Luke. It's a strappy dress in electric blue with a huge wilted rose dotted with shocking pink diamanté pinned at the front, which was probably the reason the dress hadn't sold. Removing the brooch made a whole world of difference.

What surprised me most of all was that after working such long hours, and skipping a few meals due to lack of time and money, I had lost a few of my comfort-food pounds. In fact the dress almost fitted me. But, as previously mentioned, those long hours spent indoors had done my olive skin no favours, so the success of the night hung on a bottle of Tanfastic Your World.

YES, he had spoken to Nacho. Inviting Lucia for supper was his good deed for the day—make that the year.

'Would you spoil Lucia a bit?' Nacho had asked him, no doubt overcome with relief that Luke had tracked down his missing sister.

'I'll buy her supper,' Luke had offered.

'And a card?' Nacho prompted.

He exhaled steadily before answering. 'I'll see what the hotel shop can offer.'

'Thanks, Luke.'

Nacho's gratitude made him feel guilty, and then he detected another question in Nacho's voice. 'You want me to try and buy her a little gift or something?' he said, anticipating Nacho's next request.

'Please,' Nacho said with relief. 'I'll wire you the money—'

'*Dios*, Nacho,' Luke exclaimed, slipping into the lingo they customarily used. 'It will all wash through—and I won't find much in a hotel shop.'

'Just do your best, Luke.'

He shrugged, reasoning he could throw money at it—though what a wild child with a penchant for scrubbing floors might want for her birthday escaped him.

Oh, this was nerve-racking. Her hand was actually shaking. She'd never used to be completely useless when it came to men. Quite the opposite, in fact. It had used to come naturally

to her—she'd never had to think about it before. Flirting with
hot guys, knowing they wanted her, and always, always being
in control. But now it was different. She had had a king-sized
setback that had spiralled completely out of control, but she
was determined not to let it colour her whole life. It was just
that going out for supper with a guy she'd had a crush on for
what seemed for ever, who looked like a sex god and who
probably looked on her as a nuisance at best—well, that took
a lot of preparation.

The dress wasn't bad on reflection. It was certainly colourful. *Retro*, she corrected herself, trying to imagine how her
former self would have pulled it off. Surely it was just about
confidence? If she felt confident she could make it work. *If*
she felt confident…

Who was she kidding? Lucia thought, blinking back tears
as she tried to put her lenses in. Oh, bother them—she'd just
have to wear glasses.

She parked around the back at the Grand, easing her ancient
car into a gap between a sleek black limousine and a gleaming off-roader she doubted had ever seen a field. Well—deep
breath—this was it.

She marched along the gravel path, dipping once to adjust
the heel strap on her stratospheric sandals. That brief swoop
was enough to shoot rain from her collar down the Grand
Canyon between her breasts. She didn't have a raincoat smart
enough to wear to the Grand to protect her from the elements,
so she was wearing the luminous yellow sou'wester Margaret
had loaned her for heavy work outside. With nothing to cover
her head apart from a handbag, it was probably safe to say her
make-up had washed off and her hair was a mat of black frizz.

The doorman ignored her. How could he not see the plump
girl in luminous yellow oilcloth with a handbag balanced on
her head?

Oh, well.

'Lucia.'

'Luke…' She gazed at the vision in designer jeans, a crisp white shirt and tailored jacket, standing at the open door. 'Amazing,' she breathed, squinting at him through her rain-speckled glasses.

'Are you coming in?' Luke said briskly. 'Or am I supposed to stand here all night?'

The uniformed doorman took the hint and hurried out of his regular position to take control of the door. 'My apologies, sir,' he said effusively, while Lucia blinked owlishly at the two men.

Luke linked her arm through his as if he had been waiting for this moment all his life. 'How good to see you,' he added warmly.

As Luke led her away she glanced behind her and had the satisfaction of seeing astonishment colour the doorman's face. She thought about sticking her tongue out, and then thought better of it when Luke cautioned her, 'No!' reading her with his usual ease.

Luke escorted her to the cloakroom, where he helped her with the sou'wester. 'At least you're dry underneath,' he said, ignoring the surprised look of the pretty girl behind the desk, who couldn't seem to take her eyes off Lucia as Luke handed her oilskin cover. 'Your ticket,' he said. 'Put it in your bag before you lose it,' he prompted.

Lucia was incapable of speech. She had just caught sight of herself in the ornate gilt mirror. Now she knew why the girl was staring. Her make-up was smudged, which was only to be expected after braving a rainstorm, and her hair could not have been bushier—but what she couldn't have anticipated were the tiger stripes of orange and olive where the fake tan had washed off. It was not a good look.

'Would you like to go and freshen up before we go in to

supper?' Luke suggested. Reaching into his pocket, he pulled out a clean white handkerchief and handed it to her discreetly.

Nothing would help. Her evening was ruined. Her hair was having an electrical storm and her skin-tight dress was totally unsuitable for a cold night in a posh hotel. Nothing had changed at the Grand, and as Lucia had expected every other woman there had chosen to wear outfits best described as classic and timeless. Certainly they were discreet. No one was wearing anything to compete with Lucia's electric blue Lycra number and the fake tan dripping down her arms. 'I'm so sorry, Luke.'

'What are you sorry about?' he said. Linking her arm through his again, he steered her across the lobby in the direction of the ladies' restroom. 'Go wash up. You'll be fine.'

'I'm so embarrassed...'

'Lucia,' he said firmly, 'you're not going to let a little bit of slapdash painting spoil your birthday, are you?'

A smile was hovering around Luke's sexy lips—that sexy mouth was something she must put out of her mind immediately. She had enough on her hands, concentrating on disaster management.

The disaster was too extreme, Lucia concluded. Fear of men, fear of Luke finding out what had happened in London, and now this. 'Seriously, Luke—I'd rather go home. Even if the fake tan does wash off, I'm not dressed for this.'

'It's your birthday,' he said, as if that made any fashion *faux pas* acceptable. 'I'll wait out here. Take your time, but make a thorough job of it,' he added with a crooked grin.

She could just imagine Luke's report to her brothers—*Lucia was fine the last time I saw her, if a bit liverish.*

Going into the restroom, she planted her fists on the side of the basin. She couldn't even bear to look at herself in the mirror she was such a mess. Finally, pulling herself together, she ran the taps. She was going to scrub and scrub until her skin was clean again—until she really felt clean again. And then she was going to man up and join Luke for supper as if what had happened was a regular part of any date.

'I'm sorry,' she said wryly as she exited the restroom. 'I couldn't save your hanky.'

Luke's lips curved in the same attractive grin. 'I've got plenty more.'

She gasped as he leaned forward. 'Oh,' she murmured as he removed her glasses and stood back to take a really good look at her.

'Wow…'

'Wow, good? Or wow, bad?' she said tensely.

'Wow, pretty damn fantastic,' Luke murmured.

Nodding to the *maître d'*, Luke linked her arm through his and led her into the glittering crystal and gilt dining room, where it soon became obvious that no one gave a damn what she looked like because everyone was staring at Luke. Waving the waiter away, he insisted on pulling out her chair.

'What's this?' she asked, staring at the envelope on her plate.

'Damn, that looks like an envelope to me.' Reaching across the table, Luke put his big paw over hers. 'Before you open it, can I just say you look amazing tonight, Lucia?'

'And you couldn't have been more surprised?' she supplied in a comic voice.

Luke shook his head as if he gave up. As he called the wine waiter over Lucia wondered if she had freed him from the obligation to work his way through the list of appropriate compliments her brothers must have foisted on him.

'Your best champagne, please,' Luke requested as the waiter hovered. 'Well?' he prompted, turning back to her. 'Aren't you going to open the card?'

'Of course.' She stopped as Luke reached beneath his

chair and produced a gift-wrapped present. 'You really didn't need to.'

'Just open it,' he said.

He felt guilty as Lucia's eyes lit with surprise and pleasure. He'd spent so much time teasing her over the years he had never really thought about Lucia's feelings. *He* didn't have any—why should she? But Lucia had enough feelings for both of them, he realised as she stared down at the gift. Her surprised expression touched him somewhere deep.

'Don't get too excited,' he warned. 'It's just something I picked up at the hotel shop.' *On the instigation of your brother*, he silently added. But this was the first time he'd bought Lucia anything. If he had even looked at her the wrong way when they were younger Lucia's brothers would have ripped his head off.

She opened the card first. He was sorry he hadn't been able to go somewhere with a wider selection—get something with a funny message on the front, something more appropriate for Lucia. The card was nice enough, but it was one of those 'suits every occasion' blank cards that hotels stocked. There were a bunch of flowers on the front in no-nonsense bright colours.

'Lovely,' she said, reading what he'd written inside: *To my old sparring partner—Happy Birthday, Luke.* 'No one could accuse you of forgetting the old days.' She smiled, as if that pleased her, and then turned the card over to read the script on the back. 'Anemones are for unfading love, hmm?' Her eyes were sparkling with humour as they searched his. 'I'm betting you didn't think to read the back?'

'You'd be right,' he admitted gruffly, caught out red-handed.

'Anyway, it's very nice of you to buy me a card at all, so thank you.'

'Aren't you going to open your present?' She was still touching the card with her fingertip, as if there was something meaningful to be gleaned from his bold black writing. 'Go on—open it,' he pressed. Was he getting into this?

'Luke, you shouldn't have.'

'And risk you having a strop because I hadn't got you anything?'

'I'm not fourteen any more, Luke.'

He'd reminded her of her fourteenth birthday party, which Nacho had arranged. It had been heavily policed by her brothers, who had checked up on Lucia and her friends every five minutes. Predictably, the girls had swooned when the boys had walked in, while Lucia had only craved a single glance from Luke. But the older they'd got, the more Luke had pushed her away. She had bumped into him the next day in the hay barn and screamed at him that he hadn't even wished her a happy birthday, let alone bought her a present.

'I've never made your life easy, have I, Luke?'

'At least we're on the same page where that's concerned,' he agreed.

He had bought a shawl—soft and feminine in moss-green cashmere. He'd thought it would look great against Lucia's hair and eyes—though, admittedly, it wouldn't look quite so great with a bright blue dress. 'If you'd rather change it for another colour...'

'I wouldn't dream of it,' she said, holding it to her face. 'My brothers generally buy me pieces of tack for my pony.'

When all the teenage Lucia had craved was the latest colour lipstick, or music by whatever group was in vogue, he guessed.

'I loved it that they remembered my birthday,' she went on, 'but sometimes...'

Sometimes she'd missed her mother, he silently supplied.

Closing her eyes, Lucia rested her cheek against the shawl.

'Good,' he said briskly, jerking them both out of the spell she had woven. 'Job done. Shall we order? Are you hungry?'

'Starving,' she admitted. Her cheeks fired red. 'I mean—'

'We're here to eat, Lucia,' he pointed out.

Calling the waiter over, he ordered plenty, in case Lucia didn't order enough, and when the food arrived she ate with such relish it was hard to keep up. Lucia wasn't just hungry, she was ravenous.

He tried not to dwell on this, but as she scraped up the last of the Crème Anglaise from her plate and sighed with pleasure he couldn't hold back any longer. 'When did you last eat?'

'It's been a long time since I've eaten anything this good,' she admitted, laying down her spoon.

'Is that it?' he pressed.

'Lunchtime,' she said defensively, sitting up straight. 'One of Margaret's delicious cream teas.'

He made no comment. 'Okay, so now you're fed and watered, how about coming clean about why you're working at the club?'

'It's a job, Luke.'

'Has Van Rickter been bullying you?'

'What is this? The Spanish Inquisition?'

'*Has* Van Rickter been bullying you?' he repeated, holding her flickering gaze.

'Of course he hasn't. I feel sorry for him, really. He's such a frustrated individual—not *that* way,' she said quickly, her cheeks colouring. 'Are we going to have coffee now?'

He recognised the diversionary tactic, but was more determined than ever to get to the bottom of whatever Lucia was holding back. He was close to certain that there was a man involved. He dangled some bait. 'Nacho was telling me about the hotel management job you had in London.'

'I'm taking a sabbatical,' she said quickly.

Which made no sense to him.

A fork hit the floor. It wasn't one of Lucia's better ruses. As she bent to retrieve it he waved the waiter away.

With her face hidden by the linen folds of the tablecloth,

she was trying to buy time in the hope that thoughts of what had happened in London might fade.

'Lucia?'

She exhaled with frustration, seeing that Luke had joined her under the table, his face level with hers. 'What are you doing?' she asked impatiently.

'I might ask you the same question. And we can't stay down here for ever—people will talk.'

As if Luke would care. Straightening up, she handed the fork to the waiter with an apology.

Luke remained silent until the man had gone, and then asked, 'Are you okay, Lucia?'

'I dropped a fork, Luke.'

'So you didn't have to answer any more questions about London, I presume?'

Luke's expression was one she recognised: unwavering and disbelieving. Which said he was prepared to hang in for however long it took to get at the truth. He proved this theory with his next question. 'So, what did you learn in London?'

'Plenty.'

'Such as?' he probed.

That the world without family was a hostile, angry place, and that all men didn't behave with the same chivalry towards women as Luke and her brothers. She might resent their interference in her life, but she had never realised that honour was in such short supply before.

She almost choked on her relief as their coffee arrived and there was the usual interruption as the waiters set everything out in front of them. Luke pushed a dish of chocolates over to her side of the table without another word.

Lucia devoured the chocolates as she had devoured everything else within reach, with a freakish type of nervous energy—as if she were a squirrel storing up for winter. Whatever she was hiding from him it was big. The impulse to transfer money into her account ASAP so she could buy some proper food was banging in his head, but he could just imagine Lucia's reaction if he tried. And something told him that a balanced diet was the least of her problems. But he could hope.

'Are you eating properly?'

'I eat too much.' She grimaced.

A diet of cream teas and chocolate, if he remembered Margaret's specialities correctly. And he wouldn't be surprised if any money Lucia saved from her earnings went to help Margaret out rather than any payment flowing the other way. Lucia had always had a generous heart. Too generous sometimes.

'Great music,' she said, drawing his attention to the Salsa band.

'They must have known you were coming,' he said, remembering Lucia on the dance floor at her brother's wedding. Recollections of that evening curled heat around him. 'Would you like to dance?'

'Oh, no, that's okay,' she said, pulling back in her chair.

'I wouldn't want to embarrass you with my skill,' he agreed.

She relaxed. 'Your *skill*?' One brow rose. 'Since when have polo players had any skill to speak of—unless they are mounted on a really great horse?'

'Ouch.'

'I've had the chance to practise that one,' she admitted, with a wry spark from the old days in her look.

'A few times, I imagine,' he agreed. 'Shall we?' he said, standing up.

Her lips pressed down as she stared at his outstretched hand. 'I suppose one dance won't kill me.'

As he held her chair he felt a surge of anticipation at the thought of holding Lucia in his arms that had absolutely no connection with doing a favour for her brother.

CHAPTER SIX

The first step is the hardest. And after that it's all down-hill, right?

Not this time, because tonight when Luke took my hand and led me onto the dance floor the bad thoughts took flight and all I could see in my mind's eye was Luke riding flat out across the sand. Riding bareback, bare-chested, wearing the designer jeans his mother always insisted her staff must put a crease down the front of. Luke wore them cut off and frayed, covered in hoof oil and wet with sea spray, so that they clung to his hard-muscled thighs.

He'd whoop as he overtook the last of my brothers, leaving them roaring with frustration in his wake, lying flat on his horse's neck, encouraging it to go even faster. Wings of diamond-studded mist would spread out be-hind him as if he were riding Pegasus and they might take to the sky at any moment.

At least that was what I always imagined when I was fourteen, as I sat watching him from the shadows by the rock pool.

As THEY threaded their way through the tables Luke's warm palm in the hollow of her back was a badly needed wake-up call. Luke could read her like a book, so she had to cage all her wild, unfounded, fearful thoughts and place all imaginings about a romance with Luke in the never-going-to-happen box.

'Are you cold?' he asked with concern as she shivered with a whole mix of emotions when he gathered her in.

'Just frightened for my feet,' she managed dryly.

'Don't be,' Luke murmured.

She needn't have worried. Once they reached the dance floor Luke's touch was light and impersonal, and he was careful to keep a space between them that would have made a maiden aunt feel safe.

He loved Salsa dancing. He loved the rhythm and the music and the contact—especially tonight, with Lucia moving so easily in his arms. Dance was liberating, and a great prelude to sex. Though not with Lucia, of course. He held her well away from him. But she moved so easily it wasn't long before his mind strayed onto the dark side. Dance was like sex. Trust had to be established and then limits set. Timing was all-important too.

His appetite sharpened when Lucia, having grown so much in confidence during the dance that she was almost back to the girl he knew, escaped him to execute a few hot Salsa moves of her own. Other men were watching her, and he found he didn't like that. And when she yipped, *'Ay, caramba,'* laughing as she threw her head back so her luscious hair swept the full curve of her buttocks, he knew he was in for trouble. He could have watched her all night. Private viewing would be his preference…

Most men looked awkward on the dance floor, but Luke was so well coordinated he looked hot, and they moved well together.

'You're a great dancer, Lucia.'

'For such a great hulking oaf, you're not so bad yourself.' And if she couldn't take the heat on the dance floor there were plenty of women watching Luke who could, Lucia concluded.

'We fit so well together,' he said, drawing her close.

So much of her was glued to Luke it was hard to disagree, but telling herself that Luke would never hurt her, or take advantage of her, didn't help her heart to slow down. Again, she was worrying unnecessarily, for when the music stopped Luke escorted her back to the table.

'That was so good!' she exclaimed as he pulled her chair out, feeling as if everything bad that had happened in London must have floated away.

'Will you excuse me, please, Lucia?' Luke asked once she was seated.

'Had enough of me?' she teased, angling her chin in enquiry.

Dipping his head, he murmured in her ear, 'There's something I must do. I'll be back in a couple of minutes.'

She glanced around as Luke left the restaurant, and noticed that every other woman was doing the same thing. Picking up her champagne glass, she gave a wry smile to think of so much man going to waste on her. She was about to take a sip of the sparkling wine when a man lost his balance and lurched into her table.

'I'm afraid that seat's taken,' she explained politely.

Her stomach clenched with alarm when the man ignored her and insisted on trying to sit down. He was so drunk he could barely stand, she realised. She glanced around, looking for help, but all the other diners were eating or chatting, and the waiters were busy.

It occurred to her then that before her experience with the concierge she could have handled something like this without missing a beat, but her brain seemed to have been rewired along with her confidence levels, and all she could force out of her mouth was a weak 'Please don't do that.'

The drunk ignored her.

It all seemed to be spinning out of control, just like the

day in London when the concierge had locked them both in the staffroom. Her chest felt tight. She couldn't breathe. And though a part of her brain said all this situation required was some firm action on her part she remained in a bubble of apprehension, waiting for the inevitable touch, the pinch, the grope.

Lurching forward, the drunk made a hideous munching sound as he reached for her breasts. In terror, she jerked back, and her drink flew everywhere as she rocked sideways off her chair.

Strong hands caught hold of her before she could fall to the floor. 'Are you okay?' Luke demanded in a shocked tone.

For a moment she could only stare at him in blank surprise, but then she slowly became aware that other people had gathered round and were staring at her with concern.

'Did he hurt you, Lucia?' Luke asked in a low, fierce voice.

'No… No, I don't think so.' Luke was holding her hands so tightly they'd turned white. She realised she was gasping for breath like a landed fish. 'I feel such a fool.'

'Don't.' Shielding her from the onlookers with the bulk of his body, Luke lifted her out of the chair.

'Where are you taking me?'

'Questions later,' he insisted, leading her out of the restaurant with one strong arm locked around her shoulders as he drew her into his body to keep her safe.

She glanced behind them. 'My shawl!'

The *maitre d'* handed it to Luke. Having thanked him, Luke asked for a bottle of good cognac to be sent up to his suite.

'Right away, sir. We're very sorry, sir. We'll take care of it right away.' The *maitre d'* hurried away.

'I can't believe I only left you for a couple of minutes and someone tried to spoil your birthday,' Luke grated out as he stabbed the elevator button.

Luke's eyes were full of concern when he turned to search

her face. She had really blown it now. 'Nothing could spoil my birthday.' Nothing except her weak, pathetic, shaking voice—which was more proof, should he need it, that something dreadful must have happened to turn the sexy, confident, party-girl Luke had used to know into the woman he held in his arms right now.

Needless to say, he picked up on it right away.

'Is this the girl who could stand up to four fierce brothers?' he demanded tensely. 'What has happened to you, Lucia? What happened in London?'

'Nothing,' she insisted, shivering as the elevator doors slid closed, enclosing them in the small cabin. Surely it couldn't contain so much emotion?

'Nothing?' Luke murmured, his gaze sharpening on her face. 'Why can't you trust me with the truth, Lucia? Haven't we known each other long enough?'

The tension between them increased as the lift soared up to the penthouse floor, where she stepped out with relief into a beautifully decorated hallway. A lovely fresh smell hit her immediately, and though she was still reeling from her experience in the dining room she could appreciate the muted décor. Ivory walls and a thick crimson carpet beneath her feet to muffle sound, gilt mirrors glittering beneath concealed lighting. There were prints on the wall, and decorative touches of ruby and gold on lampshades and drapes.

Warm colours to make the guests feel cosy, she supposed as Luke opened the door leading into his suite. But she was still shivering.

Luke had barely closed the door when there was a discreet tap on it. It was two waiters arriving with coffee and brandy, and there was a birthday cake on a tray.

'So that's what you were arranging for me,' she said, touched by the gesture.

Luke tipped the waiters and hustled them out.

'You're spoiling me,' she said as he poured her a brandy and insisted she take a sip.

'I refuse to be distracted, Lucia,' Luke assured her. 'Ever since I saw you at the club I've known something was wrong. And now tonight—'

'There's nothing wrong,' she interrupted. 'It's just that you've never seen me striking out on my own before. It's been a lovely evening. Can't we leave it at that?'

'A *lovely* evening?' Luke queried with a penetrating glance.

'So a drunk spoiled it briefly?' She shrugged, brushing it off. 'I can't explain why I overreacted. I'm tired. It must be because I'm tired. It's not as if I haven't seen a drunk before.' She laughed, but Luke's face remained watchful and unsmiling. 'Thank you for the shawl,' she added, stroking it as the tension between them mounted. 'I don't know when I've enjoyed a birthday more.'

'Possibly the day you celebrated by putting burrs under my saddle?' Luke suggested, but there was little humour in his voice, and his stare plumbed deep as he searched for the truth she refused to share with him.

'That was a contender,' she agreed, forcing out another laugh.

They drank their coffee in tense silence, leaving the cake untouched, and finally Luke stood up. 'I'll take you home,' he said.

And let him see where she was living? Wouldn't that be the perfect end to the perfect day?

'You don't need to. My car's parked right outside.'

'You've had a shock, and I won't let you go home alone,' Luke said flatly.

'Luke, I don't need a babysitter.'

'You've had a drink. I haven't,' he said, glancing at her empty brandy glass.

'Then I'll ask them to call a cab. Look, I don't want us to part like this.'

'Like what? You're the one holding back, Lucia.'

'Why are you so suspicious? You and my brothers are all the same.' Composing herself, she stood to face him. 'Thank you for a wonderful evening, Luke—for the meal, the gift, the card, the cake. You're very kind—'

'I *am* very kind.'

She longed to cling to that grain of humour, so she could remember how it used to be between them before she felt grubby and Luke became so far removed. She was almost at the door when she stopped and impulsively, almost as if she had to prove something to herself, stood on tiptoe to plant a kiss on Luke's stubble-blackened jaw. 'Thank you for everything, Luke.'

Luke turned to look at her at just the wrong moment—or maybe it was the right moment. Whatever happened, their lips touched briefly.

He might as well have plugged her in to the socket in the wall. She drew a shocked breath as the charge flashed through her. And, most confusing of all, it wasn't fear that held her motionless in front of him but some shadow of the girl she'd used to be. It was enough.

Instead of moving away, Luke laced his fingers through her hair and drew her closer still. 'Happy birthday, Lucia,' he murmured, repeating the shock treatment in a more leisurely fashion.

She had to tell herself that Luke was just being kind—that this was a reaction to what had happened to her with the drunk, and not some declaration of intent on his part to take things further. But it was like a dream. Only better than any dream she'd ever had.

'There's something you need to know, Lucia,' Luke said rather formally, pulling back. 'We're not kids any more and I don't think of myself as your babysitter. One more thing,' he added, catching hold of her arm when, thoroughly confused by now, she went to move away. 'If you play with fire you *will* get burned.'

With her nerves stretched as taut as a bow string, she almost laughed. Luke had no idea how true that was.

He saw something in her face that made him drag her back. And there was no mistake this time. This kiss was no accident. Luke's lips were firm and persuasively mobile, and when he held her it was with both hands resting lightly either side of her ribcage, so that his thumbs could tease the full swell of her breasts.

But as the warm wave of pleasure swept over her, driving everything bad away, he let her go. 'I'm taking you home,' he said abruptly, turning for the door.

Even after all this time she received the message loud and clear. Luke was a warrior, with a warrior's appetite, and no one should mess with that. And as a friend he was hurt that she couldn't bring herself to confide in him. It was a dangerous combination.

This time she didn't stop to argue, she just grabbed her coat.

The tension between them remained high as they drove back to the caravan park, where it developed into a full-scale snarling match about where Luke should drop her off.

'Do you seriously think I'm going to let you walk through the dark on your own?' he roared, slamming on the brakes.

'Don't you get it? I'm on my own now, and I'm fine,' she whipped back as Luke swung round to glare at her.

'I'm fine,' he mocked, in a whiney approximation of a girly voice, which made her want to launch herself at him and punch him like the old days.

But Luke was right about one thing. Those days were long gone.

'How do you think I've managed without you all this time?'

she demanded, when Luke remained tensely silent, with the steering wheel clenched in his big hands as if he'd like to rip it out of its fixings. 'Anyway, I'm getting out.'

There was still no response from Luke. And now there seemed to be a problem with the door, which rather spoiled her grand flounce off. 'Child lock, Luke?'

'If the shoe fits, Lucia.' His eyes had darkened to jet.

'Let me out right now,' she warned as he sat back, clearly not prepared to let her go. 'You can watch me as I walk to the caravan.'

'Oh, that's so kind of you,' Luke remarked sharply, reaching forward to release the locks.

The air was charged with tension, and Luke had made no mention of seeing her again. She sure as hell wasn't going to ask him. But there was a little pocket of guilt inside her that said, *Don't let the evening end like this. You'll never forgive yourself.*

She turned before stepping down. 'Thank you again for—'

'It was nothing,' he interrupted coldly.

'Well, thank you anyway.'

Luke sat immobile with his eyes narrowed on some distant horizon where she couldn't reach him. She felt wretched leaving like this. Her birthday night had been crammed with emotion and drama, which Luke had cruised through. He'd bought her a lovely gift and a card—even if at the instigation of her brother. And he had kissed her. *Luke had kissed her.* Her lips were still swollen.

Darting forward impulsively, she pressed a kiss on his stubble-roughened cheek. 'Thank you.'

'For goodness' sake, go,' he snapped, staring fixedly ahead.

He watched Lucia totter across the rutted field in her totally unsuitable shoes and her flapping yellow rubberised coat. How anyone could look quite so desirable in that get-up beat him.

But when he'd danced with her, when he'd held her, when he'd felt how warm and young and supple she was…how vulnerable… *When those full breasts had rubbed insistently against his chest*. How he hadn't dragged her to him and kissed the breath out of her lungs, he had no idea.

Raking his hair with frustration, he switched on the engine. Bang went the 'like a sister' theory. The urge to bury his face in Lucia's chest and hear her whimper with pleasure while he made love to her had almost overtaken him. It had even crossed his mind to have her in the car. With her feet up on the dash and endless adjustments available to the seats anything was possible.

Except that. Throwing the off-roader into reverse, he knew he would never throw away years of caring about Lucia for a mindless screw in a field. However much she tried his patience he would always be there for her. He had tried to blank her from his mind—goodness knows how hard he'd tried—but she never left his thoughts. She had her own little space in there.

Not so little, Luke accepted as he swung the wheel and turned the car onto the road. Kissing Lucia had been a revelation and had left him wanting more. Much more. What he needed now was distance from Lucia and a chance to put his thoughts in order so he could work out what had really happened tonight.

He made it half a mile down the road before standing on the brake. He could solve most problems with money, but not Lucia. And he couldn't trust anyone else to sort things out for her. No wonder she hadn't wanted him to see the state of the caravan she was living in. Maybe she did have something to prove—but not at the expense of her safety. Throwing the gear into reverse, he headed back.

This had nothing to do with her breasts, he told himself firmly as a mental image of his big callused hands encompassing Lucia's lush breasts almost caused him to steer into a ditch. *Concentrate,* he told himself firmly as he tickled the brake pedal at the approach to the Sundowner Guest House and Holiday Park.

St Oswalds had suffered in the recession. This was something he knew a lot about, having rescued his family's business in a recession before going on to build his own company. Fortunately he had both the means and the practical capability to revive the village he believed in. Those childhood summer holidays were as clear in his mind now as they had ever been. So, however small a project the Sundowner might seem to anyone else, it was worth a king's ransom to him for the memories alone.

He could see a dim light shining in Lucia's decrepit van. Cursing softly as an image of a naked Lucia, wet and beneath a shower, flashed into his mind, he turned off the road and drove through rotting gates hanging off their hinges. This was worse than he had imagined. Everything was overgrown and desolate. Lucia's was the only van on what had once been a well-ordered pitch full of caravans. How could she continue to live here?

With his incredulity stretched to the limit for a moment, he could only think of barging in and dragging her out—but then reason kicked in. Lucia wanted responsibility, something he'd been loaded with at an early age. It hadn't done him any harm. Perhaps he should keep a watching brief and leave her to it.

He could do something here, Luke realised as his mind turned to practical matters. Energy flashed through him as ideas crowded his brain. He was eager to begin restoring the guest house to its former glory, but first he had to make sure Lucia was safe.

Switching off the lights, he freewheeled down the track. Halting behind some trees, he climbed out. Closing the door with barely a click, he walked up to Lucia's caravan and walked round it, examining it with the light from his mobile phone. There wasn't a lot he could do in the dark without tools, but he could improvise. He found rocks to place behind the wheels to act as chocks and, knocking the dirt off his hands, decided that, whether Lucia thanked him for his interference or not, he would definitely be back in the daylight to check everything out properly.

So this has nothing to do with sexual hunger and a desire to see Lucia again?

Not much, he mused wryly.

Staring round, he let his restless gaze linger on the moon-lit beach and dramatic cliff line. Everything he could see increased his determination to do something to help the village that had once meant so much to him. It would take money and time, but…

Money he had in plenty. But time?

Maybe he could spare a few more days if Margaret agreed to his plan. He had a team of men who could turn around a place like this in no time flat. And when he went back he could steer the project from a distance, no problem, which would give him some much needed space from Lucia.

Lucia…

His concerns for her were back with a vengeance. Lucia lived in great comfort with her brothers in Argentina, so there had to be a very good reason for what she was doing here. Breaking free of four brothers he could understand, but hiding away in a tumbledown caravan out of season when there was no proper work to be had…

Her reaction to the drunk tonight had made it seem that Lucia was frightened of men, but Lucia, of all the women he knew, could handle men with both hands tied behind her back. There weren't many men as fierce as her brothers. Something didn't fit. He was going to hold that next call to Nacho until he'd made his own enquiries.

* * *

She woke the next morning, feeling something wasn't quite right. Then her brain kicked into gear and she buried her hot face in the pillow as the whole wonderful, terrible evening with Luke played out in her head. The last thing she wanted was Luke alerting her brothers to a problem. Or, worse, Luke riding in on his white charger to save her and sweeping her away. This was something she had to do alone.

As the phone trilled she tossed the pillow aside and made a lunge for it, then pulled a worried face when she recognised the number. 'Luke. I was about to ring to say thank you for last night.'

'So I beat you to it,' he said, in the low, husky voice that could always make her toes curl. 'No big deal. I take it you've just woken up?'

'How did you guess?' she said carefully, testing her still swollen lips with the tip of her tongue. 'Last night was wonderful, Luke.' She held her breath.

There was a pause, then Luke said with matching restraint, 'My pleasure, Lucia.'

'So,' she said, sitting up and raking her hair into some semblance of order, as if her brain cells might oblige and follow suit, 'what can I do for you, Luke?'

'Put the kettle on?'

'I'm sorry?'

'Put some clothes on too.'

'That's a little high-handed of you. This is my one morning off. What's the rush?'

'You might want to take a look outside.'

Wiping the condensation off the window with her sleeve, she felt her heart go into flight mode—though she gave a theatrical groan for Luke's benefit. 'Couldn't you sleep?' He was sitting outside in his vehicle.

'Not as well as you, clearly,' Luke said dryly.

Luke's voice sounded so close to her ear a blast of heat spiralled through her at the thought of his touch…his kiss…

Forget all that. Luke arriving in daylight, seeing how she was living, was the last thing she wanted. He couldn't know that she was going to clear a room for herself at the guest house just as soon as she'd sorted something nice out for Margaret. This was only the start of her new life and she couldn't risk Luke interfering.

'Aren't you going to invite me in, Lucia? Much as I love sitting out here in the rain…'

'Hang on. I'll just operate the electric gates.'

She could imagine Luke's report to her brother. She could even write it for him. But whenever she found herself between a rock and a hard place her choice would always be to stand and fight.

Tossing the phone on the bed, she grabbed her birthday shawl—which she'd slept with all night. Wrapping it round her shoulders, she arranged it carefully over a mountainous expanse of unfettered breast, crimping it into folds over her already Luke-eager nipples. Clutching her chest, as if that would somehow hold her heart steady, she remained frozen in place for around two seconds, and then sprang into action with a frantic scramble to clear up the mess. Not that there *was* much mess, as she didn't have many possessions.

Seizing a hairband from the side, she arranged her wild black bed-hair in what she hoped was a sexy, messy up-do— then groaned when she caught sight of herself in the flyblown mirror. How would Luke like her early-morning look? Not a lot, she guessed, fumbling with a tube of toothpaste. There was no time to clean her teeth, but she could rub some on her gums.

A glance out of the window confirmed that Luke had arrived from Planet Fabulous, where no one rose late or looked anything other than their best. Snug-fitting jeans moulded his powerful legs and displayed those alarming contours, while his cowboy boots only added to the sense of a man who didn't give a damn what anyone thought, let alone cared about fashion. Although the red sweater beneath his heavy-duty jacket gave a surprisingly cuddly twist to a man who looked strong enough to crush a rock in his fist.

Chomping on her lips to make them pinker, she already knew that any preparation she might make was too little too late. Luke looked amazing—even better than last night.

Sweeping a hopeless jumble of empty take-out boxes, crisp packets, chocolate wrappers and soda cans from the table onto the floor, she heeled them under the seat, making it to the door with barely a second to spare.

'Luke,' she said, forcing the tin door open with a well-timed kick. She stood, arms crossed, barring his way.

'Are we going to move inside, or are we going to stand out here getting wet?' he said, glancing up as a particularly malevolent storm cloud emptied its payload on the impossibly wide sweep of his shoulders.

'I'm sorry. Come in.'

Luke took in everything as he mounted the steps.

'Welcome to my world,' she said, fingers tensely white as she clutched the shawl.

'I hope you're joking.'

'Why would I be?' she said defensively.

'Where do I begin?' Luke cast a critical glance around.

'Well, you can leave right now if all you're here for is to find fault.'

Luke only had to ease position slightly to assure her that he had no intention of going anywhere.

CHAPTER SEVEN

He loves me... He loves me not. He loves me... He loves me not. At least not in the way I need him to love me.

LUKE'S expression might be fierce and dark, but she was ready for him. Remembering his teasing kisses, she *so* wasn't up for brotherly concern.

'Why are you here?' She tried to keep her voice light, remembering her determination that, whatever happened, somehow they must remain friends.

'Can't I even visit you now?' Luke's black brows snapped together.

'That depends.'

'On what?' He looked angrier than she had ever seen him. 'Whether I shake my head and tell you how this really looks to me, or if I pussyfoot around and pat you on the back for doing so well for yourself, Lucia?'

'That's hardly fair—'

'Can I sit down?' he interrupted.

'I think you better had,' she agreed tensely.

Luke couldn't even stand straight in the van, the ceiling was so low. And his shoulders took up most of the width. He was one of the few men, apart from her brothers, who could make her feel small. Bringing the cover down, he avoided sitting on her sheets. She liked that—but not the way Luke was acting. It reminded her too much of her brothers when they were in we-must-bring-Lucia-back-into-line mode.

'I can't believe you're living here, Lucia,' Luke ground out, confirming her thoughts.

'And what's wrong with here?' she said tensely.

'I doubt it's even safe.'

'Of course it's safe.'

'Rubbish.'

'If that's all you've come to say—'

'Not nearly,' he snarled. 'If you're working for Margaret, why aren't you sleeping at the guest house?'

'Have you been there recently?'

'It can't be any worse than here. This caravan's freezing. It's damp and the roof is leaking.'

'The roof can be repaired.'

Luke flashed a fast penetrating glance. 'By you?'

'I'll find someone.'

'Make it fast. And you'll pay them how?' he fired back in quick succession. 'You'd better ask your miracle workers to remove the spiders while they're at it,' he added, brandishing a really leggy one.

'Don't kill it.'

'What do you take me for?'

'You really don't want to know.' She watched transfixed as Luke transported the spider to the door, as if it were a price-less Fabergé egg he was holding in his large fist.

'You can't stay here,' he said, having deposited their hairy friend outside.

'Says who? You?'

'I won't let you,' Luke confirmed, resting one giant fist on his hip.

She knew that pose. It was like a big cat, kidding you it was relaxing just before it pounced. 'You can't stop me living here.' Tilting her chin, she directed a warning stare into Luke's eyes.

'Let me put this another way, Lucia. You don't have to stay here.'

'You're offering to pay for me to move somewhere better?' she guessed, trying to remember that determination to remain calm.

Luke shrugged.

'I've already told you—I don't need your help, Luke.'

'You clearly do,' he argued.

'Margaret needs me here on site.'

'If Margaret needs you why don't you clear a room at the guest house and move in?'

'I'm working on that as fast as I can.'

'Work faster.'

Luke's amber eyes had turned obsidian black, and they were very close—within touching distance. It would only take a step, a breath, one move by either of them... Luke's heat licked around her like a possession spell, or maybe a lust spell, showing him to be unashamedly male. It was far too much man for her damaged soul to handle.

She breathed a sigh of relief when Luke turned away to stare out of the window. Luke was her friend and she wanted it to stay that way. He had always been the one person she could confide in when her brothers ganged up on her. She wished she could confide in him now, one last time, and have Luke draw her into the safety of his embrace. But if he did that she wouldn't know when to stop, and then she would find herself in the ambit of Luke's world, rather than her own.

'The guest house is barely habitable,' she explained, drawing her business persona round her like a protective cloak.

'And sorting it out will be a long job,' Luke agreed turning round to face her.

'Are you about to make a move on the guest house?'

'Do *you* have some prior hold on it?' he said, watching her closely.

'So you *are* thinking of investing?'

'Margaret has expressed an interest and I have money to invest.'

If Luke and his stormtroopers moved in how real would her independence be then? As if she didn't know. 'It doesn't always come down to money, Luke.'

'Try doing anything without it, Lucia,' he flashed impatiently. 'Good intentions don't mend buildings. How are *you* going to set the guest house back on its feet?'

'By working every spare hour I've got. I've had a lot of extra shifts at the club recently.'

'I don't question your work ethic. I don't question your ability to turn things round, either, if funds are available— and I'd make sure they were. I've seen the work you've done on the *estancia*, and on the guest quarters at the family house on Isla del Fuego.'

'Desperation drove me to do that,' Lucia admitted, lightening up as she thought back. 'My brothers would be quite happy for their guests to live like horses in a barn if I didn't handle the décor and the organisation of the hospitality side of things for them.'

'Exactly,' Luke agreed. 'So I don't understand why the possibility of us working together here in Cornwall has never occurred to you.'

She couldn't have been more shocked. 'What are you suggesting?'

'Come and work for me,' Luke explained. 'I'd trust you to look after my best interests if I'm not around.'

Oh, great. Work for Luke, but without him being around. She would be just one more employee amongst the hundreds working for Forster, Inc.

She should be grateful for the opportunity, Lucia reminded herself. So how come she wasn't?

Because she wanted to paddle her own canoe, maybe?

'I've always been able to trust you, Lucia,' Luke continued, picking up on her change of heart. 'Nothing's changed where's that's concerned, has it?'

'Of course not.' She blanked London from her mind.

'Well?' he pressed.

'I'll think about it. But not if it means putting an official seal on you ordering me about.'

Luke laughed at that. 'Just don't take too long coming to a decision. I've got the money and resources waiting and ready to go. You've got the training and the flair. We both care about the guest house. It makes sense that you should work for me.'

'I could work *with* you, maybe,' she finessed.

'It's my investment on the line,' Luke stated firmly.

And Margaret's future. This wasn't about her pride, Lucia concluded. So could she work for Luke? The thought grated, but if she had an official role she could maybe dilute the Luke effect if he tried to wade in and take over. Didn't she owe that much to an old lady with no one else on her side?

'What's this?'

While she'd been thinking Luke had been making himself at home, and now he was staring at his centrefold, stuck to the wall with chewing gum. Why on earth hadn't she thought to pull the damn thing down before opening the door to him?

'That's my new dartboard,' she said lightly. 'Do you like it?'

'I didn't know you cared.'

'I don't.'

'You always were a terrible liar, Lucia.'

As Luke stared at her, she improvised, 'The girl who had the van before me must have stuck it up. I expect she used it to cover a crack.'

'Must have been a bloody big crack,' Luke murmured.

'Massive, I'm sure,' she mocked. 'I must admit I was surprised when I first saw it. I never took you for an attention-seeker, Luke.'

'Maybe because I'm not.'

'So…?'

'So your sister-in-law Holly persuaded me to let her run a magazine article to raise money for one of her charities. Holly just forgot to tell me when the photographers were coming.'

'Forgot on purpose, knowing Holly,' Lucia guessed, biting down on a smile. Holly could be ruthless when it came to landing a scoop. 'So the photographers caught you out?'

'No need to sound quite so pleased about it.'

Luke had brought his stubble-shaded face so close she could feel his heat warming her. 'You might have smiled for the camera,' she said, swinging away.

'They seemed satisfied with the shots they took, so I guess angry men sell more magazines than smiling men.'

'Well, I don't like angry men.'

'Don't you?'

'Don't act so surprised, Luke. You know I don't. I've always preferred mild-mannered men who are kind and thoughtful.'

'And who have just stepped off the cover of a book of fairy-tales? Get real, Lucia.' Luke's voice turned hard. 'Or are you going to live in that fantasy world of yours for ever?'

'My world seems pretty real to me right now.' And she knew more about the real world than she cared to, which was something Luke definitely didn't need to know.

'Does this real world of yours turn on daydreams or actions?' he demanded. 'I hope for Margaret's sake you've thought this through. And as for those hard, driven men? You're a hopeless liar, Lucia. You *love* hard, driven men. You should do. You've grown up with four of them. You just think it's fashionable to pretend that you don't.'

'Why on earth would I do that?' she flashed as the temperature soared between them.

'Hell if I know,' Luke fired back with an angry gesture.

'Since when has what I feel become your business?'

'You're right,' he said, turning for the door. 'I have absolutely no interest in you whatsoever.'

'Where are you going?' She realised as Luke swung around to stare at her that the desperation in her voice had pealed out like a klaxon.

'I'm going to check this cooker. You can't use it,' Luke added, having given the sagging heap of tin a cursory examination. 'And it can't be repaired, so don't even think of exercising your new-found practical skills.'

'Why would I be practical when you and my brothers have snatched things out of my hands for as long as I can remember?'

'Only so you couldn't beat us over the head with them.'

True. 'So why are you here, Luke? To offer me a job, or to compile a list of my failings for Nacho?'

'I'm not sure I want such a difficult employee.'

'Too much for you?' she taunted, mellowing a little.

'As it happens, I didn't come here to offer you a job. I came to tie up some loose ends with Margaret, so everything we've been talking about may have to be put on hold.'

Until Margaret had given her agreement to Luke buying into the business, Lucia surmised, knowing she mustn't do anything to spoil Margaret's chances. Maybe co-operation was the key—just so long as it was co-operation and not annihilation.

'Do you ever think back to those holidays, Lucia?'

Whoa, cowboy! That was a nifty change of tack. But Luke had always known how to reach in for her heart and squeeze it tight. And there was nothing like poignant memories that joined them both to do that. 'I think about those holidays all the time,' she said honestly. And then, because she didn't want Luke knowing how that made her feel, she added waspishly, 'You always were such a charmer.'

'You haven't changed much yourself,' Luke countered.

But she had changed. *So much.*

He was lying, thought Luke. Lucia had changed beyond all recognition. Yes, she was all grown up, but there were shadows behind her eyes that had never used to be there, and they worried him. Surely she couldn't still be upset after the confrontation with that drunk last night?

'You're over last night's drama, aren't you?' he checked. 'The drunk?' he expanded when she frowned.

'Of course I'm over it.'

But her cheeks flushed red when he held her gaze. So was she remembering when he'd kissed her? *He* was. 'Let's get back to your reasons for coming down to Cornwall,' he said, seeking safer ground.

'What about it?'

'Is there anything else you'd like to share?'

'You never give up, do you?' she said, laughing as if he was making too much of things.

Her laughter sounded hollow to him. 'No, I don't,' he confirmed.

'You always were so suspicious, Luke.'

You bet he was. 'Of course I'm curious to know why you left London, why you came back here. And why you've decided to stay.'

'That's three questions.'

She laughed again, but it still rang false.

'Confiding in a friend isn't a sign of weakness, Lucia.'

'I don't feel the need to confide in anyone, Luke. And I certainly don't need you as my shrink.'

'That is good news,' he agreed.

'Why?' she said.

'Because I'd need a sixth sense and a doctorate in divination before I could sort you out.' But as his stare dropped to the curve of her lips he wondered if it really would be all that hard to sort Lucia out.

CHAPTER EIGHT

My to-do list has collapsed. I have hardly ticked off any items, and even those I have tried to tick off I've bodged. What I really need is a relationship counsellor. Luke has stirred memories I have always tried to skirt around, making me look at some of the least comfortable of them head-on. He has made me realise that I wrote my to-do list at a time when all I could think was: If I had my time, this is what I would do with it.

I wrote that list so confidently at age fourteen, hardly realising how much more complicated life could be than a series of goals to enhance my physical appearance. What about my heart? What about a to-do list for my heart?

'WOULD you like something to drink?' she asked the warrior currently taking up every available inch of space in her caravan whilst throwing his weight around like all her brothers combined. It was the least she could do, she convinced herself. After all, Luke had offered her a job that might even have a wage attached. And he'd given the caravan a health-check—not that that had worked out so well.

'That would be good,' he confirmed. 'Just don't give me one of those glasses on the shelf over the cooker, with a coating of dust and a dead fly garnish.'

She laughed. She hadn't even noticed there were glasses on that shelf. Back to the drawing board where cleaning was concerned, Lucia concluded, and with a head full of scouring powder and dishcloths this time, instead of Luke. 'How about a can of soda?'

'Whatever you've got, sweetheart.'

'I'm not your sweetheart.' She stalled, realising she'd given too much away by snapping like that. How often had she dreamed of Luke murmuring endearments, knowing he never would? A quick glance was enough to reassure her that Luke hadn't even registered the sting in her words.

This was like trying to contain a tiger in a very small box, Lucia concluded as Luke performed the seemingly impossible feat of squeezing his powerful body into the smallest of spaces between the bunk-cum-bench and a chipped Formica table.

'What happened to this place?' he murmured, staring out of the window.

'I guess the world grew tired of St Oswalds and moved on.'

'I can't see anyone studying their reflection in a rock pool,' Luke agreed, his sweeping ebony brows lifting with amusement as he glanced at her.

'I wasn't looking at myself. I was studying wildlife, if you must know.'

'I was pretty wild back in those days,' he commented dryly.

'You are *so* full of it. I wasn't looking at *you*,' she insisted heatedly, knowing full well that the whole point of sitting sentry by that rock pool had been to make sure she was in position when Luke came thundering by.

He'd always chosen the wildest pony in the bunch so he could thrash her brothers, but when Luke had returned to the guest house he'd been all gloss and manners. An only child, idolised by his parents, Luke had never let them down. When Luke came down to dinner his necktie would be perfectly knotted, his hair neat and his shoes highly polished. Leave him with her brothers for half an hour and Luke turned feral.

It had been a kickback against his strict upbringing, she realised now, remembering how unbelievably sexy she had found the transformation from strait-laced Luke to an impossibly wild version. And now he was somewhere in between. Formidably successful in business, Luke was a barbarian, unstoppable and unbelievably sexy, on the polo field. What he was like in private she had no idea—not really.

'Those were great days,' he said thoughtfully, shifting position in a way that suggested Luke's temporarily confined body was cramped like a coiled spring.

'Yes, they were,' she agreed, trying to forget the glances that had passed between them when they were teenagers.

She'd had to be so careful not to let her brothers see how she felt about Luke. Everything about the invisible bond between them had been breath-stealing and forbidden. And had quite possibly only existed in her imagination, Lucia conceded silently, since normally Luke had barely acknowledged her existence when her brothers were around.

Her brothers weren't here now...

It made no difference. She wasn't about to throw herself at Luke and make a bigger fool of herself than she already had by flirting and then flinching when the fear came roaring back.

'Those holidays were the highlight of my year,' he admitted, shaking her out of the reverie.

'You being an only child, I guess down-time with my brothers was quite a novelty.'

'That's one way of putting it,' Luke agreed, his lips tugging as he thought back.

She picked up his empty can just for the excuse to turn away and put it in the trash. Even then she could feel the heat of his stare on her back. Just what exactly was Luke thinking?

'That's the connection between us,' he said, making her swing round.

'What is?' she demanded.

'You were the only girl in a family with four hell-raising brothers, and I was an only child in a family with ramrods up its spine. Both of us were outsiders, Lucia. We just didn't see it that way back then.'

'So fill in the gaps, Luke. What have you been doing since I last saw you?'

'Making money. Building companies. Making sure my father can retire with honour. Nursing the family's charitable foundation back to health. What about you, Lucia?'

'You first,' she said stubbornly. 'Why did you come back here?'

Luke cocked his head as he stared away from her. 'Same reason as you, I expect. I've been trying to recapture something I've lost.'

'Freedom,' she said, thinking out loud.

'I'm free enough,' Luke argued, 'but I do miss the good times we used to have here. When you can choose to holiday anywhere in the world it's surprising how you hanker after the familiar. Only St Oswalds wasn't the way I remembered it when I came back.'

'No, it's falling apart,' she agreed.

'So I'll do something about it,' he said with a shrug.

'And so will I,' she said, staking her claim.

'What are your plans, Lucia?'

She felt defensive suddenly. How feeble they would sound compared to his. Her plans included working as hard as she could and trying to get the villagers to help too. She wasn't ready to admit that her plans also included the rebuilding of Lucia Acosta, brick by unsmothered brick—preferably without hang-ups this time. But she had to admit there were possibilities to them working together. Luke was a highly successful businessman, while she understood the hospitality industry and how to make guests happy.

'Were you planning to invest your own money, or are your brothers backing you?' Luke pressed as the silence ticked by.

'I'm sure Nacho must have told you that he pays me an allowance like a trust fund brat?'

'He didn't, actually. I think Nacho cares a lot more about you than you give him credit for, Lucia.'

And now she felt guilty. 'I know he does,' she admitted quietly. 'If you must know, I divert the money Nacho gives me into a charity.'

Luke shrugged. 'You don't have to explain yourself to me, Lucia.'

But she wanted to. 'Standing on my own two feet doesn't mean I don't appreciate or love my brothers any less. I just don't want handouts from anyone, Luke—and that includes you.'

'If Margaret agrees to me buying in I'll make you earn your money.'

'Then we might have a deal.'

'Let's thrash a few things through first,' he said, standing to tug off his jacket.

'You're far too big for a caravan,' she observed as Luke ducked his head.

'And you're far too spoiled,' Luke countered. 'There's plenty of room in here for both of us.'

If they were welded together, Luke might be right. 'You think?'

'I know. You just have to be well organised, Lucia.'

'I'm trying,' she said.

'You certainly are,' he agreed. 'Why don't you sit down?' Luke patted the bed by his side.

Because there was nowhere to sit without sitting on top of

him. She settled for perching awkwardly on the very edge of the bed, but even then their thighs were touching.

Luke rested his chin on his shoulder to stare at her. 'Well, this is cosy—but there are plenty of better places I can think of to chat through your terms and conditions.'

'Like the Grand?' she cut in.

Luke's lips pressed down. He'd been sure she would fold and agree to let him book a room for her.

'Let's get one thing straight, Luke. If I work for you, I stand on my own two feet. I don't commute from the Grand. I live here—on site.'

'I won't let you stay here.'

'You can't stop me.'

'Nostalgia is a powerful force, Lucia, as I would be the first to admit, but you should never allow it to cloud your judgement. You can work here and live down the road.'

'And travel in by town car? No way, Luke. I've left that life behind, and now I'm going to live my life my way.'

Raking his hair, he somehow managed to keep his mouth shut until they had both calmed down. He had vowed not to get involved. 'Let me give you some facts, Lucia. The guest house is so far gone this project might not even work with my money backing it. The Sundowner was my first choice when I decided I wanted to reinstate Polo on the Beach, but when I made enquiries I was told the guest house had been failing for years—'

'Who told you this?' she interrupted.

'My second choice: the Grand.'

'So the small local guest house finds itself in difficulties and the nearby behemoth does its best to stamp it out of business?' She shook her head. 'I can't believe you went along with that, Luke. It's not what I'd call neighbourly.'

'If you're serious about working in the hotel industry it's

time you learned how to get on with the competition. Keep your friends close and your enemies closer, Lucia.'

'Says the oracle?'

'It's a basic rule of business.'

'Well, thanks for the advice, Luke. I guess I'll just have to make my own mistakes.'

'And if you're thinking about sleeping another night under this roof,' he said, giving it a blow with his fist that set the whole place shaking, 'I'd advise you not to. It's freezing outside and you don't have any heating. There isn't even a lock on the door.'

'Margaret has lived alone at the guest house for most of her life.'

'Because Margaret *has* to,' Luke pointed out. 'You don't have to. You didn't have to live in at the hotel in London. You could have stayed at the family penthouse.'

In spite of her best efforts the temperature was rising. 'In the best part of town?'

'It would have been a roof over your head. Just as taking a room at the Grand wouldn't kill you.'

'And how is living at the family penthouse or running up your bill at the Grand supposed to make me independent, Luke? I'm safe here. The fact that Margaret has lived alone for all these years should tell you something.'

'It does,' Luke agreed. 'It tells me Margaret has no option, because she has nowhere else to go. It tells me the Sundowner isn't just failing—it has already failed. And what are you going to do about it? You don't have any money. You've given it all away.'

'Says one of the biggest charity supporters in the world.'

'I can afford to give. You can't. You've got no practical skills.'

'I learned a lot on my degree course,' she argued.

'Like what?' he scoffed. 'Fifty ways to fold a napkin?'

'That's *it*!' Lucia exploded, completely forgetting the disparity in their size as she sprang up.

Luke stood too. 'Before I go anywhere you're going to hear some home truths, and you won't like them, Lucia. You're great at starting things, but you've never finished anything in your life.'

'Get out!' She was beyond anger now. 'I should have known better than to think you are any different to my brothers. Go on!' she yelled with a furious gesture, pummelling impotent fists against Luke's stone chest. 'Get out of my caravan.'

'I'm not going anywhere without you.' He planted himself in her way.

'So what are you going to do? Throw me over your shoulder and carry me out?'

'If I have to.'

They glared at each other. Passion had never run higher between them, but she wasn't prepared for what happened next—not nearly. Yanking her close, Luke kissed her, and his firm, sexy lips worked their magic.

Of course she fought him. Of course she tried to push him away. But Luke was a rock—a fierce, ravenous, hot rock. Her nipples tightened and heat pooled between her thighs. She'd thought she'd never be able to feel this way again, but her reaction to Luke was like the plug of a volcano blowing after centuries of hot lava building up. She had to hold her hand across her mouth when he abruptly let her go, as if that could hide the proof of her arousal. She was shaking—and not from fear. Luke hadn't given fear time to set in. She was shaking with shock, with anger and with desire.

'You're vulnerable,' Luke said flatly.

'And you were just proving your point?' she demanded incredulously. Her brain cells clinked feverishly into line. That hadn't been a brush, a tease or even a trial kiss. That had been a full-on, body-melting, fear-destroying sensual assault that could never, ever be mistaken for a brotherly peck.

'I'm just putting you back in touch with reality,' Luke said, managing to look sexier than ever as he leaned back against the door.

'Nice technique you have for doing that. Am I supposed to thank you?' It was hard to do battle with her very insistent pulse throbbing, but she drove on. 'I think you should go now.'

'I'm not going anywhere until you calm down.'

'Please yourself.'

Her chest was heaving with...yes, passion. But as they glared at each other she thought of her own climb back, her fight to regain her old self, and Margaret's dream to restore her guest house. Plus, wasn't Luke's offer of a job the perfect opportunity to take that first step on her own emotional to-do list?

'Maybe I have found it hard to finish what I've started in the past,' she admitted stiffly, 'but I'm totally committed to what has to be done here. It means a lot to me.'

'As it does to me,' Luke said quietly, his stare dropping to her lips.

'Okay,' she said, coming to a decision. 'I'll make a deal with you. When I've proved myself, maybe—just maybe, mark you—I'll kiss you back.'

Luke laughed, and the tension between them started to ease, but they both knew that any thought of them being like brother and sister in future was out of the window. Lucia only wished she could tell Luke that she would *never* be able to make good on all the sexual tension between them, but how could she admit that she was damaged and tainted and frightened? Or that she could handle a business relationship, but anything else between them was impossible?

'At least life won't be dull from now on,' he remarked,

eyeing her with humour. 'Though whether it will match up to your experience in London...'

She flinched. Damn it, she actually flinched—and Luke saw it. She hadn't seen that one coming. She should have known Luke would never let it go until she told him the truth about the day that sleazy concierge had decided a pampered Argentinian princess would be easy pickings. Just thinking about it now made her feel sick.

'Lucia?'

She must have paled. 'What?' she said, swallowing back bile.

'Why won't you tell me what happened in London?'

'You still don't get it, do you, Luke? I can handle it.'

He held his hands up palms flat in apparent surrender, and in fairness to Luke she had relied on him and her brothers for so long it was no wonder he felt the need to ride in and save her like the White Knight. But she had changed, and things would be different from now on. She needed no one to save her.

'When you speak to Nacho, just tell him you've seen me and I'm safe. You can also tell him that I've got a roof over my head.'

'A leaking tin roof.'

'And that I won't do anything stupid,' she added firmly.

Unfortunately these were famous last words. As she moved towards the door she somehow managed to spill the contents of the birthday gift bag from her friends, and as Luke stared down in dumb amazement, he saw laid out in front of him, like some offering to a *yoni* god, an industrial-sized packet of condoms, a pair of red crotchless knickers and a very adult toy.

'Nothing stupid?' he murmured.

'Goodbye, Luke.' She had no intention of explaining her gifts to him. Where the job was concerned Luke could call her to account, but the gifts from her friends were none of his damn business.

'Let me know if you're going to take the job, Lucia.'

'I think you know I will.'

'Then as soon as I have an agreement from Margaret I'll have a contract drawn up for you,' he said, giving her a keen glance before opening the door.

She closed her eyes as Luke left the van, but she could still feel him in every fibre of her being. Being with Luke was like brushing the edge of a storm she longed to be swept up in. But if she allowed that to happen everything would be out of her control and under Luke's dominion. She could work for him. She would just have to keep her feelings in check. She *must*. She couldn't bear for Luke to know the humiliating truth.

CHAPTER NINE

I'm not doing so well when it comes to ticking goals off my list—but that's only because I'm impatient and try to take things too fast. And I have my heart set on one man.

So, what have I learned?

I'm frightened of sex.

I'm frightened of Luke finding out I'm frightened of sex and why...

Were I not frightened of sex there would still be a problem, because sex with Luke Forster is never going to happen. I'm obviously not his type—maybe I'm not good enough for him. Luke has sampled several kisses and shows minimal enthusiasm at the prospect of sampling more. Fair enough. If he tried more than kisses I'd probably run a mile.

So it's back to the start of my list with an open mind. If I remain focused I should reach number ten in no time. And if number ten doesn't involve sex with Luke, that's no big deal. The way I feel about sex right now, I'd sooner have an ice cream.

The new plan:

Concentrate on practical matters and forget about my heart. Unlike the path of Cupid's arrow, practical can be planned out in bullet points.

• I have a job at the guest house.

- *The guest house has nine bedrooms.*
- *Sort out the smallest of them for live-in staff.*
- *Live-in staff—that's me! My new quarters will be fabulous when they're finished. 'When', being the operative word.*

TAKING the engine to its limits, he aimed a blow at the steering wheel. Nothing helped ease the frustration inside him.

'Thanks, Nacho,' he murmured, adding a few more choice curses.

If he hadn't gone looking for Lucia he wouldn't have found her—wouldn't want her as he did. He wouldn't have danced with her, touched her. He wouldn't have the mystery of her time in London driving him insane right now.

There was only one way forward. Once he was sure she was physically safe, he was going to retrace Lucia's tiny footsteps inch by scrupulous inch until he found out what she wasn't telling him.

The attraction between them had been on the back boiler for years. It had simmered at the wedding and boiled over in the caravan. His primal instinct told him to carry her off. Not to listen to any excuses. He could just imagine Lucia's response if he tried *that* approach.

Might be fun...

Lucia gave a happy sigh. For a girl who had grown up slaving over brothers as soon as she could hold a mop, there was nothing more satisfying than cleaning up after herself. The caravan might still be shabby, but at least there were no more dusty glasses lurking on forgotten shelves. It even smelled fantastic. She kept telling herself that cleaning would help channel the energy left over from Luke's visit. It hadn't even scraped the surface.

Flopping down on the bench, she glanced at his poster. She

grabbed a magazine. Now it was just a case of finding a page that wasn't devoted to 'Different Sex Positions for Every Day of the Month…' 'Sex Positions for Your Sign of the Zodiac…' 'Hot Sex in Surprising Places…' 'Is that all anyone thinks about?' she demanded, glaring at Luke's centrefold.

Probably, Lucia concluded, thanks to posters like Luke's. Flinging the magazine aside, she leaned back against the bench, trying not to think about sex or her hang-ups. And then she leapt up again, colliding with the shelf.

'What the…?' She jumped around, nursing her head. 'Luke?' Her heart roared into action as a vehicle door banged.

Was Luke back?

What could that mean?

She knelt on the bench to stare out. Her excitement evaporated. It wasn't Luke with his sexy, brooding look, let alone Luke bearing armfuls of flowers with an adoring expression on his swarthy, disreputable face. It was Luke in practical mode, climbing out of a humungous pick-up truck. There was a hook on the back of the truck which he was now attaching to a fixing on the front of the caravan.

He might have warned her! Bracing her hands against the walls as the van rocked up and down, she finally made it to the door. She had to bounce off it a couple of times before she could force it open, by which time she was stoked.

'What the *hell* are you doing?'

'You might want to wait in the truck while I do this,' Luke suggested, without bothering to glance up.

'I'm not going anywhere until you tell me what you're doing.'

Luke's tousled head lifted and his fierce gold stare pierced hers. 'What does it look like, Lucia?'

'You're hitching up the caravan. And taking it where?' she demanded. 'If this is just another ruse to get me to move out—'

Luke straightened up to his full ridiculous height. 'There's no subterfuge involved in what I'm doing. I'm going to tow the caravan a safe distance away from the cliff.' His eyes narrowed. 'You *must* have felt the wind lifting it?'

The cliff did seem dangerously close, now she came to look. 'I have felt it rattling sometimes,' she admitted, distracted by how thick Luke's nut-brown hair was as the wind tossed it about, making it catch on his sharp black stubble.

'And the jacks are broken so the caravan is resting on three wheels.'

That did not sound good. 'Okay, thank you.'

'Go and get something on before you freeze to death. You're soaked through. Your clothes are sticking to your body.'

They were?

And her nipples were nicely puckered too.

'I'll pack the breakables,' she called back, retreating into the caravan.

'Here!' Luke called her back. 'Before you come outside again put this on.'

He reached out to hand her his jacket, but before she could take hold of it he draped it round her shoulders.

'Now, let me go and hitch this thing up,' he said brusquely, turning away.

Wind and rain apparently made no impact on Luke's mighty jean-clad frame. She leaned her head against the doorframe for a moment, watching him, waiting until he had disappeared round the side of the caravan. His clothes were nicely moulded to his body, and as she pulled his jacket close she could only be happy when she found that it was still Luke-warm.

She packed up quickly and then went to wait in the pick-up. Resting her head against the worn leather seat, she listened to Luke's music tracks as she absorbed the scent of truck oil, spice and soap. The warmth in the cab, with its overlay of Luke, made her feel all homey and contented. Her imagination soon took flight.

And quickly came down to earth again when Luke joined her in the cab with a blast of cold air and a blaze of energy, following it up by barely acknowledging her before starting the engine. She was taking a chunk out of his day. That was obvious. Luke kissing her was a long-ago fantasy. He'd tried it and parked it.

Releasing the brake, he inched the truck forward. The sound of creaking and grinding was alarming as the old caravan moved reluctantly off its site.

'Hang on!' Luke exclaimed as they hit a pothole.

She gasped as the truck lurched and she fell into him.

Shrugging her off, Luke turned to glance over his shoulder. 'Lucky escape.'

He was probably right, Lucia thought, moving as far away as possible.

'This is the place,' he said, when they reached the shelter of some trees. 'I scouted round earlier. The caravan will be private here, and it's safe on level ground.'

Which was more than *she* was, Lucia reflected ruefully. 'Do you want me to get out and check round?'

'You stay there,' he said, springing down.

The caravan was soon unhitched, and when Luke climbed back into the cab he looked at her. 'Okay, you can go now,' he prompted, gesturing with his chin towards the door.

'Where are you going?'

'To the Grand for a shower,' Luke offered, his brooding amber gaze alive with the first humour of the day. 'Is that a problem for you?'

'No,' she said, as if she couldn't care less. She had thought he might stay…

'My jacket?' Luke prompted as she reached for the door.

If she was waiting for another kiss that experiment was clearly over, she concluded, tugging it off and handing it over.

'Let this be an end to the risk-taking,' Luke advised.

So don't come round again, she thought, staring him in the eyes. But when her gaze dropped to his lips she was prompted to promise fervently, 'No more risks of any kind.'

Slapping the side of the truck as she got out, she walked back to the caravan. She felt hollow as she watched Luke drive away. She shouldn't have kissed him. She shouldn't have flirted with him. She shouldn't have allowed herself to think for one moment that they could be anything but friends. Maybe she'd spoiled even that. Maybe Luke's offer of a job was just a way of keeping her in one place so her brothers always knew where she was.

Did she have so little confidence?

Where Luke was concerned? Yes. It was hard to feel upbeat when she felt as if she'd lost him—when she felt as if the Luke she'd used to know didn't exist any more. And she missed that man.

Lucia's heat remained in his jacket all the way back to the hotel. He tried to ignore how that made him feel, and settled into accepting some facts that couldn't be changed. Lucia was his best friend's sister. She was the closest thing he had to a sister. But he wanted her.

And Nacho?

He would tell Nacho the truth—that there was no quick fix for a woman of Lucia's temperament, and that her brother would just have to be patient for once.

And how patient was Luke?

Some things never changed, Luke reflected as he glanced into the rearview mirror, as if he might catch one last glimpse of Lucia. He would always care about her.

He smiled as he wondered how long it would be before the parcels arrived, and if she would send them straight back.

* * *

She was about to leave for the guest house when there was a knock on the door. Throwing her weight against it, she stood staring in blank surprise at the man in uniform standing outside a big green van.

'Delivery for Ms Acosta?' the man said, checking the label on one of the packages he was holding.

'That's me,' Lucia confirmed, 'but I haven't ordered anything.'

'Then it must be a gift,' the delivery man said, sticking a clipboard beneath her nose. 'Sign here, please.'

There was only one person in the world who would order a hamper from London's most famous luxury goods store. There was only one person who knew her address in Cornwall.

As soon as she had loaded everything inside, she picked up her phone and called Luke. 'What do you think you're doing?' she demanded the moment he picked up. 'Why are you sending me food parcels? I'm not that desperate.'

'I can't send a few treats for you and Margaret to share?'

'We don't need charity.'

'My PA handles returns—speak to her.'

She sat back, stung.

'Goodbye, Lucia. Enjoy the bacon and eggs.'

She stared at the dead phone in dismay. This Luke was far removed from the Luke she had provoked, teased and taunted when they were younger; she didn't even know him.

Hadn't she changed too?

And it wasn't just a hamper of food. There was everything anyone might need if they were starting out on their own for the first time—good towels, sheets, throws, decent pillows.

'This will all have to go back,' she told Luke's poster. But as his arrogant face sent a scorching challenge back and she lifted one of the pillows and held it to her face she wondered if she wasn't being just a little hasty.

And ungrateful, Lucia conceded. She tried to call Luke

again, to thank him. She wanted to tell him he should take the money out of her wages. But he wasn't picking up.

He didn't take her call until later that day, and she was rather put off her stride to hear Luke's husky tone backed by a soundtrack of languidly swishing water. Trying to blank the X-rated mental images that evoked, she said hello.

'Hey,' Luke murmured lazily, 'this is a nice surprise.'

That Luke hadn't declined her call? It certainly was. He sounded unimaginably pleased, as if something big had gone down. But far worse was listening to him groaning with pleasure as he eased his position in the bath.

'My assistant did okay for you?' he prompted. 'Do you like the stuff she chose?'

Another disturbing mental image flashed into her mind. This one involved an extravagantly beautiful PA—something like the Technicolor blonde—discussing her with Luke before rushing off to carry out his mercy mission.

'Mary said it was no trouble to pick out some essentials for you while she was shopping for her grandchildren's Christmas presents, so I hope she got it right?'

Lucia's shoulders slumped. She felt such an idiot. 'Please tell Mary I'm very grateful. And thank you, Luke. Just don't do it again.'

'Do what again?' he murmured, in a voice that spoke of warm soapy water and tropical ambient heat. 'Buy you gifts?'

She stroked the shawl. 'I don't need handouts.'

Luke's laugh was a rumble deep in his chest. 'I was just being neighbourly, Lucia. I thought you approved of that?'

There was more swishing water, until all she could see was Luke's massive body, wet, tanned and gleaming, his hard muscles flexing—along with a whole raft of other X-rated images.

'Just so long as you're not trying to buy me off.'

'Can I do that with a few rashers of bacon and half a dozen eggs?'

She smiled as she hugged the phone. 'You'd be relieved to be rid of me.'

'I certainly would,' he agreed.

'I have every intention of paying you back.'

'I would expect nothing less,' he murmured, sighing contentedly. She imagined him sinking lower in the bath as he demanded drowsily, 'Is that it?'

'Am I keeping you?'

'Yes. What are you doing for the rest of the day?'

Trying not to think about you buck-naked in a warm, soapy bath. 'There isn't much left of today, but I have cleared a bedroom at the guest house, so at some point I'll be decorating and sorting it out. I don't have time to chat.'

'Maybe I'll drop by later to see how you're getting on.'

'There's no need,' she said as her heart rate went off the scale.

'I'll bring some decent coffee with me.'

'We've got good coffee.'

'Excellent. Start grinding. I could murder a cup.'

'Call room service.'

Luke laughed as he cut the line.

Thoroughly shaken, she threw herself back against the cold tin wall in an attempt to steady her breathing and consider the facts. If Luke did come round, as he had threatened, Margaret would be pleased. And this was all about work now. Luke never backed off once he'd got the bit between his teeth, and while she didn't have Luke's money or influence, her background and training—honed by four demanding brothers— meant she could bring quite a lot to the party too.

Work with Luke?

Work she could do. And she couldn't deny that the prospect of butting heads with him on a regular basis held massive appeal.

CHAPTER TEN

There is a lot to be said for home-cooking.
   East, west, home's best?
   It certainly is. Try looking at what's been under your
nose for years.
   No! Not the moustache-in-need-of-a-wax, stupid!
Luke.

MARGARET had been baking up a storm. There was a non-stop supply of succulent sausage and crispy bacon for all the people who had turned up to work. Luke had announced his intention to fast-track the project, which was great news for everyone—apart from Lucia, who wondered if she was the only one to receive the news with mixed feelings. Luke was experienced in business, while this was her first big project, and Luke wasn't exactly noted for his tolerance levels. If she didn't make the grade she'd be out on her ear.

There were more important things than her pride, Lucia concluded as she took a spoonful of Margaret's soup. 'Your cooking is what St Oswalds has been missing.'

'Do you really think so?' Margaret smiled happily as she turned back to the cooker. 'If you stopped working at that club—stopped being Anita and started being the girl I used to know—all this would be worthwhile for me. You *have* given your notice in?'

'Yes, I have,' Lucia confirmed.

The two women had become close, and Lucia had never been anything but open with Margaret about the reason for her name-change. All sorts of busybodies frequented the club, and though Lucia had never made a magazine spread in her life, and doubted anyone knew her face, the name Acosta might have raised suspicions, since the family had spent many of their summers in the area.

'I'm so glad you're going to be working with Luke.'

Lucia's chin shot up. There was a distinct difference between working *for* and working *with*. She knew Luke would think so.

'I don't understand business, which is how I got myself into this mess in the first place,' Margaret was busy explaining, 'so I'd like *you* to be my caretaker-manager.'

'Manage the Sundowner?' Lucia exclaimed. 'Have you spoken to Luke about this?' She could already hear the thunderclaps approaching.

Margaret shrugged. 'I still have some say. You'll balance Luke out. You both believe in the Sundowner, and while you have the training and flair Luke can handle the financial side of things. In my eyes it's the perfect partnership. I want you front of house, Lucia.'

'Only until you feel ready to take over,' Lucia said firmly. 'Thank you,' she added quietly. 'I can't tell you what it means to have your confidence.'

'If you ask me, Lucia, people should have been placing their confidence in you a long time ago.'

Lucia laughed. 'You've met my brothers. They don't think I can tie my own shoelaces yet. But I won't let you down.'

'I don't think for one moment you will, and as soon as Luke returns from London I'm going to tell him my decision.'

'Luke's in London?' Lucia heard nothing else.

'Some business he needed to look into, I think he said.'

Margaret shook her head. 'I really don't know,' she said vaguely. 'Why are you looking so worried, Lucia?'

'No reason.' But Lucia's mind had started flying in all directions.

'Why don't you go into town and spoil yourself for a change?' Margaret was suggesting. 'Buy yourself a couple of suits in anticipation of the guest house opening?'

'Go into town? Good idea,' Lucia agreed distractedly, pulling herself round.

Her life was changing so rapidly it was hard to keep up. But she had to—though she doubted she could relax, as Margaret had suggested, for wondering what Luke was doing in London. Some sixth sense told her that whatever it was it wasn't good.

As the tall, imposing individual emerged through the swing doors of the exclusive London hotel pedestrians shied away. Rather than step forward to ask if the man required a cab, the uniformed doorman stepped back.

Tugging off his heavy jacket, Luke tossed it into the back of the SUV, which he'd parked aggressively in a no-parking zone. Springing into the driver's seat, he placed a call to Lucia's brother in Argentina.

'The problem's sorted,' he confirmed without expression.

He had tracked down the man he now knew had attacked Lucia, and had resolved the situation to his personal satisfaction. Cracking his knuckles, he gunned the engine and swung the vehicle into the slow-moving London traffic. In a few hours' time he would be back in Cornwall, and Lucia would be none the wiser.

He reorganised his diary on the way back to Cornwall. He wouldn't be returning home right away, as originally planned. His business interests were well managed and could survive without him for a few more days. Whether she knew it or not, Lucia needed him—and that took precedence over everything.

He was going to stay on at the Grand until the guest house project was up and running and he was sure she was okay. Learning what he had in London had convinced him that what Lucia Acosta needed was a guardian angel.

Though after today a *dark* angel might be a more fitting description, Luke concluded as his senses roared at the thought of seeing her again. So he was going to see Lucia again. No big deal.

Try telling that to his libido.

After a quick shower at the Grand he checked out the stubble situation. He badly needed to shave, but he was impatient to see Lucia again. He threw on a pair of jeans and while he was buckling the belt he thought about her. He thought about Lucia all the time. So what if she brought mayhem to his life? There was never a dull moment when they were together. And the thought that someone had hurt her…

Breaking through to Lucia was his next and most important project. She couldn't shut out what had happened in London for ever. She mustn't be allowed to. It would damage her.

Ruffling his hair in a token nod to grooming, he grabbed the phone when it rang and smiled as he checked the number.

'Margaret.' He strained to hear Lucia's voice in the background, but he couldn't make out what she was saying. 'It's never too late to eat, Margaret. Thanks for the invitation.'

The shave could definitely wait.

She was working her socks off in an attempt to forget Margaret had invited Luke for supper. Luke having mysterious business in London was something she preferred not to think about, so she'd chosen displacement activity instead. Where practical matters were concerned she already knew her strength lay in design and layout, and then in sourcing the right people to do the job, but today it felt as if she had more to prove.

Today it felt as if she had everything to prove.

It was the concierge effect chipping away at her self-confidence, Lucia suspected. Just hearing Luke was in London had brought it all back to her. Fortunately fate had played into her hands. While she was rooting around in the attic she'd found a bolt of fabric and a staple gun. A stool was a good place to start—nice and simple. And just think of the money they could save if she could upholster some of the stuff herself instead of sending it out. How hard could it be? Stool. Stuffing. Cut a template for the fabric…

She found out how hard as Luke pulled into the yard. Her increasingly urgent calls to Margaret had met with zero response as she tried frantically to detach the sleeve of her uniform from the stool. Not that her heart wasn't playing Jai-alai at the thought of seeing Luke again, but…

Be careful what you wish for?

She had wanted to surprise Margaret with her frugal ways, but had not pictured accidentally stapling herself to the stool as a possible outcome. She could just imagine what Luke would say.

And…

Oh, good. He was peering through the window.

He had driven to the guest house the same way he rode a horse—flat out. He couldn't wait to get back to Cornwall and hold Lucia in his arms to reassure her that anyone who tried to hurt her again would have to get past him first. His pulse had surged when he'd seen her at the window as he drove up. He'd expected she would get up and open the door for him, but instead she was just staring at him. And if he hadn't known better he would have said that was alarm on her face. Even having raked his hair into some semblance of order, he reasoned he probably did look like a bandit.

'I'm not interrupting anything, am I?' he demanded, finding her alone in the room.

Luke looked so gloriously wolfish for a moment she couldn't speak. She had never seen him looking this pumped off a polo field. 'Welcome back,' she said carefully. Remaining seated, she turned at an awkward angle to hide the fact that there was a stool attached to her arm.

'What have you got there?' Luke said, coming closer to investigate.

'It's an antique,' she explained offhandedly, dragging in his warm, spicy scent, laced with a refreshing shot of bracing sea air.

'An antique?' Luke murmured, his lips pressing down attractively.

'Yes…' She met his assessing gaze with a challenging look, but she couldn't read if Luke had learned anything in London from a stare that was brooding and amused. 'I thought I'd restore the stool,' she explained, clinging to something safe and mundane.

'Do you mean you're re-covering it?' Luke glanced at the remains of the fabric strewn across the floor.

She was the one who needed recovering, Lucia concluded when Luke shocked her by giving her a hug.

'Good job,' he said, springing back.

'What did you do that for?' she gasped.

'No particular reason,' Luke insisted on his way out of the room.

She was instantly suspicious. The only time her brothers hugged her was when they were worried about her—if she had fallen off a horse, or something similar. It was their way of showing relief that she was okay, she supposed. So was Luke reassuring her that they could still be friends?

There was no point wishing for anything more, she told herself firmly as she returned to battle with the staples.

It was no use. They wouldn't budge. She would just have to take her uniform off.

'Margaret says the food is...' Luke's voice died as she dived behind the door.

Tired of greying white granny pants, she had treated herself to some new underwear in town—a gaudy display of shocking-pink lace to cheer her up when she was wearing work clothes. 'You're not supposed to be here,' she pointed out, cheeks glowing red when Luke showed no sign of leaving.

'Clearly...'

She held her breath while Luke and his sexy swagger finally returned to the kitchen.

'What *now*?' she exclaimed, feeling horribly caught out when he came back again.

'For goodness' sake, Lucia, I *have* seen you in a swimming costume before,' he pointed out impatiently, advancing on her with a pair of pliers.

Agreed. Luke *had* seen her half-naked before—when she was about sixteen. And she had been wearing a bikini at the time, which was somehow different. 'How did you know I was stuck to the stool?'

'Is that a serious question?'

Having freed the stool, Luke set it aside. 'Stick to what you do best in future. No one can do everything. Not even you, Lucia. Are there any more little jobs I can do for you before I go?'

Was *that* a serious question? 'You're going already?'

'To eat,' Luke's eyes darkened with amusement. 'Oh—and, Lucia?'

'Yes?'

'Nice underwear.'

Oh-kay.

'We shouldn't keep Margaret waiting,' he prompted, holding the door.

'I'll be right there.'

Just as soon as her heart had steadied.

She hesitated outside the kitchen door and then grasped the nettle. 'Beer?' she said casually, walking in. Luke was already seated at the head of the table, she noticed, bridling.

'Sweetheart, beer is *always* good.'

'What have I told you?' she warned him on her way across the kitchen.

'I promise never to call you sweetheart again.'

She glanced over her shoulder at Luke. His face was straight enough, but his eyes were dancing with laughter. She reached for a glass.

'Can I help you do that?'

She inhaled sharply to find him at her side. *Damn.* Luke moved like a soft-pawed predator. 'I can reach, thank you.'

'I don't need a glass.'

'Then what *do* you want?' she asked breathlessly.

Luke's mouth was very close to her ear, and although if anyone could make her lose her fear of men it was probably Luke, no way would she put that theory to the test.

'Maybe I need to practise my bar skills on someone,' she suggested, pulling away.

'Practise away,' he said, shooting her one last thoughtful look.

Still none the wiser as to what Luke had been up to in London, she decided to concentrate on being a consummate professional—something tangible within her reach. Thanks to Margaret's excellent cooking she served the perfect meal. She served the perfect coffee too, and Luke was pleased.

'If you continue like this you'll have the place full in no time,' he told Margaret. 'That was delicious, thank you. I'll take a look around now, and check out what's got to be done about the décor and furnishings—'

'That's my department,' Lucia interrupted.

'Says…?' Luke's gaze narrowed.

'Says me,' Margaret confirmed. 'That's what Lucia and I have agreed.'

'Oh, have you?' Luke smiled at Margaret, but reserved another look entirely for Lucia.

The challenge made her stare him down—or attempt to. Then Luke stood and the sizeable farmhouse kitchen shrank around him. For a moment she wondered if he was going to thump the table and roar that no one decided who did what unless *he* signed it off.

'Perhaps you two could check out the place together,' Margaret suggested tactfully as the atmosphere in the kitchen took a dive. 'I've asked Lucia to be my manager,' she explained, as evenly as if she were pointing out the fact that Lucia's new bucket and mop set was in a nicer shade of blue. 'And Lucia has agreed. Isn't that wonderful, Luke?'

'We'll discuss this later,' Luke managed through gritted teeth.

'Would you like to follow me?' Lucia asked mildly.

'No, I'll lead the way,' Luke insisted. 'Having stayed here for at least ten consecutive years I'm sure I don't need anyone to lead me round.'

Message received loud and clear. But she led the way anyway.

'What the hell is this nonsense about you being manager?' Luke demanded the moment the door had closed on Margaret.

'How much experience of running a hotel do you have, Luke?' Lucia challenged. 'Exactly,' she said when a muscle in his jaw worked. 'You've got more money than Croesus, as well as endless experience in the international business arena, but I have the hands-on experience—which began around the time Nacho asked me if I could organise a polo supper for him. I think I was about fourteen at the time. Plus, I fully understand that you need to be sure your investment in the Sundowner is safe, but let neither of us fool ourselves. I know this place is a means to an end for you. You want to reinstate Polo on the Beach and the Sundowner Guest House is in the perfect position: perfect stables, perfect access to the beach—'

'You seem to have it all worked out,' Luke growled tensely.

'Let's just say I'm not the child you seem to think I am. Shall we start the tour?'

'It seems I don't have much option but to go along with this for now, as Margaret has already appointed you.'

'Not so much of the "for now",' she warned. 'I fully expect to be fired if I fall short in any way. But the one thing I don't need is for you to prop me up.'

'You'd just like to spend my money?' Luke suggested coolly.

'Margaret appreciates your investment,' Lucia countered pleasantly. 'Shall we?' she suggested.

Luke's eyes flashed a warning signal that clearly stated it was game on. 'After you,' he bit out.

CHAPTER ELEVEN

Fans self... *Hot momma, this man might not be mine
but I cannot—will not—think about anyone else making a move on him. I might be damaged goods, but I'm
still capable of admiring a fine ass. And in the unlikely
event that Luke ever made a serious move on me I can
rest assured that it could never come to anything because he'd soon realise that when it comes to sex I'm a
complete non-starter. So when he finally settles down I
shall just have to go on retreat to Outer Mongolia and
never come back...*

FOR the sake of maintaining a professional front she blanked
Luke, huge and powerful, dwarfing her completely as he
stayed close at her side as they went up the stairs. Luke in
snug-fitting jeans—a little frayed, a little ripped, a little pale
and worn in places. She refused to notice that too. Inviting
him to go ahead of her at one point, she surveyed the tight hips
and muscular thighs—purely out of clinical interest, of course.
Just as she'd thought. He was bigger than her brothers. And
that heavy Aran sweater did look great with Luke's swarthy
skin, his hunky build and brooding amber gaze.

And there it ended, Lucia told herself firmly. Luke Forster
would be the first to admit that he believed women existed to
be protected, rather than to stick their heads above the para-

pet and invade a man's world. Women were far better seen
and not heard—preferably in the bedroom, she imagined, remembering the blonde.

'You're being uncommonly accommodating, Lucia,' Luke
commented as she led the way down the landing.

'I'd like to show you the attic room,' she replied in a businesslike tone, careful to maintain distance between them.

'I'm all attention,' Luke said, moving close enough for
their hands to brush.

She led him into the huge room that took up much of the
top of the house. It had the most spectacular view through
picture windows of the endless beach and the sea beyond.
Margaret had always dreamed of turning it into a residents'
lounge and library. Lucia explained this to Luke. The room
was still full of ladders and decorating equipment, but she
threaded her way through all the tackle until she reached the
windows where they could look out over a beach the colour
of rich Jersey cream and the wild Cornish sea beyond, which
had turned from angry pewter to smooth, crystalline blue.

'What do you think?'

'Apart from the shock of discovering Margaret has appointed you manager of the Sundowner, do you mean?' Luke
enquired, hitting her with a curve ball.

'I imagine you could override that if you wanted to,' she
said, returning to the subject at hand. 'So, what do you think?'

'You know what I think,' Luke growled. 'I love this place.
But to turn it into an exclusive venue for international polo
players who are used to the best will be a complex project.'

'And you don't think I'm up to it?'

'You're not exactly tried and tested.'

Wasn't that the truth? And now she must stick to the subject at hand. 'I'm not an amateur, either,' she said. 'I may not
have your facility for figures and keeping ten thousand plates

spinning at once, but I do know how to run a hotel—and from the bottom up. I can stand in for any job you care to name.'

Except for one, he thought, remembering the concierge.

'And if anyone knows how to cater for demanding polo players,' she pointed out, 'it's me.'

He couldn't argue with that. 'So, how do you feel about us working together, Lucia?'

'How do *you* feel about it?' she countered.

As if it was going to be difficult to concentrate, he concluded, feeling his groin tighten as Lucia continued to stare at him. This was not the girl from the beach, or from the wedding. This was a woman who had been through a lot since he'd last really known her, and who had gained in strength because of it. It made Lucia a better fit with the job, and made his life a lot more interesting.

'Can you cope with my being your boss?'

Her eyes flared and then she relaxed, seeing his eyes smiling into hers. 'So long as I don't have to bow and scrape,' she said.

'I'll put a clause in your contract to that effect,' he offered dryly. 'So…?'

'So Margaret is thrilled by your investment,' she said carefully. 'Just so long as you understand that my life isn't on the agenda, Luke. I refuse to live my life by committee a moment longer.'

'I think I've gathered that.'

'Well,' she said, 'if that's it…? I hope you like the changes I'm making.'

'Why don't I take a look?' he said.

It soon became apparent that Lucia had touched things with fairy dust. Even on Margaret's limited budget the old house was already being brought up to scratch, with hours of work having been put in—by Lucia, he imagined. There were quirky touches only she could have dreamed up—driftwood from the beach arranged to look like a piece of art on a high ledge, where it cast intriguing shadows on the pale chalky walls, and bleached wooden chairs upholstered in faded blue ticking inviting relaxation in a tranquil reading room, where the only ornament was a bowl of fresh flowers set in the centre of a vast refectory table on which newspapers could be laid out flat, or books studied in the natural light of the panoramic window framing the shore.

He paused at the window to stare out at a sky rapidly changing from daytime shades of smoky-blue to a cloak of night, streaked with red-gold.

'Luke?'

He turned to see Lucia standing waiting for him in the doorway. 'You're a real homemaker, Lucia.'

'There's no need to sound so surprised,' she said, smiling. 'Anyway, if you want to linger and soak up the view I just thought I should let you know I'm going out.'

'Okay.' He ground his jaw as he listened to her footsteps fading. She couldn't spare five more minutes to talk to him? And where was she going? he wondered as the front door opened.

To the beach.

He might have known. He watched until her shadow had disappeared down the cliff path and then pulled away from the window.

She was endlessly fascinated by the busy little creatures darting about the rock pool so purposefully in their unknowable lives. Hugging herself, she leaned her chin on her knees to watch them.

'Lucia...'

She glanced around, even though she knew her mother couldn't be calling her. Demelza Acosta was long dead, so she could hardly be running across the beach towards Lucia, trailing one of those big straw hats she'd used to love, her long red hair blowing wild and free in the fickle Cornish breeze. But if Lucia closed her eyes she could almost see her mother— barefoot and laughing, calling out as she came closer for Lucia to run with her. She'd be wearing one of those dresses that were totally unsuitable for the beach. It would be long and flowing, with a dainty flower print, and would keep catching round her mother's legs. Her mother would laugh all the more as she struggled to free herself, and when she finally made it to the rock pool she would grab hold of Lucia's hand and take her running, which often meant dodging the boys on their horses. Her mother had loved that game. She'd said tempting fate was exciting.

The dream ended abruptly, because Lucia hated giving in to weakness. She preferred to laugh and make jokes.

'Lucia?'

She glanced up in surprise to find Luke watching her. 'I didn't hear you. The wind,' she explained briskly, knuckling her eyes.

'Sorry if I'm intruding,' he said, shifting position. 'I just wanted to find you and say what a wonderful job you've been doing at the guest house.'

'I'm glad you approve,' she said, putting on her flippant voice. She felt vulnerable and exposed after her emotional workout. She braced herself and stood to face Luke.

'You're not going yet, are you?' he said as she glanced at the cliff path.

'It's getting cold.'

'Have I done something to upset you?' Luke probed.

'Oh, you know,' she said, reverting to the old mocking tone.

'No, I *don't* know,' Luke said, frowning. 'I'd like you to explain. What are you running away from, Lucia?'

She drew in a fast breath as Luke took hold of her arm. 'Nothing,' she said edgily. 'I just want to go back.'

Luke lifted his hands away. 'If that's what you want.'

'If you've come looking for the past, you won't find it here,' she blurted out. 'Sorry.' She tried a laugh that didn't quite work. 'Don't know where *that* came from,' she added in a jokey voice, pulling a face.

He did. 'I always come to the beach when I want to recapture those feelings from years back. There's nothing wrong with that, Lucia—'

'I tried it,' she interrupted. 'And it doesn't work for me. I've looked for the past here, but I can't find it.'

As emotion welled behind her eyes she stared away to sea. Lucia couldn't see her handsome Argentinian father and her Cornish mother laughing together as they strolled along the beach as she had hoped, he guessed. All she had found in St Oswalds was a rundown guest house and an old lady battling to keep things afloat without any real hope of doing so. But he'd seen real prospects for change here, and found it hard to believe Lucia couldn't see how large a part she played in that. Her confidence must have taken a real kicking. And now he knew why and how. He just had to be sure he got the timing to voice his concerns and got the healing absolutely right.

'The worst thing of all,' she said, distracting him, 'was that until you came along I couldn't see how I could help.'

'You've already helped Margaret with your friendship and with your company, as well as your hard work. And we're not finished yet,' he assured her.

'It's all words, Luke.'

'No, it's not,' he argued. 'Let me prove it to you?'

'What do you mean?' she said, staring at him suspiciously, but there was just the ghost of remembered humour in her eyes and that was enough for him.

'Okay, here's the challenge,' he said. 'If I don't make you laugh and remember the good times we used to have on this beach I'll give you a wage-rise. How about that?'

'I haven't even fixed a wage with you yet,' she pointed out. 'So I've got nothing to lose.'

'You are totally shameless,' she protested.

Maybe he was, but she hadn't said no, and to see that smile still playing round her lips was enough for him.

'Luke, what are you doing?' Luke was kicking off his boots. 'Are you completely mad?' she demanded as he started unzipping his jeans. 'You can't be thinking of swimming in the sea. It's freezing! You *are* mad,' she concluded, backing away from the latest massive roller.

'Chicken?' Luke shouted back.

'Certainly not.' Well, maybe a little, she conceded as Luke started on his boxers.

She clutched the back of her head as Luke casually stripped them off. 'Luke, you can't do that! What if someone sees you?'

'You mean there are more people as mad as us?'

Swimming off a freezing cold beach at night? Hmm…

It wasn't like they hadn't done it before…

Oh, what the hell!

She was probably going to land herself with the most graphic erotic dream yet, but chicken she was not, Lucia concluded as Luke plunged into the sea. And, yes, he *was* tanned all over.

Shaking his head like an angry wolf, Luke roared back at her over the crash of surf, 'I thought you said we were equal, Lucia? Looks to me like I'm the superior being after all.'

Firming her jaw, she yelled, 'Turn your back.'

'You speak and I obey.'

'I wish,' Lucia muttered, tugging off her clothes.

She raced into the sea, shrieking and wailing as a wall of ice-cold water hit her. 'You didn't turn around,' she complained, regaining her feet. 'That shows blatant disregard of the rules.'

As if Luke cared. He was standing taking lazy inventory,

with his massive fists planted on his taut naked hips. The only thing she had to be grateful about was the fact that the sea at night provided them both with a modesty curtain. He dodged the spray as she shrieked a war cry and launched herself at him.

'Two can play at that game,' Luke confirmed.

Unfortunately it was yet another game at which Luke excelled.

'Okay, I give up,' she conceded, raising her hands in the air. 'You win!' she exclaimed, her voice shaking with tension as Luke towered over her.

'Do I?' he said, taking a firm grip of her arms. 'What's my prize?'

If she could draw breath to speak she might come up with something, but with the entire length of Luke's hot, magnificent body pressed up against hers it was hard to think, let alone speak.

'Warm now?' he murmured, dragging her closer still.

There was too much information bombarding her brain for her to spare breath for an answer. But feeling more of Luke than was safe, she pulled away.

'You still don't trust me?'

Her answer was to place her hands flat against his chest in an involuntary defensive action.

'Dry yourself, Lucia. Get dressed and then we'll talk,' Luke said crisply as he turned to stalk back through the waves to the shore. Having snatched up his jeans and stepped into them, he strode away in the direction of the guest house. 'You were right about this place,' he called back. 'There's nothing here but sea and rock and sand.'

'Luke, wait.' Tying her shirt in a knot around her waist and wearing her jeans like a shawl, she chased after him. Managing finally to catch up, she grabbed hold of his arm.

'Don't let me spoil things for you. I was in a dark place tonight—it's nothing, just a phase.'

'Take care it doesn't become a way of life,' he said, shaking her off.

Luke was frighteningly right with that remark, Lucia realised, gritting her teeth as she ran after him. 'Margaret's out late with her friend, the farmer from across the road,' she explained, skipping backwards as she spoke. She was desperate for a return to normality between them. How would she work with Luke otherwise?

'So?' he demanded, still striding on, refusing to look at her.

It was a relief when he walked past the car. 'So come to the house,' she said. 'Take a shower—put some dry clothes on. We can have something hot to drink. We'll soon warm up.'

He stopped so abruptly she almost cannoned into him. 'How long are you going to pretend that this is all about whether you're cold or I'm cold, or if there are ghosts on the beach, Lucia? You must know I had to find out what happened in London. You must know I couldn't leave it without knowing what you were running away from.'

She flinched at his choice of words. 'What are you saying?' Ice washed through her. She couldn't read Luke's expression. She only knew he was saying horribly hurtful things she had been doing her best to avoid—true things—events she couldn't face any more than she could face the cold expression in Luke's eyes.

'I'm saying that I found out for myself what you didn't trust me enough to tell me, Lucia.'

'Luke—'

'I'll make a bargain with you, and my bargain is this,' he said, speaking over her. 'We talk about the past. We don't hide things from each other. And you don't hide your tears from me. Stop,' he added grimly when she tried to protest. 'I don't want to hear your jokes or your excuses. What happened to you in London is too serious for that.'

'I know. I told the police.'

'So you told the police but you couldn't tell me?'

'I told them as soon as Margaret told me you were in London, but I guess you got there first.'

'I guess I did,' Luke agreed. 'What, Lucia?' he demanded fiercely, grabbing hold of her. 'How could you imagine I would think any less of you because of what happened in London? I only wish you'd told me.'

'I…' She couldn't find the words as she stared up into Luke's complex expression. There was anger in his eyes—hurt too—but most of all there was the strength she should have remembered was always there.

'Those were great days on this beach, Lucia. There's no shame in remembering them with laughter, and even with tears. I don't see how either of us can come here without feeling something, and I don't want you to shut me out. The past belongs to both of us. Can't you see that?'

She heaved a great shuddering breath, knowing she must find the strength to tell Luke exactly what had happened in London. He was right that the past had to be faced up to and dealt with.

'Do you remember that barbecue?' he murmured, so softly she barely heard him.

'How could I forget?'

She knew exactly the day he was referring to. As Luke turned to stare at the spot where their two families had gathered she took the chance to pull on her clothes. By the time Luke turned around his face had softened and all the anger was gone.

'My brothers nearly set fire to the table,' she said, remembering.

'The table my mother insisted must be brought down from

the guest house, complete with linen tablecloth, silver table settings and candlesticks,' Luke supplied.

'My mother burnt the food.' She began to smile.

'But your father saved the day,' Luke pointed out.

'Your father helped,' she reminded him. 'They really liked each other, didn't they?'

'Strangely, they did,' Luke agreed, remembering his stiff, unbending father forming a surprisingly easy relationship with Lucia's striking, autocratic father.

'Not sure our mothers got on so well,' she said, 'though they always made the effort—'

'Both of them were polite to a fault,' Luke cut in, 'though there was never going to be too much common ground between them,' he admitted, thinking back. His mother had always been too worried about what people might think, while Lucia's mother hadn't given a damn.

'They were good days,' she said quietly.

'Yes, they were,' he agreed, shifting position to shield her from the wind. 'You'd better get back to the house.'

Luke wanted space—just as she did sometimes, Lucia guessed, taking the hint. 'I'll head in and grab the first shower,' she said.

'Were you crying when I first came down to the beach?' Luke probed softly, returning to the subject uppermost in his mind.

'I should have remembered you're the master of waiting until you're certain your dart will strike home.' Her mouth pulled in a rueful line.

'That wind can be a real nuisance sometimes,' Luke commented, but his eyes were warm with concern.

'Yes, it can be,' she agreed, holding his gaze steadily.

He caught hold of her as she went to move past him. 'So, do we have a bargain?' he demanded, staring into her eyes.

'A bargain not to hide our feelings about the past from each other?'

'All right… Yes, we do.' She couldn't pretend she wasn't disappointed that that seemed to be the only thing on Luke's mind.

Lifting his hands away from her, he let her go. 'Margaret's been talking about a party for everyone involved in the restoration of the guest house. Have you heard anything about it, Lucia?'

'Yes,' she admitted. 'Will you be here for it?'

'I'll do my best.'

Hurt, she demanded, 'How low down on your list are we?'

'Not low enough,' Luke growled.

When he yanked her close this time she was expecting some sort of lecture, but that was the last thing Luke had in mind. All thoughts of Luke the friend, Luke the almost-brother, shot out of her head, to be replaced by Luke the man she had watched over the years growing into a formidable warrior, protector, leader, unofficial guardian angel. And, whether she wanted him in the past or not, pain-in-the-neck adviser. And unashamed sexual tiger, she was now forced to add to that list.

As emotion overwhelmed her she clung to him, standing on tiptoe to kiss him back. Luke soothed as he stimulated, and claimed her for his own even as he set her free. But he knew everything there was to know about wild creatures, and that like the wildest and most wary of them all Lucia needed the ultimate coaxing, so even as her own passion grew Luke stepped back.

'The wind's blowing up again,' he pointed out. 'You should get back to the house before you catch cold, Lucia.'

His thoughts were always for others and not himself. 'Just one thing first.'

'Name it.'

'Equals?' She held out her hand to shake his.

'Agreed,' he said.

When he clasped Lucia's hand their heat mingled. Her eyes darkened and her lips parted to suck in air, but there was still too much reserve in her—and until he got past that...

She turned for home as if nothing of significance had passed between them.

But it had and they both knew it. They had both committed to travelling the same road together for a while, with neither of them certain where that road might lead. His goal had always been straightforward: restore St Oswalds and the guest house, and then shoot back to attend to his other business interests. But then he'd rediscovered Lucia and retraced her steps to London, with everything that involved.

He should have known life was always going to be more complicated than he had originally planned.

CHAPTER TWELVE

They say that you have to get all the pus out of a wound before it can heal, but the cleansing of the wound can be traumatic.

They say that what doesn't kill you makes you stronger.

Who is this indefatigable 'they'? And have 'they' tried it? Have 'they' tried laying themselves bare in front of the one person with whom 'they' least want to share their shame?

THEY reached the house and parted without a word to find a shower. She came down to find Luke in the kitchen. He didn't waste any time—but then subtlety had never been Luke's strong point.

'Let's talk about what happened in London,' he said tensely, his eyes like shards of glass.

'Luke, please, I don't want to do this now.' Her voice rose with every syllable. Luke's expression told her he hadn't just dug up part of her life she had been trying so hard to forget, he had laid it bare, and now he was going to shake it in her face and demand a reaction. 'Please don't make me...'

Luke slammed the door shut so there was no escape from the kitchen. Leaning back against it, he said in a deceptively soft voice, 'As someone who cares about you, Lucia, I think it's important that we do this.'

'I don't care what you think. I don't need you to fight my battles for me, Luke—'

'So I'm not supposed to care that I find you working as a cleaner in a trashy club?' he broke in. 'Or to notice that you're living in a barely habitable caravan in Cornwall, out of season on a rundown caravan park?'

'You're happy enough to work with me.'

'Margaret's known us long enough,' Luke said, refusing to rise. 'And I'm giving Margaret the benefit of the doubt. Perhaps she's on to something.'

'Let me out of the kitchen now, Luke. I don't want to talk about this.'

'If not now, when?' he demanded. 'You'll never be ready, Lucia. You keep everything locked inside you until it grows like a worm and eats you from the inside out. And I won't stand by and watch that happen.'

Luke was whip-fast as she tried to slip past him. She stared in fury at his fists planted either side of her face on the door. 'If co-operation's the key to working together you're not making a great start,' she fired back. 'First you go nosing about in London, and now you're trying to—'

'I'm trying to what?' he bit out.

She had been distracted by something else. 'You've been fighting,' she exclaimed under her breath. 'Luke, what have you done?' she asked faintly.

Pulling back, he studied his bruised knuckles. 'I've been hitching up caravans and moving rocks. What?' he demanded. 'Do you seriously think I'd beat up on some sad, disgusting little man? Is that why you think my knuckles are bruised?'

'So you know...' she whispered.

'Of course I know,' Luke confirmed. 'What I can't understand is why you didn't tell me.'

'Because whatever happened in London I've dealt with it. It's over and it will never happen again.'

'*Is* it over?' Luke said quietly.

As he spoke Luke lowered his arms and stepped away from the door, but this time she made no attempt to escape. Leaning back against the wall, she hugged herself for comfort as she remembered the day her life in London had come to an abrupt end.

'Moving from getting a good degree to my new life in London was supposed to be so different from the way it worked out—so straightforward.'

He could have told Lucia that nothing in life was straightforward, but he had waited so long for her to let the poison out he wasn't going to say a single word to distract her.

She felt the shame again—of arriving at the guest house feeling pretty much like the filthy slut the concierge had called her. She remembered how her heart had raced with fear and panic that Margaret might turn her away. She had realised how it must look to the elderly owner of the guest house, but Margaret had taken her in without a word.

'It all began when I went to change my uniform,' she explained to Luke. 'I went into the staffroom. I didn't bother locking the door. It was supposed to be for female members of staff. It was a very formal hotel in London, so I should have been safe. I heard a sound, and when I turned around a concierge I thought was my friend was standing by the door, watching me.'

She had to pause. She didn't want to make this overly dramatic. She wanted to remember it exactly as it had been without any theatrical flourishes.

She shuddered, remembering. 'He was touching himself through his trousers as he watched me getting changed. When I turned and he saw me looking at him he gave himself a special firm stroke. I couldn't believe it. You'd think he'd be embarrassed—but, no… He came closer while I stood frozen to the spot. My feet wouldn't work. He stood in front of me and asked in a really normal, conversational tone of voice if I would like to touch him. When I said no and shrank back, he said, "What? A hot-blooded South American like you doesn't want to touch *me*?" And I could tell he had taken offence.'

She swallowed and turned away from Luke as she remembered the violence the concierge had unleashed.

'He undid his zip and exposed himself. He asked if there was something wrong with him when I shrank away. His voice turned ugly.' The calm beam of Luke's stare remained on her face, willing her to go on. 'He was angry when I wouldn't take hold of him. Sorry—'

Spinning around, she gagged. Clamping her hand over her mouth as her stomach heaved, she moved away, her hand up to ward him off when Luke reached for her.

'Dry gagging's no fun,' she said, trying to make light of what had happened when her stomach settled.

Luke wasn't smiling.

She steadied her voice. 'He rubbed against me. I slapped him away. I fought him with everything I had. He turned rough. He was touching me everywhere. He felt my breasts. He hurt me. He bit me. He grabbed me here. He ripped my briefs off. He poked his—'

She couldn't go on. How could she, when she saw that look in Luke's eyes?

'Go on,' he encouraged steadily.

Heaving a deep breath, she made herself go back. 'I kicked him in the knee as hard as I could. While he was howling and lurching about I somehow managed to get away. I ran back to my room, grabbed my car keys and a few things. I didn't stop to wash.'

Her eyes when they met his were wounded, tortured.

'My skin was hot. I was sure he'd put something on it—

acid or something. Of course it was nothing. Just the imprint of his hands. I got down to my car—they let us park under the hotel—and I drove out of London. I didn't even know where I was going until I reached Exeter, and then I knew I was heading back to the guest house where I'd always been happy.' She swallowed on a dry throat. 'I couldn't go to the family penthouse in London. My brothers could have turned up at any time and they were the last people I wanted to see.'

'Thank goodness Margaret was home.'

'Yes,' she agreed, finally focusing on his face. 'But I must have frightened Margaret half to death. She opened the door to a madwoman with her hair sticking out at all angles, make-up smeared with tears, ripped clothes hanging off a body covered in bite marks and scratches. I can't even imagine how she must have felt when she saw me.'

He could.

There was a long pause as she remembered that first bliss-ful, purging shower, and how she had examined her skin in minute detail under the spray, certain the concierge had put something horrible on it—something she would never be able to wash off. She had stood beneath that cleansing stream, scrubbing herself with the roughest cloth she could find until the water ran cold.

'Lucia…'

'I'm sorry.' She lifted her hands and let them drop again, by which time some warmth was creeping back into her body. 'That's all there is,' she said.

'It's enough,' Luke said gently.

'Sleeping with that concierge would have really opened my eyes, apparently.' She tried to laugh, but even to her it didn't sound right. 'And my legs, presumably, which was the bit that really freaked me out.'

This time when Luke gathered her into his arms she made no attempt to fight him off. 'Why didn't you call *me*?' he said, nuzzling his face against the top of her head. 'I would have come for you right away.'

'I felt so ashamed, so dirty. It wasn't something I wanted anyone to know. And it was my problem.'

'Not this time, Lucia,' he said, pressing her against his chest, where she could feel Luke's heart beating, regular and strong.

'It was better you didn't know,' she argued. 'You might have killed someone.'

'Quite possibly,' Luke confirmed, staring grimly away. Then, slowly and very deliberately, he dipped his head and kissed her. She couldn't say whether that kiss was soothing or loving, long or short, firm or light. She only knew that she was in a place where people were kind to each other and only meant well.

'Forgive me, Lucia,' he said, pulling back. 'That's the last thing you need.'

'It's everything I need,' she argued. 'I should have known you wouldn't rest until you found out what had happened in London. I think you and my brothers are throwbacks to some warrior race, where honour is a badge worth fighting to the death for.'

'And where those warriors believe that little girls never grow up?' he suggested gently.

'You're all guilty of that,' she agreed. 'But I can assure you this girl's all grown up.' She gave Luke's chest a half-hearted thump as she pulled away.

'Come back here.'

'Let me go, Luke,' she said, trying to be firm with him. 'I'm warning you.'

'No, you're not,' he argued gently. 'You're resting on me, because that's what you've always done when you're upset. You know you can tell me anything. You always could.'

'In the absence of anyone else to confide in,' she admitted ruefully.

'You always did know how to make me feel valued,' he teased her gently.

'You *are* valued,' she said, staring up into his eyes. 'You have no idea.'

He was all out of words.

Her mind crashed as Luke's mouth covered hers. She gave a whimper and, hearing his responding growl, shivered with the relief of a wounded animal being rescued by its mate. Luke cupped her head in one big hand as he moved his lips against hers, and kissing him back was like coming home. She had never been frightened of Luke. He might look like a barbarian—he might even act like one on the polo field—but Luke was her lodestone, her rock. She just hadn't ever risked thinking of him as a man who might want her after what had happened. And if he'd leave it at kisses...

Luke sensed the change in her immediately and pulled back.

'Why?' she whispered.

'Because you're not ready,' he said, staring deep into her eyes. 'And this is not the time.'

He left her to go and get his jacket, which he'd hung on the coat stand in the hall. He was smiling as he brought a small package back with him. 'I almost forgot this.'

'What is it?'

'I bought you something.'

'Something else?' she said wryly, her lips pressed in a questioning line.

'I don't like buying gifts from hotels,' Luke explained. 'It always feels like the easy option to me. And, okay, it *was* the easy option,' he admitted. 'Nacho asked me to buy you something. So this is from me. I found it in London. I hope you like it. Happy birthday, Lucia.'

She smiled when she saw what the elegantly packaged gift-box contained. 'Are you telling me I need to brush my hair?' she said as she examined the exquisitely crafted hairbrush.

'I rather thought I might do it,' he murmured.

'Luke, it's beautiful. I love it.'

The back of the brush was enamelled in turquoise lacquer decorated with intricate whorls in soft gold and rose-pink. The craftsmanship was so fine it took her breath away. That and the prospect of Luke brushing her hair, which was a fantasy yet to be explored and far more erotic than anything she might have dreamed up.

'You shouldn't do this,' she said, shaking herself round. 'It must have cost you a fortune.'

Luke shrugged. 'I can always take it back.

She hugged it close. 'Not a chance.'

'Well, I'd better be going.'

Luke tugged on his jacket as if nothing unusual had happened between them, while she felt as if everything had changed. 'Goodnight, Luke.'

His hand warmed her arm briefly as she opened the door, and then he walked past without another word.

Oh, well. Closing the door behind him, she leaned back against the polished wood, trying to fathom out whether all her painful revelations had brought them closer together or pushed them further apart.

Luke didn't trust himself to stay a moment longer. He had wanted to grab hold of Lucia and hold her tight and safe for ever. It had taken all the will power he possessed to leave her at the door. Whatever she thought of him, he respected her bid for freedom and her need for time to put what had happened in London behind her. But she had smelled so good—so fresh and innocent. She had aroused every protective instinct in him. And, on the dark side, he wasn't nearly done with kissing her yet.

Or with giving her gifts, Luke reflected as he climbed into his car.

It was ironic to think that Lucia had always been the risk-taker while he considered every move. Events in London had changed them both for ever, turning the world as they knew it onto its head. It would be some time before Lucia could trust a man again, and he had been so sure his soulmate would be a soothing, peaceful, calming beauty—no drama, no tempera-ment, no ruffles in the smooth waters of his life.

When he reached the Grand his head was still full of Lucia. He stormed into his suite, took another shower and dried off. Dressing quickly, he told himself not to be so rash, and that work was the answer. Raking his damp hair impatiently, he crossed to the desk and tried to focus on a line of figures Lucia had asked him to look at. They blurred into her lovely face. Anger followed at the thought of the pain she had suffered when he hadn't been there to stop it.

With a violent curse, he slammed the lid down on his lap-top. 'Crazy!' he exclaimed. She made him laugh. She made him lust. She made him throw up his hands in exasperation.

He realised he hadn't known a moment's peace since his first day in St Oswalds, when he had spotted a wild and lovely young girl on the beach. He'd never seen anything like Lucia before. To him she had seemed like some exotic bird in com-parison with the tame canaries back home. There hadn't been a day since then when he hadn't thought about her.

Lucia's family had been too busy with their own concerns to notice the tightrope she was walking, but he had.

And now she didn't need him. How did that feel?

It stuck in his craw.

CHAPTER THIRTEEN

Get a wax
*Luke is right. I have to move on. No wonder he gave up
and walked out on me. When did I turn into such a wuss?
Picking up my old to-do list, I scoured it. Apart from
more serious matters, what else have I been avoiding?*

Oh, yes.

*I drew a blank with the fast search company on the
phone—maybe I wasn't frank enough with the man on
the other end of the line? Thankfully my chat with Grace
from the club bore fruit. Not only will I not have to
brave the chi-chi beauticians at the Grand and risk
running into Luke, which would be embarrassing to say
the least, but apparently there is a new place, a local
place, a small and discreet place, tucked away in the
backstreets of St Oswalds.*

*And, bonus! If the stress of what I am about to do
gets too much for me, the salon also offers massage by
Britain's strongest woman.*

*Banker's Bonus: I have managed to score their last
appointment.*

THE lights were pink neon; the windows were obscured glass.
The words 'Power Massage' plastered over a banner didn't
exactly instil confidence in a girl who believed in preserving

her body by never using it. But she wasn't here for a massage, Lucia reassured herself as she opened the door.

'Veruschka will be with you in a moment,' the receptionist in the well-packed white uniform purred, staring up through a fringe of false black lashes as if she could read Lucia's fear and knew she was dreading it. 'Veruschka is *verrry* good… *verrry* gentle…'

Eek.

The door to the back room creaked open.

But it was only a really nice young girl, around Lucia's age, with a high ponytail, hardly any make-up and a nice clean shirt and jeans.

'Come this way, please,' she said with a friendly smile.

Oh, this wasn't going to be at all bad. What on earth had she been worried about?

Okay, so this might be a bit of a problem, Lucia conceded, holding up the paper thong when the girl had left her in the dressing room. Not that she hadn't seen a thong before, but as the thin bit was at the back and the waxing wasn't, which way round should she wear it?

Never mind. They'd given her a gown, and that nice girl would soon put her right if she'd got it wrong. 'Veruschka…? I'm ready…'

'This way, please.'

Had Veruschka turned into a man?

That wasn't a young girl's voice, Lucia reasoned, hovering nervously behind the plastic curtain.

She gasped as the curtain was ripped aside and a woman as tall as her brothers and at least as wide stood, beefy arms akimbo, waiting for her. 'I am Veruschka,' the Titan informed her.

'I'm not here for a massage,' Lucia explained in a shaking voice.

'No,' the woman said in *basso profundo*. 'You are here for waxing.'

'Correct.' Dropping her shoulders, Lucia lifted her chin. Wasn't this a rigmarole women the world over put up with? Was she less than the rest? Was she a wuss?

Yes.

She was lying prone and stiff on the hard, plastic-covered couch, just wondering how to broach the subject of the thong, when Veruschka turned.

'We start with the moustache and then we move on to the big guns.'

What?

'Oh, good… Perhaps…'

Too late. The pot, the Titan and the red-hot wax were on their way.

The wax cooled rapidly. So far so good—though she hadn't realised her moustache covered half her face before. And…

Youch!

Was it supposed to hurt so much?

'Tell you what, Veruschka. Shall we leave it there?'

She didn't wait for an answer. By the time Veruschka thundered something in reply Lucia was already in the changing cubicle, tugging on her jeans.

'Just take it,' she said, thrusting money at the dazed receptionist. 'No—no change. And definitely no vouchers for a return visit,' she insisted, waving them away.

Get a cool new wardrobe.

It wasn't all lose-lose. Now she had made a start on her to-do list another item followed swiftly on the heels of the wax. It was late-night shopping in town—the perfect opportunity to choose a couple of smart suits for when the guest house was finished and she was front of house. Being given free rein was quite a novelty after the black suit or black suit choice she had had in London. And she could put something fairly nice together without spending too much money if she shopped around…

This was so ridiculous she couldn't believe she was doing it—except it was something she felt compelled to do. It was almost dark and she was down on the beach, showing off her new outfits to her mother. She wanted her to see them. She was wearing one of her new suits—a smart, tailored navy blue number—teamed with a violet top underneath. One exclamation mark per outfit was enough, Lucia's mother had always told her.

The suit fitted Lucia like a glove. She had even had to go down a size. Not that she was back to her old self yet—far from it—but with high heels on she didn't look half bad.

'Just a minute,' she said, teetering about as first one and then the other heel sank into the sand. 'There,' she murmured, imagining her mother watching her. 'What do you think?' she said, slowly turning in a circle.

'I think you look amazing…'

She nearly jumped out of her skin. 'Luke!'

'Who else were you talking to?'

She laughed a little nervously. This wasn't the time to admit she had been communing with her long-dead mother. 'You really think so?' she said, frowning. 'You don't think the violet top is too much?'

'I think the colour combination is as unique as you, Lucia.'

Was that good or bad? she wondered wryly. She took a chance. 'I'm glad you approve.'

'Do you need me to steady you?' he asked, when she stood like a stork to take her shoes off.

'You'll never do that, Luke.'

Humour flashed across his eyes. 'It won't stop me trying.'

She rested one hand on the hard muscles of his upper arm. 'How did you know I'd be here?'

'Do you really need to ask that question?'

Luke was right. They had always been in tune with each other's thoughts. It was reassuring to know they still were—though not quite so reassuring to see the brooding look in his eyes, or to feel her body respond to it. Even she couldn't misinterpret the growing tension between them. And what if Luke wanted more than kisses?

'So?' she prompted brightly, shaking off her brush with apprehension. 'Are you thirsty? Do you want to come back to the house and have a coffee or a beer?'

'Lucia, stop babbling,' Luke advised, 'or you'll have me thinking I make you nervous.'

'As if,' she scoffed.

'Before I think about a drink,' he said, turning serious, 'I've drawn up some projected figures you should take a look at.'

'Oh…how interesting.' And now she felt flat, when surely she should be feeling relieved that Luke was only here to talk business rather than to make her confront more demons than she was ready for. 'Business comes first,' she agreed, starting up the packed sand path.

'You never did tell me what you're doing on the beach in a business suit, talking to yourself,' Luke remarked casually, strolling alongside her.

'That's right, I didn't,' she said, playing his game as she hurried on.

She was at the top of the cliff before she realised Luke wasn't following her. He was still down on the beach, watching the last blood-red rays of the sun sizzling and finally going out on a charcoal horizon.

The temperature had dropped suddenly, and a stiff wind was whipping his hair. He registered those things in some logical storage compartment in his mind while Lucia took up every other nook and cranny. How much time had they wasted?

Storming up the cliff path, he stopped dead at the top, seeing the guest house was in darkness. Where had she gone instead? He looked around wildly. There, to the left, he could see a light flickering in one of the windows of the caravan.

Jogging across the field, he stopped outside the door. There was a pause before anything happened, and then she finally wrenched the door open.

She smiled crookedly at him.

'You've been crying. Did you miss me?' His lips tugged at this suggestion.

'You're so full of it,' she said, but at least she was smiling again. 'As it happens, I'm jealous because Margaret's gorging herself on freshly churned butter and clotted cream with the farmer across the way. Are you coming in? Or do I have to stand here all night?'

'I can see the lack of clotted cream is as good a reason as any for your tears. I don't have any Cornish cream,' he said, brushing past her as he entered the van, 'but I can offer you some good, honest brawn, if that's any good?'

She gave him a look—eyes narrowed, chin up. 'You'll do, I suppose,' she said, pressing back against the side of the van to let him pass. 'You're impossible,' she murmured when he gave her a wry stare back.

And she was…*beautiful*. Her face was blotchy from crying, but that only made him want to hold her and make things right for her. 'So, come on, what's wrong?' he said briskly once the door was shut behind him.

'There's nothing's wrong,' she said, with a little too much heat.

'I don't buy that, Lucia.'

She bit down on her bottom lip, and her eyes were stormy

as she confronted him. 'Okay, so I was missing my mother,' she said angrily. 'Are you satisfied now?'

Reaching out, he brushed some tendrils of wayward hair from her face. 'Your mother would be very proud of you.'

'Do you really think so?'

'I know so. Margaret's been wearing my ears out telling me how hard you work, how great your ideas are, what a flair you have for the hospitality industry and how she can't think how she ever managed without you. Damn, this bed's uncomfortable,' he said, hunkering down on the edge of the narrow bunk. 'How the hell do you sleep here?'

'My room's nearly ready at the guest house, and this guy I know sent me some excellent throws and pillows.'

'Is this guy anyone I know?'

Scooping up a pillow, she chucked it at him. 'Does that help jog your memory?'

'There's only one thing that can help me.' Reaching out, he took hold of her.

Still laughing, she shook him off. 'Let me go, you great oaf!' She shrieked as he brought her crashing down on the bed at his side. 'This isn't the hay barn, and I'm not a child to be manhandled,' she insisted—but without much heat.

Feeling the soft cushion of her breasts beneath his arm, he thought he would happily vouch for that.

'And if this is about that work you mentioned, I've clocked off.'

'So have I,' he assured her.

'So why are you here?'

'Well, I wouldn't call this work,' he said, taking in every adorable aspect of her face.

'Are you sure?' Sitting up, she looked at him comfortably sprawled on her bed. 'Are you sure I'm not just work for you, Luke?'

'How can you say that?'

'I just have to look at your track record to date. You come. You go. You report back to my brothers, who tighten the reins until I squeak. Isn't that how it goes? Or has your role in my life changed?'

'My being here now has nothing at all to do with your brothers,' he assured her.

'Good, because when you see them you can tell them I've found something worth finishing, and I'm not going anywhere until I've done just that.'

'I'm not going anywhere, either.' He dragged her close.

'Luke, I—'

'You talk too much.' As he kissed her, he pushed the jacket down her arms and started on the buttons on her top.

'If this is one of your jokes…'

'This is not a joke, Lucia.' Her skin felt like warm silk beneath his hands, but there was still space between them, as if they both had to be sure. More than sure, they had to be certain.

'What are we doing?' she whispered.

'I'm making love to you.'

'Can we still be friends?' she asked, placing her hands flat against his chest in one final and not very convincing last-ditch attempt to hold him off.

'We'll probably argue more.'

'Impossible.'

He cut her off. Cupping her face in his hands, he kissed her tenderly and slowly. For a few seconds she resisted him, as if she didn't want to take the risk of damaging their friendship. In that moment he wondered if he'd called it wrong. He had never been uncertain in his life before, but where Lucia was concerned he was all over the place.

But just when he was about to pull back she softened against him and said, 'Again…'

'Why?' he demanded, smiling against her mouth. 'Did I get it wrong the first time?'

'I won't know until you kiss me again,' she said.

He dropped kisses on her mouth, teasing her, bringing her to a higher state of arousal, but he could sense that something still wasn't right. 'You know I'd never hurt you.'

'I know that.' She squirmed with embarrassment, and then turned her head so she didn't have to look at him as she admitted in a voice he could barely hear, 'There must be something wrong with me.'

'There's nothing wrong with you,' he insisted. 'Does this have something to do with London?'

'I don't want to talk about it, Luke.'

A bolt of fury hit him as the man who had done more damage than he knew flashed into his head. He was determined to prove to Lucia that fear had no place in her life, but before he could do anything she caught him off guard. He could only describe it as some dark side of Lucia taking her over. Locking her hands behind his neck, she dragged him down to kiss him with a fire that astounded him.

Seizing her wrists, he held her firmly beneath him, with her hands safely captured on the pillow above her head. He had never seen her like this, with her lips parted to suck in air, her eyes black with passion, but he needed no reminder that his reality did not include mindless sex with a woman he had loved since childhood.

'Lucia.' Having managed to free her hands, she had started tugging at his clothes. 'Lucia, stop that!' he said sharply.

Bringing her hands down, he held her as her expression changed from furious passion to shock at what she'd done, and then to something that stabbed at his heart, until finally she turned her face into the pillow as if she had done something wrong.

'Lucia, look at me,' he said gently. Drawing her into his

arms, he stroked her hair and kissed the top of her head. 'I only stopped you because it shouldn't be like this. Not the first time. Not for you.'

'But it isn't the first time,' she confessed, anguish at all her perceived faults making her voice break.

'I'm talking about the first time with *me*,' he said, his lips tugging wryly as he stared into her troubled eyes. 'If you really think I'm that sort of judgemental jerk, what are you doing in my arms?'

'Doesn't everyone think I'm a party girl?'

'Only those who can't see through you as I can.'

'I'm not like my mother, Luke.'

She made it sound like some sort of monumental failure, which really shocked him. He had never realised Lucia's in-securities cut so deep, or had such history.

'My mother was a free spirit, and I so wanted to be like her. But when I try to do the things she did I just make a mess of everything.'

'You don't make a mess of anything,' he argued tensely.

Lucia's mother had been more than a free spirit; she had been reckless. If Demelza Acosta hadn't insisted on going back into the *estancia* to save some silly trinkets Lucia's father wouldn't have tried to save her and they would both be alive today. He would never tell Lucia what he knew about the flood, but she was so wrong to compare herself unfavourably with her mother. Lucia had far more common sense.

He only realised now what coming back to Cornwall meant for both of them. It meant facing the truth—however unpal-atable that truth might be.

'That concierge made me feel as if I'd led him on,' she said, pulling him back to the present with a jolt. 'I keep re-running what happened through my head to see if he was right, if it *was* my fault...'

'You've got to stop that right now,' he insisted pulling her into his arms. 'That man was sick. He was bad, Lucia. Look at me.' He cupped her chin with his hand so he could stare deep into her troubled eyes. 'What you're thinking is impossible. You would never act like that. I know for certain, because I know you better than anyone. You cover everything with humour and a bold face, but inside you're as tender as a—'

'Steak?' she suggested, reverting to the jokes that had always kept her safe before.

'I was thinking more tender as a summer night,' he said, lips tugging as she stared at him in disbelief.

'Since when has the Enforcer been a poet?' she demanded, narrowing her eyes.

'I went to school, too,' he said with a shrug.

Her gaze steadied on his as she realised that he had no intention of allowing her to distract him. She frowned, then heaved a breath and said, 'Okay. I worry that I can't...you know...' Turning her face away, she said, 'I can never give you what you want, Luke.'

The thought of some bully leaving her in this state made him angry all over again. 'Maybe I don't want as much as you think.'

'You just want kisses?' she said, pinning him with a suddenly fierce look. 'No. I didn't think so.'

It hurt to see her mouth twist in that heart-wrenchingly familiar grimace. From the day her parents had drowned, Lucia had hidden her feelings from everyone. She would rather tie her face in knots than let anyone see how she felt inside. That was the look she was giving him now.

'I'm not that bad, am I?' he said. 'You make me feel like Bluebeard.'

'It's not just the concierge and what he did to me,' she admitted. Drawing a deep breath, she went on, 'I've never—' She stopped. 'Help me out here.'

'Enjoyed sex?'

'How did you know I was going to say that?'

'I applied intuition,' he said dryly.

'What are you doing now?' she said as he tugged his top over his head.

'Equalling things up a bit,' he admitted.

'But my chest isn't naked,' she protested.

'Not yet.'

CHAPTER FOURTEEN

Get a great dance teacher
Right about now you're probably thinking, 'How can she be thinking about dance teachers at a time like this?'
Well, with the best dance teacher in the world currently holding me in Perfect Hold, I feel confident in this area of my life too.
Well, sort of...

LOVEMAKING started with kisses, strokes and whispers of endearment, and that much she could do.

The lightest brush of Luke's mouth sent pleasure jolting through her body. Her dreams had been full of this since the first day she'd seen him galloping flat out on the beach—though not as good as this...not nearly as good as this. And Luke proved to be the master of the outrageous suggestion, which aroused her even more.

She worried he wouldn't find her full figure sexy, but when Luke tossed her top aside her breasts fitted his big hands so perfectly that for the first time in her life she didn't wish them to be any different. There was such a connection between them she couldn't have summoned up a gram of fear even had she wanted to. Her only wish was to be closer and to sink deeper into incredible sensation, and then have it last for ever.

Lacing her fingers through Luke's hair, she kept him where

she wanted him as he dipped his head to tease her nipple with his mouth. Each tug of his lips brought a corresponding reaction of pleasure that throbbed insistently between her thighs. She loved the feel of strong sun-bleached waves springing against her palm, and the rasp of his stubble as he raised his chin to look at her.

Seeing the look in her eyes prompted him to move down the bed, while she writhed beneath him, wondering about nerve-endings that must have been sleeping but were now leaping into life. Unable to bear the frustration a moment longer, she undid the buttons at the waist of her suit trousers and slid them down.

Dark heat was burning in Lucia's eyes. Her hunger revealed itself in swollen lips and peaking nipples. Her inhibitions were lost in the need consuming her. All he wanted was for her to forget her fear, to be able to move past the block she had created in her mind to protect herself from the pain of what that man had done to her. He tasted innocence when he kissed her, which only made him all the more determined to protect her. He took time to enjoy the pleasures of her body. He drew deeply on the fragrance of her skin and revelled in her plump, smooth softness as she pressed herself against the hard, unyielding muscles of his chest.

'You're beautiful,' he murmured against her mouth.

'You have no idea what it took to get here.'

'Stop it,' he said gently. 'Stop with the jokes, Lucia. I mean it when I say you're beautiful. You've always been beautiful to me, and you're even more beautiful now.'

She gasped when Luke's hand touched her leg, but her eye contact with him didn't waver as he stroked and reassured, aroused and excited her—though she sucked in another fast breath when his hand reached her thigh. But Luke was in no rush, and now he teased her lips apart and her brain grew woolly. Stroking his tongue with hers was the greatest intimacy she had ever known with him, and as he deepened the kiss she welcomed the thrust of his thigh between her legs. She even angled herself in an attempt to catch more pleasure, but Luke was too clever for that, and always managed to keep just that little frustrating distance away. Breath gushed out of her in an excited sigh when he cupped her buttocks. The heat of those big rough hands was holding her so safely, even as they placed her in the most unimaginable danger.

Falling in love is dangerous.

'You're such a brute,' she murmured, making it sound like a compliment, which made him laugh.

Luke knew everything about delay and how it heightened pleasure. He knew she was swollen with need and that a pulse beat greedily at the heart of that need. But all he did was to cup her with one big hand, refusing to touch her where she wanted him to, almost as if he were stealing away her chance at pleasure.

'How can you?' she whispered heatedly, in an agony of desire. This was the worst frustration she had ever known. 'How *dare* you?' she complained when Luke just gave her that crooked smile.

'How dare I?' he said, lips tugging in amusement. And he kissed her with deadly efficiency and still held back.

'Luke…'

'What's the problem?' Luke murmured, lifting his head.

'You,' she said, biting down on swollen lips. 'Why must it be like this? Why make me wait so long?'

'Because pleasure should be savoured, and I want to make sure you are ready.'

As Luke said this she decided that if there was to be no reprieve she would take matters into her own hands, but her hands were shaking as she started to battle with the buckle on his belt. At least she had the satisfaction of knowing that Luke was massively erect, and by the time she managed to get her hands to the right place the zipper on his jeans didn't so much open as explode. Maybe he was right about taking things slowly.

He rested motionless while Lucia undressed him. She was right in that compared to her he *was* a brute. He was twice her size and goodness knew how much stronger, and as he bathed in the light of her clean, bright innocence he felt like a satyr on the loose. The thought that Lucia had never known true pleasure at the hands of a man made him doubly aroused, and doubly determined to serve and satisfy, but he would wait for as long as it took for Lucia to feel confident.

With this in mind he continued to lavish attention on her breasts with one hand, while his other rested motionless in place, denying her the quick fix she thought she wanted.

'Goodness, Luke,' she breathed.

He'd kicked his jeans off and she realised she had never seen him completely naked before—except in the sea, when it had been dark and the water had covered them both. He soothed her with words and kisses, giving her just a fraction more of the pressure she craved. As he did so her eyes opened wide with surprise and a breath shivered out of her.

Staring into his eyes, she managed to utter one word. *'More.'*

At the back of her pleasure-clouded mind she realised that she had been waiting for fear, but it didn't come. Instead a heavy, erotic beat pulsed urgently between her thighs. Luke still refused to take her any closer to the edge, as if he knew exactly where her limits lay. But when she got there would she be able to take that final step? Letting go meant trusting Luke completely.

'This can't be enough for you,' she said, already worrying.

'It isn't enough for *you*,' Luke countered wryly. 'Relax,' he said, moving down the bed.

This was all new to her, and she briefly resisted him slip-

ping her legs over his shoulders. It made her feel so exposed.
But the fight dissolved at the first touch of his tongue. And
then the thought of Luke kneeling in front of her as he was
doing now, to serve her and attend to her pleasure, was such
an erotic notion she surrendered gladly and rested back.

'I want to see you come,' he said. Seeing her shocked expression, he added softly, with that humour in his eyes, 'Don't
look so worried—there's no rush.'

Exhaling shakily, she settled back again, with her heart
hammering so hard she could hardly breathe. Far from toning
things down in deference to her inexperience, Luke slipped
a pillow beneath her hips, exposing her even more as he positioned her in a way that suited him. Closing her eyes, she
concentrated on sensation. The scratch of his sharp black stubble on the inside of her tender inner thigh was a thunderbolt
to her senses.

'Look at me, Lucia.'

It was possibly the only time in her life that she had obeyed
one of Luke's instructions without argument, but this time
she did so willingly, and a cry shivered out of her as Luke's
big hand turned into the most delicate instrument of pleasure.
She couldn't hold back and screamed his name, while Luke
made sure she enjoyed every second of the violent pleasure.
The waves surging over her seemed never-ending, though at
some point Luke must have collected her into his arms, because he was holding her safely now, as he kissed and stroked
her until the last addictive ripple of enjoyment had subsided.

'Was that good?' he murmured.

'What do you think?' she managed, when she was capable
of focusing on the world again.

But a new hunger soon started up inside her. She could feel
Luke's erection pressing urgently against her thigh and was
overwhelmed by the desire to have his tongue in her mouth,

his pulsing energy deep inside her. The thought of them joined completely and in every way made her shiver with excitement.

'Greedy,' Luke murmured, though his hands were instantly at her service.

'Touch me,' she said.

'Touch *me*,' he challenged softly.

Closing her eyes, she reached for him and, stroking lightly, marvelled at the breadth of him, the incredible silken length.

'Again,' he said, 'and use more pressure this time.'

'What are you doing?' she asked, wondering if she had done something wrong when Luke broke away.

'I'm protecting us both. Help me?' he suggested.

Luke didn't have a shred of self-consciousness in him, and she fed on that. Involving her like this meant that nothing he did could come as a surprise to her. As if to confirm that, Luke dropped kisses on her mouth, and his eyes were smiling into hers with a new intimacy. This was a kiss between two people who had known each other for a lot longer than one night but who were seeing each other clearly for the first time.

A soft cry escaped her lips when somehow the tip of Luke's erection caught inside her. He was so intuitive, so tuned to her needs, that when he finally eased inside her she gasped with relief rather than fright. He rested, allowing her to become used to this new sensation, and it was she who moved again first—tentatively to begin with, and then with increasing confidence, until Luke took up the rhythm and she was mindless and free, completely free. No words could express how it felt to be one with Luke after so many years of loving him.

'You are my official sex slave now,' she informed him much later, when they were lying together on the bed with their limbs comfortably entwined.

'Do I get a contract to that effect?' he murmured, toying with her hair in between kissing her.

'An indefinite contract,' she assured him, drifting into sleep.

'Sounds good to me...'

When she woke Luke was still watching over her, with his face resting on the pillow next to hers. 'What?' she murmured when he smiled.

'You,' he said. 'At last.'

'What do you mean, me at last?'

'You, where you belong at last,' he said.

There were moments in life that were precious and would always be remembered, and this was one of them. This was the first time she had realised they both felt the same—for how long she couldn't know, since life had whipped them up and put them down in different places. But they were together now. And hungry again, she realised, seeing the smile tugging at the corner of Luke's mouth.

'No,' she said, deciding to tease him as he had teased her.

'That's fine by me,' he said, and laughed deep in his chest when she growled with frustration and threw herself on him.

He lost count of how many times Lucia had wanted him. He had never imagined she would be so passionate, or so insatiable. He would have loved her just the same without that, but it was a bonus.

Love?

Yes. Love. He had always loved Lucia. He just hadn't realised the extent of that love before, and now it only remained for him to find the right time to tell her how he felt. Now was not that time. Not while they were both basking in the afterglow of mind-blowing sex. He'd choose his time. Lucia meant the world to him, so he had to get it absolutely right.

They came out of the caravan arm in arm to find that it had somehow, mysteriously, moved several yards down the field.

'How could that have happened?' Lucia puzzled as she stared at the tracks.

'I can't imagine,' he murmured, tongue in cheek.

She looked at him blankly and then understood. 'You mean we—?'

'We'll have no bad language here,' he warned, drawing her close.

She laughed. 'You were right about the caravan not being able to withstand extreme conditions.'

'Which is why I want you to move into the guest house, where it's safer. Or there's always my suite at the Grand…'

How nice would that be? But all the more reason to continue with her plan to succeed on her own merits, Lucia concluded. Then she could book her *own* suite at the Grand and invite Luke over.

'Do you think Margaret knows about us?' Will it change things? she wondered.

Luke's answer was to pull her into his arms and stare into her eyes as he said, 'It's time to start trusting the people who love you, Lucia. You have to let people love you—and to do that you have to let them in.'

'Now you've made me feel selfish,' she said, seeing the other side of the coin clearly through Luke's eyes.

'Well, I'd never say *that* about you,' he said, pulling back to give her one of his looks. 'Awkward. Stubborn. Aggravating.'

'I get the picture,' she said.

Linking arms, they continued to chat as they stood outside the newly decorated guest house, and then Luke said, 'I've been telling your brothers how well you're doing, and that in future they should be calling *you* for advice.'

'Oh, great,' she said with a mock groan, smiling as Luke dragged her back into his arms again. 'If you think I'm going to take on the duties of agony aunt for a gang of over-sexed polo players… Tell them to write to Holly. She's the expert.'

But it felt good to know that Luke was acknowledging that the tables had turned, and that none of them would ever think she needed a knight in shining armour to ride to her rescue again. Although some knights were exempt from that rule, Lucia decided, as Luke brushed her lips with his.

'I'll e-mail them,' she murmured, knowing that if she didn't distract them both they would have to go back to the caravan and move it again.

'You do have something pretty big to share,' Luke agreed.

'Like…?'

'Like I love you,' Luke said, smiling against her mouth as she softly echoed his words.

CHAPTER FIFTEEN

Get a gag for polo-playing brothers
Okay, it seems sensible at this point to re-establish con-
tact with my brothers. Not only is it sensible, there is
no one I want to share my happiness with more. Plus,
the sooner I lay down some ground rules the better, as
I don't want them sharing embarrassing little snippets
from my childhood with Luke—though I guess it's too
late for that. He probably knows most of them anyway.
I'm going to start in order of age and work through.
And we're talking age in terms of emotional develop-
ment with regard to their sister, so that would be tod-
dler to infant—Nacho through Ruiz.

Nacho—I hope this doesn't come as a shock to you, but life
has come full circle for me here in Cornwall and Luke and I
have fallen in love. Your blessing means everything to me.
You mean everything to me. And if I haven't shown my love
for you in the past, please forgive me. Yours, Lucia.

Lucia—I couldn't be happier. Horse saddled and waiting.
Talk again soon—Nacho.

Diego—You are my inspiration. You have proved that however difficult you make it for someone to love you—and, boy,
have you and I made it difficult—there are some stubborn

people out there who can see something in us that no one else can. Luke sees something in me. Perhaps I should introduce him to Maxie? Seems they've both got what it takes to tame an Acosta.

Maxie here, babe. So thrilled for you. I *love* Luke. Will tell Diego as soon as he comes off the polo field. Let me know if there's anything I can do—anything at all…maybe plan a wedding?

Kruz—Don't start, okay? So you won't want to hear this, but it's about time you and I were back in touch, don't you think? I'm in love. With Luke. Luke Forster. And if you even *think* of telling him about the time when I ate dog food as a dare, you are *so* dead.

The Luke? Does that mean the Enforcer will be playing less polo? If Luke's still on Nero's team and playing against us, that can only be a good thing—no? Kruz.

Ruiz—No one pushed the boundaries more than you, so I wouldn't want you thinking it might be amusing to tell the man I love about the time I had to be hosed down from the roof after an argument with Nacho. Or the day I reported him to the police for confiscating my gum.

Sorry, Luce—you can guess where Ruiz is. Do you need the services of an agony aunt, or is that just me? Oops. Forgot. I *am* an agony aunt.
Love you, Luce. Whatever you want is what I want for you. And if I can do anything for you at any time you only have to ask. Xoxoxo

OKAY, so admittedly some of those responses weren't exactly what she had hoped for. It seemed the world went on turning and the only thing that had changed was how she and Luke felt about each other. Polo men were difficult, she thought, glancing at him.

Had anyone said this would be easy?

As their love affair progressed things moved fast towards the forthcoming party and the high-profile polo match on the beach. To draw the crowds Luke had arranged for several top international polo players to attend. He would head one team, while Lucia's notorious brother Nacho would head the other. Luke's parents were also expected to attend. The Fearsome Forsters, as Lucia had used to think of them when she was a child. Daddy Forster was a self-confessed stiff-backed son of old money, while Luke's mother was so posh she'd make a queen look common.

Wanting to make sure she had everything covered, Lucia had called a meeting in the cosy kitchen for a final chat-through.

'I'll leave you two to get on with things,' Margaret said when the meeting was over. She sensed love in the air, and Margaret's blue eyes were sparkling with suppressed excitement.

It seemed all her ghosts had been laid to rest, Lucia reflected as Luke reached for her hand. She had no worries about her brothers coming to Cornwall to spirit her back to Argentina, where she'd resume Cinderella duties at the ranch. Luke would never put up with it, and she had moved way past that.

Margaret stopped by the door on her way out of the room. 'There goes the old caravan,' she said, reminding them that Luke had arranged for brand-new lodges to be raised on proper foundations in the holiday park. 'I have fond memories of that caravan,' she mused as it trundled past the window.

Lucia hardly dared raise her eyes to Luke's.

If she had one worry now it was the thought of Luke's parents attending the party. Mr and Mrs Forster idolised their only son, and Lucia couldn't imagine that anyone would ever be good enough in their eyes for Luke.

As if sensing her concern, Luke put his arm around her shoulders. 'Stop worrying,' he said. 'You've got everything covered. It's going to be fine.'

Was it? Then why was she feeling a niggle of unease?

Later that day Luke was in the stables while Lucia was standing with Grace outside the guest house, waiting for the Argentinian polo circus to arrive. Grace was still working at the club, but now Lucia had left she felt guilty at leaving her friend behind. She hoped they could always be friends, and she'd thought this would be a great opportunity for Grace to meet the rest of Lucia's family, about whom Grace had heard so much.

'This is something no woman should miss,' Lucia confided wryly as the first vehicles driven by her brothers and their entourage crested the brow of the hill.

'You're not kidding!' Grace exclaimed as the parade of vehicles came closer. 'Who *is* that incredible-looking man?'

'Which one?' Lucia intoned in a mock-weary tone. She was used to fending off questions about her brothers.

'That big one with the wild black hair and tattoos.'

'I'm afraid you're going to have to be a little more specific…'

'And an earring. Oh, my goodness,' Grace breathed, clutching her chest. 'He's *totally* sex on legs.'

'I'm afraid I'm no closer,' Lucia admitted. 'I have four brothers, all with dark hair and tattoos, and at least a couple of them wear earrings. Brigands are in vogue this year, I'm told,' she added dryly.

'The one leaning out of the window of that black tank on

wheels.' Grace clutched her arm. 'Lucia—he's looking at me like he can see right through my clothes.'

'Nacho, you wretch!' Lucia exclaimed as the beast of an SUV slowed to a halt beside them. 'Do you have nothing better to do than terrorise my friends?'

'Just looking,' Nacho said without apology but with a wolfish smile. 'Nice friend…' And with one last appraisal Nacho pushed the sunglasses back up his nose and closed the window.

If only everything in life could go so as smoothly as this, Lucia thought later, hoping those would never be classed as 'famous last words' as she spotted Grace and Nacho chatting to each other in the yard.

Nacho towered over Grace, who was quite tall herself, and Lucia's typically taciturn brother seemed unusually animated today. With a smile she hurried on to make sure everything was ready inside the guest house for Luke's parents.

The Forsters arrived about an hour later, with an entourage of their own, and Lucia was hugely relieved when both Luke's father and mother declared themselves charmed by the guest house.

Well, that was two discerning families satisfied, she concluded, as Nacho added his praise to theirs.

'The Sundowner is even better than I remember,' Luke's mother was assuring Margaret. 'Always so quaint. And now *so* of the moment…'

Margaret looked blankly at Lucia.

'Thank you,' Lucia said brightly, stepping in.

'And Margaret tells me *you* were the driving force behind the restoration of the guest house?' Luke's mother commented, sizing Lucia up.

It was some time since they'd seen each other, Lucia reassured herself as she explained that putting the Sundowner back on the map had been a team effort. 'We all played our part,' she said pleasantly.

'With Luke's money...'

A million responses flashed through Lucia's head, but she countered the comment with a welcoming smile. 'Can I show you to your room, Mrs Forster? I'm sure you must be tired after your journey and keen to freshen up?'

Round one to the wild Acosta, Luke's amused eyes reassured Lucia. They both knew that at one time Lucia might have retaliated rather differently to his mother's not so veiled observation that Lucia might have been a pleasant enough fellow guest at the Sundowner all those years back, but that she was under suspicion in her new role as Luke's business partner.

'Lucia and Luke working together...' Luke's father murmured, hanging back to share an amused and kindly smile with Lucia. 'Do you two have anything else to tell me?'

'Like that we've stopped fighting?' Lucia suggested.

'I was thinking of something more interesting than that.'

'I'm sure you'll love the suite I've chosen for you,' Lucia said quickly. 'It has a marvellous view of the sea.'

'And you, my dear, are more diplomatic than you were as a child.'

Lucia flashed a glance at Luke on her way out of the room. She knew she would never fit the mould and be stamped 'Approved' when Luke's father barely approved of his own son, and Luke's mother didn't approve of anyone. But what Luke thought was the only thing that mattered, Lucia reassured herself as Luke's hand brushed her arm in a brief show of support as she left the room.

He had arranged everything to the second, so that nothing went wrong. He had the ring in his pocket and he was going to wait until the party on the beach was in full swing and no one would notice if he had a very special private moment with Lucia. The match had created an incredible buzz, which was still reverberating through the crowd. The night was warm, the moon was shining, and a top band was setting the mood with sexy South American music.

Now all he needed was Lucia, who had gone to change out of her work clothes so she could enjoy the party.

Margaret was going to mount the stage first to thank everyone for coming. Luke would speak next.

Once that was done he would find Lucia. Guessing romance had never figured very highly in Lucia's life—mainly because of her fear that her brothers would laugh at her—he wanted to do something special for her. Something that didn't involve her brothers looking over her shoulder.

Grace had helped her to choose a dress for the party, which had involved a lengthy shopping trip to the nearest town.

'Instead of hiding your voluptuous figure, you should celebrate it,' Grace had pronounced.

So instead of a dress with a yoke and enough material in the skirt for a second marquee, Lucia was wearing a red off-the-shoulder number that clung lovingly to every curve.

'You look sensational,' Grace breathed in awe when Lucia had finished her make-up. 'Your hair's glorious.'

'Luke's never seen me dressed in anything but dungarees, jeans or a suit,' she said, craning her neck to examine her rear view. *Or naked*, she silently amended.

'You look fabulous,' Grace assured her. 'You only have to see the way Luke looks at you to know that he thinks so too.'

'I just hope his mother doesn't think I look too tarty.'

'The only problem you've got is that his father's tongue will be dragging on the floor.' Grace stopped as they both glanced out of Lucia's bedroom window to see Lucia's brothers sauntering into the courtyard.

'When you grow up with that bunch it's enough to give any-one an inferiority complex,' Lucia explained wryly as Grace groaned softly at the sight of Nacho spearheading the group.

Lucia laughed. 'It's time to pick *your* tongue off the floor, I think.'

'You're right,' Grace agreed, turning away from the window. 'We've got a party to go to.'

If only she hadn't overheard that conversation between Luke's parents as she passed their room she might have been able to face the evening with all the new-found confidence that restoring the guest house and being with Luke had given her. Well...it certainly explained the sense of doom that had been dogging her, Lucia accepted as Grace hurried on ahead.

'If only she weren't one of those wretched Acostas, Donald,' Luke's mother had been saying. 'They're such a wild bunch. It's hard enough coming to terms with the fact that Luke and Lucia are working together on this tiny project, but to have Luke tell you that he has fallen in *love* with her...'

There had been a pause here, doubtless for a shocked ex-pression.

'Why couldn't Luke pick a nice, refined girl from the coun-try club?'

Yes. Why couldn't he? Lucia had wondered, not waiting to hear Luke's father's reply.

From the reflection she caught sight of in the mirror as she passed the door to the Forsters' suite now, Luke's mother was, as always, immaculately groomed, while Lucia felt more of a mess than ever. She'd styled her hair hastily, and it was al-ready falling down. She worried again that her dress was too sexy—it certainly wasn't something she could imagine any of the girls from the country club wearing. For a moment she felt sick at the thought of seeing Luke again.

'Lucia.'

She glanced up to see Luke's father coming down the stairs.

'You go ahead,' she told Grace. Lucia was managing the guest house now. She could hardly turn and flee at the first sign of trouble. 'Is there anything you need?' she asked Luke's father with concern.

'The suite is perfection—just a word or two, if you have the time…?'

'I've always got time for you,' Lucia said, remembering that the formidable Forster papa had been a good friend of her equally formidable father.

'I just wanted you to know, Lucia, how pleased I am.'

'I'm so glad you like the room—'

'I'm just trying to say, in my clumsy way,' Luke's father interrupted, 'how pleased I am that you have brought Luke out of himself, reminding him of a time when he was truly happy. By doing that you have stopped him becoming obsessive about business. At least that's what I think—and what Margaret tells me. She says she's never seen either of you so happy.'

'Working together has been surprisingly good,' Lucia admitted carefully.

'There's more to life than work, Lucia,' Luke's father said gently, 'as I'm always telling my son. Margaret says you have been through the mill, but now you're smiling again.'

'It *has* helped being here,' she admitted.

'You can't shy away from your feelings here—even if they hurt like hell,' Donald Forster observed shrewdly.

Luke's father must be hurting too, Lucia realised as she watched his face grow sad. 'I know you and my father were very close.'

'He was one of my dearest friends,' Luke's father confirmed. 'And it isn't easy for a man to make a friend. But it must have been hard for you to begin with, coming back here, Lucia?'

'Cathartic too,' she admitted.

'For me also,' Donald Forster admitted quietly. 'Anyway,'

he said, bringing her back to the present, 'I know we Forsters must seem a bit lofty sometimes, but I just wanted you to know that I'm glad you and Luke have found each other again. There is a sort of symmetry to it, don't you think?'

Was that a declaration of acceptance? Lucia wondered. Or had Donald Forster heard her hurrying past the open door to his suite earlier? Something in those kindly eyes said he had. But would Luke's mother ever be reconciled when Lucia was patently not the kind of daughter-in-law she had in mind?

She was wrong for Luke, and wrong for his family, and the last thing Lucia wanted was to buy her happiness at the expense of anyone else's.

CHAPTER SIXTEEN

Get a non-polo playing man
It seems fate has other ideas.

I might be forgiven for wondering if there is any other type of man. Even Luke's father was mounted on one of the quieter ponies for a brief canter round the field. And Luke has always been The Only Man. Even at age four-teen, when I first wrote the list, I only added 'non-polo-playing' because Luke had less and less time for me. As polo took over his life Luke could only be bothered to shoot me threatening looks and gallop on. Threatening what? I used to wonder. Well, now I know. Oh, boy, do I know...

So that 'non-polo-playing man' will just have to find some other girl to woo, because I'm hooked on tail shots, tackle and flying hooves.

THE party had started without a hitch and was still going strong. He was so proud of Lucia. All she had needed was a chance to shine in her own right, away from the glare of her four domineering brothers. Even Lucia's sister-in-law Maxie, who was a bona fide party-planner, had made a point of com-ing up to him to say what a fabulous party Lucia had arranged.

His glance swept the beach, and then the lasers flashing on a stage where a rock band was in full swing. All age-groups were represented beneath banners proclaiming, 'THE SUNDOWNER'S BACK!' and Margaret was in the centre of the dance floor, dancing with the local farmer.

Luke patted the ring box in his pocket, just to check. Tonight was the pinnacle of the lifetime he had spent loving Lucia. He turned to see her picking her way down the cliff path with her shoes in her hand.

'Luke.'

She felt limp with fatigue when he took her in his arms. 'You must be tired,' he murmured, stroking her hair. 'Must you stay much longer?'

'Until the last person goes,' she said, lifting her chin.

'Has something upset you?' He was surprised by the detached note in her voice.

'Someone,' she said, moving back.

'Who?' he demanded frowning.

'Me,' she said, already heading for the rock pool.

Kneeling down by the edge of the water, she seemed oblivious to the fact that her pretty party dress was soaking up the brine. Swirling her fingers across the smooth surface, she shattered the ribbon of moonlight shimmering on the cool surface. 'What have you told your father about us?'

'That I love you and want us to be together when this project is finished.'

'And your mother? What does she think about it?'

'What does my mother have to do with it?' He frowned.

'Quite a lot, I would think,' she said, still refusing to look at him.

Doubt coursed through him. 'Don't you want us to be together?'

'Are you really serious about it, Luke?'

'Of course. Why shouldn't I be?' His frown deepened. 'I would have thought that was obvious.'

'Well, not to me it isn't. I only know that I love you and want to be with you.'

'You must know what your mother thinks of my family.'

He swore softly under his breath. 'I know my mother's secretly thrilled to be here,' he argued. 'Danger is forbidden at the country club, which makes it irresistible. Whatever she might say for effect, just being here is a great feather in my mother's cap—'

'Rubbing shoulders with my four dangerous brothers?' Lucia interrupted.

'With your very glamorous and intriguing brothers,' Luke corrected her. 'That's how my mother will see it, I'm sure. And, more importantly, how her friends at the country club will see it. They'll be green with envy, and she will revel in that fact—'

'And me?'

'You're the only woman I want, Lucia.'

'You're sure you wouldn't rather have some chic blonde from the country club?'

Dragging her into his arms, Luke cupped her face so she was forced to look at him. 'How can you have doubts when I adore you?'

'Because I overheard your mother saying something to your father...'

She said this in her usual frank way, but her eyes were swimming with tears of hurt, and his heart went out to her for all the things he had taken for granted and which Lucia, growing up in a family ruled by her brothers, had never known.

'If your mother was here to advise you, she would tell you that some mothers find it impossible to think of another woman in their son's life. It doesn't mean my mother likes you any less. It means she feels threatened by you. It's up to both of us to help her realise that my loving you doesn't change my love for her.'

'But will I ever fit in with your high-tone lifestyle?'

Luke laughed. 'I don't think you know *how* I live. And why would you want to "fit in", as you put it, when you're gloriously unique and everyone envies you your originality? And fit into *what*, Lucia? I have my own life. My own house— houses,' Luke admitted wryly. 'And I don't want you to *fit* into my life. You have your own life, and I would never try to cage you—though I must admit you are a little wild sometimes, and could certainly do with some taming.'

To prove the point he drew her close and they exchanged a look that set both their senses soaring.

'Not here…not now,' she murmured reluctantly.

'But later,' Luke promised. 'Nothing means more to me than you, Lucia. You can believe that, or you can believe something you overheard outside a door.'

'A door left conveniently open.'

'If my mother did go to such fiendish lengths to drive you away I'll take it as a measure of her love for me. And since when have you been so easily put off? Aren't I worth fighting for?' he demanded.

'Pistols for two—coffee for one?' she suggested, starting to smile again.

'I should think my mother would be only too happy to take you on at hairbrush-fencing.'

'Which reminds me,' she said, reaching up to lace her fingers through his hair, 'I still expect you to brush my hair, as promised when you bought me that beautiful hairbrush.'

'I'll add it to my already exhaustive agenda,' he promised, though he was more interested in kissing her right now. 'I must be mad,' he conceded when they finally parted. 'Perhaps my mother's right and I *should* beware of the wild Acostas— especially as you're the only woman I've been tempted to go shopping for. Everyone else—including my mother,' he admitted, 'gets something chosen with care, courtesy of my very considerate PA.' He reached in his pocket for the antique silver filigree ring box. 'But I bought *this* for you myself.'

'Two shopping trips? What's brought this on, Luke? Are you sickening for a fever?'

'I hope you like it,' he said.

'Luke, it's beautiful,' she gasped, stroking the finely worked box with her fingertip. 'You have to stop doing this.'

'But not yet,' he said. 'Well…aren't you going to open it?'

As understanding crept into her eyes he added, 'I'd live with you in that beat-up caravan, Lucia, and teach kids to ride if that's what it took for us to be together.'

'Luke—'

'Don't look for problems,' he said, meeting her gaze. 'Look at the ring and then tell me if you like it.'

He had grounds to be confident, and as Lucia opened the lid and gazed at the ring, and then at him, he thought the past, the present and the future rested in the look she gave him.

There was silence, and then the tears came. 'This was my mother's ring,' she breathed, staring at the pretty Victorian love band studded with seed pearls and diamonds.

Nacho had told him the story of Lucia's mother spotting the ring in a jeweller's store when she had been walking down the high street in the nearby town with Lucia's father. When she had commented on how pretty it was Lucia's father had bought it for her.

'I spoke to Nacho—obviously,' he told her. 'Nacho was your guardian while you were still a minor, so I felt it my duty to tell him about my intentions.'

'Your intentions?' Lucia was sure her whole world had just tipped on its axis. 'Luke, will you stop with the formal stuff for a moment? Are you proposing to me?'

'I might be,' he said, giving her one of his looks.

'Well, either you are or you aren't.'

Luke merely raised a brow.

'You can't joke about something like this, Luke.'

'Me? Joking? You demanding a serious approach? You're right, Lucia. What is the world coming to?'

'Stop it,' she said, but without much force. She couldn't get too het up when she could hardly breathe because her heart was beating so fast. 'You actually asked Nacho if you could marry me?'

'I did,' Luke confirmed.

She half expected thunderclaps to rend the air and a screeching Mrs Forster to make her entrance on a rocket-powered broomstick. But instead the waves lapped gently at their feet and Luke looked more certain than she had ever seen him—and Luke Forster was hardly noted for his indecision.

'I asked Nacho because that was the right thing to do, and I told my parents because I love them.'

'And they were…?'

'Relieved that I had finally found someone like you,' Luke cut in as Lucia frowned with concern. 'Someone real—someone with a bit of spark about her, as my father put it.'

'And your mother?'

'My mother couldn't wait to get on the phone to her friends.' Luke's lips tugged wickedly. 'According to my father they're the toast of the country club, and my mother's friends are green with envy, as I predicted. Are you pleased with the ring?' he added gently. 'I know your mother would want you to wear it.'

'She adored you,' Lucia murmured, feeling there was still some hidden power connecting her to her mother as she studied the ring. And as for Luke giving her the ring here on this beach, where they had shared so many happy memories— it was like a blessing on their future lives together. 'Luke Forster!' she exclaimed as Luke went down on one knee in front of her. 'Are you really doing what I think you're doing?'

'Either that or my legs have given way,' Luke said dryly. 'So, what's your answer, Lucia? Will you marry me?'

Lucia came to kneel on the damp sand in front of him and, leaning forward so their brows touched, she put her hands over his and said simply, 'I will.'

Luke kept his room at the Grand, while Lucia stayed at the guest house to help Margaret recruit more staff. They had decided that while Luke would run the family business and the charitable foundation they would form a joint venture company to handle their burgeoning interests in the hotel industry.

'Everything dovetails neatly,' Lucia told Luke as she showed him the schedule she'd drawn up to take them hectically towards Christmas and the wedding they were planning to hold at the *estancia* in Argentina.

'That's a pretty tight schedule, Mrs Luke Donald Forster the Third-to-be,' Luke observed.

'Don't you dare,' Lucia warned, flinging a cushion with deadly accuracy. 'I'm not having my rampaging polo player turning into a stuffed shirt.'

'Would you rather I took the shirt off?'

'Is that a serious question? More importantly, is there time?'

'Margaret's in town,' he growled, freeing the buttons on her blouse.

'How am I supposed to concentrate on work?'

'You're not. I'll do all the work.'

'What are you doing?' she protested breathlessly as he lifted her.

'If you don't know now…'

'And what if Margaret walks in?'

'She'll walk out again.'

Breath shot from Lucia's lungs as Luke positioned her quite expertly on the sofa. 'Are you taking advantage of me?'

'This is a guest house, isn't it? I'm looking for some old-style hospitality.'

'I'm not sure I can accommodate you at such short notice.'

Luke laughed wickedly. 'Past experience says you can…'

EPILOGUE

ROCK! MAGAZINE REVIEWS OF THE YEAR,
by your roving reporter, Holly Acosta

ALL'S WELL THAT ENDS WELL
The rumours are true. The whirlwind romance between Lucia Acosta, one of the wild, untameable Acostas, and Luke Forster, scion of East Coast society, is to end in a fairytale wedding on an estancia the size of a small country, ruled over by deliciously dangerous men.

No one can accuse Luke Forster of not living up to his nickname on the polo field—the Enforcer has insisted that wedding invitations include the note: No muddy boots. No spurs. No curb bridles on spirited ponies. At least not in public!

Needless to say invitations to the wedding are highly sought-after, and with only Nacho and Kruz Acosta untamed, ladies, the race is on!

'THE *estancia* has never looked lovelier,' Lucia exclaimed as Luke drove between the wonderfully familiar gates before parking outside the sprawling house. It was the best time of year for the gardens, and the courtyard was a riot of colour. The dogs were snuffling around—a little older, but just as excited to see her—while contented cats snoozed the sunny day away beneath the shade of vine-covered canopies. 'It's the perfect season to get married.'

'Any time's good for me,' Luke observed beneath his breath. 'I couldn't care less if it's freezing cold so long as I can get you into a hot bed,' he added, holding Lucia's gaze as he lifted her down and swung her around before lowering her to the ground.

'I've always dreamed of getting married here to the man I love.' She sighed, adding with a cheeky smile, 'You're lucky I invited *you* along.'

'It wouldn't be much of a wedding night without me.' Luke gave her one of his dark looks. 'I'm going to leave you to it,' he said, as Nacho's housekeepers, Maria and Concepción, bustled out of the house to greet them.

'Let me guess,' Lucia said. 'Stables. Horses. Brothers.'

'But not necessarily in that order,' Luke agreed. 'See you at the wedding, Lucia.'

'Hey, wait.'

Dream on. This was all happening way too fast. Luke had told her he was going to stay in the *estancia* guest house until the wedding night, but she hadn't believed him. Luke knew exactly what he was doing, Lucia realised as he disappeared out of sight. Luke had demonstrated quite convincingly, on so many occasions, that delay increased pleasure, and now he was out to prove by just how much.

Lucia's friends had gathered to help her celebrate her marriage to Luke. Grace from the club was to be her chief bridesmaid. The girls had just laced Lucia into her wedding gown, and now Grace handed her the exquisite bridal bouquet, composed of white peonies, ivory roses and dainty cream orchids with a deeper, clotted cream centre, all set off by clusters of delicate lime-green Lady's Mantle, which had been the inspired suggestion of Luke's mother.

'Hello…? Can I come in?' Donald Forster poked his head around the door. 'I hope I'm not interrupting anything important?' he said, looking round. 'I had the word that you were almost ready.' He beamed at Lucia's friends.

'You know I've always got time for you,' she said, drawing her father-in-law-to-be into the room.

'You look beautiful,' Donald exclaimed when they had exchanged kisses on the cheek. 'My son's a very lucky man, and I hope you won't think it impertinent of me if I give you a token of his parents' love, to show how pleased we are that you're joining our family. You're making Luke happier than I have ever seen him,' he added, when Lucia's pleasure showed. 'It used to be all business and polo for Luke, but now he's encouraging me to ride out with him again. He even told his mother she looked lovely today. As if Luke has ever paused long enough to notice *that*. I don't know what you've done to him, Lucia, but whatever it is, long may it continue. Now…' Donald continued, delving into the breast pocket of his jacket. 'Every bride should have something old, something new, something borrowed and something blue—or so my wife tells me. So she took me shopping today.'

Lucia had to be careful not to smile at the expression on Donald Forster's face. He gave the impression that shopping was some mysterious rite most safely avoided by long stints on the golf course.

'We decided to buy you something new,' he went on. 'My wife said this gift will remind you how to deal with a wild polo-playing man. As if you need any help in that direction.'

Lucia could only stare in surprise at the small jewel case.

'You'll have to get used to being spoiled, my dear. I don't expect you've had much of that since your parents died, but Luke's mother and I will take great pleasure in spoiling the daughter we never had.'

Lucia paused, and then flipped the catch. Her friends had gathered round to see, and after the gasps came laughter.

'You are the best parents-in-law a girl could have,' Lucia said, giving the girls a closer look at the perfectly formed miniature diamond spurs. 'Thank you. Thank you both so much,' she said, brushing a kiss against Donald's taut tanned cheek. 'I shall think of you every time I wear my spurs,' she promised him—though not every time she handled her wild polo-playing man, Lucia silently amended.

'You were worth the wait,' Luke assured Lucia as he freed the cravat from his neck. Flinging it onto a chair, he opened a couple of buttons at the neck of his shirt.

They were safe in the glorious bridal suite, where the floor was covered with fragrant rose petals, thanks to Maria and Concepción, egged on by Margaret. The evening party was still in full swing, and would carry on through the night... with or without their company. Without, being Luke's choice. Lucia's too.

'You're worth waiting for too,' Lucia managed unsteadily, her breath coming faster as she leaned back against the wall to survey her new husband. 'Are you going to take your jacket off and make yourself even more comfortable?'

'What about you?' Luke said, prowling closer.

'I asked first.' Reaching up, she checked the diamond spurs glittering in her hair. *Start as you mean to go on, Señora Forster*, she silently advised herself.

'It's nice to see my mother has retained her sense of humour,' Luke observed, his keen stare following Lucia's gesture.

'Everyone has a different recipe for a good relationship,' Lucia teased him, dodging out of reach when he tried to catch hold of her.

Luke's eyes narrowed as he closed her down. 'Are you avoiding me or luring me on?'

'Which do you think?' she said. 'Perhaps I like to be chased.'

She screamed as Luke boxed her in. Thankfully he was a lot faster than she was, and soon had her pinned securely against the wall.

'Hmm,' he murmured, plucking the spurs out of her hair. Several hairpins followed, and Lucia's hair cascaded down past her waist in an inky-black cloud. 'You are seriously over-dressed for the type of hunting I've got in mind,' Luke observed in the stern voice she loved.

'Why don't you undress me?' she suggested.

Moving her hair aside, she turned to present the back of her securely laced gown, which Luke unthreaded, whipping each lace free of its confinement with the skill of a gaucho. She was trembling with anticipation by the time the cool silk pooled around her ankles.

'You're certainly dressed for the occasion now,' he remarked.

She should be. The bridal gown had the most brilliant corset built in, so she was naked underneath—other than for the blue lace garter her bridesmaids had insisted she must wear.

'Aren't you supposed to take it off with your teeth?' she challenged, balancing her foot on the seat of a chair.

'If I must…'

The garter was duly removed.

'And now it's your turn,' she said.

Luke slid off his jacket.

'And now your shirt,' she said, settling down on the bed to watch him.

Tugging his shirt off, Luke tossed it aside.

'Undo your belt.' Her mouth was dry, Lucia realised. 'Pull

down your zipper. And now your shoes. Apologies...your cowboy boots.'

Luke kicked them off.

'*Off,*' she instructed, lazing back on the pillows as Luke toyed with the waistband of his boxers. 'Nice,' she murmured appreciatively.

'Anything else?' Luke's lips tugged wickedly as he slid them down.

'Not unless there's a teeny-weeny you hiding inside the most magnificent body suit I've ever seen.' Making a circular motion with her hand she encouraged Luke to turn around. 'Perfect sex-slave material... You're hired.'

'Come here,' Luke murmured, his amber eyes dark and watchful.

'*You* come here,' she argued, reclining on the bed.

Luke shook his head. 'The bed's for when you get tired.'

'And in the meantime...?'

'You'll have to come here if you want to find out...'

The space between them vibrated with sexual energy, encouraged by the deep bass notes of a samba throbbing from the dance floor below. Slipping off the bed, she padded across the rose petals, crushing them so that their scent rose in the erotically charged air.

'You've made me wait too long,' she complained, lifting her arms to rest her hands on Luke's shoulders.

'Not nearly long enough,' he argued, teasing her as he dropped kisses on her neck.

But she forgave him when, lifting her, Luke flexed his knees and took her firmly. She fell at once, calling out his name and clinging to him as he held her safe in his powerful arms while she bucked uncontrollably.

'Was that good?' he mocked against her mouth when she had quietened.

'When I can breathe again I'll tell you,' she gasped, but

Luke gave her no chance to recover, and nothing more to do other than lock her arms around his neck as he took her smoothly and rhythmically to the edge of pleasure and beyond—not once, but several times.

'Shall we take this to the bed?' he said finally.

'If you're tired,' she teased him.

'I'm not in the least bit tired,' Luke assured her. 'I was thinking of you.'

'Anywhere, any way, any time,' she whispered.

Hours later it was dawn, and the house was quiet when she told him her news. 'I'm going to have a baby,' she whispered.

Luke stirred, and then lifted himself on one elbow to stare down at her. 'How can you possibly know?' he said.

'I know—that's all.'

'And how long have you known?' he persisted.

'About five minutes. Didn't I tell you that all Cornishwomen have magic powers?'

'You're only half-Cornish,' Luke pointed out.

'And the half that's Cornish is my witchy self,' she said, smiling. 'We're going to have a little girl, and we're going to call her Demelza.'

Luke shook his head, murmuring to no one in particular, 'I can't pretend I didn't know what I was getting into.' But then his amber gaze darkened into concern. 'Are you sure, Lucia? I don't want you to be disappointed.'

'I won't be disappointed,' she said confidently. 'In nine months' time you'll be holding our child in your arms. I can already see her, Luke.'

'In your imagination,' Luke tempered patiently. 'And we all know about your imagination—don't we, Lucia?'

'I'm a changed woman,' she said. 'I'm merely stating a fact.'

'Remind me of that fact again in nine months' time,' Luke murmured, smiling as he reached for her. 'Any views on your brothers?' he teased her. 'It may have escaped your witchy notice, but only two are left unmarried—Nacho and Kruz.'

'I *do* have a view, as it happens,' she said, putting on a dreamy stare. 'Life is going to get a whole lot more exciting for all of us—especially Nacho.'

Luke scoffed. 'Now I *know* you're wrong. Nacho's a confirmed bachelor.'

'Is he?' Lucia said, as if she knew something different.

'Yes, he is,' Luke insisted. 'But let's get back to us. I've got unfinished plans for you...'

'I have plans for you,' she countered, mounting up. 'Now... Where are my spurs?'

* * * * *

THE EX WHO HIRED HER

BY
KATE HARDY

Kate Hardy lives in Norwich, in the east of England, with her husband, two young children, one bouncy spaniel and too many books to count! When she's not busy writing romance or researching local history, she helps out at her children's schools. She also loves cooking—spot the recipes sneaked into her books! (They're also on her website, along with extracts and stories behind the books.) Writing for Mills & Boon has been a dream come true for Kate—something she wanted to do ever since she was twelve. She says it's the best of both worlds, because she gets to learn lots of new things when she's researching the background to a book: add a touch of passion, drama and danger, a new gorgeous hero every time, and it's the perfect job!

Kate's always delighted to hear from readers, so do drop in to her website at www.katehardy.com.

For Lizzie Lamb and Jasper, with love.

CHAPTER ONE

XANDRA BENNETT.

Jordan would just bet she'd changed the spelling of her name, on the grounds that it made her sound more like a marketing hotshot than plain 'Sandra'. He just hoped there was enough substance to back up the style. Maybe there would be; the recruitment agency had obviously thought enough of her to ask Field's for a last-minute interview. Though, after an entire day listening to the bright and not-so-bright ideas of the people who were desperate to become the next marketing manager of Field's department store, Jordan wasn't really in the mood for someone who was all style and glitz.

Last one, he told himself. Last one, and then I can get on with my work.

His PA opened the door. 'Ms Bennett.'

And, as Xandra Bennett walked into his office, Jordan forgot how to breathe.

It was her.

Of all the department stores in all the towns in all the world, she walked into his.

Different name, different hair, and she'd clearly swapped her glasses for contact lenses, but it was definitely her. Alexandra Porter. His whole body tingled. Last time he'd seen her, she'd been eighteen, with mousy-brown hair that fell almost to her waist when he'd loosened it from its customary plait. And she'd worn clothing typical of a shy eighteen-year-old girl: scruffy trainers, nondescript jeans and baggy T-shirts that hid her curves.

Now, she looked every inch the marketing professional. A sharp, well-cut business suit that flattered her curves without making them look ostentatious; a sleek jaw-length bob with highlights so skilfully done that the copper and gold strands looked as though they'd been brought out naturally by the sun; and high-end designer heels that made her legs look as if they went on for ever.

And she still had a mouth that sent shivers through him.

He pushed the thought away. He didn't want to think about Alexandra Porter and her lush, generous mouth. The mouth he'd once taught how to kiss.

She masked it quickly, but he'd been watching her closely enough to see the shock on her face. She recognised him, too, and hadn't expected to see him here, either…or had she? He didn't trust her as far as he could drop his pen onto the desk. Back then she'd turned out to be a manipulative liar, and that wasn't the kind of personality trait that changed with age. Was Bennett the man she'd dumped him for? Or had she then dumped *him* as soon as she'd found someone else who could offer her more?

Maybe he should tell her that the position was already filled and he wasn't going to do any more interviews. Except that would mean explaining his reasons to his co-interviewers—explanations he'd rather not have to give.

Jordan Smith.

Alexandra felt sick to her stomach. He was the last person she'd expected to see. Ten years ago, she'd vowed never to have anything to do with him again. She'd never forgiven him for not being there when she'd needed him most. For lying to her. For letting her down. It had taken her years to rebuild her life; and now, just when her dreams were in reach, he was right in her way all over again.

The tall, slightly gangly student she'd known had filled out; he was far from being fat, but his shoulders were broader and his build more muscular. His mouth still had that sensual curve, promising pleasure—not that she wanted to remember how much pleasure his mouth was capable of giving.

The scruffy jeans and T-shirt he'd usually worn back then had been replaced by a designer suit and what looked like a handmade shirt and a silk tie. There was the faintest touch of silver at his temples—well, of course hair that dark would show the grey quickly. And he definitely had an air of authority. He'd grown into his looks; more than that, he'd grown into the kind of man who just had to breathe to have women falling at his feet.

As the CEO of Field's, Jordan Smith would have the final say over who got the job.

Which left her…where? On the reject pile, because she'd be a permanent reminder of his guilt—of the fact that he'd abandoned her when she was eighteen and pregnant with his baby? Or would he give her the job, even if she wasn't the best candidate, because he felt he owed it to her for wrecking her life all those years ago? And, if he did offer her the job, would she take it, knowing that she'd have to work with him?

The questions whizzed round her head. Then she realised that one of the panel had said something to her and was waiting for a reply. Oh, great. Now they'd think she had the attention span of a gnat and would be a complete liability rather than an asset to the firm. Bye, bye, new job. Well, she had nothing to lose now. She might as well treat this as a practice interview. Afterwards, instead of licking her wounds, she could analyse her performance and see where she needed to sharpen up, ready for the next interview.

'I'm so sorry. I'm afraid I didn't catch that,' she said, giving the older man an apologetic smile.

'I'm Harry Blake, the personnel manager,' he said, smiling back. 'This is Gina Davidson, the deputy store manager.' He paused for long enough to let Alexandra exchange a greeting and shake the deputy manager's hand. 'And this is Jordan Smith, the CEO.'

Jordan had to be a good twenty years younger than his colleagues. He was only thirty now. How had he made CEO of such a traditional company that fast?

Stupid question. Of course Jordan would be on the fast track, wherever he worked. He'd always been bright; his mind had attracted her teenage self just as much as his face. A man who could speak three other languages as fluently as his own; who knew all the European myths, not just the Greek and Roman ones; who knew Shakespeare even better than she did, back in the days when she still wanted to lecture on Renaissance drama. Dreams that had shattered and died, along with—

Alexandra pushed the thought away.

There was no way round it; she was going to have to be polite and shake his hand. She forced herself to keep her handshake brief, firm and businesslike and to ignore the tingles running along every nerve end as his skin touched hers. But then she made the mistake of looking into his eyes.

Midnight blue. Arresting. His eyes had caught her attention, the very first time she'd met him. Sweet seventeen and never been kissed. Until that night, when he'd seen beyond her image of the geeky girl with the mousy hair and glasses who didn't really fit in with everyone else at the party and had come over to talk to her. He'd danced with her. *Kissed her.*

She swallowed hard, and looked away, willing the memories to stay back.

She couldn't meet his eyes, Jordan noticed. Guilt? Not that it mattered, because as far as he was concerned she wasn't getting this job. No way was she going to be back into his life, not even in a work capacity. He'd get through this interview, and then he'd never have to set eyes on her again.

As the personnel manager, Harry was officially the one conducting the interview, so Jordan sat back and listened to him take Alexandra through the same questions he'd asked the others. Her answers were pretty much as he expected, so he glanced through her CV again. And then something stood out at him. The date she'd given for her A levels was three years after the date he remembered her being due to take them. Why? She'd been a straight-A student, the last person he'd expect to fail her exams.

Had the guilt of what she'd done finally hit her in the middle of her exams, so she'd messed them up? But, in that case, why had it taken her three years to retake them? And she didn't have the English degree he'd expected, either. She'd planned to become a lecturer, so why was she working in business instead of in an academic role?

He shook himself. It was none of his business, and he didn't want to know the answers.

He *really* didn't.

'Any questions?' Harry asked his colleagues.

Gina smiled. 'Not at this stage.'

And here was Jordan's opportunity to show everyone that Xandra Bennett was completely unsuitable. 'We did ask all the other candidates to prepare a presentation on how to take Field's forward,' he pointed out.

'But the agency added Xandra to the list at the very last minute,' Harry said, with a slight frown at Jordan. 'So it wouldn't be fair to expect her to give a presentation.'

'Not a formal presentation, of course,' Jordan agreed. 'But I do expect my senior staff to be able to think on their feet. So we'd like to hear your ideas, Ms Bennett. How would you see us taking Field's forward?'

Her eyes widened for a moment; she clearly knew that he was challenging her. And it was obvious that she also knew he was expecting her to fail.

Then she lifted her chin and gave him an absolutely glittering smile. The professional equivalent of making an extremely rude hand gesture. 'Of course, Mr Smith. Obviously, if this were a real situation, the first thing I'd ask is what the budget and the timescales are.'

She was the first person that day to mention budgets and timescales; the other candidates had just assumed. And some of them had assumed much more money than was available, talking about putting on TV spots in prime-time viewing. Completely unrealistic.

'And secondly I'd ask what you meant by taking Field's forward. Are you looking to attract a different customer base without losing the loyalty of your existing customers? Or do you want to offer your existing customers more services so they buy everything from Field's, rather than buy certain products and services from another supplier?'

Both Harry and Gina were sitting up a little straighter, clearly interested. She'd gone straight to the heart of their dilemma.

'What do you think?' Jordan asked.

'I'd start by doing an audit of your customers. Who they are, what they want, and what Field's isn't offering them now. And I'd talk to your staff. Do you have a staff suggestion scheme?'

'We used to,' Gina said.

'I'd reinstate it,' Alexandra said. 'Your staff know their products and their customers. They know what sells, what the seasonal trends are, and what their customers are looking for. They're the ones who are going to come up with the best suggestions for taking Field's forward—and I'd say that your marketing manager's job is to evaluate those suggestions, cost them, and work out which ones are going to have the most impact on sales.'

'Do you buy from us, Ms P—' Jordan had to correct himself swiftly '—Bennett?'

'No, I don't.'

That surprised him. He'd been so sure she'd claim to shop here all the time. She wasn't planning to curry favour that way, then. 'Why not?'

'Because as far as I can tell your range of clothes isn't targeted at my age group, the pharmacy chains have much better deals than you do on the perfume and make-up I buy, and I'm not in the market for fine crystal, silverware and porcelain dinner services,' she said.

Wow. She was the first of their candidates to criticise the store. And he could see that she'd taken Harry and Gina's breath away, too. 'So Field's is too traditional for you?' He couldn't resist needling her.

'Field's has one hundred and five years of tradition to look back on,' she said. 'Which should be a strength; being around for a long time shows your customers that they can rely on you. But it's also a weakness, because younger customers are going to see Field's as old-fashioned. As far as they're concerned, you sell nothing they'd be interested in. This is where their parents shop. Or even their grandparents. And you need to counteract that opinion.'

'So how would you raise their interest?' And, heaven help him, she'd already raised his own interest. Her com-

ments were the best thing he'd heard all day. Her criti-
cisms were completely constructive and she'd given solid
reasons for her views. Reasons that he'd been thinking of,
himself.

'Taking myself as a prospective customer—if you
tempted me into the store by, say, a pop-up shop showcasing a hot new make-up brand I'm interested in, and
you set it up next to my favourite designer's ready-to-
wear range, then I'd realise that maybe I'd got the wrong
idea about Field's. I'd be tempted to look around the store.
If you sell what I want, at the right price, and your store
loyalty scheme's good enough to tempt me away from my
current supplier, then you'll get my business.'

He really couldn't fault that.

'And I'd also take a look at your online presence. Your
website needs to be dynamic and involved with social
media. Do you have an online community?'

'Not at the moment,' Gina said. 'How would you see
one working?'

That was the moment that Alexandra really lit up.
Suddenly she was shining, full of enthusiasm and bringing everyone along with her. 'Forums, hosted maybe by se-
lected members of staff. Not all the time, just five minutes
now and then. You could invite customers to be an expert
in their field and share their tips. And you definitely need
a plan for taking advantage of new media, if you're looking to attract a younger audience. Look at how they use
social media and mobile media, and how you could make
that work for Field's.' She rattled off a few examples—all
practical ones.

Jordan glanced at her CV again. In her last job, she'd
been responsible for online marketing, so she knew exactly what she was talking about. He made a mental note

to look up her old company's website to see what she'd done there.

'Thank you, Ms Bennett. No further questions from me,' he said.

'Are there any questions you'd like to ask us?' Harry asked.

'Not at this stage,' Alexandra said with a smile. A polite smile, Jordan noticed, rather than a triumphant one; she clearly wasn't taking it for granted that her interview had gained her a ticket to the next round.

'Then thank you, Ms Bennett,' Gina said. 'If you'd like to wait outside for a couple of minutes?'

Jordan was aware of every single step Alexandra took as she crossed to the door. And, although he tried hard not to look, he couldn't help himself. Ten years ago, she'd been sweet and shy, her beauty hidden away; now, she was polished and confident, and any man with red blood in his veins would stand up a little straighter and try to catch her eye. He hated the fact that she could still make him react physically; so it was just as well he wouldn't have to see her again. Working with her would drive him crazy.

'She's by far and away the best of the bunch,' Harry said when Alexandra had closed the door behind her.

'Seconded,' Gina said. 'She understands our business a lot more than most of the others did. And she's got some great ideas.'

Which didn't leave Jordan any room to manoeuvre. If he hadn't known her in a previous life, he would've agreed with them. But he *had* known her. And that was a problem. Maybe that was the way round this. 'Unfortunately, I need to tell you there's a slight conflict of interest. One I wasn't aware of before the interview.'

Gina frowned. 'How do you mean?'

'I knew her. At school.' He coughed. 'Under a different name.'

Harry's eyebrows arched. 'Neither of you said a thing just now.'

Jordan knew he deserved the rebuke. Either or both of them could've acknowledged that they knew each other. But they hadn't. For exactly the same reason: one that he wasn't planning to share. He sighed. 'The middle of an interview's hardly the place for a reunion.' Not that he wanted a reunion with her. He'd moved on. And he didn't have any plans to go back.

'Her CV doesn't say she was at your school,' Harry pointed out.

'She wasn't at my school. I met her at a party—a friend of a friend of a friend. Actually, I was at university at the time.'

Harry shrugged. 'So you didn't know her *that* well.'

Well enough, Jordan thought, to make her pregnant. Except, when his mother had refused to pay her an extortionate allowance, she'd cold-bloodedly terminated their unborn child without even so much as discussing it with him. She hadn't even told him she was pregnant, and he couldn't forgive her for that.

And then she'd vanished to avoid any fallout. He'd spent weeks trying to find her, to no avail. When he'd finally tracked her down, he'd been gutted to discover that she was married…to someone else. He'd had to face how little he'd really meant to her—otherwise how could she have married another man so quickly after getting rid of his baby?

Not that he was going to tell Harry and Gina about that. It was something he never, ever talked about. To anyone. He'd buried the anger and the hurt, and they were staying buried.

'She's what we need,' Gina said. 'She can think on her feet, she's full of ideas, and she's straight-talking. And she was the only one to mention a budget—she's grounded in the real world.'

Jordan couldn't deny any of that. But could he cope with having her back in his life?

Harry clearly sensed the younger man's reservations, because he asked, 'Did you clash badly with her, or something?'

Or something. She'd been the first girl Jordan had really fallen in love with. She'd charmed him utterly. To the point where he'd even planned to spend the rest of his life with her.

How stupid he'd been. It would never have worked. Then again, neither had marrying someone he'd been friends with for years, someone who had the same kind of background that he did. He'd failed there, too. So, as far as he was concerned, relationships were best kept short and sweet—and ended before they started to sour.

'Jordan?'

He made a noncommittal murmur, not wanting to explain.

'Whatever happened—and I for one won't pry—you were both a lot younger then and still had a lot of growing up to do. People change,' Gina said.

Jordan didn't think so. Alexandra had been incredibly ambitious—expecting their unborn child to give her an entry into his world and a hand up from her own—and he'd bet that she was just the same, now. That kind of personality trait didn't change.

'Let's go through the candidates and see who we're going to bring back for a second interview,' he said, wanting to shift back onto safe ground.

On three of the final candidates, they were agreed; on

the fourth, there was no way he could explain why he didn't want her without dragging up too much of the past.

Just as they finished, Jordan's PA knocked on the door. 'I'm so sorry to interrupt, Mr Blake. I'm afraid it's a matter that can't wait,' she said to Harry.

'Go,' Jordan said. 'You too, Gina. I know you're both up to your eyes. I'll do the debriefs,' he said.

'Are you sure?' Harry asked.

'Absolutely.' It meant he'd get a word with her on his own—and then maybe he could find out what she was really up to.

As soon as his colleagues had gone, Jordan spoke to the candidates in the order he'd seen them. He commiserated with the ones who didn't get through to second interview and explained why, so they could work on their skills for the future; and he gave a briefing pack to the three candidates who'd got through to the next round.

And finally it was time to face Alexandra.

All the candidates had been seen in order. Most had come out looking dejected; three had come out looking pleased. And, as the last one to be interviewed, Alexandra was the last one to be debriefed.

She had thought about leaving quietly, so she didn't have to see the expression in Jordan's eyes when he told her that she was rejected. But that would be the coward's way out, and she wasn't a coward. Plus the debriefing was going to be useful for her next interview. Even so, her nerves were strung so tightly that she stumbled as she walked through the door.

'Ms…' He paused, looking her up and down. 'Bennett.'

Then she realised that Jordan was on his own. Oh, no. This was going to be really bad. He wouldn't have to hide the fact that he was gloating when he told her that she hadn't got the job.

Well, they did say that attack was the best form of defence. She lifted her chin. 'You could've just sent a message via the agency that I didn't get the job. You didn't need to bother telling me personally.'

'Actually, you made the list for second interview.' He handed her an envelope. 'And this is the briefing pack for the situation we want you to think about and discuss with us tomorrow.'

It was so unexpected that it silenced her. He was actually giving her a chance?

Then, when he spoke again, she wished she'd just said thank you and made a run for it.

'I wasn't expecting to see *you* today,' he said coolly.

'I had no idea you worked here.' Much less that he was the CEO.

He scoffed. 'Come off it. You know exactly who my family are.'

She frowned. 'No. All I knew was that they were posh.' In a different league from her own family. The ground floor of their entire house could've fitted into the Smiths' living room.

He didn't look as if he believed her. 'Let me refresh your memory. My great-grandfather started the store,' he said. 'My grandfather took over from him. And then my father.'

So it was his family business. 'And now you're the CEO. Following in their footsteps.' That much she could work out for herself. 'But it doesn't quite add up. Since it's a family business, why isn't your surname Field?'

He shrugged. 'It's my middle name. My father refused to change his surname when he married my mother.'

Oh. So the store belonged to his mother's family. With

a heritage like that, no wonder Vanessa Smith had been so confident. And maybe she could understand now why Vanessa had made that accusation when Alexandra had gone to her for help—an accusation that even now made a red mist swirl in front of Alexandra's eyes because it had been so unfair and so unjust.

Jordan looked at her. 'Speaking of names, I notice you've changed yours.'

Was that a roundabout way of asking her if she was married? Under employment law, he couldn't ask her; marital status was nothing to do with someone's performance in their job. On the other hand, it wouldn't hurt if he thought she was still married. Just in case he was under the very mistaken impression that she wanted anything from him other than this job. 'It's my married name.' And she'd kept it after the divorce.

'Even your first name's different,' he mused. 'I knew you as Alex.'

When she'd been a very different person. Naïve, believing that she'd been lucky enough to find her soul mate at the age of seventeen. Except she'd kissed her handsome prince and he'd turned into a slimy toad. She shrugged, affecting a cool she definitely didn't feel—even thinking about kissing when Jordan Smith was sitting right in front of her was a mistake. 'Xandra is a perfectly valid diminutive of Alexandra,' she said crisply.

'Very "marketing".'

Which was what her tutor had told her when she'd started doing the evening class. Look the part, sound the part, act the part, and you'll get the part. She'd followed that to the letter. 'Is that a problem?'

'No.' He paused. 'I told Harry and Gina I knew you.'

Knew her. Yeah. He'd known her, all right. In the Biblical sense. 'Didn't that put me out of the running?'

'They liked you.'

And he'd made it very clear that he didn't. Definitely guilt talking, she thought.

Meeting his gaze was a huge mistake. The man had proved to her years ago that he had no integrity where personal relationships were concerned. He'd abandoned her when she'd needed him most, let her down in the worst possible way. How could she possibly still find him in the slightest bit attractive? She reined her thoughts back in.

'If Field's were to offer you the job, would you take it?'

If that was his idea of an apology, Alexandra thought, it was much too little and much too late.

Then again, this was a real opportunity: to be the marketing manager of a traditional, well established department store, with a brief to bring it bang up to date. If she was offered the job, it'd be a real plus on her CV. If she turned it down just to spite him, she'd really be doing herself a disservice. 'I'd consider it,' she said.

'The job would mean working with me.'

'Is that a problem for you?'

He looked straight at her. 'Not if it's not a problem for you.'

In other words, it could work if they didn't talk about what had happened ten years ago. Could she do that, for the sake of her career?

She took a deep breath. 'That depends on what you offer me.'

Pretty much what she'd said to his mother.

Alexandra might look different and have a different name, but deep down she was still the same person. Still on the make. Jordan had to fight not to scowl at her and to keep his voice even. 'That depends,' he said, 'on what you can offer us. We'll see you here tomorrow at three.'

'I'll be here,' she said.

Yeah. And he'd just have to hope that this time she managed to show her true colours and put Harry and Gina off.

CHAPTER TWO

'SHE's the one,' Harry said the following afternoon, when Alexandra left the room after her second interview. 'No question about it.'

'I really like her ideas for taking the store card to a new level, especially combining it with an app so customers can have instant access to all their account information wherever they are,' Gina added. 'And her presentation was flawless as well as enthusiastic. You'd never believe she only got the brief yesterday. She's going to be a real asset to Field's. The Board's going to love her.'

Jordan couldn't think of a single argument to change their minds. Mainly because they were right. Much as he hated to admit it, she *was* the best person for the job.

Maybe that huge ambition of hers could be harnessed to work in their favour.

Maybe.

Well, he'd never been a coward. He'd always stepped up to the mark, always shouldered his responsibilities. That wasn't going to change now. 'Let's call her in and give her the good news.'

The serious look on Jordan's face confirmed Alexandra's gut reaction. She hadn't got the job. Given that he was on the interview panel, that wasn't so surprising. Hopefully the debrief would tell her where she'd gone wrong; though she had a feeling that the real reason for her rejection lay ten years in the past.

What an idiot she'd been, putting herself in a position where he could reject her for a second time.

'Ms Bennett. Do sit down.'

She thought about defying him and remaining on her feet; but she was very glad she had taken the seat when he added, 'Welcome to the team.'

She'd got the job?

It surprised her so much that she was actually lost for words.

But her silence didn't seem to faze him. He continued, 'Mr Blake will sort out the details with you—when you're able to start, setting up an induction day so you can meet the rest of the team, sorting out your security for the store and the computer network.'

'Thank you.'

'Do you have any questions?' Harry asked.

'At the moment, only one.' She paused. 'Is the culture here always this formal? I'm more used to working on first-name terms.'

Jordan looked at her. So she was going to start challenging him already?

OK. He'd let her think she'd won this one, because it really wasn't an issue. 'No, it's not. Everyone here calls me Jordan.'

'Jordan,' she repeated.

It was the first time he'd heard her say his name in a decade, and he felt the colour rise through his face because he could remember a completely different tone to her voice, back then. When she'd cried out his name as she'd climaxed.

What an idiot he'd been. Not an issue, indeed; suddenly she'd made it one. And she hadn't just won this round, she'd completely flattened him. He needed to get out of here before he said something stupid. He glanced at his watch. 'I'm afraid I need to be somewhere. Excuse me. Thank you for your time, Ms B—Xandra.' He deliberately didn't meet her gaze and turned instead to the personnel manager. 'Harry, would you mind debriefing the other candidates?'

'Sure.'

Jordan walked out of the room without looking at her; when he reached his office he sank into his chair and closed his eyes. How the hell was he going to cope with having her back in his life?

Lots of cold showers, he answered his own question. And he'd better hope that the icy water would wake up his common sense. Because this particular woman was absolutely off limits, whatever his body might like to think.

A week later, Alexandra walked into Field's.

From today, this was *hers.* And she was going to take it from being a quiet, slightly old-fashioned department store to one that was buzzing. One that hit the news for all the right reasons. One that could deliver cutting-edge products, yet back them up with solid tradition.

And she could hardly wait.

She smiled as she swiped her store ID card through the slot by the staff entrance door, and stepped through.

Harry was there to meet her and introduced her to all the office staff, then took her round to meet the manager of each department. Jordan was conspicuous by his absence. She wasn't sure whether to be more relieved or cross; was he deliberately avoiding her? Well, he'd have to face her eventually, and she'd make sure that he didn't have a single thing to complain about. She was going to make a real success of this job.

A couple of days later, Jordan was doing his daily walkabout through the store—not so much checking up on his staff as making sure that he was visible rather than a faceless boss, and so he could see for himself if there were any issues that needed tackling or where his staff needed more support.

His body prickled with awareness and he glanced round. Alexandra—he still couldn't think of her as Xandra—was there, talking animatedly to the staff on one of the perfume counters. She was wearing another beautifully cut business suit that emphasised her curves and those high, high heels that made her legs look even longer.

As if she sensed him watching her, she glanced up and caught his gaze. She gave him a shy smile, and for a moment he was transported back to being nineteen years old, catching her gaze across a crowded party. She'd smiled like that at him back then, her brown eyes huge and slightly wary behind her spectacles.

And then she'd reeled him in. Hook, line and sinker.

He had to remember that. The shyness had been just an act, and she'd fooled him.

Though he was a fast learner. Nobody fooled him twice.

He gave her a cool, formal nod and turned away.

By the end of the week, Alexandra was absolutely certain that Jordan was avoiding her. He never seemed to visit the staff canteen—or, at least, not when she did; he hadn't dropped in to see how his newest manager was coping in the role, delegating that task to Harry; and he hadn't acknowledged her once on his daily walkabouts in the store, even though she knew damn well he'd seen her talking to customers and staff and setting up the customer audits.

Worse still, even when her back had been to him, her body seemed to have developed some kind of radar system that told her exactly where he was. And it was infuriating that she was still so aware of him.

If she was honest with herself, she knew the old attraction between them had never really gone away. But she'd just have to ignore it, because she didn't repeat her mistakes. Apart from the fact that Jordan Smith had been the second-biggest mistake of her life, her marriage had taught her just how rubbish her judgement was when it came to men. As far as she was concerned, from now on, she was married to her career. At least her career wasn't going to let her down or try to control her or make her feel bad about herself.

Though Jordan was the CEO here, and she was planning to make quite a few changes. Which meant that they were going to have to work together. They'd need to discuss her plans. Since he clearly wasn't going to make the first move and establish a decent working relationship between them, then she was going to have to be the one to do it. 'Stubborn, annoying, *ridiculous* man,' she muttered, and printed out the report she'd been working on.

It was late enough on a Friday evening for the rest of the office staff to have gone home, but she knew that Jordan would be working late. He put in a crazy number of hours—a work schedule that would strain just about any marriage to creaking point. Which wasn't her problem; she wasn't in the slightest bit interested in whether Jordan Smith was married and how happy he was. But his working habits did mean that she'd be able to talk to him this evening without anyone else being able to overhear.

Just in case it got awkward.

She walked down to the far end of the corridor—had he deliberately made sure that her office was as far away as possible from his? she wondered—and looked through the open door. He was seated at his desk, working at his computer. She'd never seen him wearing glasses before, and it made her catch her breath; right now he looked incredibly clever and incredibly sexy.

But she had to remember that she couldn't trust him as far as she could roll a ten-ton boulder up a slope.

OK, as a boss he seemed reasonable enough, and everyone she'd talked to in the department store had spontaneously mentioned what a nice guy he was and how he really cared about the staff; but when it came to personal stuff she knew he wasn't in the slightest bit reasonable or reliable. She had the physical scars to remind her. Scars that only a surgeon would see, but they were most definitely there. The physical ache had gone, but the emotional ache was something she'd learned to live with over the years.

She rapped on the door jamb.

He looked up, and his eyes widened in surprise. 'Is there something you need?'

'I just thought you might like to know what I've been working on for the last week.'

He shrugged. 'I don't believe in micromanagement. I know my managers are perfectly capable of doing their jobs.'

Ha. Considering he clearly hadn't wanted to give her the job in the first place, that was rich. 'Well, I'm telling you anyway, because I believe in good communications.' Neatly pointing out his own failings in that area, without actually saying the words. 'This is the stuff about the social media. It's a quick win and a small budget.' She walked over to his desk and handed him the report.

'You could've emailed this to me. Or given it to my PA.'

'So I could.' He wasn't even going to try meeting her halfway, was he? 'I'll remember that in future.' She gave him a cool smile and walked away.

Jordan almost called her back. Almost. But, until he'd managed to inure himself against those beautiful brown eyes, he needed to keep some distance between them.

Even so, instead of putting her report in his in-tray for later, he read through it.

There was a concise summary at the beginning, then each section had figures to back up her recommendations. She was definitely as bright as he remembered. And she was a team player: she'd acknowledged the input of every member of staff from the shop floor who'd made a suggestion. She'd suggested who would be good at hosting each of the community forums she'd recommended, and why. All the store's departments were included: home, garden, fashion, beauty, kitchen, technology, sport. She wanted sections on the website for articles giving 'how to' advice on everything from choosing lighting in a room or the right pillow for you through to make-up demonstrations and fashion tips, and she already had people in mind to write them or be filmed in action for a demonstration.

In one short week, she'd managed to spot the strengths of the team, and reinforce them. It was exactly as Harry and Gina had said: she'd be a real asset to the firm.

So why did he feel so antsy around her?

Not wanting to answer that question, he typed her a swift email instead. Headed 'Social media'.

I'll talk to the Board next week and recommend that they agree your plans. JS.

Nicely formal.

And now he could go back to what he'd been doing before she'd torpedoed his concentration.

Easier said than done, Jordan thought wryly the following day, when he saw Alexandra balanced precariously on the top of a ladder in the toy department. She was standing on *tiptoe,* for pity's sake. 'What do you think you're doing?' he demanded.

'Putting up a banner in the department to publicise the first story-time session, next week,' Alexandra said. 'What does it look like?'

'Dangerous, with a flagrant disregard for health and safety. You could hurt yourself, as well as customers or colleagues. Why didn't you ask Bill—or anyone taller than you, for that matter—to do it?'

'Bill was busy, and I wanted the banner up as soon as possible. The kids have worked hard on this.'

'Kids?' Jordan wasn't following.

'My friend Meggie's Year Two class.'

Meggie? He narrowed his eyes. He remembered Meggie. Alexandra's best friend. Ten years ago, she'd had great pleasure in telling him that Alexandra was married to someone who would treat her properly, and he could go and take a running jump. Or words to that effect. 'I see,' he said crisply.

But he noticed that the banner was composed of the words 'story time here Monday 10 a.m.', with each letter carefully cut out, painted and glued to the banner. And all around them were glued drawings of book covers, clearly the children's favourite books. The children had obviously worked really hard to make the banner bright and colourful. To make it special, for Alexandra.

Year Two. The children in the class would all be aged

seven. If things had been different, he and Alexandra might've had a child of their own in that class, as well as another in Year Five...

The thought made him snap at her. 'Will you get down from there before you fall?'

'I won't fall.'

In a suit and high heels? He wasn't going to take the risk. 'Get down,' he said again. 'I'll put the damn thing up for you.'

For a moment, he thought she was going to defy him, but then she shrugged. 'Fine. Thank you.'

He had to take his eyes off her legs as she descended from the ladder, carefully holding the banner.

Then she handed him one end. He'd just finished fixing it to the ceiling when he glanced down at her, and realised that she had a camera in her hands. 'What are you doing?'

'Taking shots for social media. To show that our CEO isn't afraid to get his hands dirty.'

'You're *photographing* me?'

'I'll let you vet the pictures, first.' She gave him a wicked grin. 'Maybe.'

Infuriating woman. He was about to say something cutting, when she asked, 'Would you mind putting the other end up for me, too, please, as you're here?'

After the fuss he'd made about her being up the ladder, he could hardly say no. He gave her a speaking look, but did so.

'My hero,' she purred.

'Don't push it,' he warned.

She just batted her eyelashes at him. And it made him want to grab her shoulders and...

Kiss her.

Shake her, he corrected himself. 'Don't take unnecessary risks again,' he said when he got down from the ladder.

'No, sir.' She gave him a smart salute.

He resisted the provocation, just, and stomped back to his office.

Later, his email pinged. The message contained a picture of him up the ladder, and a note from her.

Using this one. If I don't hear back within the hour, will assume OK.

He went straight to her office. 'How exactly are you intending to use that photograph?'

'Here.' She flicked into a screen on her computer and indicated the monitor so he could see the web page.

'What if I said no?'

'Let me see. This shows you as hands-on. All the mums are going to go weak at the knees and want to be here in case you walk by. All the grandmothers are going to think of their own sons and warm to you. The grandfathers will do the same, and the dads will see themselves in your shoes. So you're generating customer warmth. Plus you're creating links with the local community, as a local school worked on the banner—using material that Field's supplied. Now, why would you say no to that kind of PR?'

He didn't have an answer to that, because he knew she was right. 'Just stay inside health and safety guidelines in future,' he muttered.

She rolled her eyes. 'I'm not planning to have an accident and sue Field's or anything like that. I'm part of the team here. And I like being hands on.'

Hands on. He wished she hadn't used that phrase. He could still remember the feel of her hands against his skin. 'Whatever,' he said, annoyed by the fact that she could still unsettle him like that. 'If you'll excuse me. I have things that need sorting.' And he left her office before he did or said anything *really* rash.

On Monday morning, Jordan headed for the toy department. It was the first of their story-time sessions, and Alexandra had managed to get a minor children's TV presenter in to do the first one.

Except it seemed that the presenter had gone down with tonsillitis and wasn't able to appear. And Alexandra had stepped into the breach.

Jordan stood on the sidelines, watching her. She was sitting on a bean bag, with the children gathered round her and the mums sitting on chairs that looked as if they came from the staff canteen—no doubt she'd asked very nicely, with those huge eyes and the sweetest smile, and charmed the catering manager into helping. She was reading a rhyming story for the younger ones; some of them were clearly familiar with it, because she got them to join in on the chorus sections. She had a gorgeous voice, he thought, and he wasn't surprised that all the children were hanging onto every single word.

And then he found himself imagining her with their child. If she hadn't had the termination, would she have sat curled on the sofa with their toddler on her lap, pointing out the pictures and the words, gently teaching their little one to recognise letters?

Their child would've been ten, now. Nearly ready for high school. Would they have had a boy or a girl? And would they have had more children? A boy with his own dark hair and blue eyes, a girl with Alexandra's huge brown eyes and sunny smile…

Jordan was cross with himself for even thinking about it. It was pointless dwelling on what might have been, because you couldn't change the past. And right now children weren't part of his future in any case.

Quietly, without catching her eye, Jordan moved away. Alexandra was doing just fine on her own; she didn't need any support from him. And he wasn't going to crowd her.

Though he did return right at the end, just as Alexandra was finishing the story, with a camera.

She glanced up at him and for a moment he could see laughter in her eyes; she clearly recognised this as a bit of tit-for-tat. And he took more photographs of the line of children thanking her for the story and the queue of mums at the tills with books under their arms, before sliding the camera back into his jacket pocket and starting to stack the chairs.

'I saw that camera, you know,' she said, joining him in the chair-stacking.

'My marketing manager is very keen on social media and taking every photo opportunity we can,' he said.

'Good man. You're learning.' She patted his arm. 'Though I'm afraid we'll need to get all the mums to sign a release form before we can use those pics.'

Just as well there was a jacket sleeve and a shirt sleeve between his skin and hers. As it was, his skin was tingling where she'd touched him. How could she affect him like that, when he knew what he did about her?

He cleared his throat. 'I don't think anyone missed the TV presenter. You did a good job.'

'Thank you. I'm getting the staff to do a rota; they're all going to read their favourite stories.' She smiled. 'It's lovely that everyone in the store wants to get involved, whether they're from the shop floor or behind the scenes. Maureen from the canteen's even coming in on her day off to read her granddaughter's favourite story.'

'Was that a hint that you're expecting me to read a story?' he asked.

'Could be.'

She smiled again, and he noticed the dimple in her cheek. Cute. How had he forgotten that? And it really made him want to touch it. Touch *her*. Dip his head and brush his mouth against hers. Kiss her until they were both dizzy.

'Jordan?'

'Uh—sorry.' He felt the colour rise in his cheeks. She'd just caught him staring at her like a fool. 'You know me. Mind always on the next project.'

'I said, it might be a hint. If you want to read a story for the kids, that is. If you're not too busy.'

'I'll think about it.' Again, he found his thoughts coming back to the baby. Did she ever think about their baby? Did she ever regret what she'd done? Did she ever wonder what it might've been like, making a family with him?

And just what was wrong with him, suddenly thinking about having a family? Since the break-up of his marriage, he'd pushed all that sort of thing to the back of his mind and concentrated on making Field's the best department store he could.

'What made you think about having story time sessions?' he asked. 'Did your parents used to read to you a lot, or something?'

She shook her head. 'It was Miss Shields, my primary school teacher. She used to read a few pages to us just before we went home. And she took me off the official school reading scheme and lent me books that I enjoyed a lot more.'

He should've guessed it hadn't been her parents to encourage her love of reading. She'd told him once that she was the first person in her family to stay on for A-levels, let alone think about going to university.

'How about you? Did your parents read to you?' she asked.

'I had a story every night.' From his nanny. His parents had been busy at work; they hadn't had the time to read to him.

'And you read to your own children?'

'I don't have children.' Except the one he hadn't known about—the one who hadn't even been born. He knew he shouldn't ask, because he really didn't want to hear the answer, but he couldn't help the question. 'You were pretty good at that. I assume you read to yours?'

For just a second, he could've sworn that she flinched. And she turned away as she said, 'I read to my godchildren. Meggie's two.'

So she still didn't have children. Then again, pregnancy would make her face up to what she'd done when she was eighteen. And he was beginning to think that maybe Alexandra was a bit less hard-boiled than he'd believed her to be. How did she feel about the prospect of starting a new family, knowing that she'd deliberately chosen not to have a family before?

'Excuse me. I'm sure you're busy and I need to get some things sorted here. Thanks for your help in stacking the chairs.' And then she fled.

CHAPTER THREE

BUT Jordan couldn't stop thinking about it all evening. Thinking about *her*. Alexandra still didn't have children. Why? Was it the guilt about what she'd done to his baby stopping her, or had her husband not wanted children anyway?

Her husband.

The words dropped into his thoughts like a clanging bell. Alexandra was married. Jordan didn't believe in cheating. And, even if she hadn't been married, she worked with him. How many times had he seen an office romance end in tears? And then there was the kicker: been there, done that and she'd destroyed his trust. Never again.

No, what he needed to do now was to establish a working relationship with her; maybe then he could move on and leave the demons of the past behind, locked away where they belonged.

On Tuesday night, Jordan was working late as usual. He went to make himself a cup of coffee in the staff kitchen, and noticed the light shining through Alexandra's open door at the far end of the corridor. She was working late again, too. Now he thought about it, she'd worked late every night since she'd started. Was she trying to prove

herself to him? Or was she struggling with her workload,
unable to cope with the demands of the job?

He walked down the corridor, knocked on her open door
and leaned against the door jamb. 'Won't Mr Bennett have
something to say about you working this late every night?'

She looked up and simply shrugged.

She was so ambitious that she'd put her job before her
marriage? he thought, stunned.

Then she gave him a cool look. 'Won't Mrs Smith have
something to say about *you* working this late?'

'Touché.' He gave her a wry smile. 'Actually, I didn't
come in to fight with you, just to say that I was making
coffee and to ask if you wanted a mug, too. And, for the
record, I don't expect my staff to work the same hours as
I do.'

'I'm fine. I'm just settling in and enjoying the challenges
of my new job.' But she returned his smile, her expression
softening slightly. 'Sorry, I didn't mean to snap at you just
then.' She glanced down at her left hand. The ring finger
was defiantly bare. How hadn't he noticed that before? 'I
guess I should tell you that there isn't a Mr Bennett. Well,
there is,' she amended, 'but he's not married to me any
more. I just kept his name.'

She was single?

For a moment, he forgot to breathe.

Oh, for pity's sake. That wasn't what this was meant to
be about. He was simply trying to set up a decent working relationship between them. And maybe he should offer
her the same honesty. 'There isn't a Mrs Smith, either,' he
admitted. 'She went back to her maiden name after the divorce.' And then she'd remarried.

'I'm sorry it didn't work out for you.'

'And you.'

It was the most civil they'd been towards each other

since she'd walked back into his life, and Jordan was surprised at how good it felt.

The harsh overhead light showed that there were shadows under her eyes. He remembered her looking like that years ago, when she'd been studying too hard. 'When was the last time you ate?' he asked.

She blinked, looking surprised. 'What?'

'It's nearly eight o'clock. You've been here for more than twelve hours. Did you actually have a lunch break today?'

'Yes.'

Though the slight hesitation in her voice told him the truth. 'It was a sandwich at your desk while you were working, wasn't it?'

She spread her hands. 'Busted. But there's just not enough time for lunch. There's so much I want to do.'

He knew that, from the wish list she'd emailed him. Pop-up shops, chosen by the consumer through an online poll; a Christmas bazaar showcasing local craftspeople, held in a marquee in the courtyard café; an events programme including demonstrations that would also be broadcast on the Internet; and a dozen more ideas, some of them completely off the wall but he had a feeling that she could make them work. No, she wasn't struggling with her job. She was struggling with prioritising things—and only because she'd had so many good ideas. He'd be doing the same, in her shoes.

'If you don't pace yourself properly, you'll burn out,' he warned.

Her expression said very clearly, *Right, as if you give a damn about that.*

'Actually, I do give a damn,' he said. 'We look after our staff at Field's.'

'Everyone I've spoken to is happy.'

That was completely out of left field. He blinked. 'You asked my staff if they were happy?'

'No, that wasn't my brief. But I can tell they're happy by the way they talk. They're enthusiastic, they're full of ideas, and they love the new staff suggestion scheme. You should see my inbox.'

'Why don't you tell me about it over dinner?'

'Dinner?'

He pushed aside thoughts of damask tablecloths and the light from vanilla-scented candles glinting on antique silver cutlery. This was a working relationship; they weren't picking up where they'd left off, before she'd vanished. Before the bombshells had dropped. 'I have to eat. So do you. We might as well eat together while we discuss it.'

She shrugged. 'I was going to stop in ten minutes anyway. I was going home to make myself an omelette.'

'An omelette's fine by me.'

Her eyes narrowed. 'I don't remember inviting you back.'

He blew out a breath. 'Sorry. That was pushy. How about a compromise?' he asked. 'There's this trattoria just round the corner. It's pretty basic, but the food's excellent.'

She leaned back in her chair, eyes narrowing even further as she stared at him. 'You're asking me out to dinner?'

'A *working* dinner,' he clarified. 'To make up for the fact that I haven't had a chance to spend any real time discussing your ideas with you.'

They both knew that wasn't what he was really saying. He'd been avoiding her, and they were both well aware of the fact.

'So you'll listen to my ideas.'

'And give you feedback. Yes.'

Her expression showed that she was considering it.

Weighing up the pros and cons. So she was just as wary of him as he was of her, then. Guilt talking? he wondered.

'OK,' she said eventually.

'How long will it take you to get ready?'

'As long as it takes to back up my files and shut down the computer.'

Ha. Well, of course she wasn't going to change, or re-touch her make-up, or spritz herself with perfume. This wasn't a date. It was simply discussing work while they ate. Multi-tasking.

'Meet you back here in ten minutes?' he suggested.

'Sure.'

Ten minutes later, when he met her outside her office, he was pretty sure that she'd reapplied her lipstick, but he didn't make a comment. He simply ushered her out of the store and down the side street to the little trattoria he'd discovered a couple of years before.

'Red or white?' he asked as the waiter arrived to take their drinks order.

She shrugged. 'I don't mind. Though I would like some water as well, please. Still, with ice.'

He remembered her preferring white wine; her tastes might have changed over the years, but he decided to play safe and ordered a bottle of pinot grigio and a jug of water. 'Thanks, Giorgio.'

'*Prego,* Jordan.' The waiter smiled back at him.

'If the waiter's on first-name terms with you, I assume you eat here a lot?' she asked.

Jordan shrugged. 'It's convenient. And, actually, he's the owner. His wife's the cook.'

She gave him a sidelong look. 'So you haven't actually learned to cook, yet?'

He knew what she was referring to. The time he'd taken her back to his place when his parents had been out. He'd put some bread under the grill to toast—and then he'd started kissing her on the sofa and forgotten all about the toast until the smoke detector had started shrieking. He couldn't remember how to turn the alarm off, so they'd had to flap a wet towel underneath it and open all the windows; even then, the house had reeked of burnt toast for a whole day afterwards.

'It's convenient,' he repeated. After Lindsey had left him for someone who didn't have workaholic tendencies, he'd discovered that he really didn't enjoy cooking a meal for one, even if it was just shoving a ready meal in the microwave. He tended to eat at lunchtime in the staff canteen, then grabbed a sandwich at his desk in the evening; and on days when he didn't have time for lunch, he grabbed a sandwich on the run and ate at the trattoria after work.

'What do you recommend?' she asked, glancing over the edge of the menu at him.

'Pretty much everything on the menu. Though the lasagne's particularly good,' he said.

'Lasagne it is, then. Thank you.'

He ordered the same for both of them when Giorgio returned with the wine and water. 'Bread and olives?' Giorgio asked.

He glanced at Alexandra. At her nod, he smiled. 'Yes, please.'

If anyone had told Alexandra six months ago that she'd be having dinner with Jordan Smith, and enjoying it, she would've laughed. Really, really scornfully.

But Jordan was excellent company. Charming, with good manners. And she was actually having a good time.

Then she reached for another piece of the excellent bread at the same time as he did; when their fingers touched, her mouth went dry. Oh, hell. She could remember him touching her much more intimately, and it sent a shiver of pure lust through her.

She mumbled an apology and withdrew, waiting for him to tear off a piece of bread before she dared go anywhere near the bread basket again.

'The bread's good,' she said, hoping to cover up the awkwardness—and hoping even more that he wouldn't guess what she'd just been thinking about.

He raised an eyebrow. 'I did wonder if you'd stick to just the olives.'

'Why?' For a moment, she looked puzzled. 'Oh. Because of the carbs.' She gave him a wry smile. 'You're obviously used to dating twig-like women who exist on a single lettuce leaf—and maybe a nibble of celery if it's a special night out.'

'I don't date twig-like women.' He couldn't help the slight snap in his voice. It was none of her business who he dated.

'Another elephant,' she said softly. 'At this rate, we're going to have a whole herd.'

'How do you mean?'

'The elephant in the room. Screened off. Things we don't talk about, things that are absolutely off limits. The past. Your marriage. Mine. The women you date who don't eat.' Her gaze held his. 'Would you like to add any more to the herd?'

He really hadn't expected this. 'That's very direct.'

'I find it's the easiest way. It cuts out the lies.'

Was she admitting that she was a liar? Or was she accusing *him* of being a liar? Right at that moment, he couldn't tell. But he wasn't the one who'd behaved badly. He wasn't the one who didn't even bother to say, 'You're dumped,' but simply went incommunicado. Then, when he'd heard what his mother had to say about the situation and tried to find out what the hell was going on, Alexandra had simply vanished. He hadn't been able to find her and drag the truth out of her.

'By my reckoning,' she continued, 'that leaves us the weather, work or celebrity gossip as our next topic of conversation. Would you like to choose?'

There was the slightest, slightest glint of laughter in her eyes, and suddenly the tension in his spine drained away. 'Work, I think,' he said. 'Before we have a fight.'

She inclined her head in recognition. 'That's direct, too.'

'Yeah.' He couldn't bring himself to echo her words back at her. Because she was the one who'd told the lies; and they'd just tacitly agreed not to discuss it. He still wanted to know why—why hadn't she told him about the baby? Had she ever loved him, or had his mother been right and she'd just seen him as a meal ticket for life? But he wasn't sure he was going to be able to handle the answers to his questions; and anyway, whatever had happened in the past, right now he knew that Alexandra Bennett was going to be really good for Field's. And his family business was the whole purpose of his life nowadays.

'Tell me about your ideas,' he said instead, then sat back and watched her blossom as she talked. As she expounded on her ideas her eyes shone and her face was completely animated. She clearly loved her job; this was her passion, the reason she got up in the mornings.

And then he wished that word hadn't slipped into his head. Passion. He could remember her being passionate in bed with him, once she'd got past her shyness. Once she'd got past the embarrassment and awkwardness of her very first time, started to learn how she liked him to touch her, and what gave him the most pleasure when she touched him...

Oh, hell, he really needed to stop letting his thoughts run away with him like this.

'So why did you pick marketing?' he asked.

She blinked. 'Sorry?'

'I thought you were going to be a lecturer.'

'That's not relevant.'

And he'd hit a nerve, judging by the expression on her face. 'OK. Ignore that. I just wondered what made you pick marketing as a career?'

She shrugged. 'I was in a bit of a rut in my job. A friend who worked in HR persuaded me to let her practise on me and got me to do some tests. The results said that marketing would suit me as a career, so I found myself a job as a marketing assistant and started studying for my professional exams.'

Exams, he remembered from her CV, where she'd gained distinctions in every paper. And she'd done the whole lot in less than a year. 'So was your friend right? Are you happy?'

'Yes. And this job is a challenge. I'm glad I went for it.' She paused. 'Though I really didn't know you were anything to do with Field's.'

Her eyes were very clear; maybe she was telling the truth.

'The agency put you in at the very last minute.'

'I'd just signed up with them. I was looking to make my next career move,' she explained. 'They said there was the perfect job for me, except the application date had already passed. And then they said they'd see if they could do something about it.' She spread her hands. 'I really wasn't expecting them to ring me and say I'd got an interview, so I didn't bother doing any research on Field's. When they said I had an hour and a half to get there, it was too late to do more than read the factsheet they sent me and then spend five minutes walking round the store before the interview.'

He couldn't leave it. 'If you'd known I was going to be doing the interview, would you have turned up?'

'I don't know,' she said. 'I would've had to think very hard about it.'

'But you came back for a second interview.'

'Because I wanted the job. This sort of challenge doesn't come up that often, and I realised it'd be pointless cutting off my nose to spite my face.'

He could appreciate that.

'So why did you give me the job?' she asked.

Even though he hadn't wanted her back in his life? 'Fair question,' he acknowledged. 'Because you were the best candidate. And you said it wouldn't be a problem working with me.'

'It won't be.'

He wasn't so sure. 'This elephant in the corner thing isn't going to work. We're better off getting everything out of the way. We need to talk about what happened. And then we can move on and have a chance of a decent working relationship.'

Her face went white. 'You want to talk about it *here?*'

She had a point. The trattoria was quiet, but not that quiet. 'After we've eaten,' he conceded. 'Your place or mine?'

She shook her head. 'Neutral territory. Isn't there a park or something near here?'

'On a March evening? We'll freeze. Your place or mine?' he repeated inexorably.

She sighed. 'Yours.'

So she could walk out when it got too much for her? he thought cynically. 'That's settled, then.'

The lasagne was good. Probably the best she'd ever tasted. Except Alexandra was so nervous, she could barely swallow. Why hadn't she kept her mouth shut? Why had she had to make that stupid comment about him dating twig-like women? Why hadn't she kept the conversation strictly to business and insisted on discussing marketing ideas for the department store?

She really didn't want to drag up the past. To rip the top off her scars and let all the pain come flooding back. She'd reinvented herself, worked hard to make something of her life.

But maybe he was right. Maybe they did need to get all this out of the way. And in some respects it would be good to have closure. To hear him apologise, even though it was way too late and nothing could fix what had happened.

She toyed with her food.

'Don't you like it?' Jordan asked.

'I do. I've just…' She might as well be honest with him. 'I've lost my appetite.'

He blew out a breath. 'My fault.'

'Yeah.' There was no point in telling fibs.

'OK. I'll get the bill.'

She frowned. 'You haven't eaten your own meal.'

He shrugged. 'I'm not that hungry any more, either.' For the same reason as her. He wasn't looking forward to their conversation. But it had to be done. Like lancing a boil. Letting the poison out.

She took a couple of notes from her purse and handed them to him. 'My half of the bill.'

'Not necessary. I think I can just about afford to buy my marketing manager a meal.'

She shook her head. 'I don't like being beholden to anyone. This was business.' At least, they'd planned to talk business. Even though in the end they hadn't ended up talking about any of her ideas. She lifted her chin. 'So I'm paying my share. It's not up for discussion.'

For a moment, she thought he was going to argue. But then he shrugged. 'OK. Purely to keep the peace.'

A peace they were both about to destroy, she thought wryly.

'Do you have a problem with me ordering us a taxi?' he asked.

'No.'

'Good.'

The silence between them as they waited for the taxi was painful; it was a relief when the car arrived. Though the silence in the taxi was just as bad. She wasn't willing to break it by chattering about something inconsequential; when she stole a sidelong glance at him, there were tense lines around his mouth, so he clearly felt the same.

By the time the driver pulled up outside the building where Jordan lived in Notting Hill, Alexandra felt as brittle as the most delicate glass. One wrong touch, and she'd shatter.

He tapped in a code to let them into the lobby. Ushered her into the lift with a gesture. Unlocked the front door to his flat and motioned with his hand for her to walk inside.

'Coffee?' he asked as he closed his front door behind them.

It would've choked her. 'No, thanks.'

'Come and sit down.'

His flat was just as she'd expected. Masculine, plain— and everything was utterly luxurious. Carpet deep enough to sink into, making her feel guilty that she hadn't re- moved her shoes; cream leather sofas that were incredibly soft to the touch; and state-of-the-art television and audio equipment.

Without comment, she sat on the sofa, and was relieved when he took the chair opposite her rather than sitting next to her. If they were going to get through this, she didn't want him too close. Didn't want him distracting her.

'So,' he said. 'Time to talk.'

And she had no intention of letting him take the upper hand. She lifted her chin. 'So you're finally going to tell me why you cheated on me?'

CHAPTER FOUR

Jordan looked as if she'd just poleaxed him. He sat down and stared at her in what looked like utter incomprehension. 'I *what?*'

'You cheated on me,' Alexandra repeated.

He shook his head. 'No, I didn't. Why on earth would you think I'd do something like that?'

'Even if I hadn't been told outright, I could see the signs.' She folded her arms. 'You weren't that serious about me—you were just messing about with me until Miss Right came along, weren't you?'

He frowned. 'I don't get any of this. What do you mean, told outright? And I wasn't messing about with you.'

'Jordan, you never rang me in term time. You never came back to see me, or invited me to come down to Oxford for the weekend.'

'You *know* why. The terms at Oxford are short and intense. I was studying all the time and I had tutorials on Saturday mornings. I wanted a Double First, and that meant putting in the work. I barely had time to breathe.'

'Would it have killed you to text me? To email me? To let me know you were thinking of me?'

His frown deepened. 'I don't remember any of this being an issue at the time. You were studying for your exams and I was studying for mine. If you weren't happy with the way things were, why didn't you say?'

'Because I was scared I'd push you away,' she said. 'Or that you'd laugh at me. I mean, my background was nothing like yours.'

His face tightened. 'So now you're saying I'm a snob?'

'No. I'm saying I was eighteen, I wasn't exactly confident in myself back then, and I'd seen my best friend messed about by someone who went away to study, wasn't faithful to her and left her struggling as a single mum. So, yes, I worried that it'd be like that with you. That it'd be a case of out of sight, out of mind, and you'd find someone else.'

He shook his head. 'That's completely unfair. Not all men are the same.'

'I know that. But what happened to Meggie made me wonder. Would things change between us when you were at Oxford and I was still at home? Would you meet someone else while you were away, someone more suitable, and dump me?'

'I'm still not following. What do you mean, more suitable?'

'You never let me meet your family, we never hung out with your friends when you came home, and part of me wondered, why on earth would someone like you date someone like me—someone who wasn't from your world and would never fit in?'

'Of course you'd fit in. And I didn't keep you away from my family on purpose. My friends, yes, purely because I didn't want to have to share the time I had with you. If anything, I neglected them for you. But I never kept you away from my family. My parents worked long hours; they weren't home that much. That's the only reason you didn't get to meet them properly.' He stared at her. 'I still can't believe you thought I cheated on you. So who said I did? Meggie?'

'No. A woman who said she was your girlfriend.' Alexandra took a deep breath. 'I called you at Oxford, and a woman answered your phone. I asked to speak to you, and she asked who I was. And then she made it very clear that she wasn't happy about some random woman phoning up her boyfriend.'

'I don't have the faintest idea what you're talking about. *Who* you're talking about. What was her name?'

'I didn't ask. I wasn't exactly thinking straight,' she admitted.

'You're telling me! Alex, you knew I lived out in my second year. I shared a house with four other students. People were always just dropping in. And, just because some girl answered my phone, you assumed I was cheating on you?' He shook his head. 'That's incredibly unfair.'

And childish. The implication stung. 'I didn't assume anything. It's what she *said*. That she'd left you in the shower and had come downstairs to make coffee for you both. She made it very obvious that you'd just had sex. And she told me not to ring you again.'

'I didn't have sex with anyone in Oxford when I was seeing you. Not in the shower or anywhere else.' He raked his hand through his hair. 'How could you believe something that a complete stranger told you—someone whose name you didn't even know?'

'Remember I was eighteen, Jordan. And I was panicking.' She'd been full of self-doubt and raging hormones, worrying about what he'd say when she told him the news that she was pregnant. Worrying that he'd dump her, the way Meggie's boyfriend had dumped her when she'd told him about their baby.

'So is that why you didn't tell me about the baby?'

'No.' She wrapped her arms round herself. 'That's why I rang you in the first place. To tell you about the baby. I tried to wait until you were home for the holidays and not disrupt your studies, but I just couldn't. What was happening—it was too big for me to deal with on my own. I needed to talk to you. And then, when I thought you had another girlfriend in Oxford…' She could still remember how she'd felt. Dismayed. Shocked. The way the hurt had seeped through her, numbing her. 'I didn't see that there was any point in telling you about the baby after that, because I didn't think you'd want to know. And it wasn't as if you called me back.'

'I didn't call you back because I had no idea that you'd phoned in the first place. Nobody gave me a message that you'd tried to get hold of me. You weren't even shown on my phone as the last caller.'

'But I must've been. Unless…' A nasty thought struck her. 'Maybe she deleted the record from your call log. To cover her tracks. Because if you'd called me back, I would've had a fit about you cheating on me with her.'

'And then I would've told you the truth—that I was doing nothing of the kind.' He stared at her. 'But obviously you thought I didn't call you back because I didn't want to.'

'What else was I supposed to think? I'd called you, and you didn't call me back.'

'Whoever that woman was, I wasn't sleeping with her.' He looked awkward. 'I admit, I had offers. There was one particular girl who threw herself at me a few times, but I turned her down. I told her I had a girlfriend at home and I wasn't interested. She still hung around our house a bit too much.' He shook his head. 'I can't even remember her name now. It was ten years ago. But I most definitely didn't have any kind of relationship with her, or anyone else, while I was seeing you.'

Looking at him now, she believed him. He hadn't been cheating on her. All these years, she'd believed a pack of lies from someone who'd clearly tried to manipulate her way into Jordan's life and make sure his real girlfriend stayed out. Alexandra had been so mixed up, full of hormones; the woman's lies had been so close to her own fears and doubts that she hadn't questioned them. She bit her lip. 'I know it's a bit late, now—but I'm sorry. I should've believed in you. I should've called you again instead of thinking the worst of you and backing off.'

'As you said, you were eighteen and you weren't particularly confident. You were so shy when I first met you— so, yes, I can understand that.' His expression hardened. 'But what I really can't understand is why you did what you did next.'

It was her turn to frown. 'How do you mean?'

'You didn't tell me about the baby—but you told my mother.'

'Because I thought she might help me.'

His lip curled. 'Don't you mean, pay you?'

'*Pay* me?' She stared at him. 'I don't understand.'

'You asked her for money. And when she wouldn't give you anything, you decided to dump me—without even bothering to tell me—and had a termination.'

He'd thought *that* of her? Alexandra was too shocked to say anything at first. And then anger flooded through her. Yes, she'd been wrong about him—but he'd been far more wrong about her. 'You bastard.'

'I'm just telling it like it is.'

'No. Absolutely not.' She shook her head emphatically. 'How could you possibly believe I'd ever do something like that?'

'Let's see.' His face was grim. 'When I got back from Oxford, my mother said that you'd told her you were pregnant with my baby and you asked her for money. True, or not true?'

'True,' she muttered.

'So I tried ringing you, but your mobile phone was permanently switched off. I couldn't get hold of you. I went to see your parents, and they told me you didn't live there any more. I asked about the baby, and they told me you were no longer pregnant. They made it clear I wasn't welcome. So then I got in touch with Meggie, thinking she'd tell me where you were—and she said you didn't want to see me ever again.'

Alexandra was shaking. How, how, *how* could he have put the pieces together and got the picture so wrong?

'Well? Isn't that what happened, Alex?'

'Not like the way you're making out it happened. Yes, I told your mother about the baby and I asked her to help me. I needed money for nursery fees, so I could still go on to do my degree and know the baby was being looked after properly while I was studying.' Back then, she'd still thought she could do it. Go to university, take her degree, then teach; and she'd manage to support their baby on her own, once she'd graduated. 'She refused. And yes, I left home. And yes, I wasn't pregnant any more when I left home. And yes, I told Meggie and my parents I never wanted to see you again. I hated you, Jordan, because when I needed you most you just weren't there. All of that's true.' She lifted her chin. 'But I didn't have a termination. I had an ectopic pregnancy.'

'You had a what?' He stared at her, looking completely confused.

'An ectopic pregnancy. It's where the egg gets stuck in the Fallopian tube and grows there instead of in the womb,' she explained. Just as the doctor had explained it to her, all those years ago. The reason why she'd been in such agony. 'You don't know it's happened until the foetus grows big enough. Then the tube ruptures.' She swallowed hard. 'I guess it hurts a bit.'

Horror filled his expression. 'Oh, my God. Alex.' He stood up and moved to wrap his arms round her, but she lifted her hands to tell him to back off.

'Don't touch me, Jordan.' The full impact of his words had just sunk in. He'd thought she'd used their baby as a bargaining ticket to get money—and that, when she failed, she'd deliberately had an abortion. Did he think she'd deliberately got pregnant, too? That she was the gold-digger his mother had accused her of being? 'I know we didn't plan to have a baby, but I can't believe you thought I'd ever have a termination. That I'd get rid of our baby without a second thought. I loved you so much, and you let me down. I didn't think you could let me down any more than you did back then…but you just have.' She felt sick.

'What was I supposed to think, Alex? I had to find out about our baby from someone else—and then I was told that there was no baby any more. You vanished. Nobody knew where you'd gone—or, if they did, they weren't going to tell me—and I couldn't find you. I couldn't get in touch with you to find out your side of things.'

'I couldn't bear to be at home, not afterwards. My parents…they couldn't see why I was so upset about losing the baby. The way they saw it, with me losing the baby, the problems had all been solved. There was no baby to get in the way of me doing my exams and going to university.' She drew her knees up and wrapped her arms round them. 'I hated the fact they were relieved. Every day, it hurt more. I couldn't bear it. So I left home.'

'Where did you go?' he asked.

'A hostel, for the first few days. I stuck it out for nearly a week, but I hated not having any privacy. Though I had some savings.' She shrugged. 'And I knew I wasn't going to university any more, so I thought I might as well use them. I scoured all the small ads and managed to find myself a bedsit.' She grimaced. 'It was damp. There was this huge patch of black mould on the ceiling and I couldn't get rid of the smell, but even so it was better than the hostel. It was mine.'

Jordan hated to think of her struggling like that, living in a damp, poky bedsit. Even his student house in his second year had been dry, clean and spacious, thanks to the generous allowance his parents had given him.

'And I found a job so I could support myself. It was fine as long as I could do a bit of overtime.'

No, it wasn't fine at all. She should've been enjoying her life as a student, the way she'd planned, not working all hours to make ends meet. Her life had been turned upside down—and his had been endless privilege. There was nothing he could say, nothing he could do. He couldn't even put his arms round her now to comfort her, because her body language was screaming 'keep away'—and anyway it was ten years too late.

He'd never felt so helpless, so useless, in his entire life.

'What made you think you couldn't still go to university?' he asked, focusing on the one bit he didn't quite understand.

'I knew I hadn't got the grades. I missed three papers while I was in hospital, and I was on so many painkillers for the next couple of days that I couldn't think straight. I have no idea what I wrote in my exams, but I'm pretty sure it was garbage.' She shrugged. 'I knew I'd blown it and my dreams had gone, so what was the point of waiting for my results to confirm it? So I left home the day after my last exam.'

When she still hadn't recovered physically from losing the baby, let alone dealt with the emotional pain. He hated to think that she'd been so alone. 'I understand why you wanted some space from your parents, but why Meggie? I mean, she was your best friend and she'd been through... well, something similar. Couldn't you have stayed with her for a bit?'

Alexandra shook her head. 'I couldn't bear seeing the pity in her eyes every time she looked at me. I'm not proud of myself, but I cut myself off from her as well. Until I got my head together again.'

Or so she'd thought at the time. She'd been swept off her feet by Nathan Bennett, and then—filled with delight when he'd placed the diamond ring on her finger—had phoned Meggie, wanting to share the news with her best friend, apologise for going AWOL and asking Meggie to be her bridesmaid. She'd had no idea that she'd gone from the frying pan straight into the fire.

'Alex, if I'd known...' He looked tortured.

'But you *did*,' she said. 'That's the whole point. You knew. I collapsed at school, the day after my first exam. They called an ambulance; my mum and dad came to the hospital and I begged them to get hold of you. I gave them your number—your parents' number as well as your mobile. Dad went to phone you. Then he came back and told me you wouldn't come.'

He frowned. 'I never spoke to your parents.'

'So you're saying they lied to me?'

'You're saying my mother lied to me?' he countered.

'Your mother twisted things. She said there was no way I could prove the baby was yours, and she wasn't going to let me foist it on you and ruin your life. And I was a cheap little gold-digger who saw you as a meal ticket for life, but I was mistaken because she wasn't going to give me a penny.' She shivered. 'It wasn't like that. I loved you. And it *was* your baby.'

At least he didn't try to deny that.

She dragged in a breath. 'I didn't ask her to pay me off, Jordan. I asked her to give me a loan, because I knew my parents couldn't afford to help me. I was going to pay her back once I'd graduated and had a job.'

'That's not what she told me. She just said you asked for money.'

'Technically, I did ask for money.'

'But not in the way she made me think you did. Oh, hell.' He closed his eyes briefly, as if shutting out the pain, then stared at her. 'Alex, I'm so, so sorry. If I'd had any idea…The second she told me about the baby, I came to see you and find out what was going on.' He paused. 'Your parents didn't say you'd been in the emergency department and lost the baby. They just said you weren't pregnant any more.'

'And you assumed that I'd got rid of the baby deliberately.' She shook her head in disgust. 'I can't believe you'd think that of me.'

'What can I say? I was twenty years old and I still had a lot of growing up to do. Alex, all I knew is that you were pregnant with our baby, and then you weren't, and you didn't want anything to do with me. You hadn't told me *anything*. I was furious with you. I thought you'd dumped me without even bothering to tell me that you wanted to end it—and that's why I believed the worst of you.' He dragged in a breath. 'I guess it was easier than digging to find out the truth. And I'm sorry. I'm sorry I was such an arrogant bastard who didn't think any further than his own

ego. I'm sorry I wasn't there for you.' He came to kneel
in front of her chair and placed his hand over hers. 'If I'd
known about the baby earlier, believe me, I would've been
right there by your side.'

'You were in the middle of your second-year exams.
And they counted towards your degree.'

'That doesn't matter—I could always have resat them
if I'd needed to. But *you* mattered, Alex. You did.' His
voice was full of anguish, as if he were desperately trying to make her believe how much he'd cared about her.

'You weren't there,' she whispered. 'My whole world
blew apart, and you weren't there. I was so desperate, I
asked my parents to contact you—and you didn't come.'

'Your dad didn't ring me. I had no idea that any of this
happened, Alex. You have to believe me.' He stroked her
hair back from her forehead. 'I'm so sorry you had to go
through that without my support. And yes, I would've
walked out of my exams to be with you. Everything else
would've sorted itself out later.'

'You didn't even send me a message. A card.'

'Because I didn't know what was going on. Anyway, I
wouldn't have sent you a card. I would've been with you.
End of.'

The worst thing was, she believed him.

She'd got him so badly wrong—just as he'd got her
badly wrong. They'd both been too young to trust each
other completely. And they'd lost half a lifetime together
because of it.

'You were just eighteen, and you had to go through all
that alone. That's awful.' He raked a hand through his hair.
'And I can understand now why you acted the way you did.
You'd just found out you were expecting our baby—something that was going to change your whole life, maybe turn
all your plans upside down. And you rang me, only to get

some strange woman who told you a pack of lies at a time when you were vulnerable enough not to question them. If you hadn't been scared and pregnant—not to mention full of hormones—you wouldn't have believed a word she'd said. You would've called me back later and demanded to know what the hell was going on.'

'And nobody told *you* the full truth, either.' She swallowed hard. 'I'm still furious that you thought I could ever—' she couldn't quite bring herself to say the words again '—do something like that, but I think now I can understand why you came to that conclusion.'

'That, and then Meggie telling me that you'd got married. Only a short time after you'd been pregnant with my baby.' He looked straight at her. 'What was I supposed to think? Obviously I wasn't that important to you, if you could marry someone else so fast.'

Nathan. The biggest mistake of her life. 'It wasn't quite like that.' She sighed. 'Let's just leave it that I was a bit mixed up at the time.'

'A bit?' he asked, sounding bitter.

'My life had changed completely. I was living in a damp little bedsit and working ridiculous hours to earn enough to support myself. I'd lost the man I loved, I'd lost our baby, and when someone sweeps you off your feet and makes you feel special and offers to take all the worries away...' She grimaced. 'I don't want to talk about my marriage.' She didn't even want to think about how bad her judgement had been. How much of herself she'd lost over those three years. 'Let's just leave it that it didn't work out.'

'For what it's worth,' he said gently, 'I'm truly sorry.'

His apology disarmed her. And he wasn't the only one at fault. She needed to take her share of the blame in what had happened. 'Me, too.'

'What you said about your Fallopian tube—did the doctors manage to fix it?' he asked.

She shook her head.

'So what does that mean for you?'

She'd known he'd ask that. Typical Jordan: she'd seen him in meetings and he always cut straight to the heart of the problem. She took a deep breath. 'If one of the tubes goes, it means that getting pregnant will be harder. And you have a slightly bigger risk than average of having another ectopic pregnancy next time round.'

'Is that why your marriage broke up?' he asked softly.

'Partly.' She swallowed hard. 'Please, can we just leave this now? I want to go home.'

Some of the pain in her voice must have touched him, because he nodded. 'I'll drive you.'

'A taxi's fine. If you don't mind me waiting here until it turns up.'

'In the circumstances, I think driving you home is the least I can do,' Jordan said. 'And yes, I know you're an adult and you're perfectly capable of ordering your own taxi. But right now I'm feeling bad about the way I believed the worst of you for all those years.' He looked awkward. 'I guess I'm better when I'm doing something practical.'

She could understand that. It was like that for her, too. That was one of the reasons why she was so hands-on in her job. 'Just as long as you don't expect to be offered coffee the other end,' she warned. 'Not because I still hate you, but because right now I'm all talked out and I can't handle any more tonight.'

'Understood. Shall we go?'

When she stood up, he moved to put his arms round her; she took a swift sidestep.

Pain flickered across his face. 'That wasn't a come-on, Alex. What you've just told me must've brought back a lot, and it couldn't have been easy for you. I thought…' He looked hurt. 'I just thought you could do with a hug.'

Yes. She wanted to be held. But then she knew she'd start crying and make a fool of herself. There would be no crying until she was back in her own flat, with a locked door between her and the outside world. Nobody saw her vulnerabilities, nowadays. *Nobody.* 'I'm fine.' But she stole a glance at him and felt guilty; he looked drawn and miserable.

They went to his car in silence; but this time the atmosphere was resigned rather than tense. Life had made them both jaded and wary, she thought. And the way she'd disappeared and then married someone else so quickly had definitely played a part in making Jordan the way he was now. The man she remembered had been full of laughter, enjoying clever jokes and wordplay. The man he was now…She'd seen him smile, but he'd become so serious. A workaholic.

Though who was she to judge? She knew that she was just as bad.

'I'd better give you directions,' she said.

'No need.' He tapped her postcode into his satnav.

'How come you know my postcode?' she asked.

He shrugged. 'Your address was on your CV. I only need to read things once to remember the salient points.'

Of course. He'd always been bright.

When they reached her flat, he insisted on seeing her to her door. 'This isn't a bid for coffee. It's simply good manners,' he said.

She didn't argue. But she nearly cracked when he said gently, 'Are you going to be OK? Do you want me to call Meggie for you?'

'I'll be fine,' she fibbed. 'But thanks for asking.'

'OK. I'll see you tomorrow.'

'Yeah. Thanks for the lift.'

'Pleasure.'

She closed the front door behind her, then leaned against the wall and sank down to the floor, wrapping her arms round her legs and resting her head against her knees. If things had only been different…

But they weren't.

And she and Jordan just had to put everything behind them, forget about tonight's revelations, and learn to work together.

CHAPTER FIVE

THE next day, Alexandra was in the office early. Though not early enough to avoid Jordan; when she walked into the staff kitchen, he was already there.

He looked at her, then took down another mug and spooned coffee into it. 'Morning. How are you doing?'

'Fine,' she lied. She noticed that he had dark smudges underneath his eyes; it looked as if he'd spent as bad a night as she had last night. 'Are you OK?' she asked.

He gave her a weary smile. 'I'm in meetings all day today. But text me if you need me, OK?'

Which didn't answer her question; and right now she didn't want to push. She didn't want to hear him say that he felt as bad as she did—and know that she was the cause of it.

'Coffee.' He pushed the mug along the worktop towards her.

'Thanks. I'll see you later. Enjoy your meetings.'

She didn't text him. Even though she was tempted. Going through everything again last night had stirred up all kinds of things—most of them unwelcome. Not just the memories of the pain she'd gone through, but things that she could barely admit to herself. Like the fact that she still found Jordan Smith attractive. Not just physically: she liked the man he'd become. Straight-talking, yet responsible and thoughtful.

Which was another reason why she ought to avoid him. She couldn't afford to let herself fall for him again. She'd fought so hard for her independence and she didn't want to lose a single iota of it. Jordan was used to being in charge, and she'd had her fill of controlling men.

But the idea wouldn't go away, and her face grew hot when he walked into her office at the end of the day.

'Had a good day?' he asked.

'Fine. You?'

'Fine.' He paused. 'You didn't text me.'

She shrugged. 'I didn't need to. I'm perfectly capable of doing my job.'

'I know. Otherwise I wouldn't have hired you.' His gaze held hers. 'And I didn't mean about work.'

Yeah. She knew that. She sighed. 'Jordan, what's past is past. We can't change it. Only accept it.'

'Even though it makes me feel like pond life?'

She smiled. 'I don't see any signs of gills. Or slime.'

He inclined his head. 'Thank you for that. I wasn't fishing.'

'Well, no. If you're pond life, you'd be the one being fished for.'

He smiled, then, and she wished she'd kept her mouth shut. Because his smile was genuine, causing little crinkles at the corners of his eyes. Crinkles she wanted to smooth away with the tips of her fingers, before...

The blood rushed to her face as she realised what she was thinking about. *Kissing Jordan.*

Interesting. She'd just gone really, really red. What was she thinking about? Jordan wondered. But if he asked her he knew she would back off rapidly. She was incredibly wary of him; though that was hardly surprising, given what had happened to her. In her shoes, he'd be the same.

To make it easier for both of them, he brought the conversation back to business. 'How's the staff suggestion scheme going?'

'Good. I've had some really great ideas through it already,' she said.

'And I hear that every one of them has been acknowledged with a personal note, along with a chocolate Neapolitan that says "thank you" on the wrapper.'

She frowned. 'Is that a problem?'

'No. I was just wondering how big the chocolate bill is going to be.'

'It's not a marketing department expense. I bought them myself.'

Now that he hadn't expected. 'Why?'

'Because I want people to feel that they're appreciated— it's a small gesture, unexpected enough to please people but not expensive enough to embarrass them. And almost everyone likes chocolate.'

Yeah. He could remember lying in the park under the trees with his head in her lap, with her feeding him squares of chocolate. He could almost smell her light, floral scent, taste the sweetness of the chocolate, feel the silkiness of her hair against his face as she dipped her head to kiss him…

'Not expensive?' he said, trying to keep his thoughts on business instead of remembering what it was like to kiss the woman who sat at her desk, all cool and professional.

'I have a friend who produces promotional chocolates. If you choose a stock wrapper, like the one I use, you can buy them in reasonable quantities at less than the cost of, say, a small box of chocolates from Field's deli.'

'Define reasonable.'

'A box of fifty—so there isn't a storage problem like there would be if you had to buy a couple of thousand at a time.'

'Where do you store them?' he asked, curious.

She smiled. 'That's classified information, given how many chocoholics work on our floor.'

Including him. He fought to push the memories back. 'You've certainly made a hit.'

'And that's what I want Field's to do with our customers. Make them feel they're appreciated.'

He raised an eyebrow. 'You're going to send them chocolate, too?'

'No. I was thinking more along the lines of a points system. The more they interact on the website, the more points they get—and when they reach a certain level they'll get a store voucher.'

'Which we send out?'

'No. We give them a code they can use either online or at a till point in the store. And it's a unique code so it doesn't leave us open to fraud.'

She'd clearly thought this through properly, and he was impressed. And she'd follow it through, too, with her enthusiasm; he knew she'd carry the board of directors with her when she explained it to them.

Though all he could think of was how beautiful her mouth was as she spoke. And how that mouth had felt against his skin. And how the last time he'd really been happy was ten years ago, before they'd broken up.

Crazy. It couldn't work between them. No way would she let him close after what had happened. And he wasn't looking for a relationship in any case. He'd learned that lesson the hard way: they didn't work if you went in with your heart, and they didn't work if you went in with your head. Besides, he had enough on his plate with a department store to drag into this century.

Though he was having a seriously hard time getting Alexandra out of his head.

It got harder still during the rest of the week. She wasn't avoiding him, exactly—she was busy with events, and he had a week full of meetings—but when he did see her he realised that he liked the woman she'd become: bright, sparky, enthusiastic. She was good at her job; she came to him with solutions, not problems; and her ideas were creating a real buzz among customers and staff alike. Footfall in the store was up, and so were sales. Hiring her had definitely been the right thing for Field's; and he needed to keep his own feelings in the background.

On Friday evening, he dropped in to her office. 'Are you busy on Sunday?'

'Why?' she asked, looking wary.

'I was planning to go for a walk by the river in Greenwich. I wondered if you'd like to join me.'

'Is that a good idea?' she asked, looking warier still.

'Probably not,' he said. 'But I thought it might be nice to go for a walk and have an ice cream.'

She licked her lower lip, and a surge of longing filled him.

'That's a really bad idea,' she said, as if she'd guessed at his thoughts.

'OK.' He shrugged. 'Forget I asked.'

'I didn't say no,' she pointed out. 'Just that it's a bad idea.'

'So was that a roundabout way of saying yes?'

'A walk by the river and an ice cream,' she repeated.

Which was his version of an olive branch. 'Or a coffee if it turns out to be wet and freezing.'

'Wet and freezing works fine for me, where ice cream is concerned. What time?'

'Two? Three?'

'Two. Meet you outside the gates to the Royal Naval College—the ones nearest the Tube,' she said.

Funny how her agreement warmed him.

He was almost late. She was leaning against the iron railings, and she tapped her watch as he hurried to meet her. 'Tut. You're cutting it a bit fine, Mr Smith.'

'Blame the siren song of the spreadsheet,' he said, and she laughed.

She looked utterly gorgeous. Instead of the sharp business suits and high heels he was used to seeing her in, she was wearing faded denims, low-heeled boots and a bright red cashmere sweater beneath her open jacket. It made her look softer, younger—*touchable*. To the point where he had to jam his hands into the pockets of his own jeans to stop himself acting on the urge to pull her into his arms.

This was crazy. He shouldn't want to hold her, touch her, kiss her until they were both dizzy. But seeing her like this made the old desires flood all the way back.

They headed for the path by the river and walked together in silence for a while. Not an awkward silence, to his relief; more as if they were both wondering where this was going. As if they were both weighing up all the options.

'I've always liked this bit of London,' she said. 'Those gorgeous buildings. The domes.' She smiled. 'I always thought Rome would be like that.'

He remembered Italy being top of her travel wish-list when she was a teenager. Rome, Venice, Capri, Florence,

Pompeii, Vesuvius, Juliet's balcony in Verona: she'd wanted to see all of them. 'Did you ever get to see Rome?'

'Last year. A long weekend in Rome, seeing the Colosseum and the Pantheon and the Trevi Fountain. And the Sistine Chapel. It's the most beautiful city.'

'Yes, it is.' He found himself wondering who she'd gone with.

As if she'd guessed his thoughts, she said, 'Meggie told me I was crazy, going on my own. But I loved it—it meant I could see the places I wanted to see on *my* schedule, nobody else's.'

'There's nothing worse than having to rush round something you want to see because someone else thinks museums are boring,' he agreed.

She raised an eyebrow. 'That sounds personal. Did your wife—?' She broke off. 'Sorry. That was intrusive.'

'No, it's fine. She wasn't into museums. But she did like shopping, so we compromised in Rome. She enjoyed herself in the Via Condotti with my credit card, and I had the afternoon in the Capitoline Museum, among the sculptures.' He looked at her. 'Was your husband not keen on museums, either?'

'No,' she said, her voice crisp.

'Sorry. I didn't mean to pry.'

'It's OK.'

But he knew it wasn't; the wariness was back. Her marriage clearly hadn't been happy, or she wouldn't be divorced now. Or, he suddenly wondered, had she wanted to stay married but her ex had been the one to end it?

Not that he could ask her. She'd find it way too intrusive, and pushing would make her back off even more. And he didn't want her to back off. He wanted to get to know her again.

'So do you come here often?' she asked.

'Usually when I'm a bit out of sorts,' he said. 'I guess it's the flow of the water that makes me feel calmer.' He gave her a wry smile. 'And it's quicker to get to the Thames than it is to drive to the nearest beach.'

'I haven't been to the beach in years.'

She sounded wistful, and Jordan had the craziest idea. They'd managed a couple of days out to Brighton, that summer. OK, so you couldn't repeat the past. But you could still enjoy things second time round. Maybe he could take her to the beach for the day and it would bring a real smile back to her eyes.

He found a kiosk and bought them both an ice cream, then tempted her to take a taste of his. As their eyes met he remembered the times they'd done this in the past; he was pretty sure she was thinking of it, too. About how he'd lean forward and lick the smear of ice cream from the corner of her mouth. And then she'd turn her head very slightly towards him, lips parted, so his mouth could glide over hers. He'd nibble her lower lip until she sighed and slid her hands into his hair, letting him deepen the kiss.

He saw her eyes widen. Was she as close as he was to repeating it? What would she do if he leaned forward and kissed her? Probably run a mile, he acknowledged wryly. Now wasn't the right time. He'd know when that was— when they were both ready.

He kept the conversation neutral as they strolled along beside the Thames, and finally saw her home.

'Thank you. I've had a lovely time,' she said outside her front door.

'Me, too.'

She gave him a wry smile. 'Maybe I'll invite you in, next time.'

His heart skipped a beat. So there was going to be a next time. She felt it, too—and it wasn't just the past. It was who they were now. 'Sounds good,' he said, keeping his tone as light as possible.

He knew this was his cue to say goodbye. But he wasn't ready to leave her, not yet. Unable to help himself, he cupped her cheek.

Her eyes widened. 'Jordan.' Her voice was slightly deeper and huskier. Just as his would be, if he said her name. Almost rusty with desire.

His thumb was so close to her lower lip. All he had to do was move his hand. Very, very slightly stroke the pad of his thumb over her lower lip. Lightly, gently…

Risky. It might make her bolt.

On the other hand…

It was too much for him to resist. Barely making contact with her skin, yet feeling as if every nerve end were sizzling, he brushed the pad of his thumb over her lower lip.

Her pupils dilated even more, and her lips parted. He could feel the warmth of her breath against his skin, and it made his head spin. 'Alex,' he whispered, and dipped his head to kiss her. Sweet, soft, asking rather than demanding.

She kissed him back—tiny, nibbling kisses that heated his blood even more. But when his hands slid under her coat, drawing her closer to him, she pulled away.

'We shouldn't be doing this.'

He was about to tell her that she'd known damn well this would happen, when he noticed the panic in her eyes. No. It was going to happen. Both of them knew it. He just needed to give her a little more time to get used to the idea.

'I'd better go.' Even though he didn't want to. Every fibre of his being was begging him to stay. 'I'll see you later.'

The panic in her eyes started to ebb, and he knew he'd

made the right decision. And he also knew that she was going to be worth waiting for.

From that point, it felt as if they'd reached a truce, and it was a lot easier to work together. Jordan didn't feel as if he had to watch what he said all the time, and she didn't seem quite so reserved with him. Keeping his libido under control was harder, though, and it didn't do his temper much good.

In the middle of the week, Alexandra came into Jordan's office. 'Can I run something past you?'

'What, now?'

She raised an eyebrow. 'Sorry. Is this a bad time?'

He sighed. 'No. Sorry. I shouldn't take my bad mood out on you.'

'Problems?'

'No.'

'It sounds as if you need carbs.'

He frowned. 'What?'

'When did you last eat? A sandwich at your desk, was it?'

'Don't make a big deal out of it. You do exactly the same,' he said.

'True,' she admitted with a smile. 'OK. I'll leave you to your bad mood.'

Except she didn't. Fifteen minutes later, she walked in with a box of something that smelled delectable.

'Pizza?' he guessed.

'Yes. I went to that trattoria.'

'But they don't do takeaway food.'

'They do for you. I told Giorgio we were having a late meeting and couldn't leave the computer. He says this is your usual. *Funghi e prosciutto.*'

He really, really hadn't expected her to do that, and it threw him. 'I…Thank you, Alex.'

'Prego.' There was a hint of a teasing smile. 'As Giorgio would say.'

He wasn't surprised that she'd charmed the trattoria owner. She'd certainly charmed him. And he desperately wanted her to stay here a little longer. 'I hope you'll share it with me.'

'I…' She gave him a wary look.

'I don't bite,' he said softly. 'I know I growled at you earlier, and I apologise. I'm just out of sorts. And you're probably right, my blood sugar's a bit low.'

As they shared the pizza, once, his fingers brushed against hers, and it felt as if he'd been galvanised. He just hoped it hadn't shown on his face, because he didn't want her to bolt.

Then again, she could've made some excuse not to stay, not to share the pizza with him.

He looked at her hands. Beautiful hands, and such delicate fingers. She'd been able to bring him to his knees with her touch. He noticed a smear of tomato sauce on her thumb, and it was too much to resist. He picked up her hand and drew it to his mouth, licking the sauce away.

She dragged in a breath, and her eyes had gone wide.

Unable to stop himself, he drew the tip of her thumb into his mouth and sucked.

Oh, dear God. If Alexandra hadn't been sitting down, she would've fallen. Jordan had always been able to make her tremble with that beautiful, clever mouth. Pictures bloomed in her head; she could see herself sweeping everything off his desk. Pushing him across it. Straddling him…

She was practically hyperventilating now.

'Jordan. This is a bad idea.' She did her best to drag her

common sense from where it was hiding. 'I...this wasn't meant to be a seduction.'

'No. But it could be.' He moistened his lower lip with the tip of his tongue, making her wish it were her skin he was moistening. 'Alex.' His voice was low and sexy—and it made her wet when he said her name like that.

Oh, God. She was seconds away from losing her self control. From losing her mind, He'd stopped sucking her thumb, but his fingers were caressing her wrist, feeling the pulse thudding here.

She tried again. 'The pizza—I was just being nice. Doing what I'd do for any colleague.'

Liar. He didn't actually say it, but then again he didn't need to. They both knew.

But the panic must have shown in her face, because he released her hand. 'Thank you.' He paused and held her gaze. 'Lindsey certainly wouldn't have done that.'

'Lindsey being the former Mrs Smith?'

He sighed. 'Yes.'

She bit her lip. 'Sorry. I didn't mean to drag things up.'

'No, it's OK. The divorce was three years ago now. I'm fine.'

'Are you?'

'Actually, yes.' He grimaced. 'In hindsight, I shouldn't have married her. But at the time I thought I was doing the right thing. Dad was having chest pains, and I knew he was worrying about me settling down and being ready to take over from him.'

'Is your father OK now?'

'He's absolutely fine and enjoying retirement,' Jordan reassured her.

'That's good.' She paused. 'So you got married to keep your parents happy?'

'Not happy, exactly. But I knew they wanted to be sure

that I was settled.' He shrugged. 'I'd known Lindsey for years. She'd gone to the girls' school next door and we were friends.'

Given how badly things had gone wrong with Alexandra, Jordan had decided to choose his bride with his head rather than his heart. When he'd kissed Lindsey, his head hadn't filled with fireworks, the way it had when he'd kissed Alexandra, but he'd told himself that that was a good thing. He'd learned from Alexandra that love didn't stop you getting hurt, and so he'd chosen his wife *sensibly*. Someone from the same background as his own; someone who wanted the lifestyle he could give her and would be a corporate wife for him. 'I thought that our marriage would work out just fine.'

'But it didn't,' she said softly.

'No.' He sighed. 'It was my fault. I worked too many hours, didn't pay her enough attention, and she got bored waiting for me. She found someone else who was willing to give her what she needed, and she's much happier now.'

'Hard for you, though.'

Not as hard as it had been, losing Alexandra. Because, if he was honest about it, he'd never really loved Lindsey. Love hadn't been on his agenda. He'd thought that his head would steer him in the right direction, unlike the way his heart had steered him with Alexandra. And he'd still got it wrong. Ended up being hurt. Admittedly, his pride had been bruised slightly more than his heart, but it had still been a miserable time in his life. Since then, he'd kept all his relationships short and sweet. Non-existent, for the last six months, because he'd been concentrating on work.

'It wasn't great at the time, but I got over it.' He shrugged. 'As I said, I'm fine now.'

'Bored waiting for you.' Alexandra made a face. 'Didn't

she have a job, or at least do some charity work to stop herself being bored?'

'No.'

Alexandra's expression was unreadable. 'So she was a full-time WAG. Looked after financially by you, and her day was her own.'

He raised his eyebrows. 'Are you telling me you disapprove of WAGs?'

'Not all women like being looked after and told what to do.'

'I didn't tell Lindsey what to do,' he said dryly. 'But isn't that meant to be the dream? Not having to drag yourself out of bed every Monday morning and know you're going to spend the week having to deal with office politics or difficult customers, not to mention worrying about whether the company's going to go under and you'll still have a job at the end of the week?'

She thought about it. 'Maybe for a couple of days it'd be nice not to have any worries or responsibilities. But the idea of every single day being the same—a session with a personal trainer, then off to be pampered at the beauty parlour, then lunch with the girls, then mooching around the shops, then waiting for my husband to come home so I could tell him all about my, oh, so exciting day...' She shook her head. 'I'd be bored to tears within a week. Not to mention the fact I'd rather earn my own money and not have to be accountable to someone else for every penny I spent.'

That sounded a bit heartfelt. 'Are you talking from experience?' he asked.

For a moment, he thought she was going to back away, but then she gave him a sad little smile. 'Yes.'

She'd said that her marriage hadn't worked out. Clearly she'd been unhappy with Bennett. But Jordan didn't understand why she'd had to account to her husband for every penny she'd spent, when she'd been earning. There'd been no gaps in her CV. She'd always had a job.

'Jordan,' she warned, 'your thoughts are written all over your face. Don't ask.'

'OK.' Clearly it was too painful for her to talk about. 'For what it's worth,' he said, 'I'm sorry your marriage didn't work out. I was hurt and angry when I found out you'd got married to someone else so soon after me, and I hated you for a while—but I wouldn't have wished you anything else but happiness.' Her eyes were suspiciously shiny, and he saw her blink back a tear. 'And I'm sorry. I didn't mean to rip open any scars just now.'

'Not your fault.' She took a deep breath. 'I rushed into getting married. I thought Nathan would give me everything you and my parents hadn't. What you said about being looked after—that's what I wanted, back then.' She bit her lip. 'Except it didn't turn out quite how I thought it would.'

Accountable for every penny she spent. Clearly the man had taken 'looking after' to the extreme. Jordan had never expected Lindsey to tell him what she'd bought; he'd simply picked up the bills, thinking that as long as she was happy everything would be fine.

He reached across his desk and squeezed Alexandra's hand. He kept holding it for just long enough to let her know that he was on her side, then withdrew his hand again so she'd know he wasn't going to crowd her. Wasn't going to push her, the way he had when he'd drawn her thumb into his mouth. 'It's easy to be wise with hindsight,' he said. 'But you just have to do the best you can, based on the knowledge you have at that moment.'

'I guess so.'

'Sometimes you have to stop beating yourself up about

things you would've done differently.' He gave her a rueful smile. 'And that's easier said than done. I'm still finding it hard to forgive myself now I know what happened
to you.'

He didn't know the half of it, Alexandra thought. And she
wasn't ready to tell him the rest of it. About how she'd
struggled to support herself. How she'd been so ready to
fall for Nathan's promise of a happy-ever-after. And how,
when she hadn't been able to hold up her side of the bargain, Nathan had never let her forget how she'd failed him.
She'd failed to give him the family he wanted, failed to
suppress her own needs and make him the centre of her
world instead of dreaming about finally taking her degree,
failed to be the dutiful and biddable wife he'd expected.

'It wasn't all your fault. I made some bad choices, too.'
She lifted her chin. 'And we're both in danger of getting really maudlin. So I'm going home.' She paused long enough
to make it clear that it wasn't an offer for him to join her.
'And I hope you're not intending to stay at your desk until
midnight.'

'Not quite. Though there was something I wanted to
finish tonight,' Jordan said.

'Don't work too late.' She took the pizza box with her,
and disposed of it in the bin in the staff kitchen, then
headed back to her own office, backed up her files and
switched off the computer. And then, on impulse, she took
something from her filing cabinet, placed it in a small
envelope from her recycling tray, and walked back into
Jordan's office.

'See you tomorrow,' she said.

'See you tomorrow,' he echoed. 'And thank you for the
pizza.'

'Pleasure. Oh, by the way, I have something for you.'
She handed him the envelope.

'What's this?'

She simply smiled. 'Open it later.'

When she'd gone, Jordan opened the envelope. It contained
one of the infamous chocolate Neapolitans she sent out
with her acknowledgement notes for the staff suggestion
scheme. *Thank you.* What was she thanking him for? he
wondered. For listening to her tonight, or for not pushing
her to go to bed with him, or for not pushing her to tell him
everything about her unhappy marriage? Clearly whatever
had gone wrong had left deep scars—and he didn't have a
magic wand to whisk them away. If he'd taken proper care
of her in the first place, she wouldn't have ended up marrying the guy, so he definitely had a share in the blame.

Where did they go from here? He really didn't know.
But she'd given him an opening with the chocolate, and
he intended to make the most of it.

CHAPTER SIX

THE brown envelope on Alexandra's desk contained a small box and a sticky note that said, *Chocolate: raise you one.*

Jordan hadn't signed the note; then again, he hadn't needed to. His handwriting was bold and confident, like the man himself.

She opened the envelope to discover a small box containing a single gold-foiled chocolate. So he was claiming this was better than her Neapolitans, was he? As if. She smiled, and left it in the box until her mid-morning coffee.

The chocolate melted in her mouth; she'd never, ever tasted anything so good. She could brazen it out and pretend that she thought it was perfectly ordinary, but that way she wouldn't find out what it was and where she could get more. And she had to push away the sudden vision of him feeding her the chocolates one by one—in bed.

She emailed him.

You win. Stockist details required, pls.

The reply came back swiftly.

Field's deli. Tut. I expect my marketing manager to be a *bit* more observant.

Though there wasn't an edge to his tone. She could imagine him laughing as he wrote the email. And she liked this fun, teasing side of him. More than liked. If she wasn't careful, she could find herself falling for him again. Not that she'd act on it, this time round. Her life was back on track, and she intended to keep it that way. Yes, she could go to bed with him; and yes, it would be good for both of them. But she couldn't trust herself to keep it just physical—and no way did she want to risk her heart again.

The wonderful chocolate turned out to be Italian. So how did she top that? She went for a walk during her lunch break, still thinking about it, and found a tiny market stall that sold handmade chocolate by a local chocolatier. Chocolate that, according to the notices on the stall, had won awards. A quick chat with the chocolatier netted her something that she was confident might just raise the stakes. Back at the store, she discovered that Jordan was in a meeting, so she left him an envelope containing a dark chocolate praline and a white chocolate square scented with lavender, plus a sticky note saying, *Raise you two*.

She'd just finished double-checking a set of figures for a report when her computer pinged to tell her that an email had arrived.

This isn't ours. Why not?

She typed back.

Clarification required. Why not = why use a competitor, or = when can we make them a stockist?

Jordan didn't waste words.

Both. Can you get samples and contact details to
Sally? Thanks.

Sally was the deli manager, a real foodie who loved her
job; and Alexandra had thoroughly enjoyed talking to her
about her idea for developing specialist hampers—particularly as sampling had been involved.

Sure.

The chocolate—and the talk they'd had over takeaway
pizza at his desk—had gone a long way to thawing out their
relationship; not just the business side of things, showing
them that they could work together for the good of Field's,
but personally, too. A couple of times, Jordan talked her
into going to the trattoria with him; although they spent
most of their time talking shop, more personal stuff had
started creeping in.

It really didn't help that she found him so attractive still.
Why couldn't he have turned into a short, overweight, middle-aged businessman with greasy hair, terrible skin and
bad teeth? Then she might not have found herself thinking about him so much...

There was a rap on her door, and she looked up from
her desk to see the subject of her thoughts standing there.
'Got a second?'

'Sure.'

He walked into her office and sat down on the chair
next to her desk. 'Are you busy tomorrow evening?'

'No.'

'Then I wondered if you might come somewhere
with me.'

Work, she presumed. 'You're going to see a new supplier? Sure.'

'Not a new supplier.' He took his mobile phone from
his pocket, flicked into the Internet, and passed the phone
to her. His fingers brushed against hers as she took the
phone, and every nerve ending in her skin tingled.

She stared at the screen, really hoping that she wasn't
blushing, because her face felt incredibly hot. *'Antony and
Cleopatra.'* A seriously good production, too. It had been
one of her A level set texts and she'd loved the play. Was
this simply a coincidence, or did he remember? 'You've
got tickets for this?'

He nodded. 'I was going with a friend, but she can't
make it now.'

A friend. A *female* friend. His girlfriend? No, of course
not. She knew now that he wasn't the kind of man who'd
cheat. But she still couldn't help the question. 'Will your
girlfriend mind you taking me?'

'Siobhan's not my girlfriend. Just a friend.'

'I see.'

'She's married to my best friend,' he explained. 'And
the reason she's not coming is because she has morning
sickness that seems to last all day. Our tickets are in the
middle of the row and she's terrified she won't be able to
escape to the loo in time if she starts feeling ill.'

'I see,' Alexandra said again. Her heart contracted
sharply at the mention of morning sickness. It wasn't something she'd ever suffered; both times she'd been pregnant,
things had gone wrong well before she'd reached that stage.
Then she realised that Jordan was waiting for her to say
something. She tamped down her feelings and tried to
sound sympathetic. 'Poor woman.'

'She's really disappointed about missing this. Hugo
loathes Shakespeare—which is probably Siobhan's fault

for taking him to see a really avant-garde version of one
of the minor plays, years ago, instead of breaking him in
gently—so the deal is that I go with her to any Shakespeare
she wants to see and he goes to all the comedies and lighter
dramas with her.'

His best friend's wife. *Really* just a friend, then. Though
she didn't quite understand why Jordan was still single.
The man she was getting to know was the man she'd
wished he'd been, ten years before.

'So would you like to go with me?' he asked.

'Yes, please. As long as I can pay for my own ticket.'

He sighed. 'That's not necessary. I've had the tickets
for months, so they would've been wasted if you'd said
no—and actually it'll be nice to share it with someone
who knows the play as well as you do.'

So he *did* remember that it was one of the texts she'd
studied.

'I'll pick you up at seven,' he said.

Too close to Nathan, organising her and always being in
charge. She'd rather make her own way there. 'How about
I meet you in the foyer at seven?'

'If that's what you'd prefer.'

'Thank you. Seven it is, then.'

Alexandra found it hard to concentrate on work for the
whole of Friday, and she agonised all the way home about
what to wear. She knew that people didn't dress up so
much for the theatre nowadays, but even so jeans would
feel wrong. In the end, she decided on a little black dress,
the designer shoes that always made her feel confident, and
minimum make-up and jewellery; that way, she wouldn't
be so dressed up that she'd draw attention to herself, but
she wouldn't be too casual, either.

Jordan was already waiting for her in the foyer; like
her, he was dressed smart-casual, in dark trousers and a

cashmere sweater that brought out the blue in his eyes. Alexandra's heart skipped a beat as he raised a hand to acknowledge her and walked to meet her, smiling.

Oh, help. She really had to remember that this wasn't a date; it was simply a matter of not letting good tickets go to waste. Being practical.

'I'm glad you could make it.' For a moment, she thought he was going to kiss her cheek; then he clearly thought better of it and moved back just a fraction. Just as well, because she wasn't sure she could cope with the feel of his lips against her skin. She might do something truly stupid—like turning her head slightly so his mouth met hers, and...

'Can I get you a drink?' he asked.

'I'm fine, thanks.' And it was ridiculous to feel so nervous. They were colleagues. Maybe even starting to be friends.

'I took the liberty of getting you a programme. And don't you dare offer to reimburse me,' he added, 'because I would've done the same for Siobhan.'

'Thank you.' She'd accept his kindness. To a point. She still wasn't going to compromise her independence. 'And in return you can let me buy you a drink in the interval.'

'Sure. Shall we go and find our seats?'

He placed his hand under her elbow to guide her through the crush, and Alexandra instantly regretted wearing a sleeveless dress. The touch of his skin against hers sent desire licking all the way down her spine. A thick woollen sweater would've been much safer. Or maybe a full suit of armour.

The seats were close enough together that, when the row was full, Jordan's leg was forced against hers. The lick of desire grew stronger; at this rate, Alexandra thought, by the end of the evening she was going to be a complete puddle of hormones.

To her relief, the safety curtain finally went up and the play began. The cast was strong, and she was soon absorbed in the sheer poetry of the words.

On stage, Enobarbus waxed lyrical about the queen. 'The barge she sat in, like a burnish'd throne...'

Jordan's fingers curled round hers. Lost in the magic of the play, she didn't pull away; but when the curtain came down for the interval she realised that they were still holding hands, their fingers tightly linked.

Oh, help. This wasn't on the agenda for either of them.

'Um, shall we get a drink?' she asked brightly.

She could see in his eyes that he was tempted to call her on her refusal to mention the fact that they were holding hands. But then he disentangled his fingers from hers without comment. 'Sure.'

She bought them both a glass of wine; and she was aware that she was drinking hers much too fast. That, or Jordan's nearness was making her head spin. Where was a cold shower when you needed one?

To her relief, he didn't take her hand again when they returned to their seats. She lost herself in the play again, until the moment when Antony died and Cleopatra realised what she'd lost. 'There is nothing left remarkable Beneath the visiting moon.'

Alexandra remembered exactly how that felt. The bleakness of the days when she realised exactly what she'd lost—the love of her life, their baby, and her future. Days when nothing could touch her or drag her out of the pit of despair, not even the books she'd once loved so much. She hadn't taken them with her when she'd left home; she wondered if her parents had kept them for her in the attic.

Or maybe they'd taken them to the nearest charity shop, to get all the clutter out of the way.

She felt her eyes fill with tears; frantically, she tried to blink them back, but it didn't work. She dared not rub her eyes and draw Jordan's attention to the fact she was crying, in case he pushed to find out why—yes, the play was moving, but he was bright. He'd work out that there was more to it than that. He'd ask what was wrong. And he'd ask until he got a proper answer.

She blinked as hard as she could, but several tears escaped and slid silently down her cheeks.

Outside the theatre, he noticed immediately that her eyes were red. 'You were crying,' he said softly.

'Sorry, that play always moves me. Even though I think Cleopatra's a selfish, manipulative attention-seeker, she really did love Antony.' Just as she'd loved Jordan. With all her heart. Before he broke it into tiny pieces. 'It's been a very long time since I've seen it.' She drew in a shaky breath. 'Thank you so much for bringing me.'

'My pleasure.' He looked awkward. 'I'd better get us a taxi.'

He managed to hail one almost instantly. 'I'll drop you off first,' he said.

'Thank you.' She gave the taxi driver her address.

Jordan wasn't holding her hand in the taxi, but she could still feel the warmth and pressure of his fingers curled round hers. And, when the car pulled up outside her flat, she gave in to the mad impulse and said, 'Do you want to come in for a coffee?'

Jordan looked at her. 'Are you sure?'

No. This could turn out to be a huge mistake. 'I'm sure,' she fibbed.

'Then thank you.' And his smile made her knees feel as if they'd just melted.

'Make yourself at home,' she said as she unlocked the front door and ushered him into her flat. 'I'll bring the coffee through.'

Alexandra's flat was small, Jordan thought, much smaller than his own, and decorated in neutral tones. Her living room was only just big enough for a sofa, a TV, an audio system, and a single bookcase. There was a framed print of a Whistler nocturne on one wall, but the only photographs on the mantelpiece were of her with Meggie on what was obviously Meggie's wedding day, two more of her holding a baby—which he guessed were the godchildren she'd mentioned at the story-time session—and what were obviously the latest school photographs of the two children, one of eleven or twelve and one who looked about six. But there were none of Alexandra's parents, which struck him as odd; he remembered her being reasonably close to them, ten years ago.

She'd told him that things had been strained after she'd lost the baby, but clearly their relationship hadn't been repaired. Why? Because of her divorce? Had they approved of the man she'd married, or had he come between Alexandra and her family? He didn't have a clue, but he didn't want to scare her off by asking her. Not now she'd actually asked him into her flat, let him that little tiny bit closer.

There also weren't many books; that single bookcase also held a selection of music and films. Again, it surprised him; he could still remember the time when Alexandra's parents had been out and she'd sneaked him up to her room. There had been two huge bookcases in her bedroom, completely stuffed with books, as well as a big pile next to her desk. But there wasn't a single academic book on her shelves now. No poetry, no Shakespeare, no plays.

Most of them were marketing textbooks. And it just didn't feel right. Didn't feel like *her*.

He wandered into her equally tiny kitchen. There was barely enough space for both of them in the room. He could smell the vanilla base of her perfume, and it made him want to taste her. He'd promised himself he'd give her time, but his resistance crumbled like sand. 'Alex,' he said softly.

She turned round to face him, her eyes huge, and he was lost; he dipped his head and brushed his mouth against hers. Her lips were so soft; he couldn't resist doing it again and again, catching her lower lip between his and sucking. When her lips parted, he deepened the kiss, sliding one hand against her nape and the other at the base of her spine, drawing her closer to him.

Heaven.

It had been so long since he'd felt like this. Years.

Kissing Alexandra...

Oh, God. He wasn't supposed to be doing this. He broke the kiss and dropped his hands, though there wasn't enough room for him to take a proper step back from her. 'I'm sorry. That wasn't meant to happen.'

'No.' But she was staring at his mouth. She glanced up at him again, just like the first time he met her, and he couldn't resist. He needed to kiss her. Here. Now. Before he imploded. He bent his head again to kiss her, and this time she slid her arms round his neck and was kissing him back. It felt like coming home after too many years away, which was utterly crazy. What happened to keeping some professional distance between them? What happened to being just close enough to have a decent working relationship?

'Alex.' Her name was ripped from him.

'It's Xandra nowadays,' she reminded him.

He shook his head. 'You'll always be Alex to me.'

'I'm not the person I was back then,' she warned. 'I'm not looking for love any more. I'm older and wiser.'

'I know. Me, neither.' He stroked her cheek.

She swallowed hard. 'This thing between us. We can ignore it.'

'Of course we can. We're both intelligent adults.'

And he really, really needed to kiss her again. Preferably in the next nanosecond.

Things felt much, much better when her mouth was moving against his. She was kissing him back; her hands slid underneath his sweater, stroking his skin, and it felt so, so good. He loved the feeling of her skin against his, though he wanted more. He was burning up with need and desire.

Then she broke the kiss. 'Jordan. We can't do this.'

'No?' His head was swimming.

'It went wrong between us before. I don't want to complicate things at work.'

Work. He'd forgotten about that. Completely. How? Field's was the centre of his life; it had been for years. How had he completely blocked that out? He dragged in a breath. 'OK. You're right. We'll be sensible. We'll keep things strictly business between us. And I'd better not stay for coffee.' He couldn't trust himself not to kiss her again.

'Let me call you a taxi.'

'It's OK. I'll find one. I need some air.' To clear his head. Hell, if he had to walk back to his flat in Notting Hill, it wouldn't matter. And it probably still wouldn't be enough fresh air to wipe the memories from his head. 'I'll, um, see you at Field's.'

'Yeah.'

'I'll see myself out.'

* * *

Alexandra waited until he'd closed her front door behind her before she sank down on the kitchen floor, drew her knees up to her chin and wrapped her arms round her legs. The tears she'd tried to stem in the theatre slid down her cheeks, unchecked.

If only things could've been different.

Even though she knew now that he hadn't cheated on her—that she would've been able to rely on him—her marriage had corroded her ability to trust. She couldn't take the risk of a relationship with another man who was used to being in charge, a man who'd boss her around and tell her what to do. Maybe with the best of intentions, but he'd still tell her what to do.

And there was the other issue, too. Jordan had said nothing about whether he'd wanted a family with his wife—or in the future, for that matter—but she knew that he was the fourth generation of his family to head up the business. So it was more than likely that he'd want an heir—an heir she couldn't give him without an awful lot of medical intervention. Intervention she just hadn't been able to face, no matter how much Nathan had gone on and on and on about how she was being weak and feeble and pathetic and a coward. Maybe Jordan's reaction would be different; but she really didn't want to see the pity in his eyes when he knew the full story.

So she was just going to have to be strong. Resist everything her heart was telling her. Her heart had got things so wrong in the past; from now on, she was only listening to her head. And her head was definitely telling her the right thing. The sensible thing.

Stay away from Jordan Smith.

CHAPTER SEVEN

JORDAN found himself reading the same page of the financial report for the third time. And it still made no sense, because all he could think about was Alexandra. The way he'd kissed her. The way she'd responded. And the way she'd run scared.

He was the one who'd said it would be strictly business between them from now on.

What an idiot he was. How could it possibly be just business between them, when every day he worked with her was torture? Being in a meeting with her, when he was close enough to smell her scent or feel her fingers brush against his as she handed him a piece of paper…The last week had driven him crazy. He was aware that he'd been snapping at everyone; Alexandra, on the other hand, had managed to stay absolutely professional and treated him exactly the same way that she treated everyone else.

Except, despite what he'd said to her, that wasn't what he really wanted. And he'd caught her eye enough times, seen the wistfulness in her face that she hadn't been quite quick enough to mask, to think that it wasn't what she wanted, either.

It made no sense. Last time they'd been together, they'd crashed and burned. How could it possibly be any different, this time round?

Yet he wanted her. More than he'd wanted anyone in his entire life.

He glanced at his watch. Half-past seven. Everyone else on their floor would have gone home by now; the only people here were the security team. And Alexandra.

He backed up his files, turned off his computer, and went to her office, pausing in the doorway. She clearly hadn't heard him because she simply continued working; he could see how much she was concentrating, because she'd caught the tip of her tongue between her teeth.

Her mouth was driving him crazy.

Everything about her was driving him crazy.

And he needed to do something about it.

He knocked on the open door, and walked in as she looked up.

'Did you want something?' she asked.

Yes. He wanted her.

He sat on the edge of her desk. 'This isn't working.'

There was a flare of panic in her eyes. 'What isn't?'

'We have unfinished business, Alex, and you know it.'

'No.' She dragged in a breath. 'We agreed we'd keep it to just work between us.'

He shook his head. 'I don't think I can do that any more. I'm not sure you can, either.' He looked straight at her. 'And I don't want to talk about it here. Your place or mine?'

'Just to talk,' Alexandra said.

In answer, he spread his hands, as if to say, *What do you think?*

No, it wasn't going to be just talking. The two of them, alone, in a private space…it was obvious what was going to happen. What had been waiting to happen for days. What had been making her pulse race, every time she was in a meeting with him. What she couldn't get out of her head.

She licked her dry lower lip. 'Yours,' she whispered.

He picked up her phone and ordered a taxi; it was all she could do to keep her gaze off his hands. Beautiful hands. Hands that she so desperately wanted to touch her—even though she knew that this was the worst idea either of them had ever had.

As soon as she'd backed up her files and switched off the machine, he said, 'Let's go.'

The taxi was already waiting outside. Neither of them said a word on the way to Jordan's flat. He still wasn't talking when he ushered her into the lift. But she could practically feel the tension radiating off him; so he wasn't as cool and calm as he was trying to make out. Just as she was trying to preserve a façade of coolness and control, when inside she was shaking with need and anger and desire, all mixed up together.

He unlocked the front door and gestured for her to go inside. The second he'd closed the door behind them, he pulled her into his arms and jammed his mouth over hers. It wasn't a sweet, gentle, persuading kiss. It was an angry kiss, full of frustration and desire and need. A kiss that she matched, touch for touch and bite for bite.

When he lifted his head again, they were both shaking.

'This is insane. It shouldn't be happening.' He shook his head in seeming exasperation. 'I shouldn't want you this much.'

The confession undid her. 'Me, neither,' she whispered.

'Alex, I haven't slept properly in a week. All I can see is you. All I can feel is you. I even dream about you, for heaven's sake.'

She lifted her hand and laid her palm against his cheek. 'We said we'd keep it strictly business.'

'It's a hell of a lot easier said than done.' He looked tortured. 'I'm starting to think about opening a branch in

Australia and going there to set it up myself. Being half a world away from you might just help.' Though then he turned his face so his lips were against her palm. Pressed the softest, sweetest kiss against her skin. And it made her want to cry. Why were they both making this so complicated when it should be so simple?

'Opening a branch on the moon wouldn't help,' she said, her voice ragged. 'Or on Mars. Or even on the other side of the Milky Way. Because I'd still be thinking about you.'

Her admission made him crack. He cupped her face in his hands and brushed his mouth against hers in the sweetest, most cherishing kiss; then he bent to scoop one hand behind her knees, lifted her up and carried her down the corridor to his bedroom. When he set her back on her feet again, he made sure that her body was pressed against his all the way, leaving her in no doubt of just how much he wanted her.

She wanted him, too. Wanted to feel his hands on her body, his mouth on her skin. She wanted to touch him, too—so much that it made her ache for him.

He undid her shirt, taking it slowly, keeping his gaze fixed on hers. Once he'd pushed the soft cotton over her shoulders, he took a step back and just looked at her. And it was just like the very first time he'd done that, the weekend she'd turned eighteen. When he'd slowly undressed her, touched her, taught her body exactly how much pleasure he could give her.

Now, as then, the intensity of his gaze made her feel shy—and yet, at the same time, it made her feel hot. Thrilled that she could turn this gorgeous, clever man to mush, push everything out of his mind except her.

'You're beautiful, Alex.' The admission was almost ripped from him, and heat pooled in her stomach. He reached out, moulding her curves with his palms.

Back then, she'd been a girl. A shy virgin. When he'd stroked her to her very first climax, she'd been shocked by how he'd made her feel, as if the universe were splintering round her.

She wasn't a shy, naïve teenager any more. She knew what to expect. And although it had been years since they'd touched each other this intimately, she knew it was still going to be the same between them—that same flaring, intense heat.

'Jordan. I want you,' she whispered, and drew her tongue along her lower lip.

'Good,' he said.

He drew each shoulder strap of her bra down in turn before kissing his way along her exposed skin. So slowly that it was driving her mad; she wanted to be skin to skin with him. Here. Now. *Right now.*

'So soft. So smooth. So kissable.' He kissed his way along the edge of her bra. 'And here…' He nuzzled the peak of her nipple, and the friction of the lace against her sensitised skin made her gasp.

And then she stopped thinking at all as his mouth closed over her nipple. Hot. Wet.

'Jordan,' she whispered. 'Now.'

'I know.' His voice was husky as he straightened up again and looked her straight in the eye. 'I want you so much, it hurts. I want to be inside you right this very moment. But at the same time I want to take it slowly, savour every second of this.'

Fast and slow, all at the same time. She knew exactly what he meant: it was the same for her. She wanted everything, all at once.

The intense look of desire in his eyes gave her licence to do anything she pleased. She removed his tie, then undid the buttons of his shirt; she took her time, retaliating for the way he'd undressed her so slowly. The pads of her fingertips teased his skin, moving in tiny circles in a way that she knew would arouse him to fever pitch, the same way he'd aroused her.

He was shaking slightly, clearly trying to stay in control—and she needed him to lose it as much as she had. She let his shirt fall to the floor, then leaned forward and pressed a hot, open-mouthed kiss against his throat. He arched his head back, giving her better access, and closed his eyes in seeming bliss as she nibbled her way across his skin.

She took her time removing his trousers; finally, his control snapped, and he kissed her hard. The next thing she knew, they were both naked, she was in his arms, and he was lifting her onto the bed.

She reached up to trace his lower lip with a fingertip.

He moved to catch her finger between his lips, and sucked.

'Oh, my God, Jordan. That's…'

'Yeah. Me, too.' He kissed her throat, nuzzled the hollows of her collarbones; in turn she stroked him, touched him, urged him on.

He moved lower, took one nipple into his mouth and sucked. This time, there was no lace in the way: just his lips and his tongue and his teeth, teasing her and arousing her until her hands were fisted in his hair and her breathing was fast and shallow.

'I'm not finished with you yet. Not by a long way,' he whispered against her skin. He moved lower, nuzzling her belly, and slid one hand between her thighs.

Her pulse rate spiked. 'Please, Jordan.' When he skated a fingertip across her clitoris, she was completely lost. She tilted her hips, needing him deeper, harder.

He went still. 'We need a condom.'

No, we don't, she thought. The bitter irony wasn't lost on her. What broke them up in the first place couldn't happen at all now. She couldn't get pregnant just by making love. She couldn't make a baby—not without a huge amount of medical help and an even bigger bit of luck. It wasn't a real option for her any more.

But it hurt too much to say it. Her throat felt as if it was closing up.

'Alex—hold on.' Luckily for her, he misinterpreted what had made her freeze. He stroked her face, then climbed off the bed and rummaged in his pocket for his wallet. He gave a sigh of relief as he took out a foil packet, ripped it open, slid the condom on to protect her. Then at last, he eased inside her.

And it was heaven.

She wrapped her legs round his waist to draw him deeper. It had never been like this with anyone else. Only with Jordan had she felt this soul-deep connection.

'You feel amazing,' he whispered.

'So do you.' Her voice sounded shaky, even to herself. How long had it been since someone had said that to her—had made love to her just for herself, instead of trying for a baby?

He stopped moving and propped himself on his elbows so he could look her in the eye. 'OK?' he asked softly.

She nodded, not trusting herself to speak.

'If you want me to stop, I will.' He touched her cheek with the backs of his fingers. 'This isn't just about me. I want you with me all the way.'

She shook her head. 'This shouldn't be happening,' she whispered. 'We should stop this right now.' She dragged in a breath. 'Except I don't want you to stop.'

'I don't want to stop, either.' He lowered his mouth to hers in a warm, sweet, reassuring kiss.

Pleasure started to spiral through her; as if he knew, he slowed everything right down, focusing on the pleasure and stretching it out. She gasped as he pushed deeper, deeper. 'Jordan, *yes*.' And then she felt her body begin to tighten round his, pulse after pulse of sheer, mind-drugging pleasure.

'Alex,' he sighed, and she felt his body surge against hers.

He stayed where he was, just holding her close; finally, he eased out of her. 'I'll just deal with the condom.'

While he was in the bathroom, Alexandra's doubts flooded back. No way was she going to be able to stay naked in his bed. She retrieved her scattered clothing. Everything looked horribly crumpled, but the dry-cleaner would be able to sort out her suit later. She'd just finished buttoning her shirt when Jordan walked back in—completely naked. Not even a towel wrapped loosely round his hips.

'Right. So I'm at the disadvantage now,' he said dryly.

'Should I, um, turn my back while you get dressed?'

'Whatever,' he drawled.

'I, um…I'll just get myself a glass of water in the kitchen. If you don't mind.' She could feel her face turning crimson.

'Sure.'

She grabbed her shoes and fled; but the cold water did nothing to ease the heat in her face. Why the hell hadn't she had more self-control?

Jordan joined her in the kitchen, wearing dark trousers and the same cashmere sweater he'd worn to the theatre. The one that had made her want to touch him. Her fingers itched to stroke the soft material, but that would be a liberty too far. Especially as she knew that she wouldn't be able to stop at just touching the cashmere.

'OK. So this was a mistake. But it doesn't have to affect us at work,' she said. 'We just got a bit mixed up and forgot who and where we were. We'll just pretend on Monday morning that it never happened.'

'I'm not sure I can do that.'

She bit her lip. 'So what, then?'

'Neither of us can keep our hands off each other.' He looked at her. 'Every time I see you, I want to touch you, kiss you until we're both dizzy and carry you to my bed. And don't tell me it's not the same for you, Alex.'

She was about to protest that it wasn't, when he circled her hardened nipple with one fingertip. Heat burned through her face.

'Admit it. You want me as much as I want you.'

'Yes.' She couldn't lie. Not with the physical evidence so damn obvious to both of them. 'But I'm not looking for a relationship.'

'Neither am I.' He held her gaze. 'But I can't get you out of my head.'

'Maybe it's just a physical thing and it'll burn itself out.' She dragged in a shaky breath. 'Maybe we should…' The words stuck in her throat.

'Avoid each other?' He spread his hands. 'That's not an option. We can't avoid each other at work. And we need to talk about this, Alex. Ignoring it won't make it go away.'

She leaned her forehead against his. 'This whole thing scares the hell out of me.'

'If it helps, you're not the only one,' he said dryly. 'Here's an idea. I'll drive you home. You ring me tomorrow morning when you wake up. I'll bring breakfast over. And then we'll decide what we want to do for the rest of the day.'

She frowned. 'It's Saturday. Aren't you going to be at work?'

'I do take the occasional day off. And I happen to know you don't have any events on tomorrow, so you're not in work either. So, is it a deal?'

A whole day with Jordan. Doing anything they liked. Free just to be themselves, to be with each other. It was so very, very tempting…

'Is it a deal?' he repeated.

She nodded. 'Deal.'

'Let's go. And be clear about this, Alex—I'd rather you stayed here with me tonight. Much rather.' His gaze held hers. 'But I think you need a bit of space, and if that makes the difference between you running scared and you spending tomorrow with me, then I'll live with that.'

'Thank you,' she said softly.

He kissed her. 'Let's go. While I still have some control over myself.'

CHAPTER EIGHT

THE next morning, Alexandra rang Jordan at eight.

'You've only just woken up?' he asked, sounding surprised.

'No, I've been up for a couple of hours.' She'd barely slept; not that she was going to tell him that.

'So have I.' His voice softened. 'Why didn't you ring me earlier?'

'Because I didn't want to be too pushy,' she admitted.

He laughed. 'I nearly drove over at six without ringing you first. I wish I had, now. Still. I'll see you in twenty minutes with breakfast.'

Alexandra had already showered and dressed, and had been trying to distract herself with a mug of coffee and a cryptic crossword. Not that it had worked; she hadn't been able to stop thinking about him. Wanting him. 'See you in twenty minutes,' she said.

It gave her enough time to tidy the flat for the second time that morning, put the kettle on and lay the kitchen table for breakfast; but all the while butterflies were stampeding in her stomach. Today was the first real day of their fling. Would it turn out to be the best idea she'd ever had—or the very, very worst?

Jordan turned up dead on time, carrying two brown paper bags. 'I'm parked outside, completely illegally. Do you have a visitor permit, or is there a non-resident parking zone somewhere nearby?'

'I've got a visitor permit,' she said 'You just need to fill in the time and your registration number.'

He followed her into the kitchen; she took a visitor permit from the drawer where she kept them and handed it to him.

'Thanks. Maybe you can deal with these while I sort out the car.' He set the bags on the table.

The bags contained a selection of still-warm Danish pastries, ripe nectarines, a pot of Greek yoghurt and two paper cups of coffee. And a single red rose.

'What's this for?' she asked when he came back in.

He smiled. 'I was going to get you a proper bouquet, but I thought you might refuse it. Whereas a single rose... it's what you'd have on a breakfast tray, and I brought you breakfast. Just without the tray.'

She couldn't help smiling at him. 'Thank you. Though I can't believe you brought take-out coffee. Or, in fact, *any* of this,' she said. She rested her hands on her hips. 'Unlike you, Mr Smith, I happen to keep a properly stocked fridge. I could've provided breakfast.'

He inspected her fridge. 'OK, Ms Bennett. So the food police would give you a gold star and me a compliance notice. But sometimes it's fun to have a takeaway breakfast. And this coffee's excellent.'

He cut one of the nectarines into slices, and juice pooled on the plate. He grinned. 'Good. This is even better than I hoped.'

'How do you mean?'

He fed her a slice, making sure that a tiny rivulet of juice ran down from the corner of her mouth. Then he leaned forward and licked the juice away.

Alexandra was speechless and wide-eyed by the time they'd finished breakfast. And there was no way her legs were going to hold her up.

'Result,' he drawled.

She blew out a breath. 'You don't play fair. This was meant to be just breakfast.'

He shrugged. 'Sometimes you have to push the boundaries.'

And he was definitely pushing hers.

'So what are we going to do today?' he asked.

'I don't know. I...' Her voice faded.

'Can't think straight?' he asked softly.

'No,' she admitted.

'That makes two of us. Remember that day by the river, when you said you hadn't been to the sea for years? We could do that, if you like.'

'What, now? There are all the breakfast things to sort out.'

'They're not going anywhere,' he said. 'They can wait until later. The sunshine can't. Let's go to the sea.'

The Jordan she'd got to know at work was a planner, who'd thought through every possibility before he made a move. This man—spontaneous, playful—was a hell of a lot more dangerous. And he'd thought about what *she* wanted to do. Put her first. Which completely bulldozed her resistance.

'Seriously?' she checked.

He smiled. 'Seriously. What do you need? Flat shoes?'

'And a towel.'

He raised an eyebrow. 'You're planning to *paddle*? In March?'

Yes, and hopefully the coolness of the water at this time of year would help to bring her common sense back. 'How can you resist a paddle at the seaside on a sunny day like this?' she asked. 'The water's going to be gorgeous.'

He smiled, his eyes crinkling at the corners. 'Go and get your stuff, then.'

Alexandra had looked put out at the idea of leaving the breakfast things. Jordan quickly ran some hot water into the bowl, added detergent and dealt with the washing up while he waited for her to get ready. He could hear her humming, 'Oh I Do Like to be Beside the Seaside' as she got her things together, and it made him smile. This was the Alexandra he remembered, sweet and funny and so good to be with.

They'd both been through bad times. Now maybe it was time to have some fun. Although she still wasn't talking to him about her marriage—so he still didn't know what had gone wrong—he'd already worked out that her ex had hurt her badly. Maybe that was why she'd become a workaholic. Pretty much for the same reasons that he had: feeling that he'd failed in his personal life, and work was the only place where he really shone.

The little she had said was that Bennett had swept her off her feet at first. That she'd thought he'd look after her. And then that she'd had to account for every penny she'd spent. Which told Jordan that nobody had really made Alexandra feel special or been the thoughtful, romantic lover she'd dreamed of.

Last time, he'd let her down. Maybe this time he could get it right and be the man she wanted. A man who'd make her feel beautiful and special—not by what he bought her, but by how he treated her.

'Jordan, I didn't expect you to clean my kitchen,' she said when she came back in, carrying a tote bag. 'You didn't have to do that.'

He flapped a dismissive hand at her. 'All I did was wash up a couple of plates and knives. There wasn't that much to do.'

'Thank you, anyway.'

'Let's go.' He waited for her to lock the front door, then ushered her over to his car.

She skated her fingers over the edge of the sleek dark-blue bonnet. 'I still can't get over your flash car.'

'Hey, I'm allowed a vice or two.' And this was his only real indulgence.

'Why don't you drive it to work? No car-park space?'

'I live near enough to walk in. It clears my head in the mornings and puts me in a good mood. Endorphins.'

'We took a taxi back from the store to your place, last night,' she mused.

'Only because I couldn't wait long enough to walk you back.' He smiled wryly. 'And I also couldn't trust myself not to pin you to every wall on the way home and get us both arrested for public indecency.'

She flushed. 'Um.'

He unlocked the car. 'Sorry. I shouldn't have said that. Get in.'

She put her bag on the back seat, then settled herself in the front next to him.

He indicated the sound system. 'Put whatever you want on the radio.'

'Thanks.' She chose a commercial station playing the kind of pop music you could sing along to, then settled back to enjoy the drive.

Once they were round the M25, he headed south.

'So where are we going?' she asked.

'Brighton's the easiest beach to get to from London,' he said. 'Is that OK with you, or would you prefer to go some-where else?' He had the feeling that Bennett had made all the decisions—and she was clearly over-compensating now by being so independent—so he was careful to give her the choice. Especially as Brighton was bound to bring back memories for her, just as it did for him.

'I haven't been to Brighton for years,' she said. 'Not since we…'

He reached over to squeeze her hand briefly. 'Alex, I know it all went wrong, but we had some good times as well.'

Yeah. 'I remember.' The weekend after her eighteenth birthday, they'd spent the Saturday in Brighton. Paddling in the sea, enjoying the rides on the pier, sharing fish and chips on the pebbly beach. And then Jordan had driven her back to London, with his left hand resting on her thigh whenever he didn't need to change gear. The heat and desire had built and built and built, because she'd known exactly what was going to happen.

Thank God her parents had been out.

They'd gone straight up to her room, ripped each other's clothes off—and made love properly for the very first time.

The sound of the sea, the taste of salt in the air, always made her think of that day.

'Alex.' His voice was husky and he let his hand rest on her thigh for just a moment. Telling her without words that he remembered, too.

The nearer they got to the sea, the more she wondered. Was he deliberately trying to recreate that day. Or was this…?

'Stop thinking,' he said softly. 'Today is just you and me and fun, OK?'

'OK.'

* * *

'Shall we start with the pier?' Jordan asked when he'd parked the car.

'Sure.'

He reached for her hand as they walked along the pier; to his relief, she didn't pull away. This was like being a teenager all over again. In some ways, it was unnerving; in others, it was remarkably freeing. Today was all about having fun and forgetting the mess of the past.

'How brave are you feeling?' he asked as they reached the end of the pier.

'How do you mean?'

He indicated the thrill rides. Years ago, she'd always ducked out of them, too scared to go on them. 'Come on, Alex. It'll be fun. Let yourself go.'

She gave him an insolent shrug. 'Lay on, MacDuff,' she quipped.

He bought tokens and they queued up for the roller coaster. When they went through the vertical loop, Alexandra gripped his hand tightly, but she didn't scream the way that some of the other passengers on the cars were screaming. He could see how white her knuckles were, though. And when he glanced at her face he could see that her jaw was clenched. Her entire face was rigid; it was clear that she was absolutely petrified.

He'd hoped that she'd give in to the sheer thrill of the ride, let the adrenalin pump through her and then let herself go with him—but he'd miscalculated badly. 'You hated that, didn't you?' he asked, noting that her legs were slightly wobbly when they got off the ride, and slid his arm round her shoulders to support her.

'I'm OK.'

No, she wasn't. Her voice was shaking, and she was clearly trying to be brave and pretend that she was fine. The roller coaster had obviously terrified her past the ability to scream. He looked regretfully at the ride promising a full-on G-force experience in a matter of seconds. He would have loved to do it, but he knew she wouldn't; and it wouldn't be fair to make her join him on something that extreme. 'Let's do something a bit more traditional. How about an ice cream and that paddle you wanted?' he suggested.

She looked grateful. 'Sounds good to me.'

Alexandra had noticed the speculative look on Jordan's face when he'd seen the newest thrill ride at the end of the pier. No way could she have handled that; and he'd clearly realised it, suggesting that they move off the pier and do something else.

She'd thought that she could handle the roller coaster. But she'd never been on one as terrifying as that one— one where you actually had to go through a loop-the-loop. *Upside down.* She was just glad that Jordan wasn't teasing her about being so feeble; he was being nice, and not making a big issue about it.

She stopped at the beginning of the steeply shelving pebble beach and took off her shoes, then allowed him to hold her hand again as they headed down to the sea. Once at the shoreline, she rolled her jeans up to the knees, put her shoes in her tote bag, and stepped into the water, drawing in a sharp intake of breath as the cool water lapped round her ankles.

'Cold?' he asked.

It was March. What did he expect? 'Actually, it's good. Come on in—the water's lovely,' she said with a grin.

He shook his head. 'You're mad.'

'And you're chicken,' she retorted. 'It's practically summer.'

'What, with spring blossom only just coming out everywhere?' But all the same he took his shoes and socks off, rolled his jeans up and stood at the edge of the sea.

Thought he was going to get out of it, did he? A mischievous impulse made her bend down, scoop up some water in her cupped palms, and fling it at him.

'Oh, my God, that's *cold*!' And then an equally wicked look lit his eyes. 'Right. You asked for it.' He marched straight into the sea, scooped up some water himself, and aimed it straight at her, soaking her T-shirt across her breasts. He tipped his head to one side, surveying his handiwork. 'Mmm.' A grin spread across his face. 'I'd give you first place in a wet T-shirt competition.'

Her face flamed as she realised just what effect the cold water had had on her body. And why he was looking so appreciative: her T-shirt was clinging to her. 'I only splashed you a little bit. *That* was a declaration of war.' She chopped her arm into the water, soaking his jeans up to his thighs.

'War it most definitely is.' He whooped, and a full-scale splashing contest began, ending only when they were both soaked.

'Um, I don't suppose you brought any spare clothes with you?' he asked.

'No.'

'We could go and buy some.'

She shook her head. 'They'll never let us through the door of a shop, looking like this.'

'Guess we'll have to dry out in the sun.' He took her hand and walked up the steep pebbled slope. 'Sorry. I went too far.'

'No, it was fun. I can't remember the last time I had a water fight.'

'I believe we have some new water pistols coming in to the toy department this week. They really need testing by a member of staff,' he mused. 'How about it? You, me, Hampstead Heath and a water fight, next weekend?'

'Regressed to being fourteen, have we?' she teased.

'Yep.' He moved closer so he could whisper in her ear, 'Apart from the fact that I don't have to imagine what you'd look like when I peel that T-shirt off you.'

She went hot all over. 'Behave.'

'Sure.' He spread her towel out on the pebbles, waited for her to settle herself, then stretched out next to her. 'Perfect. You, me, the sun and the sound of the sea.'

'Don't forget the gulls.'

'No.' He propped himself up on one elbow. 'I'm sorry I scared you on the roller coaster.'

She shrugged. 'I'm a wuss.'

'No. I just wanted…I guess, for you to be full of adrenalin and just let go with me today.'

She shifted onto her side so she could face him. 'I don't need a roller coaster for that.'

He looked interested. 'What would make you let go with me, Alex?'

She smiled. 'You were the one pointing out attributes for a wet T-shirt competition.'

His gaze grew hot. 'Were you thinking of getting me naked?'

'No. I was…' She stopped, feeling her face heat. She wasn't sharing *those* thoughts—the picture in her head of Jordan rising from the water, soaking wet and dressed like Mr Darcy in the film that she and Meggie had watched more times than she could remember.

'Penny for them?' he asked.

'Nope.'

He dipped his head so his mouth was close to her ear. 'You'll tell me later.' He nipped her earlobe gently. 'I'll seduce you into it. And that, Alex, is a promise I intend to enjoy keeping.'

'Yeah?' she challenged.

'Yeah.' He stole a kiss. Then he groaned, dipped his head again, and kissed her properly. A kiss that promised as much as it demanded.

She was near to losing it completely. 'Jordan, this is a family beach.'

'And I wish to hell it was private. Because right now I want you naked, with me inside you,' he whispered back.

She could just imagine them on a private beach. Nobody around, just the two of them drying off from the sea. And there would be no reason to stop when he kissed her, touched her…

A moan of need escaped her. 'Are you trying to drive me crazy? Because you're succeeding.'

'You're right. It's a family beach.' He sighed. 'And you look like a really, really sexy mermaid. This is hopeless. You'll have to handcuff me to something so I don't touch you.'

That put even more pictures in her head. She groaned. 'I'm going to be thinking of that all day, now. Sometimes, Jordan Smith…'

'It's an hour and a half back to London.'

'And no way are you going to let us sit in your precious car while we're soaked in sea water.'

'I could get the car valeted.' He stole a kiss. 'But actually, we can lie here and dry off in the sun. Be patient.'

And go quietly insane in the meantime. 'I need distracting. From you,' she clarified.

His eyes lit. 'How about the G-Force thing?'

'Uh—no.'

He smiled. 'I was teasing. I think fish and chips might be a better idea.'

Except it didn't distract them; they ended up feeding chips to each other, tasting each other and stoking their desire to fever point.

Even another paddle—this time without a water fight—didn't manage to cool them down.

'I don't care if we're still wet and I don't care about my car,' Jordan said, pulling her close. 'We're going back to London. Now.'

CHAPTER NINE

How he got them back to London without getting a speeding ticket, she'd never know. But somehow he did, and he parked as close to her door as he could.

He kissed her on the back of her neck as she opened her front door, and desire surged through her. 'Jordan,' she gasped.

They just about made it to her bedroom.

Jordan closed the curtains, then came to stand behind her, wrapping his arms round her waist and hauling her back against him. Even through their clothes, she could feel the warmth of his body against hers. It wasn't enough. She wanted to feel his mouth against her skin, his hands. She wanted everything.

'Jordan. Touch me,' she invited, her voice husky. 'Before I go insane.'

'Touch you.' His hand was splayed across her ribcage; slowly, he moved it upwards until he was cupping one breast. 'Here?'

The breath hissed from her. 'Yes.'

His thumb and forefinger teased her nipple through the fabric of her T-shirt. 'Alex.' His voice sounded husky, lower than usual. He traced a path of kisses along the nape of her neck. 'I want you.'

'Do something about it, then.'

He nibbled the curve between her neck and her shoulder. 'What a good idea.' He slid his fingers underneath the hem of her T-shirt and slowly peeled it off her. Then he reached round to cup her breast properly. 'Oh, yes. The perfect fit,' he whispered huskily, teasing her nipple through the lace of her bra.

Her heartbeat kicked. She wanted him so badly, she was going to implode.

'Turn round,' he said, and dealt with the button and zip of her jeans. He dropped to his haunches as he helped her out of the denims, then nuzzled her abdomen while he undid the clip of her bra and let the lace fall to the floor. 'Mmm. I like having you like this.'

'Practically naked, while you're fully dressed?' she asked.

He laughed and threw her earlier words back at him. 'Do something about it, then.'

'Me?' She smiled. 'No. I have a much better idea.' She went and sat cross-legged on the bed. 'Why don't you un-dress for me?'

'Strip for you?' His eyes lit with amusement. 'If that's what you want.'

'It is.'

He undressed so slowly that Alexandra was close to climbing off the bed and ripping the rest of his clothes off—but patience was a virtue, she reminded herself, and she was most definitely going to get her reward.

At last, he was completely naked. And utterly beauti-ful.

He joined her on the bed. 'Alex. I'm not sure whether I want to start by touching you, tasting you, or just looking at you.' He reached out to touch her shoulder, smoothed the flat of his palm down over her upper arms. 'Your skin's

so soft, so smooth—so perfect. And you're all curves.
Gorgeous, feminine curves.'

He shifted so that he was kneeling before her, and
cupped her breasts. 'Perfect,' he whispered huskily. 'The
perfect size, the perfect shape…You feel wonderful.' He
rubbed the pad of his thumb across her nipples, making
them peak and harden under his touch. 'And I need to taste
you, Alex.' He took one nipple into his mouth, teasing it
with his tongue.

His mouth was hot against her skin, and Alexandra
could feel her temperature rising. 'Jordan.' She slid her
hands into his hair, urging him on, and closed her eyes so
she could concentrate on the sensations washing through
her.

In one fluid movement, he moved them both so that
she was lying back against the pillows. He kissed his way
down over her belly, then gently parted her legs and kissed
her inner thigh. He pulled the lace of her knickers to one
side, and she felt his tongue glide along the folds of her
sex.

She gasped as he found her clitoris and teased it with the
tip of his tongue; her arousal deepened, spiralling within
her and spreading need through every nerve end. 'Oh,
God, yes, Jordan—yes. Please.' She didn't care that she
was begging, now. She needed the release so badly. He'd
teased her all day, and she was so hot for him.

After the last awful year of her marriage, when Nathan
had insisted on scheduling sex purely during the most fer-
tile phase of her cycle, with the sole aim of making babies,
it felt amazing to be making love with a man purely because he wanted to make love with her. Because he wanted
to give her pleasure, and take pleasure in return.

And it was as if Jordan could read her mind; he continued to pleasure her, sliding one finger inside her to ease the

ache and flicking the tip of his tongue rapidly across her clitoris, varying the speed and pressure until she couldn't even remember where she was any more.

Her climax hit unexpectedly, intense and sharp, and she gasped his name and went still. He held her while the aftershocks bubbled through her, then shifted to lie beside her.

'Right now,' he said, 'I really want to be inside you.' He kissed her lightly, retrieved his wallet and removed a condom.

He was kneeling between her thighs again; he still hadn't bothered removing her knickers, and simply pushed the material to one side. She felt the tip of his penis nudge against her entrance—and then he was inside her with one long, slow, deep thrust.

The perfect fit.

He rolled onto his back, taking her with him. 'You're in charge,' he said softly.

So different from the way it had been in her marriage, when Nathan was always in charge. When he'd always insisted on the same position: the one that, according to him, was the best one for conception.

And she found she loved being in charge, setting the pace. His hands were gripping the pillow tightly as she raised and lowered herself over him, taking it so slowly that he was almost whimpering, then speeding up until he was gasping her name.

In his eyes, she could see the exact moment that his climax hit—the moment when her body started to tighten round him, pleasure rippling through her over and over, tipping him into his own release. He moved to a sitting position, wrapping his arms round her and holding her close; she could feel his heart thudding hard and fast, slowly settling down as his climax ebbed away.

He went to the bathroom, then came back to bed, drawing her back into his arms so her head was pillowed on his shoulder and her fingers were linked with his, resting across his heart.

'So are you going to tell me what you were thinking about? When you went all dreamy?'

'You as Mr Darcy. Wet. Emerging from the pool.' The words slipped out before she could stop them.

'That can be arranged,' he said. His eyes glittered with amusement. 'And I guess that would be fitting, Ms Bennet.'

'With two Ts, in my case. And it's Alexandra, not Elizabeth.'

'Alexandra's a prettier name.' He kissed her lightly. 'Why did you keep his name?'

The question was straight out of left field—and so unexpected that she blurted out the truth. 'I'm not Alex Porter any more. I'm not that naïve, innocent teenager.'

'He hurt you, Alex,' Jordan said softly. 'Did he hit you?'

'No.' It had been much more subtle than that. All smiles when she did what he wanted, and cold criticism when she didn't. 'I guess,' she said, 'it's to remind myself.'

He said nothing, simply held her. And that gave her the courage to finish the sentence. 'To remind myself never to let anyone control me again.'

Jordan hated seeing the pain in her eyes. 'That sounds like a very hard lesson.'

She nodded. 'It was.'

'I'm sorry you had to go through that. How did you meet him?'

'At the bus stop. It was raining, my umbrella broke, and he offered to share his.'

Looking after her, Jordan thought. He would've made

the same offer if someone in the queue next to him had had the same problem.

'He asked me out to dinner that night.'

Jordan felt a flicker of jealousy, but tried hard not to show it. Now she'd started opening up to him, he didn't want to make her clam up again. Especially as he had a feeling that this was something she almost never talked about. Maybe not even to her best friend, Meggie.

Clearly Nathan Bennett had been a charmer, because back then Meggie had been one of the most spiky and suspicious people Jordan had ever met—and she'd seemed to approve of Bennett. He could still remember the words she'd flung at him when he asked her where Alex was. *She's married to someone who'll treat her properly.*

How wrong they'd all been.

'I turned him down.' Alexandra's brown eyes were huge. 'I didn't think I could ever face getting involved with anyone again, after you. But he asked me the next day, too. And then I started thinking, why shouldn't I? And he was *nice*, Jordan. He made me feel special, swept me off my feet. He did all the little chivalrous things like holding doors open for me, holding my chair out, bringing me flowers.'

All the things *he* should've been doing for her.

'He was eighteen years older than me, but the age difference didn't matter.'

Twice her age, Jordan thought. And that kind of age difference mattered when you hadn't quite finished growing up. Alexandra had still had years of change ahead of her—which didn't bode well for her marriage.

'I guess I thought he'd look after me,' she said softly. 'That he'd support me, the way you and my parents didn't.'

Jordan flinched inwardly, but he knew he deserved that. From her point of view, he hadn't been there. He hadn't supported her—though only because he hadn't known the truth.

'But he didn't.'

'No. And…' She blew out a breath. 'I don't want to talk about him, right now.'

She'd already told him much more than she'd told him before. She'd let him closer to her. And although he really wanted to know the rest, so he could wipe the shadows out of her life, he knew that now wasn't the time to ask. He didn't want to risk making her back away again. 'OK. Let's change the subject.' He paused. 'Are you going to ask me to stay the night?'

'I don't think that's a good idea,' she said carefully.

The last time she'd said something was a bad idea, she'd let him persuade her into it. Though this needed to be her choice, not pressure from him. He needed to show her that he wasn't like Bennett. He wasn't going to try to control her. He stole a kiss. 'Would that be in the slightest bit negotiable?'

'No.'

And it sounded as if she was already backing away. Although it was a bitter disappointment—he wanted the teasing, playful Alex who'd started a water fight in the sea—he knew that this wasn't the time to push her too hard. 'OK. I'll take your lead on that. But will you at least have breakfast with me tomorrow?'

She frowned. 'But you had today off. Aren't you going to be catching up in the office tomorrow?'

'Not first thing. Though I am supposed to be going to my parents' for lunch.' He stroked her face. 'Maybe you could come with me—if you'd like to, that is.'

'I don't think your mother would be too pleased at that idea.'

'Actually, I think she would.'

Alexandra scoffed. 'Considering what she said to me the last time we met, I'm not buying that.'

'She was horrified when I told her what really happened back then. Really upset. And she's been trying to work out how she can get to see you and apologise properly. Lunch would be a start.'

Alexandra sat bolt upright as his words sank in. 'You *told* her?'

'She was wrong about you, and I needed to put her straight.'

Some of her fears must've shown on her face, because he added, 'Don't worry, she's not going to be broadcasting your private business to everyone she knows.' He held her close. 'She jumped to conclusions and thought the worst.'

'You're telling me.' Alexandra couldn't quite keep the bitterness from her voice.

'You and I did that too—so, although she was completely in the wrong, you and I don't exactly have any high moral ground to stand on between us.'

She felt her eyes narrow. 'I'm not a gold-digger, Jordan. I never was.'

'I know that. She knows that, too.' He stroked her face. 'I learned something else I'd never known before—something that she gave me permission to share with you. The reason I'm an only child isn't because my parents were workaholics. My mother had four miscarriages after me, and after that work was the only thing that kept her sane.'

Alexandra froze. Jordan's mother hadn't been able to have more children.

She knew how that felt. She couldn't even have *one*.

Did it mean that Vanessa was putting pressure on Jordan to give her grandchildren? Did Jordan want children? It was something she was going to have to face; and it would be easier on both of them if she found out now. So she could back away before they got in too deep. 'You said about getting married and settling down when your father was ill. Did that include having children?' she asked carefully.

'Lindsey and I didn't get to that stage.'

'But you want children?'

'It's not something I've thought about very much,' he said. 'When my marriage went wrong, I concentrated on work. Though I admit, since you've been back in my life, I've thought about it. Especially at that first story-time session, seeing you with the children. Our baby would've been ten years old, now. And it made me think maybe there would've been a brother or sister in Meggie's class, someone who took part in making that banner.'

She swallowed hard, willing the tears to stay back. If things had been different, if she hadn't lost the baby… She wouldn't have failed her exams or left home, Jordan would've come to find her and discovered the truth, and together they could've worked something out. She would never have met Nathan. Never have had that second ectopic pregnancy. Never have…

'Alex?' He brushed a gentle kiss against her mouth.

'I need some time.' Time to absorb what he'd told her. Time to think about where this was going, what she wanted—what *he* wanted.

'OK. I'll take the hint and go home.' He held her gaze. 'But one thing I want you to be sure about. I'm not Bennett and I never will be. This thing between us—wherever it goes, whatever happens, I want it to be on equal terms.'

She managed a shaky smile. 'So tomorrow it's my turn to bring breakfast to you?'

'If that's what you'd like to do. It doesn't mean you have

to. I can go to the supermarket on my way home tonight and stock my fridge properly.'

This time, her laugh was genuine. 'When do you ever go to the supermarket? Your kitchen's full of takeaway menus, with a few bits of fruit stuck in a bowl on the worktop to make it look as if you eat healthily.'

'I do eat healthily. I just don't happen to cook what I eat, that's all.' He climbed out of bed and dressed swiftly. 'You don't have to get up to see me out. Stay there. You look cute. And comfortable.' He stole a last kiss. 'See you tomorrow. And remember, we're just doing the simple stuff right now.'

The simple stuff, Alexandra thought as she heard the door close behind him. Why did she have the nasty feeling that it was just going to start getting complicated?

When Jordan opened his front door to Alexandra the next morning, he was wearing a pair of faded, close-fitting denims. And nothing else.

It made her mouth water and her pulse race. She couldn't help looking him up and down. God, the man even had sexy *feet*. Everything about him made her want to rip off the few clothes he was wearing and drag him off to bed.

'Do you always answer your door looking like that?' she asked.

'If I happen to know it's you...maybe.' He kissed her lingeringly. 'Good morning. And it's a much better morning now that you're here. You brought the sunshine with you.'

She laughed. 'Jordan, it's raining on and off.' She'd got caught in a shower, walking here from the Tube station. Just to prove it, she shook her wet hair, so droplets of rain splashed over his bare chest.

He laughed back. 'It *feels* sunny. Even if it is wet outside.' His eyes lit up. 'Are you suggesting another water fight?'

'No.' She handed him the paper bags. 'Breakfast, as promised.'

He peeked inside the first one. 'What do we have here? Oh, nice. Proper butter, posh jam, warm croissants…' He raised an eyebrow. 'But I smell no coffee.'

'Other bag,' she said.

He looked inside and frowned. 'What's this?'

'A pack of proper coffee.' She paused. 'I assume you *do* possess a cafetière? And milk?'

'Yes to the milk, no to the cafetière,' he said cheerfully. 'I usually drink decaf instant at home. It's quicker.'

'OK, we'll improvise.' She was good at thinking on her feet. 'Do you have a tea strainer?'

'Nope.'

She shook her head. 'How can you get to thirty years old and not even have the basics in your kitchen, Jordan?'

He shrugged. 'Because I don't cook. If I hold a dinner party, it's at a restaurant.'

Maybe, Alexandra thought, Lindsey had taken most of the kitchenware when she'd left. Jordan's flat definitely felt more like a bachelor pad than the family home pared down. 'OK. Decaf instant it is.' And she was *so* buying him a cafetière. The deli at Field's sold thirty different types of coffee, and she intended to try every single one. Preferably with him. And not as a marketing exercise: just for fun.

She busied herself setting things out on the table. He came to stand behind her, slid his arms round her waist and drew her back against him. He nuzzled the neck of her long-sleeved T-shirt out of the way and kissed her bare skin. 'Now you know the real reason why I buy take-out coffee in the mornings.'

'Uh-huh.'

'*And* you brought the Sunday papers with you, you wonderful woman.' He nibbled her earlobe. 'How do you fancy breakfast in bed?'

She turned round to face him. 'That depends on how persuasive you are.'

He laughed. 'Now that's a challenge I'm going to enjoy.'

Ten minutes later, she was naked and in his bed.

Half an hour after that, he reheated the croissants in the microwave, made them both a mug of coffee, and brought a tray in, with the newspapers tucked under his arm.

They fed each other croissants, except butter kept dripping onto their skin and needing to be licked off. Licking led to kissing, kissing led to touching, and the coffee was cold before they got round to drinking it.

'I'll make some more,' he said.

'No, it's fine—if I'm busy I sometimes forget to drink my coffee until it's cold,' she said.

'That's so uncivilised, Alex.'

She kissed him lingeringly. 'Maybe I just don't want you to get out of bed. I'm warm and I'm comfortable. Stay put,' she invited softly. 'Please?'

'Since you asked so nicely, sure.' His eyes crinkled at the corners, and he settled back against the pillows.

Alexandra thoroughly enjoyed lazing the morning away in bed with Jordan and the newspaper. Tackling the cryptic crossword with him, laughing over the answers, and feeling slightly smug when she solved an anagram before he did.

Eventually, he sighed. 'I have to go. Have you thought any more about coming with me?'

'I'm not ready, Jordan.' She took a deep breath. 'But I appreciate the olive branch. Can you apologise for me?'

'Sure.'

'Thank you. Give me three minutes to get dressed, and I'll be out of your hair,' she said.

'Did you drive over?' He looked horrified. 'I forgot to ask—you might have a parking ticket by now. If you do, I'll pay the fine.'

'Don't worry.' She smiled at him. 'I don't have a car. I took the Tube.'

'Then I'll give you a lift back.'

'No, you're late already. I'll be fine.'

'So what are you going to do for the rest of the day? Go and see your parents?'

Hardly. She couldn't even remember the last time she'd spoken to them on the phone, let alone seen them. Probably her father's birthday. The rift between them had grown wider and wider over the years—firstly with her leaving home, hurt by their lack of support, and Nathan hadn't encouraged her to mend the rift. It had suited his purposes for her to be more reliant on him. *You don't need anyone else. Only me.* And as her confidence had eroded she'd come to believe him.

Until one of her clients had made her take a long, hard look at her life.

But her parents hadn't tried to get closer to her after the divorce. And she'd learned that she was better off just relying on herself and a couple of close friends. Friends who would no doubt think she needed her head examining for getting involved with Jordan Smith again.

'No,' she said. 'I think I'm going to wander round the V&A for a couple of hours. And then I'm going home to watch a really girly film. And then I'm going to cook myself a risotto.'

'Would there be enough for two?' he asked, looking hopeful.

It was tempting, but she'd already spent too much time

with him this weekend for her own peace of mind. 'No. Go and see your parents,' she said. She softened her words with a kiss. 'I'll do the washing up before I go.'

'Leave it. I'll do it later.' He kissed her back. 'Enjoy your museum.'

Rather than going back to her flat, she went straight to the Victoria & Albert Museum in Kensington. Though as she wandered round her attention was snagged away from the exhibits; she was acutely aware of the other visitors to the museum. Nobody seemed to be on their own. They were either in couples, in family groups, or in a group of friends.

Right at that moment, she really missed Jordan and she was cross with herself for feeling that way. She absolutely couldn't allow herself to fall for him. Hadn't he broken her heart badly enough last time? And she'd promised herself after the misery of her marriage that she'd never let her heart get involved again. That she'd protect herself from all the pain of a broken relationship. Ever since then, she'd kept everyone at a slight distance, even friends. So why was she being so reckless now?

Alexandra wasn't in the best of moods when she got back to her flat, and although the film was one of her favourites she found herself drifting off into her thoughts partway through. Even the risotto seemed tasteless, and she ended up putting most of it in the bin.

Funny how the world seemed smaller and two-dimensional without Jordan around.

And she was the biggest fool in the world for letting herself think like this. She'd just spent a perfectly nice afternoon doing something she enjoyed. So what if it was on her own? She didn't need a man to make her life complete. And she most definitely didn't need Jordan Smith.

* * *

Later that evening, Jordan called. 'Hi. Just checking to see if there was any leftover risotto?'

'No. And don't try to con me that your mother didn't feed you.'

'She fed me.' He sighed. 'Though I would much rather have gone to the museum with you.'

'Maybe, but you would've hated the film.'

'How do you know? Maybe I like girly films.'

She laughed. 'Now you're *really* trying to con me.'

'I probably wouldn't have been paying enough attention for you to grill me on the plot or what have you afterwards,' he admitted. 'But I would've been quite happy to keep you company. You, me, your sofa…Now that sounds good.'

'Maybe next weekend.'

'I can work with maybe. See you tomorrow,' he said softly. 'Sleep well.'

Over the next three weeks, Jordan found himself getting much closer to Alexandra. He was careful to be completely professional with her at work, when anyone else was around, though he sent her the occasional text to make her blush and laugh. And when she realised that he meant it about giving her a choice and not insisting on choosing every film they saw and every place they went, she seemed to relax with him more.

She'd even bought him a cafetière, wrapping it up in white tissue paper and tying a deep red ribbon round it, then teasing him about his lack of domestication when he unwrapped it. They had breakfast together at the weekends, and they'd fallen into the habit of alternating an evening meal at the trattoria with a meal at her place. He enjoyed pottering round in her kitchen, just watching her cook.

But the one thing she consistently refused to do was to

spend the night with him. No matter how late it was, she insisted either on going home or sending him home. And he really wanted to break that last barrier between them, to wake up in the morning with her in his arms. For her to be the first thing he saw when he woke.

Maybe, Jordan thought, he needed to take her somewhere that had no memories for them. Somewhere he knew she really wanted to go—and then when they got back really, really late she might decide to stay over for once.

The following Friday night, he told her, 'I'm going to take you on a mystery tour tomorrow.'

'Mystery?' She smiled at him. 'Sounds fun. What's the dress code?'

'Smart-casual. Oh, and shoes you can walk in.'

'Flat shoes.' Her eyes gleamed. 'Is there any chance this might be the seaside?'

'You'll definitely see the sea,' he promised. He just wasn't telling her *which* sea. She didn't need to know that he was thinking of the Adriatic rather than the English Channel. 'I'll pick you up at six tomorrow morning.'

She blinked. 'The crack of dawn?'

'Yes. Oh, and you need your passport.'

'My passport? Why? Have you booked us tickets to Paris, or something?'

He grinned. 'Tut. Someone needs to brush up her geography. Since when has Paris been on the coast?'

'Well, you might be able to see the sea from the train on the way there,' she pointed out.

'We're not going to Paris.'

She frowned. 'So where are we going?'

'I told you—it's a mystery tour.' He stole a kiss. 'You'll find out, tomorrow.'

She kissed him back. 'Tell me now?'

'No.' He waltzed her to her front door and kissed her

again. 'Sleep well.' He knew he wouldn't; he'd be restless and fidgety. But maybe tomorrow night, he would. With Alexandra in his arms.

CHAPTER TEN

JORDAN arrived with a taxi at precisely six o'clock. Despite what he'd said the previous night, Alexandra was still half expecting the taxi to take them to St Pancras to catch the train to Paris; but when they ended up at the airport instead, she was completely thrown. 'Jordan, where are we going?'

He simply smiled. 'All in good time.'

She didn't have a clue until Jordan took her to the check-in desk.

'We're going to Venice, just for the *day*?' she asked in disbelief.

He spread his hands. 'OK, so it's a bit decadent—but if I remember rightly it was top of your wish list after Rome, wasn't it?'

He remembered that? 'Jordan, this is the best surprise ever. I really don't know what to say.'

'My marketing manager, lost for words? That's a first,' he teased. Then his face softened. 'You don't need to say anything, Alex. I wanted to do something nice for you. And I've been panicking all week in case I got this wrong.'

'How can you get Venice wrong? Jordan, it's…' She could feel her eyes filling with tears, but they were happy tears. It was the nicest thing anyone had ever done for her.

Though part of her was panicking. Whenever Nathan

had done something for her, she'd paid for it with a little bit more of her independence.

As if he guessed her thoughts, he said softly, 'Shall I tell you what I'm expecting from today? You, me, and a whole lot of fun. And that's it. No strings attached, no conditions. Just you and me.'

'Thank you.' The words sounded cracked, but she meant them.

He held her hand all the way on the plane.

'So we're going on the *vaporetto* now?' she asked when they'd gone through Customs at the airport.

'Better than that. I booked us a *motoscafo*.'

'Which is, in English?' she prompted.

'A water taxi. Apparently this means we get a fabulous first view of the city—and it's just you and me.' He took her down to the jetty and handed in a docket for the water taxi.

'Wow. The water really *is* turquoise. Just like in all the photos I've seen,' she said as the *motoscafo* brought them into the city. And he'd been right about the *motoscafo*. The views of Venice were amazing. The sunlight glittering brilliant white on the water. The sprawl of houses and bridges and domes and towers, all covered in stucco the colour of ice cream. Ancient buildings with their stucco peeling off and worn exposed brickwork rubbed shoulders with smart, renovated buildings whose windows were protected by ornate ironwork grilles and whose window-boxes were filled with flowers. And, above all of it, there was the bluest sky she'd ever seen.

'*La Serenissima*. Venice, the most serene city,' he said softly.

She sucked in a breath. 'Jordan, this is really special.'

He smiled. 'Isn't it just? And I really wanted to share this with you.' His fingers tightened round hers.

The *motoscafo* took them right down the Grand Canal; gondolas and motor boats were tied up at jetties, and buildings jostled next to each other, five storeys high, with narrow arched windows and stone balustrades picked out in white against deep reds, ochres and golds. Some of the buildings were familiar to her from TV programmes, films and photographs; but, in the flesh, they were even more lovely. She was utterly entranced.

'Oh, wow, and that's the bridge. "What news on the Rialto?"'she quoted.

'Such a romantic setting for the most *un*romantic play Shakespeare ever wrote.'

She laughed. 'Absolutely—oh, Jordan, this is just how I imagined it. No, actually, it's better. I… Thank you so much.' She flung her arms round him and kissed him.

He'd chosen the right place, then. Even behind those sunglasses, he knew her eyes were sparkling. Her face was lit up, and she looked completely thrilled to be here. Just as he'd hoped.

The water-taxi driver moored at the jetty by the Rialto Bridge and helped them both out.

'*Mille grazie,*' Jordan said, leaving him a tip. Then he turned to Alexandra. 'Do you want to go exploring?'

'You bet.'

He took his mobile phone from his pocket and flicked into the book he'd bought the previous evening. 'I thought we could do with a map and a tour guide so we know what we're looking at.'

She looked surprised. 'So you haven't been to Venice before?'

'No.'

'How come?'

Because your ghost would've followed me here. Not that he was going to tell her that.

He shrugged. 'I guess it's one of those things. There are so many places in the world you want to see, you can't do them all at once.'

'I guess not.'

She followed him up the steps of the bridge. The marble nearest to the inside of the bridge was smooth and shiny from years of tourists leaning across it while they admired the view; Alexandra skimmed her fingers across it. 'I wonder how many thousands of people have done this before me?'

'More than either of us could guess. It's a beautiful view,' Jordan said. 'Hey. Indulge me. Lean into the bridge and smile.' He took a photograph of her on his camera. The same photograph that most of the other tourists on the bridge were taking, though it felt as if it were just the two of them there. And she looked so beautiful, with the sunlight glinting on her hair and that wide, wide smile— a smile just for him.

'Do you want me to take one of you?' she asked.

'No, you're fine. Let's go and see the market.'

He took her hand and they wandered over to the other end of the bridge and through narrow side streets. The area opened up unexpectedly to the market place, where stalls were heaped high with produce and shoppers were haggling with the stallholders.

'This is amazing, Jordan.' She stared at the stalls in delight. 'Every fruit and vegetable you can think of, fresh herbs sold by the handful...'

'And these. Wow, just look at these.' He took her over to a stall that sold tiny wild strawberries no bigger than the nail on her little finger, and bought a punnet. 'Alex, close your eyes and open your mouth.'

Despite the fact they were in the middle of a crowded market place, it felt oddly intimate; it sent a kick of desire through him, seeing her eyes closed and her face lifted to his and her lips parted like that. He didn't know whether he wanted to kiss her, first, or feed her the strawberry; she made his head swim.

Be sensible, he told himself. His fingers brushed against her lips as he slid one of the tiny strawberries into her mouth, and every nerve end in his skin tingled at the contact.

'The sweetest thing I've ever tasted,' she said, and then laid her palm against his cheek. 'Except maybe you.'

'Is that a fact?' he drawled.

In response, she grinned. 'Close your eyes.' She teased him by brushing the fruit against his lips and then pulling it away as he reached for it.

He opened his eyes and grabbed her hand. 'You, madam, are not playing fair.'

'I know.' She fed him the strawberry, not looking the slightest bit abashed.

He smiled, loving this teasing, relaxed side of her. 'You're right. The sweetest thing except you.'

She reached up on tiptoe and brushed her mouth against his. 'That's on account.'

'I'll hold you to that.'

'I can't believe we're actually here, in Venice.' She gazed around in wonder. 'Jordan, it's incredible.'

He agreed. Completely. And how glad he was that he'd waited to share this with her. 'Let's go to the fish market,' he said when they'd finished the strawberries.

They followed their noses. 'Wow. I don't think I've ever seen so many kinds of fish in one place before.' Tiny octopuses and spider crabs and grey shrimps, alongside other kinds of fish they couldn't even name. One of the fishmongers tipped a stream of chilled water from a red watering-can onto the display, cooling the fish down and making it glisten invitingly to the shoppers. 'Hey, we could do that at Field's,' she said.

'And you'd get a health order slapped on me straight away. You're not getting that one past me, let alone the Board,' he said.

'Spoilsport,' she teased.

Once they'd had their fill of the market, they bought *gelati* from one of the little kiosks and crossed back over the Rialto Bridge, following the signs for San Marco through the network of paths and narrow stone and wrought iron bridges. They window-shopped along the way; Alexandra exclaimed over the filigree masks, then stopped him by a glass shop.

'Look at this bowl—it's gorgeous. That deep, intense blue shading to the same turquoise as the Venetian lagoon.' She sighed as she looked at the price tag. 'Unfortunately, that's way out of my price range, but our customers might like it.'

'Maybe, but we're not here for work,' he said, surprising himself; he didn't usually think twice about bringing business into his time off. But today was different. Today was just for them, and he resented the idea of anything else intruding. 'We're playing hooky. This is just for you and me. Right now, work doesn't matter.'

She nodded. 'Got it.'

As they walked under the clock tower into St Mark's Square, the onion-shaped domes of the Basilica glittered white against the bluest sky he'd ever seen, and the Doge's Palace was like a beautiful layered pink-and-white wedding cake.

'Just...wow. There really are no words to do this place justice. It's like no other city I've been to,' she said softly.

'And are those the famous bronze horses up there on the balcony of the basilica?'

He consulted the guidebook on his mobile phone. 'Apparently they're reproductions—the original ones are inside.'

'Can we go and see them?'

He smiled at her. 'Sure. That's what today's all about: doing whatever you—*we*,' he corrected himself, 'want and enjoying every second.'

The inside of the basilica took Alexandra's breath away; there were literally thousands of glass tesserae shaped into mosaics, their colours still as bright as the day they were made. She could quite understand why the tourists obeyed the notices asking them not to talk, because they simply wouldn't have words when they saw all this for the first time. She certainly didn't—and neither, it seemed, did Jordan. He just held her hand, his fingers twined through hers.

She paid for their tickets to go up to see the original bronze horses; after sighing over their beauty, they headed out to the loggia to see the reproductions and stood outside in the sunshine, looking over the square and the lagoon.

'I can see why they keep the original inside, to preserve them. But these are perfect reproductions. Utterly beautiful,' she said.

'So are you.' He stole a kiss. 'Stand there. I'll take your picture.'

'Excuse me,' an elderly woman asked. 'Would you like me to take a picture of you together?'

'Yes, please.' She took her mobile phone from her handbag and showed the older woman how the camera worked, then posed with Jordan next to the horses.

'Are you on your honeymoon?' the woman asked.

Alexandra went very still. No, they weren't, and she still wasn't sure where this was going. She was starting to think that she knew where she wanted it to go, but she hadn't told Jordan everything yet. And it scared her that things would change when he knew the truth about her; even though she knew he wasn't like Nathan, things had gone really badly wrong once Nathan realised that she couldn't give him the children he wanted. Would it be the same with Jordan?

Jordan wrapped his arms round her waist and drew her back against his body. 'Sort of,' he said. 'We're not married, but this is a special time for us.'

That much was true; it was a day just for them. For doing what they wanted. No strings and no conditions. The tension seeping out of her, she looked up at him and smiled.

'Venice is the most romantic city in the world,' the older woman said. 'We came here on our honeymoon. My husband can't manage the steps up here now, but we always come back to Venice for our anniversary. And I always look out from here, just as we did on our very first visit.'

'Happy anniversary,' Alexandra said.

'Thank you, my dear. And I hope you both find the same magic we have in Venice.'

Alexandra had a feeling that they might just have done that.

When they'd finished looking round the basilica, they found a little kiosk selling *piadina*, toasted flatbread stuffed with prosciutto and pecorino cheese. A short wander brought them to a bench in a quiet little square overlooking the canal.

'Thank you,' Alexandra said. 'This is really special. I

mean, I loved going to the seaside with you at home, but here…'

'There's nowhere in the world like Venice.' Jordan laced his fingers through hers. 'How about *really* playing hooky?'

'How do you mean?'

'Let's not go back until tomorrow. Let's stay the night.'

'But—Jordan, we don't have anywhere booked. Or anything with us. Or—'

He cut her words off by the simple expedient of kissing her. '"Peace, I will stop your mouth,"' he quoted softly when he broke the kiss.

'Indeed, Signor Benedick,' she responded dryly.

'It's all doable, Alex. I can change our flights to tomorrow afternoon and we can find a hotel. We can buy a change of clothes, and the hotel will have all the toiletries we need.' He drew her hand up to his mouth and kissed it. 'So we get to spend the night in Venice, maybe take a ride on a gondola, have dinner, dance through St Mark's Square when it's all lit up…whatever you fancy doing. How about it?'

'As long as I get to pay my half.'

'You're so stubborn.' He sighed. 'Look, I've got a pretty good idea why you feel that way, but there really aren't any strings attached. I earn more than you do, and it's not fair for you to pay half—that wouldn't be equal. I can afford a hotel room, and I just want to do something nice for you, Alex. Give you some good memories.'

To help wipe out some of the bad ones. And she knew he wasn't like Nathan and wouldn't expect anything from her in return—but she still needed to feel that she'd given him something back. 'How about a compromise?' she suggested. 'We stay in Venice tonight, but you let me take you out to dinner.'

'OK. It's a deal.' He paused. 'So do I book one room or two?'

Since the beginning of their affair, she hadn't let herself spend the night with Jordan, knowing how easy it would be to fall in love with him all over again. Not actually sleeping with him was the only way she could think of to retain some kind of distance between them.

But this was Venice. And, as he'd said to the woman who'd taken their photograph by the bronze horses, this was a special time for them. Time to be together without any pressures. No past, no future: just the present. She could allow herself tonight. Just tonight, to fall asleep in his arms and wake up next to him in the morning.

'One.'

'Are you sure about that?'

She swallowed hard. 'I'm sure.'

He brushed his mouth lightly against hers. 'I promise you won't regret that. Give me a moment.' He grabbed his phone from his pocket and looked something up on the Internet, then made two calls—one of which was in rapid Italian and she couldn't follow it.

'OK,' he said when he cut the connection. 'We have a room, and our flights have been changed to tomorrow afternoon. And I think we need to go shopping.'

While Alexandra was trying on a little black dress and high-heeled shoes, Jordan spotted a pendant shaped like a starfish in turquoise glass, shading to intense blue and laced with silver. He knew she'd love it—both the colours and the style—so he bought it and slipped it in his pocket.

Then he went over to her cubicle. 'Alex?'

'Yes?' Her voice was faintly muffled.

'Do I get to see what you look like?'

Her face appeared round the curtain. 'Are you saying you want to choose my dress?'

'No.' He bent closer. 'I'm saying I'd like to see you try the clothes on.'

'A private show?' She blushed. 'Not here.'

She wasn't saying no. Just not here. 'Where, then?'

'The hotel.'

He stole a kiss. 'I'm so going to hold you to that.'

Her blush deepened. 'Jordan. I hope the assistants don't speak good enough English to know what you just said.'

He had a feeling that they wouldn't need a translation. The way he felt about Alexandra was written all over his face, in letters a mile high. He brushed another kiss against her mouth. 'OK, I'll behave and wait outside. Take your time. No rush.'

Eventually she emerged with an expensive-looking carrier bag. 'So that's something for tonight, something clean for tomorrow, clean underwear…and I think we're going to need a small suitcase to get this stuff back to England.'

'Something small enough for hand luggage. It'll save hanging around by the carousel when we're back in England,' he said.

It didn't take long to find a suitable case.

Then he handed her the box. 'For you.'

She looked taken aback. 'For me?'

'I thought it might go with your dress.'

She opened the box and her eyes widened. 'Jordan, it's beautiful, but you didn't have to buy me anything.'

He sighed. Her independence drove him crazy; since she'd opened up to him about Nathan, he could understand why, but she knew he wasn't like her ex. And she was taking the independence thing way too far. 'Alex, it wasn't that expensive. Besides, you're my girlfriend. Which means I'm allowed to buy you jewellery.'

She actually flinched.

'Alex?'

'No. Ignore me.' She shook her head. 'I'll shut up. Thank you, Jordan. It's gorgeous.'

What had made her flinch like that? She'd said before that she'd had to account for every penny. Had she bought herself some jewellery and her husband had been furious about it?

Part of him didn't want to push her, in case she put up the barriers again. But part of him knew that this was a wound that needed lancing. Giving her time to brood would put a shadow over a day he wanted to be filled with sunshine.

'Come on. We've been walking for ages. We need a sit-down and a coffee,' he said. He found a *caffè*, ordered them both a cappuccino, and then found them a quiet corner where they could sit down and talk without being overheard.

'You're going to ask, aren't you?' she said, looking miserable.

'Yup.'

She sighed. 'I guess I owe you the truth.'

'You don't owe me anything,' he said softly. 'And I can assure you now that whatever you say isn't going any further than me. But maybe telling me might help you—because I get the impression you've bottled an awful lot of things up. And eventually they're going to have to come out before they hurt you any more.' He reached over and took her hand. 'Was he angry with you for buying yourself something?'

She gave a weary nod. 'We always had to do things his way. I went along with it for a while, because it was nice not to have to be the one making all the decisions, but gradually I started to feel I was losing myself. I couldn't make a decision without wondering what he would think, first. And it made me feel more and more of a failure.' She bit her lip. 'I wanted to retake my A levels. He kept talking me out of it, saying that I didn't need them because I had him and he'd always look after me. But looking after turned into—well, smothering me.'

'Retaking your A levels was something you wanted to do. Something for *you*. Why didn't he support you?'

'I guess he was worried that it was the thin end of the wedge. That I'd start to better myself, so I wouldn't need him any more and I'd leave him.'

He frowned. 'But that's crazy. That's not who you are.'

She gave him a wan smile. 'Thank you. But he couldn't see that. Looking back, I think he was as needy and insecure as I was. And I could've handled it better.'

'You were eighteen, Alex. He had a lot more life experience than you did.'

'Maybe. But I started lying to him, just to give myself some space. I told him I was going out with the girls once a week, and I went to an evening class instead. I guess it wasn't a total lie—one of my friends was taking the same class, so I was sort of going out with one of the girls. But he assumed I was out with a different group of friends, and he assumed I was doing girly stuff instead of studying.'

How desperately sad that she'd been forced into lying, Jordan thought.

'But then one of my friends rang me when I was out at class—and Nathan had thought I was out with her. When I got home, he accused me of having an affair. And when I told him what I'd really been doing...' She shook her head. 'He wasn't any happier about it. That's when he started making me account for every penny I spent. We had a joint bank account, so my wages were paid straight into it—and he could see on the statement if I'd bought something on our debit card, or if I'd taken some money out. So I had to lie even more. I bought all my books second-hand, hid them round a friend's and told him I'd spent the money on…' She swallowed hard. 'On jewellery.'

'Oh, Alex.' No wonder she'd flinched when he'd mentioned jewellery. He squeezed her hand.

'And whenever he bought me jewellery…' She closed her eyes. 'There was always a reason. Not because he wanted to do something nice for me. Because he wanted to soften me up a bit. And he expected…'

Jordan was truly shocked at what she was implying. 'He *forced* you?'

'No. But he wanted a baby. He decided that we were going to start a family—he thought that would keep me too busy to think about my A levels and my career.'

Jordan remembered what she'd said last night about the ectopic pregnancy, how it made falling pregnant that bit more difficult, and he had a nasty feeling what was coming next. 'And you couldn't?'

She closed her eyes. 'Maybe if we'd had a baby, he would've been happy and we could've rubbed along better.'

'No,' he said gently. 'Having a baby wouldn't have papered over the cracks in your marriage. The cracks would've been made bigger by the sheer strain of broken nights and feeds and nappy changes, not to mention all the worries until you get used to being a parent.'

She looked at him. 'If you hadn't already told me you don't have children, that'd sound a bit personal.'

'Not me. One of my friends from university…he and his wife were having problems. They had a baby, thinking it would bring them closer together and save their marriage. That's when it got seriously messy.' He sighed. 'Lindsey did suggest it, but I remembered what had happened to Mark and said no.'

'I should've said no, too. Or at least told Nathan about our—' Her voice cracked. 'Our baby.'

'You didn't tell him?'

She shook her head. 'I couldn't. I was trying to block it out. I know it was unfair of me. I know I should've said something. But I couldn't.'

'And I'd guess he didn't make it easy for you.' He squeezed her hand. 'I wish I'd known the truth all those years ago, Alex. It would've been different. I wouldn't have been able to do anything about the ectopic pregnancy, but I could've spared you what you went through with Bennett. And I would've encouraged you to retake your exams, go on to do your degree.' He paused. 'Just so you know, a degree doesn't make any difference to your job now. You have the professional qualifications, the experience and the enthusiasm. They're what count. And we're damn lucky to have you.'

'Don't be too nice to me,' she said. 'Because I don't want to cry.'

'It's not weak to cry,' he said softly. 'And, just so you know, my shoulder will always be there for you. Always.'

'Thank you.'

Her voice was thready, and he could see her blinking back the tears. Tears he knew she didn't want to shed in public. He'd already pushed her far enough. 'Come on. Let's go and find somewhere to eat tonight.'

'St Mark's Square?' she suggested.

'Sounds great.'

They wandered into the square, looked at menus, and

booked dinner for two at one of the oldest *caffès* in Venice. And then he took her to their hotel, so they could change.

She stopped dead outside the hotel and stared at him. 'Jordan, even I know that this is one of the most expensive hotels in Venice. Everyone's heard of this place.'

He shrugged. 'And?'

'And…' She shook her head. 'Where do I begin?'

'What you do,' he said softly, 'is just enjoy it. I thought, since we're playing hooky, we might as well do it in style.'

She still looked worried, and he sighed. He knew now that Bennett had always had some kind of hidden agenda, and it had stopped her enjoying things because she wondered what was going to be required of her in return. 'Alex. You're with *me*. There aren't any hidden agendas. We're having one night in Venice, and I just wanted it to be somewhere a bit special. Not because I expect something from you, but because I want to make you feel like a princess.'

'Sorry. I don't mean to be ungrateful.' She gave him a rueful smile. 'Thank you. It's lovely to be spoiled.'

'Let's go and find our room,' he said, taking her hand and drawing her with him to the reception area.

When he opened the door to their suite, the first thing he noticed was how huge the bed was. The bathroom was pure marble with a large, deep bath, and there were exquisite antique glass chandeliers and mirrors everywhere. Voile and silk curtains hung at the windows, and the bed coverlets were also silk. The table and dressing table were exquisite gilt ormolu, with Louis XIV chairs upholstered in smoky blue velvet, while the carpet was definitely deep enough to sink into as you walked.

'Wow. This is incredible.' She went over to one of the windows, twitched the voile aside and exclaimed in delight. 'Jordan, we've got a view of the Grand Canal itself. It's amazing.'

He stood behind her and wrapped his arms round her waist, resting his chin on her shoulder as he looked out at the view. 'Yes, it's really something.'

But the real thing for him was sharing this with her. The woman he loved.

And there were no two ways about it. He did love Alexandra. He'd loved her when he was nineteen, little more than a boy—and he still loved her now he was a man. It wasn't just the physical attraction; being with her made him feel different. With her, he could be himself and know that she understood him.

But did she feel the same way about him? Had Bennett damaged her so much that she'd never be able to love or trust someone again?

He kissed the nape of her neck. 'Alex?'

She shifted round to face him. 'We need to get ready.'

'So we do.' He gave her a wolfish grin, then scooped her up and carried her into the bathroom. She was about to protest, when he lowered his head and kissed her. And then everything went haywire.

She had no idea who took whose clothes off—everything was blurred by need and desire—but then they were both naked, both standing in the huge marble bath, and he'd turned the shower on so that warm water was spraying down over them.

'You're all tense.' He turned her so that her back was to him, and she felt him smooth shower gel over her shoulders. 'Here, and here.' He worked the knots out of her muscles, and she was surprised by how good it felt. Then he slid his hands round to her midriff, spreading his fingers, and drew her back against him. She could feel his erection pressing against her, and desire licked all the way down her spine. If only he'd move his hands up. Cup her breasts properly, ease the ache in her nipples.

'Your wish is my command,' he said softly against her ear, and she felt colour shoot through her face when she realised she'd spoken aloud.

'Sorry.'

He turned her to face him. 'For being demanding?' Amusement glittered in his eyes.

'I don't normally...'

'Well, you should.' He stole a kiss. 'I like it when you tell me what you want.' He poured more shower gel over her breasts, then stroked it into lather. 'Like this?'

She caught her breath as he teased her nipples into tight points. 'Yes.'

'Good.'

Here she was, need coiling tighter and tighter, to the point where she was almost begging him to take her now, finish it, because the tension was too much for her. And he was completely in control.

So not fair.

She wanted him in the same state that she was. Desperate.

It was time to take some of the control back. She grabbed the shower gel and smoothed some across his chest.

'Oh, now, that's nice. I like having your hands on me,' he said, his voice deepening.

He reminded her of a perfume ad, with his hair plastered back like that and his skin wet. Sexy as hell.

'How about here?' She let her hand drift lower, brushing over his abdomen—and it pleased her to note that he seemed to be having trouble breathing.

'Keep going, Alex.' His voice was deeper, too, slightly rougher with desire.

'You want me to touch you?' She curled her hand round his shaft. Stroked.

He closed his eyes and tipped his head back. 'Careful,' he warned. 'Carry on like this, and I'm not going to be much good to you.'

'Then perhaps I'd better stop.' She gave him her wickedest smile, and put her hands behind her back.

'That,' he said, 'is so…' He dragged in a breath. 'Alex. I need you. Now.'

'Now,' she agreed huskily.

It was a matter of seconds for him to step out of the shower, grab the wallet from his jeans and take a condom from it. It didn't seem to bother him that he was dripping water all over the floor and all over the tangle of their clothes—and it stopped bothering her, too, when he returned to the bath and lifted her up so that her back was against the tiles and the water was pouring over both of them. Automatically, she wrapped her legs round his waist for balance; and then he was pushing inside her, filling her, taking away the ache of frustration.

Her climax hit sooner than she'd expected; as her body tightened round his, he kissed her hard and she felt him shudder against her.

'I think,' he said shakily afterwards, 'we both needed that.'

'It feels as if I can breathe again.'

'Yeah.' He stroked her face. 'Come on. We'll look like prunes if we stay in here much longer.' He wrapped her in a fluffy towel and dried her.

And then she realised that half her clothes were soaked.

'Sorry, my fault,' he said. 'I was, um, thinking about other things.'

Like how quickly he could find a condom and be inside her. Yeah. That had been uppermost in her mind, too.

He looked at the mess on the floor. 'Just as well we bought clean stuff for tomorrow,' he said, but he was smiling. 'Could've been worse. I'll sort it out in a minute. Come on, we need to get changed or we'll be late for dinner.'

'I think,' she said, 'we'd better get changed in separate rooms.'

'Mmm, because you're too tempting.' He stole a kiss. 'Alex. You know the thing I'm most looking forward to, tonight? Falling asleep with you in my arms.'

So was she. Too much so. But she wasn't going to spoil tonight with worries. She was just going to let herself enjoy it. Store up the good memories. 'Go and get changed,' she said with a smile. 'I'll see you in a bit.'

CHAPTER ELEVEN

JORDAN took one look at Alexandra when she emerged from the bathroom, and his jaw dropped. 'Wow. That dress is gorgeous. And I can't wait to take it off you.'

She just laughed. 'Patience is a virtue. And a business asset.'

'I can be patient.' He pulled her into his arms and drew a line of kisses along the curve of her neck. 'I bet I can be more patient than you.'

'In your dreams.' She kissed him lightly. 'You don't scrub up so badly, yourself, Mr Smith. I like this shirt.' She skated her fingertips along the soft cotton. 'It brings out the colour of your eyes. Gorgeous.'

'The shirt, or my eyes?' he teased.

'Stop fishing.' But her eyes were glittering with amusement. 'Both.'

'Come on, we've got enough time for a walk before dinner.'

When they walked along the Grand Canal, a gondolier wearing the traditional black and white striped jersey and straw boater came over to them. 'Gondola, sir, madam, gondo-laaaa?' he asked hopefully.

'I guess if you're in Venice, you really have to take a ride in a gondola—it's something you can't do anywhere else,' Jordan said. 'Shall we?'

'That'd be nice.' But when Alexandra stepped in, the boat rocked wildly. 'Whoa,' she said, putting a hand out for balance.

Jordan stepped down beside her and steadied her. 'OK?'

'Yes. It just feels a bit—well—rickety,' she said in a whisper, not wanting to be rude to the gondolier.

He smiled. 'It's safe. Really. These boats have been sailing the canals of Venice for hundreds of years—well, obviously not this particular one, but boats just like it.'

She sat on the padded seat in front of where the gondolier stood. Jordan joined her, put his arm round her and drew her close.

As the gondolier poled them along the canal, she could see the sky fading from blue to rose pink at the horizon. Venus rose, shining almost as brightly as the moon; and then there were the first pinpoints of stars peeping through the velvety deep blue sky.

'Oh, wow, it's just…' Words failed her. This was like nothing else she'd ever experienced. Romantic didn't even begin to cover it.

And she was so glad that she was sharing this with him.

As the boat glided silently under a bridge, Jordan kissed her, his mouth warm and soft and sweet and tender; it started out reassuring, but she could feel the tension in his body, telling her that he was trying to hold back.

But the narrow little canals they were gliding through weren't lit by streetlamps, like the main thoroughfares; there was just the occasional glow from a window. Meaning that this was much, much more private than either of them had expected—just them and the starlight. And so, under the next bridge, she kissed him, nipping gently at his lower lip until he let her deepen the kiss.

God, she loved kissing him. The way he responded to her. The way he made her respond to him. The way her blood felt as if it were fizzing through her veins. He made her feel as if she had a permanent fever.

He broke the kiss as light started to draw nearer; as they reached the end of the canal, Alexandra realised what it was. The Grand Canal, its ancient buildings spot lit against the night. She glanced at Jordan; his mouth was slightly swollen from kissing her, and it was a fair bet she was in the same state. But she just hadn't been able to stop herself. 'Sorry,' she muttered.

'I'm not,' Jordan whispered in her ear. And then he gave her an incredibly wicked, sensual smile that made her feel a hell of a lot better. It hadn't just been her.

Eventually the gondola stopped by the Rialto Bridge; the gondolier helped them both out and wished them a nice evening. Hand in hand, they wandered back to St Mark's Square. The piazza was all lit up with huge round lanterns in the lower arches of the arcades and smaller ones in the two upper layers. String quartets and pianists performed in pergolas outside the *caffés*, filling the square with soft jazz and gentle classical music. Some people were sitting outside at the tables, listening to the music and sipping wine; couples walked through the square with their arms wrapped round each other; and others were actually dancing through the square.

'We have to do it,' Jordan said. 'Especially to this song.'

One of the quartets was playing 'It Had to Be You' and the vocalist had a smoky, sexy voice. Jordan spun her into his arms and danced with her through the square, spinning her round.

'I had no idea you could do ballroom dancing,' she said.

'I don't exactly advertise it,' he said with a grin. 'And this, my sweet Alexandra, is a foxtrot we're doing, I'll have you know.'

'A foxtrot?' She didn't have a clue how to do a foxtrot—she'd never done any kind of ballroom dancing—but Jordan led her so well that dancing with him was effortless. And fun. To the point where she didn't mind the fact that he was in control, because she knew he wasn't going to hurt her the way that Nathan had. And she loved the fact that he was singing the song to her—even the bit accusing her of being bossy. Which she could be. He'd never sung to her before, so she'd had no idea that his voice was so nice: a warm, soulful tenor.

'I would've made you sing "O Sole Mio" on the gondola, if I'd known you were this good,' she teased.

'Ah, so the lady would like to be serenaded? It can be arranged,' he teased back. 'But first…' He bent her back over his arm and kissed her. Thoroughly. She was flushed and laughing when they straightened up again.

'Dinner,' he said, still holding her gaze.

She was still smiling when they finally walked through the door of the *caffè* to claim their table in the restaurant.

'Today has been amazing,' she said softly, 'just amazing. This is everything I always thought Venice would be, and more. Thank you so much.'

'My pleasure. And I mean that. I'm glad I'm sharing it with you,' Jordan said.

The food was perfectly cooked, a riot of textures and flavours. But Alexandra especially liked the Venetian cookies that came with their coffee: thin slices of almond sponge, the layers coloured delicately green, red and white like the Italian flag, wrapped in melted chocolate. 'I'm going to talk Giorgio into making some of these for us when we get back to London.'

'Mmm. And I'm going to feed them to you bite by bite.' His gaze held hers. 'In bed.'

Her pulse rate kicked up a notch. 'I think I'm done with coffee.' All she wanted was him. Naked. Beneath her.

'Me, too.' He moistened his lower lip with his tongue. 'We need to get out of here.'

He wrapped his arm round her shoulder as they left the *caffè*, and she slid hers round his waist; he shortened his stride to match hers, and they got back to their hotel in record time.

'I rushed you back here,' he said in the reception area. 'And it's not even late. I should've taken you out for Bellinis.' The mixture of sparkling wine and puréed peach was one of the most famous cocktails in the world. 'Except right now I don't want to have to share you with anyone else.'

She knew exactly what he meant. She just wanted to be with him, too. It wasn't the same kind of possessiveness that Nathan had shown; it felt different. And she knew that Jordan wouldn't try to choose her friends and put barriers between her and the people who knew her best.

'So what do you suggest?'

'The balcony in our room. Bellinis, watching the night. And…' He didn't say the rest of it, but she knew exactly what he had in mind, and her body tingled with anticipation.

'Yes,' she said huskily.

He ordered their drinks at the bar, then came back over to her. 'Room Service is bringing them up,' he said. 'Let's go.'

Though when he opened the French windows and they stepped out onto the balcony, they discovered that it was a little cooler than they'd both expected.

The sky had darkened while they'd been eating and the waters of the lagoon had turned from turquoise to inky black, reflecting the lights from the building; the churches were lit from below, making them seem almost ghostly. And all around was silent, the soft lapping of the tide—

no noisy engines or roaring exhausts. She loved seeing the Thames lit up at night, but that paled into comparison with this, with the reflections of the lights on the lagoon and the occasional gondola or night *vaporetto* going past. The whole scene before them was just magical.

'Are you cold?' he asked.

'I'm fine,' she fibbed.

Though clearly he noticed the goose-pimples on her arms, because he smiled and wrapped his arms round her, drawing her back against his body. 'Time to share some bodily warmth, I think.'

She relaxed against him, her head against his shoulder, and his hands splayed across her midriff. His thumbs brushed the undersides of her breasts through her dress, and the thought of what he was going to do next made her nipples harden.

Slowly, softly, he moved so that he was cupping her breasts. She closed her eyes as his thumbs circled her nipples, teasing them; and then she felt his mouth against the curve of her neck, making her arch back against him.

Just as she was about to turn round, kiss him and walk him backwards into their room, there was a knock at the door.

He groaned. 'Bad timing. Room service. I'll get it,' he said. 'Stay here.'

He returned carrying two Bellinis in champagne flutes, each decorated with a single strawberry.

'To us,' he said softly, raising his glass. 'And to tonight.'

'To us,' she echoed, raising her own glass, then took a sip. She'd expected the cocktail to be a little over-sweet, but the dryness of the sparkling wine cut through the sweetness of the fruit and gave the drink depth. 'This is gorgeous.'

He kissed her. 'And so are you.' He took her glass and

placed it on the coffee table next to his. 'I'm really glad that your dress doesn't have a tight skirt.'

'Why?' She wasn't following this. At all.

He walked her back out to the balcony and spun her round so that she was facing the Grand Canal. 'Because, even though I'm pretty sure we can't be seen from here…' And then she realised what he was doing. Slowly, gradually, tugging the hem of her dress up to her waist.

Adrenalin kicked through her. She'd never, ever done anything like this before. He was going to make love to her on the balcony overlooking the city? 'Jordan, we can't.'

'Yes, we can.' He kissed the nape of her neck, and then stroked one hand down to her thighs. 'Stockings?' His fingers found the lacy edge of her hold-ups and he exhaled harshly. 'If I'd known about this, we wouldn't have made it to dinner. And I might just've had to find a deserted *calle*.'

'And got us both arrested. Jordan, if someone looks up—'

'They'll see you, looking out over the lagoon. They'll see me standing behind you. And this balcony is waist-high.'

'Wrought iron.'

'Covered in plants. The perfect screen.' He nibbled her earlobe. 'Neither of us is a screamer. Nobody's going to know. Just you and me.'

Making love on the balcony of the poshest hotel in Venice. He had to be crazy.

His hands were spread across her midriff again, and he'd moved so she could feel his erection pressing against her. Her mouth went dry. 'Jordan. Yes.'

It took him seconds to protect them both. 'Hold on to the balcony rail,' he directed.

She did so, and he positioned himself at her entrance, then slowly pushed inside her.

'Oh, my God,' she breathed.

'Good?' he asked softly.

'Yeah. Unbelievable.'

'Keep watching the lagoon,' he said.

Though she couldn't. As the tension built and built and built inside her, she squeezed her eyes shut and tipped her head back. And then wave after wave of sensation rippled through her as she hit her climax.

He was careful with her afterwards, walking backwards into their room and drawing her with him, and then closing the French doors. And then he carried her to their bed and undressed her achingly slowly, caressing every centimetre of skin he revealed before making love with her again.

As her pulse slowed and he drew her into his arms, cuddled against her, she actually found herself crying.

Jordan kissed her tears away. 'Don't cry, Alex,' he urged softly.

'They're happy tears,' she said. 'I promise.'

Though there was a hint of sadness, too. How she wished that the past couldn't cast its blight on her future.

She was going to have to tell him the truth. But not yet. She wanted to have tonight and tomorrow morning. Such precious memories.

She fell asleep in his arms, thinking, *I love you. If only there was a way for us to make this work.*

The next morning, Jordan woke first. He lay there for a while, just watching Alexandra sleep; the wariness had gone from her face, and in repose she was beautiful.

Funny, before, he'd been so sure that his life had direction and purpose and meaning. But, now that Alexandra was back in his life, he realised just how much he'd been kidding himself. He'd been working silly hours to distract himself from the fact that his life was empty and he envied the hell out of his best friend and his wife, who were so much in love with each other and were expecting their first child.

He could imagine Alexandra like that, radiant in pregnancy, her belly rounded by their child, and the thought made his head spin. Alexandra and their baby. A family. The family that they'd so nearly made all those years ago.

He kissed her awake, and she smiled at him.

'Hello.' Her brown eyes were all soft and warm, and for a moment Jordan was sure that they were full of love.

Then the wariness came back. He could even see it happening, and sighed inwardly. She'd told him more about her past, she'd let him close enough to actually spend the night with him—but he could tell that there were still more barriers. More things she hadn't told him.

Would he ever be able to teach her to trust again?

'Good morning.' He kissed her gently. 'Shall I order room service or, since the sun's shining, shall we go and have breakfast on the terrace? Apparently, the views are stunning.'

'We could have room service absolutely anywhere,' she said. 'But breakfast on the Grand Canal… That's a once-in-a-lifetime thing.' Her smile was bright—and, to his relief, genuine. 'I think we have to do it, Jordan.'

The terrace had amazing views over the lagoon, and the sun was so warm that Alexandra could barely believe it was only April. She enjoyed every second of it, from the ruby-red freshly squeezed orange juice to the plate of warm pastries to the huge silver pot of coffee. 'This,' she said, leaning back in her chair, 'is what I call being pampered. And it's wonderful.'

'Good. Our flight isn't until this afternoon, so we still have a bit of time to go exploring. Would you like to go over to Murano and see the glass being made?' Jordan asked.

'That'd be lovely.'

When they'd finished their coffee, they headed out to the Grand Canal and took the *vaporetto* over to Murano. They were both entranced by the glass blowers and how quickly they could turn a ball of orangey-yellow glass into a rearing horse with a windblown mane and tail—and then how a similar ball of glass could be blown into the most beautiful vase.

After the demonstration, they wandered through the glass warehouses. Alexandra noticed Jordan picking up a paperweight for a closer inspection; the expression on his face told her he loved it, but for some reason he put it down again.

She sneaked a glance at the glass; it was the same colour as the bowl she'd sighed over in Venice and the starfish pendant he'd bought her. She managed to distract him, then bought it swiftly, and had it wrapped and hidden in her bag before he could notice anything had happened.

They stopped off in Burano on the way back; Alexandra loved the pretty painted houses and took photographs of the buildings' reflections in the canals. They wandered through the main street, looking at the lace, and stopped to buy some of the lemony S-shaped biscuits the island was famous for.

And on the way back to their hotel on the *vaporetto*, she handed him the beautifully wrapped parcel.

'What's this?' he asked.

'For you.'

He frowned. 'You don't have buy me anything.'

She shrugged and threw his words back at him. 'I'm your girlfriend. I'm allowed to buy you something if I want to.' She softened the words with a smile.

'Thank you.' He opened the parcel and sucked in a breath. 'Alex, that's gorgeous. How did you know that was the one I had my eye on?'

Because she'd been watching him. Not that she was going to tell him that. 'Lucky guess,' she fibbed.

'It's gorgeous,' he said again. 'Thank you.' He kissed her lightly.

Back at the hotel, they prepared to leave for London. Their clothes from the day before were still slightly damp from their soaking in the bathroom, but he shoved them all into the case anyway.

Alexandra started laughing.

He looked at her. 'What's so funny?'

'I can't believe someone as pernickety as you packs like that.'

'It's all going straight into the washing machine or the dry cleaner's when we get back to London, so what's the point of packing neatly?'

'I guess you have a point.'

At the airport, she was relieved to discover that that their case was indeed small enough to count as hand luggage. Jordan held her hand all the way back to London, except this wasn't like coming to Venice, when she'd been so thrilled at the idea of finally visiting the place that had been top of her wish list. Now, they were going back to reality, things that couldn't be escaped. And she was going to have to tell him the rest of it.

Dread settled into a hard knot in her stomach when they landed, and her feet felt as if they were dragging as they went through Customs.

Outside the airport, Jordan hailed a taxi and gave the driver her address.

'We need to sort out our luggage,' she said as the taxi driver pulled up outside her flat. 'Do you want to come in for a bit?'

'Thanks. That'd be nice.'

Home. Except it never really had been, she thought as she opened the front door. It had been just a place to live. Somewhere to cook, somewhere to sleep. Whereas Venice—Venice had felt like home. And she knew why. Because she'd been with Jordan all the time. She'd fallen asleep in his arms, been woken by him in the morning with a kiss…

What an idiot she was.

'Penny for them?' he asked.

She shook herself. 'Just that London feels a bit cold and flat, after Venice.'

'Yeah. I know what you mean. Though I guess, to a Venetian, London would seem exotic. All the green spaces and gardens we have instead of courtyards and jetties and bridges.'

'I'd better sort out the case.' She opened it in front of her washing machine, then paused and looked up at him. 'You know, I might as well put your stuff in with mine.'

This was the opening Jordan had hoped for. A chance to move another step closer. 'And I'll collect them tomorrow night? Thanks. That'd be good.' He waited a beat. 'Or I could keep them here. As spare clothes. Just as you could keep some things at mine.'

She said nothing, but went very still.

Oh, hell. He'd taken it too far, pushed her too fast. 'It was just an idea,' he said lightly.

'Mmm,' she said, and started putting the laundry straight into the washing machine.

And now he felt completely awkward. 'Shall I make some coffee, or something?'

'As you wish.'

Hell, hell, hell. That offhand tone was deliberate, he was sure. She was putting every single barrier back into place.

There was only one thing he could think of to do to stop her. He dropped to his knees beside her. 'Alex.'

She looked up. 'Yes?'

He dipped his head. Brushed his mouth oh, so lightly against hers. His lips tingled, and he did it again. And again, until her arms were wrapped round his neck and she was kissing him back, opening her mouth to let him deepen the kiss. His pulse was hammering so hard, he could practically hear it, and his temperature had gone up several degrees.

'Forget the washing,' he said, pulling her to her feet, then scooped her up and carried her to her bedroom.

'Jordan, sex isn't the answer to everything,' she protested as he set her back down on her feet.

'No, but I can't think of any other way to stop you putting the barriers back up between us.' He stroked her face. 'Last night, I fell asleep with you in my arms. This morning, you were the first thing I saw when I woke. And I don't want last night to be a one-off.'

She sucked in a breath. 'So what exactly do you want?'

'You,' he said. 'I know I'm rushing you. I'm trying not to. But this weekend's been so special to me. I don't want to go back to how things were, having to leave you in bed and going home to a cold, empty flat.' He stole another kiss. 'It's too soon to move in together. I know that. I'm not asking for that.' Not yet. 'But I'd like to be able to stay over, and for you to stay at my place. Not every night—just sometimes.' He stole another kiss. 'Preferably starting tonight.'

'You want to stay tonight.' It was a statement, not a question.

'Which isn't a string attached to Venice.' He sighed. 'It's got nothing to do with Venice at all. Well, I suppose it has.' He stroked her face. 'I enjoyed waking up with you and it's made me realise how much I want to do that again.'

She bit her lip, looking worried.

'Let's keep it simple,' he said softly. 'I like being with you, and I think you like being with me.'

She nodded.

'So can I stay tonight?' When she said nothing, he added, 'I don't want you to say yes because you feel any obligation to me for Venice. I want you to say yes because you want me to stay. Because you want to fall asleep in my arms. Because you want to wake up with me tomorrow, just as I want to wake up with you.'

For a moment, her eyes glittered with tears.

And then she whispered, 'Yes.'

CHAPTER TWELVE

WITHIN a week Jordan had a shelf in Alexandra's bathroom and space in her wardrobe, and she had the same at his flat. What she'd promised herself would just be an occasional night spent together turned out to be every night, because now they'd actually slept together and woken up together, they discovered that they just couldn't bear to be apart.

And every day Alexandra realised she was falling more and more in love with Jordan.

She was going to have to talk to him. Tell him the bit she'd kept back. The longer she left it, the harder she knew it was going to be—for both of them.

She left work early on the Friday night; the plan was that Jordan was coming over for dinner and to watch a movie when he'd finished at the office. He texted her to let her know that he was on his way; when he arrived, he kissed her lingeringly. 'OK?'

No. She was very far from OK. But she forced a smile to her face. 'Sure. Just a bit tired.'

It felt like the last meal of the condemned prisoner; her stomach was in a knot, and she couldn't eat. She toyed with her food. Eventually Jordan laid down his cutlery, his own meal only half-eaten, and reached over to take her hand. 'What's wrong?'

Where did she start?

'We need to talk,' she said.

'I had a feeling you were going to say that. You've been antsy for a week.' He squeezed her hand. 'Tell me,' he said softly.

'It's about Nathan.'

'He's been in touch with you?'

She shook her head. 'It's about the reason why my marriage broke up.'

He frowned. 'I thought that was because he was a total control freak who bullied you, kept you apart from your friends and your family, and tried to push you into what he wanted to do regardless of what you wanted.'

'That was part of it,' she said, 'but I can't let him take all the blame. Part of it was me. I let him down.'

'How?' He looked puzzled. 'Because you wouldn't let him use you as a doormat?'

'No. I couldn't give him a child.' She dragged in a breath. 'Our baby…it wasn't the only one I lost. I lost Nathan's, too. Except I didn't realise I was pregnant at the time.' Every word felt as if she were cutting into the scars. But she knew it had to be done. She had to be honest. Tell Jordan the whole story, so he knew what he was getting in to if he stayed with her. To give him the option to leave. 'I had what I thought was just a really light period. And then, two weeks later, I collapsed at work.' She shivered. 'I knew what that pain meant. I'd been there before. And I didn't get to the hospital in time. I lost the baby and they couldn't save the other tube.'

She lifted her chin, aiming for defiance, but then the whole thing was undermined because she had to blink back the tears. 'That's what you need to know. I can't have a baby now. Not unless I do it through IVF.' She closed her eyes. 'And, after two ectopic pregnancies, I just can't face that.'

He released her hand. Just as Alexandra had expected: he couldn't handle this any more than Nathan had been able to. She couldn't look at him; she couldn't bear to see the mingled pity and disappointment in his face.

But when she felt herself being scooped out of her chair, she opened her eyes again. 'What are you doing?'

'This is a conversation where I think you need to be held,' Jordan said, sitting down in her chair and settling her on his lap. 'So that's what I'm doing. Holding you.'

'Didn't you hear what I just said? I can't have a baby.'

'And?'

How could he sound so casual? 'But—don't you want children?' She frowned. 'Don't you need a child, an heir for Field's?'

'Not necessarily.'

'But Nathan…'

'I'm not Nathan.' He looked hurt. 'Alex, the last few weeks—I thought we'd got closer.'

'We have. Which is why we need to have this conversation now. So I can let you go, and you can find someone who'll give you the child you need.' Her voice was thick with tears. 'I'll be handing in my resignation, first thing Monday morning.'

Jordan could barely believe what he was hearing. She was walking out on him and she was going to leave Field's? 'Why?'

'I can't stay at Field's any more. I can't work with you, Jordan.'

He frowned. 'I'm missing something here.' They'd developed a good working relationship. They were a team. 'Why can't you work with me?'

Her breath hitched. 'Because I'm not nice enough to be

able to stand by and smile and be pleased for you when you find someone else.'

What? Where was this all coming from? 'I'm not going to find someone else.'

'Of course you are. You just have to smile at women and they melt.'

'That's crazy. Of course they don't. And, more importantly, I don't want anyone else.' He sighed. 'Alex, it's you. It's always been you—even when I thought I hated you. I never loved Lindsey, and I guess that's the real reason why my marriage didn't work. She wasn't you. I should never have asked her to marry me.'

Alexandra looked anguished. 'But I can't give you an heir for Field's, Jordan. I can't conceive without IVF, and besides there are no guarantees that IVF will work.' She bit her lip. 'And I can't live with the guilt and the strain of another failure. I just can't.'

'You don't have to,' he said softly. 'I'm not Nathan. I'm not going to make you go through something you don't want to do.' He paused. 'So I take it he didn't support you when you lost the baby?'

She swallowed hard. 'He said I'd lied to him. Lied by omission. Which was true—I should've told him about our baby. I should've been more careful. I should've taken a pregnancy test anyway, because my period was lighter than normal and I should've realised there was a chance I might be pregnant.'

How had the man managed to make her feel that everything was her fault? Why hadn't he shown the slightest bit of sympathy? Why hadn't he put her needs first, at a time when she'd been at her most vulnerable? 'Don't blame yourself,' Jordan said fiercely. 'The way I see it, he should never have pushed you like that. You were only eighteen when you married him, you'd already had a really rough time without the support you needed from me or your parents, and he should've talked to you and found out how you felt about starting a family. And then he should've waited until you were ready instead of pressuring you.'

'I thought he would wait,' she whispered. 'That first year, when he was so good to me—I actually thought I could be happy. And then it changed. After the fight about my exams…we didn't make love any more. It was just sex, to make babies. We only ever had sex when it was the right time of the month, the time when I was most likely to conceive. And I felt he wasn't seeing me any more; all he saw was someone who could give him a child.'

'Why didn't you leave him?'

'Because I'd lost myself,' she said. 'Day by day, I'd let him take over more and more. When it's gradual like that, you don't realise how bad things are getting until you're right at rock bottom. And I'm so ashamed that I let someone control me that way.' Her breath shuddered. 'I deferred to him in everything. I hate it that I was so weak, so pathetic.'

'You weren't pathetic. You were young. And when you stopped letting him make all the decisions—when you'd finally started to get over how I let you down and wanted to do things for yourself, retake your exams and get on with your life—he couldn't handle it. So it was his problem, not yours,' Jordan said.

'It didn't feel like it,' she said. 'I felt as if I was the selfish one. He'd done so much for me, he'd given me a home and a future; and I wouldn't even give him the one thing he wanted, a baby. I tried to tell him about you, about what happened to our baby. But every time I tried, I saw the way he looked at me—he despised me, Jordan.'

'You're worth a million of him. And he was the one with

the problem, not you,' Jordan repeated. 'Couldn't you have told Meggie what was going on? Your parents?'

'I hardly saw my parents. I—' How could she explain? 'We grew apart, after I left home. Nathan didn't try to build any bridges with my parents because he said I didn't need anyone else except my husband. And Meggie…he didn't like her.' She bit her lip. 'In the end, I could only see her at lunchtime, and even then I had to make up an excuse about where I'd been.'

'I'd like to break every bone in his body—twice,' Jordan said.

Then he saw the fear in her eyes.

She'd said that Bennett hadn't hit her. Maybe she hadn't told him the whole truth about that, either. Wasn't that how bullies worked, making their victims feel as if it was their fault and they were completely worthless?

'But I wouldn't do that,' he said, trying to make his voice gentle, 'because violence doesn't solve anything. And what he really needs is professional help, because the way he treated you wasn't normal. That isn't how an equal relationship works, Alex.'

'He couldn't forgive me,' she said, 'for not giving him a child. For not being a proper wife. He went on and on and on about IVF. How, if I really loved him, I'd book myself in to a clinic and start treatment.'

'And if he'd really loved you,' Jordan said dryly, 'he wouldn't have asked you to do that. He would've realised that you'd been through more than enough. If you'd wanted to do it, if you'd been desperate for a child of your own, then fine. But it's not an easy procedure. And, like you said, there are no guarantees it'll work.'

'That's not how Nathan saw it. He went on and on and on about it. It was only one of my clients that kept me sane.'

'Clients?' Jordan asked.

'Didn't you read my CV when you interviewed me? I was a cleaner for three years.'

'I don't remember seeing anything like that on your CV.'

'The agency probably put a spin on it and called it domestic client management or something. I worked for a domestic agency when I left home. It meant doing a bit of cleaning, doing their shopping, and maybe making them a sandwich or heating through some kind of ready meal.'

A job that needed no academic qualifications. And Alexandra had been so academic. Why hadn't she held out for a job that would stretch her more?

As if the question showed on his face, she said softly, 'Jordan, I needed to earn a living and I'd failed my A levels, remember. My savings weren't that huge, so I wasn't in a position to be fussy. And actually, I liked my job. I liked meeting different people and making a difference to their lives.'

Now that he could understand. Because the Alexandra he remembered—the Alexandra he'd got to know again— had always been kind, making the effort to help people. 'So you had a nice client?'

'I had several nice clients, but Jude was the best. She used to be an actress. She had this parrot, Jasper, who used to quote Shakespeare. She'd gone through several lots of domestic help because they were terrified of him—he used to sit on your shoulder, say, "No bitey", and then nip your earlobe. And sometimes he'd land on your head, just to freak you. But he made friends with me, and I loved it when he sang a little song or quoted Shakespeare.' She smiled at the memory. 'And one day I forgot myself and spoke the next few lines of the play he'd been quoting.'

He could imagine that. It was a game they'd played so

many times themselves, when he'd been helping her study. He'd rewarded her with kisses when she got it right.

'Jude heard me. She made me sit down with her over a cup of tea and tell her how come I could quote from the middle of *The Winter's Tale*. Eventually I told her the whole story. And she made me see that I wasn't doing everything I could with my life. And my friend who'd been taking the classes with me…she said the same thing. She was the one who made me do the career tests. To see that I was worth more than Nathan let me think I was.'

'You're worth a hell of a lot more,' he said.

'It didn't feel like it at the time. It felt like yet another in a long line of failures. He wanted a baby; I couldn't give him one. I was a failure as a wife, a failure as a mother— everything I touched, I failed.' She dragged in a breath. 'I didn't tell him I was doing my exams. I made excuses, told more lies. I took the exams. And then I got my results.'

'Top marks.' Even if Jordan hadn't seen her CV, he would've known that.

'I knew I wasn't going to university, but it made me think that maybe I could still do exams. Maybe I could do some kind of vocational or professional qualification.'

'Like the marketing exams.'

'The ones my friend suggested.' She nodded. 'When I told Nathan I was going to change my job and do my professional qualifications, he said I couldn't study and have a family. I told him there was no way I was going through IVF. After two ectopic pregnancies, all that pain and all that loss, I couldn't face it. Month after month of having to inject myself with hormones and then going through all the procedures, hoping that they could collect enough eggs and fertilise them, that a viable embryo could be put back and then…' She swallowed hard. 'I'd already lost two babies, and there's only a one in four chance that IVF will work. Every cycle that didn't work would've brought that back to me, and I just couldn't handle it.'

Jordan held her closer. 'Of course you couldn't.'

'Things got worse and worse between us. He said I was a failure as a wife, a total failure. And he was going to divorce me for unreasonable behaviour.'

'What? But he was the one being unreasonable.'

'I waited until he'd gone to work, one morning, then packed my stuff and walked out. I left him a letter saying I was sorry, I couldn't stay married to him any more so I was leaving, so he could find someone who'd give him what he wanted.'

The same kind of thing she'd just said to him, Jordan thought. Except what he and Bennett wanted were very, very different things.

And she clearly hadn't finished, because she was shaking. He stroked her hair, hoping that it would give her the strength to go on. To tell him the rest, and let him help her wipe the rest of the shadows out of her life.

'He waited for me outside the office, knowing I'd have to go there to give in my time sheet, and he told me that I had to come back to him. I said no. My boss heard all the shouting and came out. He called the police. Nathan threatened to hit him. And it just got messy.' She blew out a breath. 'He ended up being taken into custody. I got an injunction so he couldn't come anywhere near me, before or after the divorce. And I swore I'd never let myself get in that position again. I'd never let my happiness rely on someone else. I'd never let anyone control me again.'

'I can understand that.' He held her close. There was one really important question he needed to ask. 'Do you know your own worth now?'

'Yes.'

'I'm glad.'

She looked miserable. 'It took me a lot of hard work to get to that point. And a fair bit of nagging from Meggie, Jude and Amy—my friend who suggested doing the marketing exams.'

'That's what friends are for,' he said lightly. And thank God she'd had some people to fight her corner when she needed it. 'Just for the record,' he said, 'I think you're bright—you have great ideas and they're grounded in reality. I think you're brave, because you've gone through hell in the last ten years and you don't whine about it to anyone, you just get on with things. I respect your judgement. And, most of all, I love you.' He stroked her face. 'Which isn't me pressuring you to love me back. I just don't want you to be in any doubt about how I feel about you.'

'You love me?' she asked in seeming wonder. 'Even after everything I've just told you?'

'I love you,' he repeated. He stole a kiss. 'I fell in love with you when you were a geeky seventeen-year-old. I loved everything about you. Your mind, your smile, your body. And it never really changed, even when I was angry with you, when I didn't know the truth about what was happening. Then, when we started working together, it drove me crazy—my common sense told me that I should keep you at a distance, but all I wanted to do was kiss you.' He smiled at her. 'Of all the department stores in all the towns in all the world, you walk into mine.'

She grimaced. 'That's the worst Bogart impersonation I've ever heard—and I hate that film anyway.'

'Ilsa walks off and sacrifices everything she had with Rick. Is that what you're going to do with me?'

She blew out a breath. 'Right now, I can't think straight—I can't make a sensible decision about anything.'

'Then don't make a decision now,' he said gently. 'And

please don't think that any of what you've just told me changes a single thing between us.'

'But—you need someone who can give you children.'

'We've already been through that, Alex. The way I see it, you've been through hell and more than enough pain. I'm not Bennett. I'm not going to make you go through a lot of painful, intrusive medical procedures just to boost my ego. If you want children, then there are other ways. We can adopt. We could foster. We could look into surrogacy. Or we could even not have children at all. We'll still be happy together.'

She blinked. 'What about Field's?'

'We can work something out. But I know what I need. I know what I want. And she's right here in my arms.'

She stroked his face. 'I wish I could believe that. But how do you know you're not going to regret that decision? Maybe not today. Maybe not tomorrow, but soon and—'

He stopped her protest by kissing her. 'For someone who says she hates *Casablanca*, you know an awful lot of the lines.'

'It was one of Nathan's favourites,' she said drily. 'One of the things we had in common—we both liked classic films. But I came to hate that one. The way Ilsa was trapped. Whatever she did, she lost. And I felt like that, too. Even though I wasn't seeing anyone else and neither was he.'

'Trapped between your marriage and your career.' That wasn't a mistake he was planning to make. As far as he was concerned, there was no reason why she couldn't have both. He'd back her, whatever she wanted to do. 'I'm sorry he didn't listen to you and let you do what you needed. But please don't think that all men are the same.'

'I know they're not,' she said dryly.

'And I want you to promise me something. If I say or

do anything in the future that makes you unhappy, challenge me. It might be crossed wires, or I might be being
an idiot. But as long as we keep talking, we'll work it out.
Together.'

'I'm not used to spilling my fears,' she said.

'I understand that. The important thing is that we'll listen to each other. Or try to—neither of us is perfect.'

'You're telling me.'

'I love you,' he said softly.

She held him close. 'I love you, too.' She took a deep
breath. 'But if I'm honest, I'm really scared that I can't
give you what you want. That I won't be enough for you.'

'All I want is you,' he said. 'You're enough for me. And
I'm going to tell you that every single day, until you finally
believe me.'

He could still see the wariness in her eyes. She wanted
to believe him, but she couldn't make that step. Not yet.

Well, it wasn't going to happen instantly. She just
needed to learn to trust him—and he knew that would
take time.

The following weekend, Jordan came back from the office
to find Alexandra brooding. Outwardly, she was simply
brainstorming a project at her kitchen table; but he could
see how spiky her handwriting was, how firm the strokes
were. Something was bugging her. And the only way he'd
find out what was by asking her directly.

'What's wrong?' he asked.

'Nothing. Just thinking about something,' she said.

'It's not nothing, or you'd look me in the eye.'

She sighed. 'OK. I talked to my parents this morning.'
She bit her lip. 'I owe you an apology. Dad didn't ring
you from the hospital. He—' her voice caught '—he said
you'd already hurt me enough, and he thought it was bet-

ter just to draw a line under the whole thing and not have you making it worse and dragging things out.'

And now she was wondering what would've happened if her father had phoned him. If things would've been different.

Jordan put his arms round her. 'Remember, we can't change the past. Just forgive it.'

'Mmm.' She really didn't sound in a forgiving mood.

'Want to know what I think? He was doing his best to protect you. He did what he thought was right at the time.' He kissed her. 'OK, he got it wrong, but he didn't do it out of malice. He did it out of love.'

She sighed. 'I guess so.'

'You used to be close to your parents,' he said softly. 'And I think you miss that. My guess is that they miss you, too, but they don't have a clue how to make things right between you—and they're scared of getting things even more wrong and making the rift wider.'

'So what are you saying?'

He scooped her up and sat down, settling her on his lap. 'Nobody's perfect. Maybe we need to start building bridges. Give everyone a chance to put their mistakes behind them. I know my mum's desperate to make it up with you, and I'd guess your parents are just as desperate.'

'So I need to make the first move?'

'We do,' he corrected gently. 'You're not on your own any more, Alex. I'm with you, every step of the way. Let's get rid of the bad stuff and make room for the good.' He kissed her again. 'I'm not saying you should do it right this minute. Just don't leave it to fester and hurt you.'

She sighed. 'You're right. I'll call them. We'll start building those bridges.'

'And that's another thing I love about you,' he said softly. 'Your bravery.'

'I'm not brave,' she said.

'You are in my eyes. And I love you.' He smiled at her. 'Always.'

Over the next month, Jordan told Alexandra that he loved her in every possible way. With a single red rose delivered to her desk. With a handwritten copy of a Shakespearean sonnet on marbled paper. With the CD of a song that had really appropriate words. With chocolate, hand-iced with the message JS ♥ AB. He stopped just short of hiring a skywriter, knowing that she'd have a tart comment to make about environmental damage; but every day he found a different way to tell her that he loved her.

And every night, he told her in words; just before she fell asleep in his arms, he whispered, 'Alex, I love you. Always.'

As the days went past, the look of disbelief in her eyes that she always quickly tried to hide gradually started to fade. Until one day it wasn't there any more. She just smiled back at him. 'I love you, too.'

Tonight might just be the night, he thought, curling his fingers round the velvet-covered box he'd had for a week.

And he just hoped she'd listen to what he had to say.

A quick phone call ensured that his plans were workable—at least from a logistics point of view. Now he had to convince Alexandra; and he knew that would be the hardest part.

He sent her an email.

Taking you out straight from work tonight. Can you be ready at half seven?

Two minutes later, she knocked on his office door. 'Where are we going?'

He spread his hands. 'I can't tell you.'

'Why not?'

'It's a surprise. One you'll like,' he added hastily. Or at least one he hoped she'd like.

'Can you at least tell me the dress code?'

'You're perfect as you are.' He blew her a kiss from his desk. 'Now go away and stop distracting me.'

'Yes, sir.' She gave him an insolent little salute.

He grinned, and waited until she was halfway out of the door before saying, 'Alex?'

She looked over her shoulder. 'Yes?'

'I love you.'

She smiled back. 'I love you, too.'

And hope bloomed in his heart.

The taxi was there dead on seven thirty, and Jordan refused to be drawn about where they we going. Until they rounded the corner and could see the London Eye, all lit up.

'Jordan?'

'It's the last ride of the night,' he said. 'And we have a ticket. I thought it might be fun.' Even though he managed to keep his tone relatively cool, his heart was hammering. *Please, please, let her say yes.*

'Do you know, I've never actually been on the London Eye?' She reached up to kiss him. 'This is a really lovely surprise, Jordan.'

This wasn't actually the surprise, he thought. And he had absolutely no idea how she was going to take this. It wasn't like an exam or a business deal, where he always had a pretty good idea how things were going. He just had to hope he'd got this right.

They went to the priority gate into the capsule. There was only one other person there.

She frowned. 'Jordan, shouldn't there be more people getting on?'

'No. It's a private capsule. Apart from the host being

there—' very discreetly in the background '—to keep the health and safety people happy, it's just us.'

And a bottle of champagne and two glasses. Which he really, really hoped they were going to use.

He waited as they rose up on the wheel and could see London all lit up below them. And then he took a deep breath. 'OK. Here's the thing. When I was twenty, I had plans to get married. It didn't work out—for a lot of reasons—and I got married to someone else. So did the girl I originally wanted to marry. It didn't work out for either of us. And I think that's because we married the wrong person—we should've married each other.'

Her face was white.

'Alex,' he said softly. 'We've both made mistakes. And I can understand if you don't ever want to get married again. So I'm not asking you that. I'm just asking you to be with me.'

At the top of the curve, he took the velvet-covered box from his pocket, dropped onto one knee and took her hand. 'Alex, you're the one who completes me. When I'm with you, everything fits and it's in the right place. I love you. And I want to be with you.' He opened the box. 'I'd marry you in a heartbeat, but this isn't an engagement ring to pressure you. It's an eternity ring, and I've spent weeks talking to that designer who did the pop-up shop you organised.'

Alexandra's face cleared. 'So that's why she's been running all those designs past me?'

'Yup. I wanted to give you a surprise—but I wanted it to be something I knew you would choose to wear, not someone else's thoughts of what you ought to wear.'

'Oh, Jordan.' Her eyes filled with tears.

'I've always loved you. I'll love you for the rest of my life. That's what this ring is about. It's not a shackle, it's a promise. Every time you doubt me, you can look at this ring and know that I'll love you for eternity.' He dragged in a breath. 'We don't have to get married and it doesn't matter if we don't have children. What matters to me is being with you. I love you, Alex. And I think you love me. So how about us giving each other a chance to be really happy?'

She nodded. 'Oh. Jordan. The ring's absolutely beautiful.'

She'd said yes. He only realised then that he'd stopped breathing, waiting for her answer. He kissed the fourth finger of her right hand and slipped the ring over the top of his kiss.

'Actually, I do have a question.' She waited for him to look her in the eye. 'Jordan Smith, will you marry me?'

It was the last thing he'd expected. He stared at her in utter disbelief. 'You're asking me to marry you?'

'You have a point. We both had a marriage that didn't work out because we married the wrong person.' She stroked his face. 'You're not Nathan. You'd never try to control me. You'd be bossy, yes, but you'd expect me to be just as bossy back. And I trust you. I know you'd never hurt me, never try to make me be anything other than who I am.'

'Never,' he confirmed softly.

She took the ring off her finger and handed it back to him. 'So are you going to do this thing properly, this time?'

'But—Alex, this isn't an engagement ring.'

'It's beautiful. It's exactly what I would've chosen. And if we're going to finish building those bridges with our parents and have dinner with them to celebrate our engagement, that ring really needs to be on my left hand, don't you think?'

She was really going to do it. She was going to marry

him, and finish building bridges with both their families. Make their future whole. Jordan's smile was so wide that it felt as if it reached across the whole of London. 'Alexandra, I love you. Will you do me the honour of being my wife?'

She smiled back at him. 'I thought you'd never ask. Yes.'

He slipped the ring onto the fourth finger of her left hand, this time. And he was laughing as he got to his feet, pulled her into his arms and kissed her.

* * * * *

MILLS & BOON®
By Request

RELIVE THE ROMANCE WITH THE BEST OF THE BEST

A sneak peek at next month's titles...

In stores from 14th January 2016:

- **A Forbidden Passion** – Dani Collins, Kelly Hunter & Catherine George

- **Her Exquisite Surrender** – Melanie Milburne, Lucy Ellis & Joanne Rock

In stores from 28th January 2016:

- **The Dante Legacy: Seduction** – Day Leclaire

- **If The Ring Fits...** – Kate Hardy, Marion Lennox & Jennie Adams

---

Available at WHSmith, Tesco, Asda, Eason, Amazon and Apple

Just can't wait?
Buy our books online a month before they hit the shops!
visit www.millsandboon.co.uk

These books are also available in eBook format!

0116/05

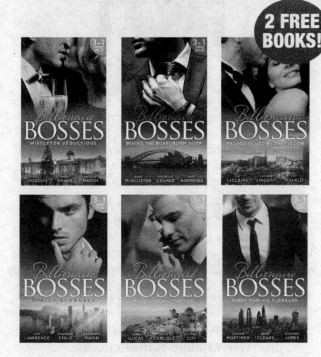

MILLS & BOON®

Man of the Year

Our winning cover star will be revealed next month!

**Don't miss out on your copy
– order from millsandboon.co.uk**

Read more about Man of the Year 2016 at

www.millsandboon.co.uk/moty2016

**Have you been following our
Man of the Year 2016 campaign?**
🐦 **#MOTY2016**